PENGUIN BOOKS

The Frost Queen's Blade

Meg Smitherman writes science fiction, fantasy and horror books (all of which involve kissing). She studied Creative Writing at Brunel University London, where she obtained both her MA and a staggering amount of student loan debt. When not writing, Meg spends her time playing video games, reading fan fiction and couch rotting. Based in Los Angeles, she shares her life with a chihuahua, a cat and a handsome Englishman.

CW01500824

By Meg Smitherman

The Frost Queen's Blade

Thrum

Swallowed

Entity

Shattered City Series

Destroyer

Sanctifier

The Frost Queen's Blade

MEG SMITHERMAN

PENGUIN BOOKS

PENGUIN BOOKS

UK | USA | Canada | Ireland | Australia
India | New Zealand | South Africa

Penguin Books is part of the Penguin Random House group of companies
whose addresses can be found at global.penguinrandomhouse.com

Penguin Random House UK,
One Embassy Gardens, 8 Viaduct Gardens, London SW11 7BW

penguin.co.uk

First self-published by Meg Smitherman 2024
First published in Great Britain by Penguin Books 2025
001

Set in 12.5/14.75pt Garamond MT
Typeset by Falcon Oast Graphic Art Ltd
Printed and bound in Great Britain by Clays Ltd, Elcograf S.p.A.

The authorized representative in the EEA is Penguin Random House Ireland,
Morrison Chambers, 32 Nassau Street, Dublin D02 YH68

A CIP catalogue record for this book is available from the British Library

ISBN: 978-1-405-98704-2

Penguin Random House is committed to a sustainable future
for our business, our readers and our planet. This book is made from
Forest Stewardship Council® certified paper

Over the centuries, scholars have called
Queen Elma I of Rothen many things. Some
brand her a hero, some declare many facets of her
life the stuff of fantasy and legend, while some still
insist she ought to go down in history as a traitor.
It is easy, if you have read the usual histories, to
label her a monster. But if one takes a moment to
study the accounts of those who loved her, most
notably the letters from her husband, one can
see a new narrative beginning to form.

What most historians routinely fail to
understand or, for that matter, convey, is that
Queen Elma I of Rothen was neither hero,
nor traitor, nor figure of legend.

She was simply a woman.

From *The Ice Queen* by Harriet Moss (1532),
Cornelian Tower archives

I

Seven Years Ago

News of her mother's death came without ceremony in the form of a hastily scribbled note. The pageboy hadn't wanted to say the words aloud, presumably, afraid of embarrassment or hurting Elma, whose mother was gone.

She held the letter in her hands long after the page handed it to her. Long after she read it. She sat in her favorite garden, the one with fruit trees and large firm plants shaped like artichokes, plants that thrived under a year-round sun. The stone bench beneath her was cool in the shade, her outstretched feet warming in a ray of sunlight.

You are summoned home, read the note. *Your mother is dead. The king requires his heir.*

You are summoned home.

Of course, Elma's father did not write a letter of his own. No, Elma thought – the moment his wife's last breath had passed her lips, the king would have ordered a messenger to send for his only daughter. Heir to the throne of Rothen. And thus, a messenger had arrived that morning with word of the queen's passing, and upon hearing it, Elma's pageboy scribbled a note and brought it to the garden.

So here Elma sat, finally crumpling the note in her fist.

This moment had always been inevitable. Elma knew her life in Mekya was temporary, knew that the caress of hot dry air on her skin, golden sun against her eyes when she closed them, scratchy grass tickling the soles of her bare feet – it was all temporary. She was only in Mekya for safekeeping, to stay out of her father's way, to give him peace and quiet. To be someone else's problem.

Until she wasn't.

Elma had not thought that her mother would die before Elma came of age. She was only fourteen now. She had imagined returning home to her mother and father together, on the first day of her eighteenth year, as was tradition. Not with warm embraces, but with a distant formality, cold enough to fit the city of her birth.

'Your Highness?' The pageboy waited, uneasy, near the edge of the garden.

Elma shoved the note into her bodice – her dress was light and gauzy and not substantial enough for pockets.

'Don't call me that,' she said under her breath, not loud enough for the page to hear. She was next in line to the throne whether she liked it or not.

'I didn't quite catch that, Your Highness,' the pageboy said, his forehead shining with sweat. He clearly wanted to go back inside, where cool stone kept the heat from permeating. Out here, there was no escape from summer's scalding touch.

Elma loved the heat. Her naturally pale skin had long since browned in the sun, her thick black hair cut short to her chin to keep her neck cool. She was born of the north, but she had bloomed in Mekya, so Mekyan she would always be in her heart.

'I said thank you,' she lied, standing. 'Would you be so kind as to send a tea service to my rooms?'

'Very good, Your Highness.' The pageboy strode inside, his shoulders back, always with an air of confidence and efficiency that Elma wished she might emulate one day.

But she was only fourteen. She hadn't yet learned confidence. She felt as if she had only just begun to know the kingdom of Mekya and its walled city of Lothyn. But she hadn't learned who she was and still hated to be called *princess*.

Clenching her jaw, Elma slipped on her sandals. The leather was sun-warmed, and she sucked in a breath at the sudden heat. But instead of kicking them off again, like she wanted to, she marched out of the garden, away from the sun and a dry breeze in the leaves.

In a moment, she was inside, cloaked by shadows and cool air. There was no door to step through, only an arch of white stone that led into a brightly tiled vestibule. This was Orchard House, the only home she had ever known. Here, she had been raised by her mother's cousins. Three sisters, each loving and motherly in her own way.

Elma passed through the vestibule into a corridor lined with tall arched windows, open to the world beyond. It was never cold enough in Lothyn to require glass panes or outer doors – everything opened itself to the giving sky.

When Elma came at last to a carved wood door decorated with a wreath of yellow flowers, she flung it open and went inside, self-indulgently slamming the door in her wake. She heard a muffled thump as the wreath hit the floor outside. She didn't care. This was her room, *her* sanctuary.

Tears pricked her eyes, and she bit her lips, willing

them to go away. She plucked the pageboy's note from her bodice. The ink was smeared now, her sweat dampening the paper.

She read it again, vision blurred.

Your Highness —

Your mother is dead. The king requires his heir. You are summoned home.

Elma was happy in Lothyn. She was safe. Her mother, she was certain, had died of some natural cause. If she had been murdered, the king would have left Elma in Mekya, far from danger. Instead, he wanted her close. He would say that he wanted her in Frost, the capital city, where he could ensure that she understood her birthright. But Elma was certain, though he would never admit it, King Rafe did not want to be alone.

Elma bit back a sob as reality sunk in.

She did not remember her parents. The last time she'd seen them, she had been an infant. There were no memories, no blurred recollection of a pair of faces, of voices, of hands holding hers. She had been too young, sent away at the first possible moment, as was tradition. Babies did not fare well in Rothen. And so, everything Elma knew of her parents had been told to her or learned in rare letters from the northern kingdom. All she knew was Orchard House. And now, she was to be ripped from it, forced into a world of long nights and frigid snows and thick, dark windows.

Tears streamed down her face.

You are summoned home.

There would be no denying the king, her father. She

4

had never met him, not truly, but she knew what he would expect of her. She knew her basic duty as heir to the throne of a kingdom – to do her father's bidding.

She made a strangled sound of frustration, gritting her teeth.

Couldn't her mother have been more careful, for Elma's sake? The thought washed bitterly down her throat. No. Whatever had stopped the beating of her mother's heart, whatever ailment had taken her soul prematurely, was the work of fate. Nothing could have prevented it; Elma knew that much. She had spent enough time lighting candles under the moon, hands clasped with her three stand-in mothers, speaking to the world's heart.

She knew things like this never happened by chance.

A knock sounded at the door, the soft rap of a knuckle.

'Come in,' said Elma, pressing her eyes with the heel of a palm.

The door opened slowly, revealing first a tray of tea, and then Tammire, one of her mother's cousins. She caught Elma's gaze as she entered, closing the door behind her. There was love and warmth in her eyes, and a steady knowing – she had heard of the death of the queen.

'I'm sorry,' said Tammire, not waiting for any formalities to pass between them before she set down the tea tray, gathering Elma into her arms.

Finally, Elma gave way to grief. She wept loss into the embrace of one of the only mothers she had ever known. Racking sobs escaped her mouth, a stream of hot tears falling from her eyes until her nose was clogged and her breath came ragged.

She wept for the loss of Mekya, the garden kingdom,

the place she would love with every piece of herself until her dying breath. The loss of Tammire, Dae, and Sharra – the women who had shaped her, nurtured her from infancy. The loss of Lothyn, its narrow streets, crowded shopfronts, expansive ponds and gardens, the libraries, the musicians, the flocks of green parrots that cackled in droves atop swaying palms.

But mostly, she wept for the impending loss of a youth that had been so fleeting, fragile in the knowledge that it would be taken away.

'Cry, cry, let it out,' said Tammire, and Elma heard in the woman's voice that she, too, wept. 'There is no shame in grief.'

'I don't want to go,' Elma said, desperate, over and over into her mother's shoulder. 'I don't want to go.'

'I know,' said Tammire.

And even those two words, soft and helpless as they were, calmed Elma until her sobs lessened, until her breathing slowed. Had Tammire told her to stop crying, she would have wailed even louder. If Tammire had tried to assure her that things would be all right, Elma would have shoved her away, disbelieving. But Tammire, Dae, and Sharra had only ever shown love. Understanding. Compassion.

Dread caught at Elma's throat. Would there be compassion in Frost? Would there be love, understanding, even acceptance? Or would her life become hard-edged, carved from ice like the glaciers that moved unendingly across Rothen like frozen seas?

'Come,' said Tammire, holding Elma at arm's length so they could see one another clearly. 'Have some tea. I'll send for the others, and we'll say our goodbyes.'

Elma said nothing, afraid to speak, should she start crying again.

'It won't be forever, love.'

The next day, Elma set off for Rothen. She had three bags full of belongings, all piled neatly on top of the carriage that would bear her across one kingdom and into another. Her gauzy dresses would stay behind, just like her sandals. They wouldn't be needed in Rothen. Instead, she wore plain trousers, a tunic, and a long woolen cloak to keep her warm at night.

The journey would take weeks. A small contingent of guards was hired to protect her, in addition to a personal maid and various other members of the traveling party whom Elma couldn't identify and had never met.

Tammire, Dae, and Sharra hugged her all as one before she left, their bodies nearly smothering her with unadulterated love. They were much like Elma, physically. Tall, graceful, their faces lined with decades of laughter and expression. They wore their hair long, thick, and gray. Tammire's hair was plaited, a thick braid down her back. Dae and Sharra wore theirs loose about their shoulders.

Elma breathed them in desperately. They smelled of cloves and orange honey, their soft embraces a lifelong comfort. She had felt so safe, so loved and protected in her fourteen years at Orchard House.

'I love you,' she said, muffled by the embrace, through the tears that streamed down her cheeks. 'I love you, I love you.'

'We love you, Elma,' they said, kissing her on the forehead, taking her hands, speaking soft prayers in the pale morning. 'We'll light a candle for you and keep it lit until we know you're home. Safe.'

Elma climbed into the carriage at last, biting back the wails of sorrow she wanted to unleash. *Home.* Home was here, in Orchard House. But she was a princess. She was on her way to fulfill her role as the heir of a kingdom. She must compose herself.

Her mothers blew kisses as the carriage rolled away, bumping over uneven cobbles. Elma watched until the three figures disappeared around a bend in the road, the last she would see of them.

'It won't be forever, love.'

The memory of Tammire's words cut her like a dull knife. Because Elma knew, deep down, that they were untrue. She had always known that the moment she left Mekya, she would never return.

2

Present Day

Boredom was too kind a word for what Elma felt. *Resigned disgust* would be a more accurate descriptor. Only her father's presence beside her, his large-knuckled hand propped against a vacant face, kept her dutifully seated. Otherwise, she would have excused herself hours ago.

They were in the Frost arena, presiding over the Death Games. It was the king's privilege, and his daughter's as well, to watch over whatever revelries occurred from day to day. King Rafe Volta always chose to indulge in the Death Games. It was his particular favorite pastime, the brutal battles that were carried out in dramatic fashion in the snow-swept arena far below.

Elma only ever saw her father truly eager when there was a smell of blood in the air.

Had it not been Elma's twenty-first birthday party, with nearly all of the Frost court in attendance, she might not have felt so miserable. If this were a typical Death Games, she would have amused herself by wandering into the underbelly of the arena to joke with the arena men, and maybe even catch a glimpse of one of the champions on his way to dismember someone.

But it was her birthday, and abandoning the celebration would be rude.

'No storm today,' her father had said that morning over breakfast, stray beads of hot wine clinging to his graying mustache. 'Your twenty-first year will be plentiful and easy.'

'Yes,' Elma had said, her thoughts elsewhere as they always were. And anyway, *no storm* meant very little in Rothen. Snow still fell, relentless and white. Though today there were no harsh winds to batter it against the fighters in the arena, or against the Frost Citadel where it perched above the city, a gargoyle of black stone and sharp steeples against a jagged mountain peak – the seat of the King of Rothen.

From her covered seat in the stands, Elma watched as a man eviscerated his opponent, a slop of gore falling out onto the dirty snow below.

Her father slammed his fist on the arm of his chair, leaning forward, teeth bared. He rarely took sides at the Games – he only cared to see brutality. It was the Volta way. The Death Games had never enticed her the way they were supposed to. They were repetitive and dull; the same champions always won in the same brutal ways. Elma leaned back in her chair, trying not to glower.

'Don't be so grim,' said King Rafe, leaning close so no one but his daughter could hear above the din of the arena crowd, the excessive indulgence here in their sheltered box seats. 'They will suspect you don't like your gifts.'

Elma glanced at the pile of trinkets next to her chair, gold and jewels, gifts of wealth that she didn't want or need. 'I don't,' she said. Her father was no stranger to Elma's insouciance, which tended to border on sullenness.

The king's frown deepened: a warning. But Elma's verbal punishment was cut short as a well-dressed young man approached their seats. He was smiling far too brightly, an expression that was as obviously forced as his deep bow and stiffly styled hair. Elma recognized him as one of her cousins, a lordling by the name of Jarian, or . . . Jedner.

'Lord Jarlen,' said the king.

Jarlen, thought Elma. *Close.*

'Your Majesty,' said Jarlen, straightening from his bow. The grin remained plastered to his white face.

He wasn't a fighter then, but one of the sheltered noblemen who preferred to stay indoors and attend parties in favor of protecting the realm from whatever horrors came out of the snowstorms. Elma's uncle had taught her, upon returning to Rothen, how to recognize a warrior. He would be sun-tanned from being outside all day, where the sun reflected a million ways off the snow. And he would hold himself in a way that spoke of ease, comfort, a man whose body and mind worked in concert.

Lord Jarlen's body could not have been more awkward, as much as he tried to appear relaxed. He swept his fur-lined cape aside in a dramatic gesture and managed to catch it on his sword pommel. Flustered, he fiddled with it for a moment, tassels swaying from his hat.

'What is it you want?' the king asked, his tone unchanging.

Elma glanced at her father. He was not a kind man, but she had become almost fond of him in the past seven years. And she was grateful that he allowed her to sit in silence in these moments, saving her from the pain of interacting with distant third cousins who couldn't even bow without causing a tangle of themselves.

'I've come to wish Her Highness Princess Elma well on this, her twenty-first birthday.' He swept another bow, this time managing to avoid tangling his cape in his sword.

'She extends her deepest thanks,' said King Rafe.

Normally, courtiers like Jarlen would smile politely, turn, and depart. But Jarlen only stood there, smiling. His gaze found Elma's, and she had to fight not to wrinkle her nose at him. 'Your Highness, I thought . . .' said Jarlen, his words tumbling over themselves as if he were reciting a rehearsed line, 'I thought I might perhaps offer you a gift on this most, ah, auspicious of birthdays.' He lifted one arm and extended it outward and behind him.

This gesture piqued the interests of the courtiers who had been milling about in the stands nearby, watching the exchange with sideways glances, their hot wines sloshing. Small gasps broke out as those gathered saw what was making its way through the crowd toward the dais.

A well-clad pageboy – clearly Jarlen's – holding a delicate gold chain in one hand. Behind the pageboy, their wrists bound and attached to the chain, were a pair of scantily dressed men.

They wore flimsy gold cloths across their hips, and jewels adorned their fingers and hair. Heavy fur cloaks fell over their shoulders, shielding them from the worst of the weather. Their bare chests were utterly hairless. They were fair-skinned and lovely and close to Elma's age. Her gaze alighted on the delicate bindings about their wrists and the chain. She didn't look away.

'For you, Princess Elma,' said Jarlen, bowing again.

Elma said nothing.

'They are bed slaves,' said the king, looking at her sidelong. 'No small gift.'

'And well trained,' said Jarlen. He snapped his fingers, and at once, the two beautiful men drew toward one

12

another, embracing, exploring one another as if the entire court of Frost weren't watching.

It was obvious from the gasps and titters that those present did not object to this display.

Elma swallowed, her mouth suddenly far too dry. This felt somehow obscene, even compared to the Death Games' letting of blood for enjoyment.

'From Slödava?' The king's voice rang out over the arena's noise.

The snow had begun to fall thicker now, giving their covered section of the stands an almost cave-like feeling.

'Where else?' said Jarlen, his confidence seemingly growing. 'They're beautiful, are they not? Pure white hair and made for pleasure. We only feed them once a day; they're far too weak to fight. The princess would be utterly safe.'

Slödava. Elma had seen the elusive northern men before, captured spies and assassins from that remote enemy enclave. Slödava was a city-state swathed in shadow and ice, a place that Elma might not have believed existed at all were it not for the prisoners she'd seen.

I don't want them, Elma wanted to say, unable to look at the bed slaves. *Get them away from me*. But she rarely spoke in front of the court. The less she interacted with the people of Frost, the less she believed she might one day rule them.

'Would Her Highness like further demonstration?' Jarlen asked, snapping his fingers again.

At that, the slaves began to kiss, slow and deep. Elma watched, horrified, as their hips rocked together, as their breaths grew shallow. Public displays of intimacy, even orgies, were not uncommon in the Court of Frost. Elma had attended but only observed, yet she had never seen two people *forced* to touch one another. Forced to become aroused.

'That will be enough,' said the king.

Jarlen snapped his fingers, and the slaves drew apart. Elma turned her eyes away from their obvious shared arousal, though she knew she was one of the few who did. His demonstration finished, the lordling continued to watch Elma with an uneasy eagerness.

'Your Highness,' he said, almost vibrating like an excited child, 'does my gift please you?'

Elma sighed. So, *this* was the point of all that flaunting, all that bowing, and the ridiculously showy gift. Lord Jarlen had not taken his eyes off her, and she ought to have recognized his intent immediately. Men of Rothen had been courting her since her arrival at the citadel, and Elma had refused each of them out of hand. Jarlen would be no exception.

A flaming brazier near them, an enormous thing that could have housed a whole family, roared hotly. Elma felt its heat too keenly.

The king shifted, lowering his meaty hand from his chin.

Everyone was waiting for her to respond. To say something. Just one word would do.

Countless glazed eyes gazed at her from the stands nearby, drunk on bloodshed and wine, all in celebration of their princess. Elma Volta, a woman who wanted nothing to do with them. Who might have given anything to be rid of them, of this life.

'No,' said Elma. Her voice, rough from an evening of disuse, was hoarse. 'Your gift does not please me.'

Jarlen's grin crumpled. Amidst the low hubbub, the gasps and muttering that fanned out through the seated courtiers, Jarlen gestured at his pageboy to take the slaves away. Elma heard his hissed commands, though she couldn't parse the words.

King Rafe frowned but said nothing. Perhaps, Elma thought, he was recalling the time he had forced a fiancé upon her, only for the man to be poisoned in his sleep within a fortnight.

This place is a grave. Fed up and miserable, as she was on each of her birthdays, Elma stood to go.

The attending courtiers rustled in response, a whisper of fabric as they stood and bowed low, as hats were removed from heads, as skirts spread out around bent knees.

'Thank you for coming,' Elma said, trying to speak above the sound of battle and death below. She considered saying something about a headache, or asking her father for permission to leave, but it would make no difference. He would be in a rage the next morning, and she'd face the consequences of her insolence one way or another.

Elma paused, bending to pick up one of her gifts, a gold and tourmaline necklace, before sweeping out of the box, head held high.

Cora, Elma's maid, met her in the arena's inner corridor.

'Leaving early again?' Cora said, hurrying to keep up with the princess's long strides. 'What happened this time?'

'Here,' said Elma, holding out the necklace and deftly sidestepping the question. 'My father will keep the rest as part of my dowry, or I'd let you have every last cursed trinket.'

Cora took the necklace with a pinched smile, shoving it deep into her bodice. 'One day he'll notice you're stealing your own birthday gifts.'

'He won't.' Elma stopped short as a thought occurred to her. This caused a slight pile-up in the dimly lit corridor, as she was being followed diligently by not only Cora, but four citadel guards. Her father never let her go anywhere alone, and his paranoia had only worsened as he aged. Where once he had been satisfied to let Elma roam the citadel with only one guard at her heels, with each passing year, his fears had increased, and thus, so had the guard detail.

'Sorry,' said Luca, the youngest yet most competent of her guards, who had nearly stumbled into her. The others were grumbling to one another about trod-upon toes, but Elma hardly heard them.

'I left the slaves,' said Elma.

Cora and the guards all shared a look.

'You . . . changed your mind?' Cora ventured, not sounding confident in this guess.

But Elma had already turned and was striding back toward the arena, where the roar of bloodlust and wine-addled laughter grew louder by the moment. She wasn't quite sure what she was doing or why she cared so much. Those slaves were her enemies. Many of her father's men had been slaughtered by Slödavan weapons.

In the first year of her life in Rothen, just before her fifteenth birthday, her father had brought Elma the severed head of her favorite guard. His skull had been sliced from top to bottom at an angle, so that only an eye remained, and part of a nose, and a bloody mush that was his brain. As she stared at the remains of his face and the insides of his skull, Elma remembered laughing with the guard over games of dice, sipping wine from his flask. He had been the only thing she had that was even close to a friend in Rothen.

'This is the brutality of Slödava,' King Rafe had said, as blood and brain dripped on the floor, splattering Elma's silk slippers. 'This is what I protect you from. What I must crush into dust.'

The bed slaves might have been sent as spies, for all Elma knew. They might have Lord Jarlen under their thumbs. It would be an elegant assassination – the princess, murdered in the throes of pleasure, strangled while the killer's cock was still inside her. She imagined it all with a sort of thrill, the kind of horrific pleasure that could only come from a life so cold that anything, even death, seemed exciting.

For some elusive reason she couldn't name, Elma did not like the thought of those two men alone with Jarlen, with her father, with the Court of Frost. They were defenseless and nearly naked, bound to one another, and now . . . useless. Rejected. Would they be killed?

I don't care either way, Elma thought, as the sound of the arena grew louder, the chill air constricting her chest. *I just don't want them to die on my birthday.*

As Elma emerged once more into the stands, her guards and Cora close behind, she could sense immediately that something was wrong. The sounds of revelry were too loud, too piercing. Odd shouts pierced the air. And . . . was someone wailing? But it was so crowded, courtiers and servants alike were everywhere, and no one seemed to notice that Elma had returned. She shoved her way through men and women, treading on booted feet and fur-draped skirts.

'Your Highness!' her guards called, following after her.

She ignored them. There was no sound of battle from below; for some reason, the fighting had stopped. As she made her way through the throng, Elma realized belatedly that everyone's attention was focused on where she had been sitting with her father. Pausing to stand on tiptoe, she saw . . . nothing. Two empty chairs.

Her heart constricted.

Two empty thrones.

'Father,' she said, a whisper in the chaos.

It felt like years before Elma reached him. She stopped at the edge of the crowd, caught in indecision. Her father lay at the foot of his chair. She couldn't see his face – someone was in the way. All she saw were his feet, the toes of his boots pointed toward the sky.

'Your Highness,' someone said breathily. 'Come away.'

Elma did not come away. She shoved away the hands that tried to protect her, stumbling forward to see. At last, the figure who had been crouching at her father's side – an arena physician, she now realized – turned and stood to face her.

'You shouldn't be here,' said the physician, her features pinched and raw. 'You shouldn't see this.'

'I'm the princess,' Elma said, as if that meant anything. 'Let me speak to my father.' It was a ridiculous thing to say about someone who was clearly dead.

The physician, nearly as tall as Elma, set her shoulders. 'You should be prepared to –'

Elma pushed past her. She had seen death. She'd cheered it here, in the great arena. She had watched, her father grinning beside her, as heads rolled on red-stained snow. She had seen him execute Slödavan invaders with his own broadsword, teeth bared as he severed their spines. And Elma was no stranger to loss. But nothing, somehow, had prepared her for the sight of her father, the king, in death. His face was purple and blotchy, his eyes open too wide. Spittle crusted the corners of his mouth.

'Who did this?' Elma said, the words coming by rote. It was the thing you always asked when someone died in Rothen. Before grief came revenge.

'No one,' said the physician, softly. 'His heart gave out.' Someone wailed.

I'm the one who should be wailing, thought Elma. 'How do you know?'

'I've seen this many times,' said the physician. 'There was no poison. The royal tasters are alive and well.'

Elma said nothing.

'The slaves,' someone said from the crowd of courtiers, which had quieted in Elma's presence. 'They did this.'

'Yes,' came another voice. 'The Slödavan slaves poisoned him!'

In a moment, the cry was taken up by the entirety of the surrounding courtiers, a chorus of rage and impotent grief, no doubt fueled by the bloodthirst of the arena.

'Stop them,' Elma said, turning to Luca and her guards. 'Silence them.'

'Only you can do that,' said Luca, apologetic.

Elma stood over her dead father and watched as the Court of Frost worked itself into a blood frenzy. *Only you can do that.* The words rang in her ears. Her father was dead. King Rafe Volta was dead. She was all that was left of the Volta bloodline.

'The slaves!' came the boiling cry.

No one was left to stop this. Elma's hands clenched into fists, her breaths fighting against a too-tight chest. She could not stop this. She wasn't meant for it.

'Your Highness,' said the physician, matter-of-fact, her voice cutting through the chaotic noise. 'Your father's body. What are your orders?'

Elma stared at it, the thing that had been her father. Part of her wondered if the slaves were still alive or whether they'd already been torn limb from limb, disemboweled right there in the stands of the arena.

'Your *Highness*.'

'Take the king to his bedchambers.' A deep, resonant voice cut through the chaos, and the noise abated until it was nothing but a dull hum.

Elma looked around for the source of the voice, relief and fear and grief all threatening to drown her. Because she would have known that voice anywhere. Her uncle, Lord Godwin, appeared at her side in his military garb. He must have been called in from his post atop one of the arena battlements. Tiny icicles clung to his dark beard.

Elma opened her mouth to speak, but her uncle's hand fell heavy on her shoulder, silencing her. That gesture alone, the weight of his presence, soothed her.

'King Rafe will be seen by the kingdom's best physicians,' said Godwin, addressing the room at large. They hung on his every word, for he was the king's general, his brother by marriage, and trusted as the sovereign's right hand. 'There, the method of his death will be determined. While this is being done, the Slödavan slaves will be held by my own men. I can promise you that justice will be carried out, and your king's memory will be honored as he so deserves.'

Then Godwin turned to Elma, his voice far lower, and said, 'Go back to the citadel. There's nothing more you can do here.' He made a sharp gesture for Luca's benefit – *keep her safe, get her home.*

Elma did not object. She didn't want to spend another second in that arena, that horrible blood-stained place where her father had been and where only a body remained. And as she hurried into the arena corridor once again, Cora and her guards at her sides, she felt distinctly that she had been subjected to some kind of test. A test that only a queen could pass, and that Elma – a mere princess – had utterly failed.

3

Elma was allowed to see her father's body just past midnight on the day of her twenty-first birthday. It seemed as though no one in the citadel slept; the halls were so brightly lit. Even the shadows were full of solemn servants and courtiers. Silken handkerchiefs dabbed at wide eyes as Elma passed.

Elma was relieved to see that her father's wing of the citadel was quiet, empty of prying eyes and listening ears. Only her guards accompanied her until she was left alone at the door of the king's rooms.

Indecision gnawed suddenly. Was she meant to knock or simply enter the room? A queen would do the latter, but Elma had been King Rafe's obedient daughter. She tapped a knuckle softly on the heavy wood.

At once, the door swung open, aided by a pair of solemn pages. She went in, aware of how she moved, the set of her chin, and every nuance of her expression. They would be watching, curious, or hoping for guidance.

Without her father, Elma was about to be the highest power in Rothen. She would be their mother, their war chief, their protector, their judge, and their jury. In her hands, she held a power unwanted, writhing in its eagerness to undo her. She had never wanted to be queen.

As she came to the bed, the physicians moved away from it in tandem, heads bowed. 'Your Majesty,' they murmured, using the title out of deference, even though Elma had yet to be officially crowned.

The words fell on her ears and sat like a rock in Elma's gut.

She studied her father's face. He was not as he had been in the arena, twisted in pain. Somehow, they had made him look peaceful. His thick arms were folded over his chest in repose, and he still wore the ring that had always been his prized possession, a trophy of war: a silver band set with a blue-black stone. His eyes were closed, and his face had been washed, his silver-flecked beard trimmed. The scent of cloves permeated the room, too strong and yet not strong enough – the reek of death cut through.

Elma's fingers curled around the tasseled edge of one of the many blankets on her father's bed and twisted. 'May the winter star guide you,' she whispered.

'May the winter star guide him,' intoned those in the room.

Elma recited the rites as best she could, the words an heir was expected to speak over her predecessor. But in her heart, she was pleading, clutching at him, begging him not to go. Not to leave her here, alone in this frostbitten waste.

This is your birthright, he had often said, admonishing. *You are the sole heir to the throne of Rothen. The sooner you learn to accept it, the less miserable you'll be.*

But Elma had always clung to misery. She enjoyed it. What else did she have here but resentment?

'Your Majesty,' said the nearest physician, and Elma blinked, jolted back to the now. 'The funeral . . .'

'Yes,' said Elma, the true weight of her new station beginning to crash over her. 'The funeral. Is two weeks enough time to . . . prepare?'

24

The physician nodded.

'Two weeks, then.'

Elma returned to her room. When she was alone at last, she went to the window and watched the snow fall. Even then, shivering and afraid, she did not cry.

Inertia kept Elma under the fur-lined blankets of her bed the next morning, a strange coldness seeping from within her as opposed to without.

She had been fond of her father. As fond as one was of a half-rotted meal that would pain the stomach yet stave off starvation for another day. For the past seven years, she had watched the lines of his face deepen, his knuckles swell with every new winter, his breaths become labored with every new spring. But somehow, she had believed, with the conviction of naivete, that he would be with her until the end of her days. He was a king, after all. Kings did not die. They ruled the land because that was their duty.

It was Cora who was finally able to rouse Elma from her morning stupor, bringing in a tray of breakfast and bitter, steaming coffee.

'Your father's . . . I mean your advisors are waiting for you,' Cora said, her face wan, lips tight. 'Godwin and the rest.'

'Godwin's a general,' Elma said automatically. She found it difficult to meet Cora's eyes, afraid she would see pity there. Or perhaps even impatience. Elma did not have the energy to contend with Cora's feelings on top of her own, whatever they were. She could not seem to access her own emotions, and she was afraid that in seeing emotion in others, they might infect her.

'He may be a general, but he's been locked in that room

25

with the other advisors all morning.' A warning tainted Cora's words.

'If you want my dowry,' Elma said, her fingers flexing on the velvet embroidered coverlet, 'it's yours. Father doesn't need it. Your family does. Your sisters . . .'

Silence stretched between them.

'I have the necklace,' Cora said at last.

'I'm not leaving my room.'

'They will make decisions without you. You'll be trodden on by your own men. You need to assert your power. You are the queen.'

A spark of anger cut through the fog of Elma's mind. She turned sharply, at last meeting her maid's gaze. Cora's eyes were wide, red-rimmed as if she hadn't slept. 'I am the queen,' Elma said.

'Yes.'

A crushing weight, as if the whole of the mountain's snow had cascaded down to bury her in its suffocating depths, fell over Elma. Cora and her family depended on Elma. Countless more souls dotting the frozen kingdom of Rothen depended on her. She was their queen.

Elma wanted, in that moment, nothing more than to let the entirety of Rothen freeze and die and take her with it. What difference would it make? There was no escape for her. This was her birthright. As surely as the winter storms, her reign would come.

'Unless you'd like a full battalion of Slödavan soldiers on our doorstep before the crown is laid upon your head, Your Majesty, I suggest we move forward with a coronation this week.'

Elma listened, heavy-lidded, as Lord Bertram insisted – not for the first time that morning – upon a swift coronation.

'Such haste speaks of desperation,' Godwin said. It had been his reply each time as the conversation went around in circles, Elma at the center of it. 'A prosperous kingdom in peacetime does not rush to crown its monarch. We need at least a month of planning and another for festivals. Celebrations. Parties and tournaments.'

'A ball, perhaps,' said Lord Ferdinand, the youngest and most genial of the advisors, spinning a large silver ring around one finger. 'The young men and women of Frost might benefit from . . . levity.'

'I don't think anyone in Rothen knows the meaning of levity,' said Elma.

The room went quiet. It was the first time she had spoken in hours, and she was convinced some of the men gathered had forgotten she was still there. She couldn't blame them – she had never found the need for her voice before, had never found it important to disagree or to weigh in. What need did a prisoner have of an opinion when her chains might never break?

A log snapped in the hearth, sending up a shower of sparks.

Godwin, no longer dressed as a general but as a lord of the citadel in a tunic and cape of fine silk and fur, broke the silence with a chuckle. 'Her Majesty has a sharp tongue. A boon for the kingdom.'

'What good does a tongue do if we are overrun by Slödavans?' grumbled Lord Bertram. His hair and skin were gray, and he was set in his ways. Elma tended to see him as an embodiment of the kingdom: old and stalwart and brutal, rotting from the inside.

'Licks its wounds,' said Lord Maurice. Half-shrouded in shadow where he sat at the far end of the table, he had said little that morning. His craggy countenance and dark eyes had always made Elma uneasy. He was a man who seemed to have always been ancient, as if a part of the mountain had crumbled off and become a man.

'Do we have evidence of an impending Slödavan invasion?' Elma asked.

She knew there was more to the aggression between Rothen and Slödava than some long-standing, pointless feud. Slödava had something that Rothen wanted – Rime Ice. Her father had waxed poetic on the subject countless times. The magic-imbued weapons were supposedly forged directly from the ice of a glacier in the far north, which only the people of Slödava could access. They were indestructible weapons of legend. It was said that the damage these weapons inflicted was far beyond any a mortal blade could cause, their wielders granted unnatural strength and speed.

King Rafe had desperately wanted Rime Ice, but Slödava had refused to even acknowledge its existence. But Rafe, and the kings before him, had never stopped hunting it, as if obsessed. Their intermittent attacks on the kingdom of Slödava were unending.

This was why, Rafe had once explained to Elma, the Slödavans battered themselves against the walls of Frost in snow-born raids, why the Queen of Slödava would do anything to put an end to the line of Volta and take the throne of Rothen for her own, and to prevent the knowledge of Rime Ice from ever reaching the southern kingdoms.

'Every month we are attacked,' said Lord Maurice, somehow subsiding further into gloom as he spoke, though his eyes shone darkly. 'They come out of the snow and assault the walls; they scale ice as if born to it. They are inhuman, bloodthirsty, unrelenting.'

'It has been decades since a full-scale assault was launched upon Frost,' Godwin said. 'To cross the Frozen Sea alone would be a feat for any army.'

'Not impossible,' said Lord Bertram. 'We must strike first, and decisively.'

Elma rested her chin on folded hands, more than ready for this discussion to end. 'No evidence, then.'

Lord Maurice said nothing. Lord Bertram spluttered, as if about to protest, but Godwin held up a hand. 'Unless there is a pending threat of attack, I see no reason to rush the coronation. Her Majesty became queen the moment her father's heart ceased to beat. A coronation is a formality.'

'A formality that bears legal weight,' Bertram insisted. 'If we declare all-out war on Slödava, which I say we *must*, then Rothen would be in a position of weakness. An uncrowned queen declaring war without an heir? None of our allies would have reason to support us. The laws of the land and the kingdom would not yet bind her, and Frost Citadel would be open for the taking.'

Elma listened, her own thoughts muffling the lords' words. A delayed coronation meant more formal events, invitations to host far-flung family members, a parade of miserable pretending and smiling. She would be forced to grin all the way to the chopping block. Yet a quick coronation meant an ax at her throat before she was ready. If one could ever be ready to rule a kingdom.

'Your Majesty,' Godwin said, turning to Elma. His eyes were softer than they had been all morning, though it might have been the firelight. Or the reflection of late morning sun glancing in through the window, pale and weak off the drifts of snow. 'When shall the coronation be held?'

The question caught her off guard. Since returning to Frost, Elma had seldom, if ever, been asked for any meaningful input. She had been asked questions, of course – what would Her Highness like for breakfast? What color dress would she like to wear to the Death Games? How many logs would she like in the hearth? But the real decisions, the ones that affected her life, had never been left to her. The only true rebellion she had ever been allowed was the length of her hair, which she had refused to grow long since leaving Mekya.

Now that a true decision was left up to Elma, she found that she hated every option. Would she prefer to hurdle headfirst into queendom, to rule a kingdom before she had even accepted that her father was gone? Or would she rather delay the inevitable, allow time to crawl all over her uneasy skin until she ached for the release of finality?

What do you really want?

The question came softly, from a place of longing that Elma had tried hard to forget. From the memory of her mothers at Orchard House. A ghost of warmth, of tenderness and love passed over her. For a brief moment, she felt Mekya's hot sun, Orchard House's cool stone under her bare feet, and drew her fingers along a broad green leaf.

I want to go home.

'Your Majesty?' Godwin said.

Elma knew what she wanted. And she could never have it. She glanced at Godwin. 'In a month,' she said, the end of her words upturned like a question.

Godwin nodded once. 'Very good, Your Majesty. Let the coronation be held in a month. Two weeks from the day of King Rafe's funeral. There will be time enough for preparations, a ball,' he tossed Lord Ferdinand a generous smile, 'and for a tournament. Even if an army were on its way to Frost now from Slödava, which is unlikely, an army in full force would not evade our notice. There is always the option to hasten the coronation if need be.'

The gathered lords seemed to find no reason to object. Why should they? It was Godwin who had spoken the words, who had made the real decision. Perhaps Elma could rule this way, allowing Godwin to guide her, to speak for her. It would be a pale life, but what did Elma know about being queen?

Everything your father taught you, she thought, her mouth twisting. *Would you fail his memory so quickly?*

'I will see to it that the preparations are carried out,' said Godwin, magnanimous.

'Thank you,' Elma said tonelessly.

It didn't matter to Elma whether she was crowned in a month, or in five, or that afternoon. As soon as the crown was hers, she would become like Bertram and Maurice, these aging men who clung with gnarled fingers to the snow and black rock of Frost. And when she died, her flesh would remain forever preserved in the frozen earth, never rotting, never changing.

*

31

'You did well today.'

But Godwin's words fell on unwilling ears. Elma had done nothing. She walked with him to one of the small dinner rooms, a retinue of guards and pageboys swarming at their heels. Elma's duties for the day would be finished after this meal, after what felt like a day that would never end. She regarded her uncle sidelong. He had shown no sign of grief or shock since her father's passing. She was grateful for it.

'One more dinner,' he went on, 'though it may be a quarrelsome one.'

'What's that supposed to mean?'

'It means that your advisors will be in attendance, and . . .' he looked pointedly straight ahead, 'there is one last matter of diplomacy to discuss.'

Elma stopped in her tracks. Luca and her guards, watching more closely now, halted behind her. 'We've been discussing diplomacy all day,' she said, her tone treacherously close to petulance.

'And what's one more hour on top of so many?' Godwin grinned, a wan baring of teeth. He extended a hand. 'Come, Your Majesty. You are needed.'

The advisors were in good form that evening, laughing uproariously at their own middling jokes, fingertips oily with goose fat and noses red from hot wine. Elma sat at the head of the table. She felt like a child playing monarch in her father's chair. She had worn her best gown, a sweeping thing of dark red, with draped sleeves and a gold braided belt that hung low over her hips. It had seemed queenly in her rooms, when Cora had fastened gold and pearl webbing over Elma's black hair. Now, it seemed silly.

What good was a gown when a kingdom lay at her feet, hoping she wouldn't trip and stumble, crushing it beneath her awkward gait?

'I've never seen anyone so jolly in mourning,' Elma said, watching as Lord Bertram laughed so hard, he choked, forcing Lord Ferdinand to slap him on the back.

The room went quiet, save for the crackle of the fire, the distant howl of wind outside.

'We celebrate the life of a great king,' said Lord Maurice. He peered at Elma over the top of a hammered gold goblet.

Elma knew these men. She had known them for seven years against her will. And while she knew they had respected her father's reign, loved him as a man might desperately love a father who withheld affection, they had never liked King Rafe. They were, like all men adjacent to the throne, happy to wait patiently until the opportunity arose to take some of it for their own. And Elma knew that she was the only thing that stood between them and a fistful of raw power.

'You celebrate the death of my father,' she said.

When the men began to protest, spluttering and wide-eyed, Godwin raised a hand to quiet them. 'Her Majesty is in mourning,' he said. 'As are we.'

The others muttered agreement, nodding and glancing between one another with solemn expressions. Elma's pulse quickened. With a flash of satisfaction, she imagined what it might be like to take her dinner knife and plunge it deep into Lord Bertram's neck, right where the vein throbbed against the papery skin of his throat.

Only the memory of Orchard House, of her three mothers' arms around her, brought Elma back to earth.

'What is the final matter you wished to discuss?' Elma asked, failing to hide her ambivalence.

Godwin lowered his chin. 'Majesty, you must be aware that King Rafe was not a diplomat of great renown. At best, he was feared by our neighboring realms. At worst, hated. And Rothen is not rich in natural resources. Our only asset has ever been . . .'

'Weapons,' Elma finished for him, bored already. She knew what Godwin would say next. That she ought to declare war on some nearby nation, raid their villages, steal their crops and burn their homes. It was all the same with these men – war, the answer to every one of life's mysteries.

'Indeed,' said Godwin. 'Frost's blacksmiths must be fed, their people housed and cared for. Our ties with Navenie and Mekya are unstable, our trade and commerce are hanging by a thread. Your father did his best, but . . .'

'But clearly he didn't,' Elma said, almost resigned. 'And here I am, about to sit on the throne of a starving country. What did you have in mind, Godwin?' She was tired, her words more liberal and cutting than the advisors were used to. Lord Ferdinand had the sense to look slightly abashed. The rest only regarded her with a touch more shrewdness.

'A mission of diplomacy,' said Godwin, folding his fingers together. 'Rothen's heir, arriving in person to broker a trade deal with the King of Navenie . . .'

'Rothen's queen,' Elma corrected him.

Lord Maurice cleared his throat. 'We think it prudent, Majesty, to withhold the news of King Rafe's death until after your coronation.'

Godwin nodded. 'We say he's fallen ill. On the mend, of course, but not able to make the journey to Ordellun-by-the-Sea.'

Elma glanced from lord to lord, realization dawning. 'You want me to travel all the way to Ordellun-by-the-Sea? Now? With no one on the throne while I'm away?'

'It would be a grand statement,' said Lord Bertram, clearly wanting to appear involved. 'The heir ambassador, so devoted to her people that she journeyed far and —'

'Be still,' Lord Maurice growled, his dark eyes silencing the other lord.

Godwin watched Elma unwavering, and she knew he was assessing her behind those eyes. Gauging to see what she would agree to, what sacrifices she'd make. Ordellun-by-the-Sea, the shining southern city of Navenie, would take almost a week to reach by horseback. The way would be treacherous, cutting through mountain passes and remote old-growth forests. Godwin knew this, and he knew that Elma understood the request.

Elma had seen paintings of Ordellun-by-the-Sea. It was a city of splendor and riches, with libraries and palaces and beautiful gardens. It was said to rival even the beauty of Lothyn. Despite the warmth of the room, she shivered at the thought of seeing the city first-hand.

'I will require my maid, Cora, to accompany me,' she said. She caught and held Godwin's gaze. *The rest is up to you.*

Her uncle inclined his head, understanding her. 'Very good, Majesty. I shall select three of Rothen's best swords, as well as working models of our ballista and the trebuchet. I'll ensure they're outfitted appropriately. King Alaric of Navenie will require evidence of what Rothen provides.'

'Thank you, Godwin,' said Elma. 'The rest of you may go. I wish to speak with my uncle alone.'

The lords seemed eager to leave, and the room was quickly empty but for Elma and her uncle.

'I see your father taught you well,' Godwin said. 'Queenhood suits you.'

'Thank you for the flattery,' Elma said, 'but there's no need to lie.' *I don't know what I'm doing.* Her father had taught her to be cold, to build a wall of ice around her heart. But there was more to being queen than being frozen from the inside.

Godwin chuckled. 'Well, you've certainly made me proud, niece.'

'You speak as if I'm a child.'

'I know very well that you're not,' he said, pouring himself another goblet of wine. 'And I also know that, despite your status as sole heir of Rothen, you never actually believed you'd find yourself in this position. Are you ready for it?'

Elma raised her chin. 'Yes.'

He took a slow drag of wine. 'I know when you're lying, Elma. Though I'm certain you'd convince anyone else. Soon, you'll have the other lords quite tightly wrapped 'round your finger. It is good that you can lie. That you can twist truths convincingly. It is a difficult skill to learn.'

'What a lovely compliment,' said Elma. She glanced at her wine goblet, still full. 'Honesty, a good heart, a conscience . . . What use are those to a queen?'

'You better serve your people with cunning than with compassion,' said Godwin. 'A compassionate ruler allows enemies to outsmart her, to overrun her. A cunning one cannot be bested.'

'I suppose you refer to battle *and* diplomacy.'

'Naturally.'

'I believe a queen should be loved by her subjects. That she ought to protect them as if they were her own children.'

Godwin frowned. 'Why?'

'Isn't that what it means to be a monarch? That we're selected, ordained perhaps by the gods, to feed and house and protect a kingdom full of people? Otherwise, what are we but despots, power-hungry inbreds with coffers of gold?'

'Is that what you believe?' Godwin's amusement was obvious.

Elma sighed, impotent in her frustration. 'I'm duty-bound to serve this kingdom. That, I believe.'

'You are duty-bound to *rule*.'

'I'm tired, Godwin.' Elma stood and moved to the door.

'Wait,' said her uncle, still seated, fingers playing with the stem of his goblet. 'When you sent away the others . . . was there something you wished to ask me?'

Pausing by the door, Elma frowned. She wasn't sure she wanted to know. But it would eat at her until she made herself sick. So, she said, 'Those Slödavan bed slaves. My birthday gift. Did they . . . ?'

Godwin's expression did not change when he said, 'They were executed.'

Elma swallowed, her throat constricting. 'I see.'

She hurried from the room, teeth clenched, determined not to let Godwin see her pain.

4

Goodbyes were easy in Rothen. With Cora accompanying her on the journey, Elma had no one to miss. Anyone who could have been considered a companion, a friend even, would be making the journey to Ordellun-by-the-Sea with her. If all went well, they would return just in time for King Rafe's funeral.

Her father's funeral.

Elma sat shivering on her horse, despite the mountain of furs that draped over her and the horse's back, despite the heated rocks tucked into every pocket and nook of her clothing. She would have preferred to be in the covered wagon with Cora, but to ride away on horseback seemed more queenly. Elma rode alongside Luca, despite his urging that she'd be safer in the wagon. 'I'd rather see my death coming,' she said and was allowed to stay on the horse.

Godwin and the advisors had gathered to see them off. There was very little fanfare, for the kingdom was officially in mourning. So, Elma rode away in silence, flanked by her guards and her servants, a wagon full of weaponry clattered behind them. A quiet snow began to fall, though it was hard to tell in the fog.

'May the winter star guide us,' Elma said, her voice muffled by furs.

The descent from the Frost Citadel was one of the most treacherous legs of the journey. The road was cut into living rock, with a sheer drop on one side and the jagged mountain on the other. The way was kept clear by industrious citadel guards, but fatal falls, deadly storms, and avalanches were common.

They rode two by two as the wind cut through to their bones. Elma had always hated this stretch of road.

She remembered the first time she came down from the citadel, in a burst of teenage rebellion. It had been a frightening experience, and she had needed rescuing by her father's guards near the base of the mountain, where at last she had succumbed to terror and sat crouched against the mountainside, unable to go near the road's edge.

Elma's heart only stopped racing, knuckles still white on the reins, when they were safely off the mountain and back on flat land.

'I thought for sure the wagon was about to blow off the road,' Cora gasped, her eyes still wide. They had stopped to assess any damage to the wagon's wheels after the rough road and to ensure that no one had plummeted from the mountain without anyone noticing. Elma clasped her maid's hand tightly. They stood huddled together near the wagon, which shielded them from the icy wind.

'You should have ridden with me,' said Elma.

Elma squinted into the thick snow and thought she could see glimpses of dark shapes against the sky, far off. 'Is that the city?' she said aloud.

'No, Majesty,' said Luca, pointing in an entirely different direction. '*That's* the city of Frost. You can't see it in this snow. Only a few minutes' ride though, in good weather.'

'What was I looking at, then?' Elma asked, frowning.

'The mountains, Majesty.'

Elma frowned. She had become so turned around in the snow, set on edge by the descent from the citadel. 'Did we lose anyone? Is the wagon all right?'

'All the men are accounted for,' said Luca. 'The wagon is all right.'

'I'm not getting back in that death trap,' Cora said, her voice wavering.

There weren't enough horses for Cora to ride too, Elma knew. The wind was harsh, and the men didn't need to be under the watchful eye of their queen at every moment. Elma took Cora's arm, holding it tight. 'I'll ride in there with you,' she said. 'If it falls off a cliff or into a ravine, at least we'll go together.'

This seemed to appease Cora, and they crawled into the wagon together. It was filled with furs and pillows and hot bricks, even a cask of hot wine that would be cold by now. The rocking of the wagon was jarring at first, but after a few swigs of wine and a hot brick against her stomach, Elma found herself relaxing. She thought she might even sleep, if she were lucky.

When Elma woke in the dark, she knew immediately that something was wrong. She was cold, achingly so – her hot brick was no longer warm, which meant she had been asleep for hours. And the wagon was still. If they had stopped to camp, Cora or Luca would have roused her. Elma waited in silence for her eyes to adjust.

'Cora?' she said, her voice so soft she almost didn't hear herself. Fear rimed her heart. She heard no sound from outside, none of what she might expect – horses shifting in the snow, guards unpacking for the night, a bonfire crackling.

All she heard was the wind.

Cora, if she was still in the wagon with Elma, did not respond.

The darkness was no longer blinding – Elma was beginning to see shapes emerging, though just barely. The lumpy furs. The tiny round window on the far side of the wagon, through which a pale moonlight made its way. The snow had abated, then, but not the wind.

Elma dared not move. She tried not to breathe. If something had come out of the wilds and attacked them, it might still be nearby. The stories she'd heard . . . she tried not to think of them, of the human-shaped forms that were said to dwell in the ice storms, with elongated arms and grasping hands, howling jaws, and eyes that rolled white and unseeing. Of winged things that burst from the clouds and stole children from the streets, of great slavering wolves that were bigger than they ought to be.

'You're good at this.'

The voice, so sudden in the quiet dark, frightened Elma nearly out of her skin. Her pulse sped, heart in her throat.

Something shifted across from her. A man's figure, barely visible in the shadows. If he hadn't moved . . .

Elma found she couldn't speak, couldn't move. Was he one of the snow demons of folklore, here to toy with her?

'Most of the time,' said the voice, 'people make a break for it. Foolish. Or they try to fight me, even more foolish. I can't guess *what* you'll do, which is exciting for me.'

This was no snow demon. His voice was cocky and well-bred, judging by the accent. 'My maid,' Elma said, not caring that her voice shook, that her throat was so dry her voice broke on the last syllable.

'I don't kill women,' said the voice, as if that should be an obvious fact. 'Unless I have to.'

'Then where is she?' Elma demanded, growing bolder. This man sounded like one of the fops at court, some brat looking for a payout. Was this a half-baked coup attempt? She began mentally listing every courtier who might betray her so soon after her father's death.

A sigh came from the shadows. 'Your maid is perfectly safe. I can't say the same for some of your guards, but they *did* attack me first. If they'd only let me get to you unhindered, they'd all be alive right now. Their faults, really.' He paused. 'Are you going to cry now?'

'No,' said Elma.

'Good. It's off-putting. I'd rather enjoy this.'

She didn't dare reach for the blade she had hidden in the belt of her dress underneath her cloak. He would be watching, waiting for just such a movement. But if she could distract him . . .

'I hear you thinking over there,' said the stranger, a grin behind his words. 'What do you suppose you'll do? What schemes are unfolding in your head? I hate to do it, I really do, Your Majesty, but . . . I haven't a choice in the matter.'

'Who sent you?' Elma said, now certain that this man was an assassin, and loquacious to a fault. With luck, he might talk.

'That's a boring one,' said the stranger, shifting again in the darkness. She caught a glint of moonlight on steel and knew he'd shifted that way on purpose. 'Who do you *think* sent me, Queen of Frost?'

'You're stalling for something,' Elma said. 'What?'

There was a slight pause in the silence, as if she'd hit a

nerve. She sat up, shifted, and immediately, the stranger moved to mirror her.

'Now, now,' he said, his voice a low growl. 'Don't go and try to flee on me, snow rabbit. I'll catch you in a second and rip out your throat with my teeth.'

In the darkness, he saw too much, every movement, every shadow. In the light, there was more to distract, more to show him until he missed what she was really doing. 'I was looking for my tinderbox,' she lied. 'Don't I deserve to see the face of the man who would kill me?'

A low chuckle. 'Already given up, then? Smart.'

Elma waited. He didn't sound like a lowborn ruffian or a bloodthirsty monster. He would honor her request.

He sighed, a long-suffering exhale of breath. 'Oh, all right,' he said, 'if you insist.' There was movement in the dark, and he shifted sideways until a beam of moonlight illuminated him in ethereal blue-white.

Blinking, Elma stared across at the stranger.

He grinned wolfishly, gesturing at himself with a leather-gloved hand. 'Take it in, Your Majesty.'

And she did. He was not, as she had initially feared, a snow demon. Nothing but a man sat across from her, so relaxed in his bearing that he could have been on a holiday jaunt instead of a killing mission. He was dressed head to toe in black leather, with a fur-lined cape affixed to his shoulders. Long fingers emerged from leather half-gloves, twirling a wicked blade as if it were a child's toy.

He was handsome, beautiful even, despite the shadows under his eyes and a broad scar that ran from just above his right eyebrow down to his cheek. His grin was as wicked as his blade, and probably just as deadly. But these weren't the details that caught Elma's eye, made her heart sink, and made the blood drain from her face.

It was his hair – bone white and starkly pale in contrast with his tanned skin.

'You're Slödavan,' Elma breathed.

He flipped his knife into the air and caught it. Tilted his head. 'None other. And now, Queen of Frost, I'll give you a choice. How would you like to die?'

5

Not at all, thought Elma, almost surprising herself. She didn't want to die.

'At least tell me your name, before you kill me,' she said, sitting up straighter in the furs. If she could angle herself correctly without drawing attention to it, she might be able to access the dagger. Might be able to draw it in time.

A line formed between the assassin's brows. 'Why would you need my name at a time like this?'

Before Elma could track his movement, he leapt forward across the wagon, crouching over her, his blade only inches from her throat. In the quiet night, just above the endless howl of wind, she heard him breathing. It was an eager, hungry thing, the breath in his lungs. A predator's anticipation.

'How about a blade across the throat?' He said, pressing his thumb to the space below her ear. He leaned close, so close she felt the faintest touch of warm breath on her skin.

She closed her eyes.

'Don't be frightened,' he murmured, settling himself on his knees so that he straddled her where she sat. 'It won't hurt a bit. I keep my blades sharp. You'll feel a little pinch, that's all. I'll hold you 'til it's done. And if it makes you feel better . . .' he leaned so close that his deep voice hummed in her ear, 'I'll hand deliver your head to the Crown Prince of Slödava myself.'

Elma was panicking. She couldn't help it. She felt her body betraying her even as she tried to slow her breaths, to calm her mind. Fear, her father had taught her, led to death. Fear made you sloppy; it made you weak.

'Or maybe,' said the assassin, tracing his finger from her throat to her chest, between her breasts, and resting it on her stomach, 'I ought to gut you like a pig. Wouldn't that be fun? We could share facts and stories about ourselves until you eventually bleed out. I'd enjoy watching the life fade from you, minute by minute. I could make it painful, if I wanted to. I could twist the blade. Reach in, play with your . . .'

'Don't,' Elma bit out.

I'm useless, she thought, even then. *You're the Queen of Rothen. Do something*. But tears burned her eyes, threatening to fall. In the face of death, alone and helpless, there were no kings or queens. Only people, fragile bones and pumping hearts, blood beneath paper-thin skin.

'Don't eviscerate you?' asked the assassin, still too close, his finger pressed against her abdomen. 'Fine. If that's what you want, but it's boring. What if I . . . hmmm . . .' he tapped the knife against his teeth. Then his face brightened, his ice-blue eyes beaming with sadistic glee. 'What if I stab you in the heart. A bit cliche, and it *will* hurt. But think of the romance. The drama. Come to think of it, I might bring your heart back to the prince instead of your head. Easier to travel with.'

Elma sniffled, her nose clogged with unshed tears. As she did, she wriggled, just slightly, moving her arm just enough so that it looked thoughtless. 'Fuck you,' she said, knowing that insults were the true mark of impotence. Of giving up.

48

'Fuck me?' He made a low sound in his throat, leaned in slowly, and licked her neck.

His tongue was wet and hot, and Elma closed her eyes in disgust.

'Not *now*, you sick thing,' he said, pulling back, his eyes darkening. 'Don't you have a preference? There are so many ways I could kill you. Each one, unique and lovely. And no matter what death you pick, don't worry. I'll enjoy it.'

'I know how I want to die,' Elma said at last. It was a quiet admission, strangely vulnerable in the dark, her voice raw.

The assassin sat back, just enough to study her face, as if he had meant to play with her, goad her, for a long time. He hadn't expected her to pick a death. 'Oh? What is it, then?'

She made a show of arching her back, slowly, her eyes never leaving his. She had never been more grateful for her ability to lie with conviction. 'I want you inside me when you do it. I've always wondered what it would feel like, to die at the height of pleasure.'

The assassin froze, his expression almost comically shocked. But it was only for a moment. He collected himself in half a breath, grinning wolfishly. 'You know, I didn't think you Volta were half as –'

But he never got to finish his sentence. Elma drew her dagger lightning fast, driving it toward the assassin's neck in one swift, practiced move. But the assassin was faster, deflecting the blade before it became a killing blow. Even so, blood flowed freely from a gash just above his collarbone.

Elma, already wet with her attacker's blood, shoved him off her, relying on the element of surprise. He stumbled, but quickly recovered as she scrambled to stand. There was so much blood.

'You *tricked* me,' gasped the assassin, as if it were the first time in his life he had been fooled. He touched a hand to the wound on his neck, and his glove came away glistening red. He frowned. 'That could be a problem.'

'It is a problem,' Elma said, breathing hard, brandishing her knife. 'If that wound keeps bleeding, you'll be dead in minutes. You can try to kill me, but if you make one move, this blade is going straight into your eye.'

'You think you can outmaneuver me?'

'I don't need to,' said Elma. 'You're already stumbling. Getting weaker. If you'd wanted to overpower me, you should have done it while you were straddled across my lap. You're bleeding too much and too fast now.'

'Yes,' he said, pressing his palm to the gushing wound, his cockiness undercut with desperation, 'but you don't know who I am.'

'Who are you?'

He bared his teeth in a cocky grin. 'The man who killed the Queen of Rothen.'

Elma only just had time to sidestep his rush attack, and even then, his blade caught her arm, staining her dress red in a burst of pain. But as she'd predicted, he was slow and sloppy. His own blood spattered the wagon floor, dotting Elma's shoes.

The rest was too easy. He came at her again from the other direction, and she turned to face him, easily kneeing him in the groin. Elma let him fall to his knees in agony, and only then did she kneel across from him, pressing one finger into the gash on his neck.

He screamed, a guttural, animalistic cry of pain.

At once Elma pulled back, sick with herself, sick with the seemingly endless gush of blood. She was breathing too fast, too shallow. The assassin, meanwhile, was leaning into her as if for dear life. Then she realized he had lost consciousness, his body falling into hers, and the weight of him brought her back to reality. She sprang to her feet, a ringing in her ears.

She leapt from the wagon, numb to the icy wind, to the snow that filled her shoes as she cried out for Cora and the guards. Stumbling and half-sobbing, she tried to wipe the blood from her hands as she went.

At last, she found Cora and her men, bound together not far from the wagon. Some of them were even half out of their bonds, having wriggled free while Elma and the assassin faced off. It was almost as if he had meant for them to escape, aware that he would be long gone by the time they freed themselves.

When the guards were free and accounted for, minus the two who had been slain by the assassin, Elma turned, almost sobbing, to Luca.

'He's in the wagon,' she said. 'Bleeding to death. Stop his bleeding at once. Then bind him. He must make it back to Frost alive.'

'But the mission –'

'There is no mission,' Elma cut him off, relishing the vengeful rage that had already begun to wash away her fear. 'Not anymore. That assassin is the most important thing in the world to me. *Keep him alive.*'

She didn't say it because she didn't have to. Keep him alive so that she could bring him back to the citadel. Keep him alive so she could question him. Keep him alive so that she, with her own bare hands, could kill him the way he'd so gleefully tried to kill her.

6

Elma insisted on riding in the wagon with the assassin. She knew Luca and his men had him under control; there was no fear of his escape. The Slödavan was bound with chains, a blade at his throat at all times.

Not that he could have made an escape in his condition. He was in and out of consciousness, head lolling on the furs like a newborn infant. But Cora had managed to slow the bleeding, applying a poultice of herbs and snow and whispered words of strength and vitality.

Elma studied the assassin from where she sat across from him, a mirror of how she'd woken in the dark. Now, she held the upper hand, and she would not give it away. She tamped down a heady excitement that rose in her, the anticipation of hurting him. Of carving into his flesh.

Her father would have encouraged it. He *had* encouraged it, loved the rare occasions when she found the Death Games enticing rather than dull. 'We live in a cruel world,' King Rafe had said to her, time and time again. 'But we Volta embrace the cruelty, the bloodshed, until we thrive in it.'

She told herself she didn't yearn to hurt the assassin for the sake of it, because she enjoyed it. No, she wanted to know why he'd come, and what her death meant to him. She would wrench every last secret from his dying lips.

Elma had always suspected the tales of Rime Ice to

be exaggerated, specters of fear created by soldiers in the thick snows of battle. A blade might come out of the white and strike a man down, and his comrades might remember things differently, more fantastical than they were. She often wondered if her father's obsession with the stuff was a delusion of age.

'Rime Ice may well change our destiny,' her father had often insisted. 'A king of Rothen who wields such a weapon would be a thing of legend. A king who commanded an army of such blades . . . this man would never be forgotten.'

Yet, even in the seven years since Elma's arrival in Rothen, her father had never declared open war on the Slödavans, nor had he succeeded in stealing any Rime Ice for himself, despite several attempts.

The assassin's eyelids fluttered, his brows furrowed even in unconsciousness. He was so different to the rugged browns and grays of Elma's guards, his stark white hair painting him as almost ethereal. As if he were a ghost, come down from the frozen glacier alone. As if he might dissipate into mist at the slightest touch.

He did not wield a Rime Ice weapon, Elma noted. Perhaps there weren't many in use, if they existed. Or maybe they were reserved for only the greatest soldiers. This was but a lowly assassin, after all. A man who, in repose, appeared strikingly youthful. Sweet, even, with strands of white hair falling over his forehead.

All at once, he shivered, a wracking, violent movement, and groaned in pain.

'Is he dying?' Elma asked, eyeing Luca, who sat nearest the assassin.

Luca glanced sideways at the Slödavan. 'Hard to say. They're hearty folk, the men of the north. If the wound remains clean, and the bleeding is controlled, he has a good chance. You just missed the artery, Your Majesty.' This last was said with a hint of pride.

'He deflected me,' Elma said. 'It's a good thing he did, or we'd be questioning a corpse.'

Cora shivered against Elma's shoulder. She had been quiet since the attack, her eyes wide, and her lips pressed in a thin line. Elma knew that her maid had never seen war, had likely never experienced death in such a manner, with blood on the floor of the wagon, in Elma's hair, under her fingernails, flecking the skin of her face. Death in the city of Frost came slowly, insidiously, with a hunger ache or a shiver in the night. Those were familiar deaths, a horror that dulled over time. Even the Death Games were contained, a dramatic play of gore and brutality carried out behind a sheen of unreality. Because Elma, Cora, and all those who lived in the Frost Citadel – they knew they would always be above, watching. They would never be below.

They would never shed blood for the kingdom in the arena or on the battlefield.

'Explain it to me again,' said Godwin. 'One more time. Slowly.'

Elma, dressed in fresh wool and velvet, draped in fur and smelling of the bear fat and pine soaps the servants used to wash her, took a steadying breath. 'You heard me the first time, Uncle. I wish to question him myself.'

It was so dark outside, the sky heavy with snow, that Elma couldn't tell whether it was night or day, morning or some middle hour, dusk or the gloom before sunrise. They had ridden nonstop back to the citadel, and things had transpired in a blur.

Snow fell upon dark glass windows. Godwin's study had always been bleak, by Elma's standards. But now it felt claustrophobic, a room of heavy beams and hardly any windows, a too-large fire, and far too many scrolls and parchments lying about. A full suit of armor, decades old, hunched in one corner on display.

Godwin half sat on his desk, arms braced against its edge, eyeing Elma with disapproval and no small amount of pity. His deep-set eyes were limned in red. 'It's not the questioning that gives me pause,' he said, as if Elma were silly not to have guessed his feelings already. 'It's the fact that you want to interrogate him *alone*.'

'I don't see that it makes a difference,' Elma said tightly. She didn't. The assassin was bound so thoroughly that not even a sorcerer – gods forbid – might free himself from the restraints. 'What are you afraid of, Uncle? That I'll conspire with him?'

'That you'll – for the love of gods, Elma, be serious. I'm concerned for your *safety*. You are the queen. And uncrowned. And though it makes little difference to you and me, it makes a world of difference to Slödava. If they overthrow us now, with no heir to contest it, there will be no one, no law or army, to stand in their way.' He shook his head, glaring at a pile of scrolls to his left. 'You should not have come back here, Elma. You've put us all in peril.'

'What should I have done, then?' Elma said. 'Continued on to Ordellun-by-the-Sea as if nothing were amiss?'

'Yes. You did not need to accompany the assassin here.

It is under control. We need you to broker a new trade deal with Navenie before our people starve.'

Elma exhaled sharply, ignoring the telltale prick of emotion in the back of her throat. Her uncle had lit a defiant fire in her, and she would not back down easily. 'If our people are hungry, give them grain from the citadel's stores. Our kitchens are stocked.'

'A temporary –'

'And when I'm finished with the Slödavan, I will write personally to Queen Antigone,' said Elma. 'I would rather we take advantage of our trade alliance with Mekya than charm King Alaric.' *I'd rather lean into the alliance that doesn't require me to ride through mountains for a week*, she thought, but honesty in this matter served neither her nor her uncle.

'As you know, trade negotiations with Mekya are ongoing,' said Godwin, 'They offer us little.'

'Little beyond food, you mean?' Elma said. 'We don't need military might, no matter what Bertram says. Even if I were to win over King Alaric, Navenie would never grant us soldiers in addition to the food we so badly need. And for what war, Uncle? Does Lord Bertram expect to fight snow demons?'

The atmosphere in Godwin's study was thick with tension. Elma had begun to sweat beneath her furs, but she refused to shift, to rearrange herself more comfortably. Godwin would see her discomfort and equate it to weakness.

After a long moment, Godwin ran a scarred hand over his face. When he again caught Elma's eye, his gaze was searching. 'Let's not argue, Niece. Not while your father's spirit remains to hear us. We'll spar about trade after his body is put to rest. Get some sleep. You look pale. Tomorrow, we'll talk.'

'If I sleep,' Elma said, desperate, 'you and I both know that when I wake, the assassin will be dead.'

'We would never –'

'You executed the slaves,' she cut in. 'They were my birthday present. They were helpless. And you had them killed.'

Godwin's gaze sharpened. 'I suppose you've forgotten that they share blood with the man who nearly murdered *you*. Elma, there is war in Rothen's future, just as her past is rife with it. Slödava has all but declared, signed, and sealed it. Had they taken your life . . .' he paused for a moment. 'Rothen would have had no choice but to declare open war for the first time since your father, gods rest him, was a young man.'

'We've been at war with Slödava since I was a baby,' Elma said.

'A war of attrition,' Godwin replied, almost pained. 'Raids in the night, assassins, thievery, lies, and plots. Nothing that required an army to cross the Frozen Sea. You know that such a campaign against Slödava would take months, perhaps years. And the number of resources . . . it would be untenable, as you are well aware. You should have continued to Navenie.' This last was said to himself, laced with regret.

'You will let me question the assassin,' Elma said, with as much of an air of queenliness as she could muster. 'I'll find out who sent him. He may be working alone, or with some splinter group that has nothing to do with –'

'You're grasping at straws,' Godwin said.

Elma stared at her uncle. He had always been a teacher to her, a guide in this frozen citadel, a friend. But he was only a general. She was Queen of Rothen. And it was *her* life the assassin had almost taken. She deserved to question him.

'Godwin,' Elma said, meeting his gaze with a ferocity she hadn't known she possessed, 'This isn't a request. I will interrogate the prisoner now, alone.'

For a moment, her uncle returned the strength of her stare, as if he might try to deny her. Then the tension broke, and he shrugged one shoulder. 'As Her Majesty wills it,' he said.

The Frost Citadel dungeons were a slow and miserable death sentence. Just cold enough to cause frostbite and misery but not cold enough to kill with haste. They were warmed by a series of massive and generally ineffective hearths along one wall; cell blocks lined the other, and there was an unending howl as the wind swept angrily past tiny cell windows.

Elma was led past cells that held things she refused to look at: huddled shapes, dark stains on dark stone, muffled and broken sobs. Or was it the wind? Elma chose to believe it was the latter, keeping her gaze locked on the back of Luca's head as he led her down the entire length of the dungeon.

'Here,' he said at last, turning to indicate the last cell in the row. It was also furthest from any fire, and an icy draft cut through Elma's thick wool stockings, licking at her ankles.

Elma almost didn't want to see. He remained a ghost

to her, a spirit of the snow. To see the assassin here, in the confines of her world, threatened to make him solid. Even so, she turned to look into the cell. It was dimly lit, as the torches in the dungeon were few and far between. The sight of him was a blow to the chest.

He was almost more striking here, somehow brighter and stranger in the dingy muck of the citadel dungeon. He sat in the far corner of his cell, arms flung out to rest on bent knees, his head hanging down between them. His hair, matted with dirt and blood and sweat, was still so white it seemed to glow in the low light.

As she studied him, he raised his head. The movement was not without a clear amount of pain and effort, and yet when his icy gaze met hers, fear bloomed in her chest.

I'm in over my head, she thought before she had a chance to silence her own doubt.

A faint smirk hovered at the edge of the assassin's mouth. As if he knew what she was thinking and agreed.

'Bring him to a private interrogation room,' Elma said. She waited with the rest of her guards while Luca unlocked the cell, while he unhooked the assassin's chains from the cell wall. She stood stiffly, hardly daring to breathe as Luca dragged the prisoner past her and toward the interrogation room. The Slödavan's icy blue gaze met hers for a split second, and a sharp pang caught in her chest.

She refused to admit to herself that she had no idea what she would say to him when they were finally alone. She had been angry, and still was. Not just angry – enraged. This was a man who spoke gleefully of carrying her disembodied head back to his crown prince. This was a man who wanted to see her dead, would see her legacy destroyed and her kingdom laid low. What else could a Slödavan want but the utter annihilation of Rothen? It was all they had ever wanted.

And because it was the only thing in the world that was truly hers, she refused to let him have it.

'He's ready.'

Luca's voice startled her. Elma blinked, drawing her furs tightly around her shoulders. She murmured her thanks and allowed Luca to escort her to the interrogation room, where she instructed him and her guards to wait just outside. They tried to fight her on it, but she was queen now, whether she liked it or not. So, she gave the order, and they obeyed.

And when the heavy wooden door slammed behind her, she was utterly alone with the assassin.

The room was empty of furniture but for a chair, various torture devices crowded against the walls, and a tray of metal implements that Elma didn't want to look at too closely. The assassin was in the chair, his ankles bound to its legs, his arms behind his back.

Before Elma had a chance to collect herself, to decide what to say, the assassin smiled. 'Come to finish the job, Your Majesty?'

'Speaking of unfinished jobs,' Elma said, not daring to get any closer. She stood just inside the door, perhaps ten feet from the prisoner. She wondered if he could break his bonds, even though they were iron. Wondered if he could turn into snow or fog like some of the old folk tales said.

'I underestimated you, little queen,' said the assassin, tilting his head. Blood flecked his face, and the scar over his eye was starkly white against his skin. 'I thought you'd be such an easy kill. I dreamed of your blood on my fingers, sticky and hot.' He smiled wider. 'But you surprised me.'

'Don't call me *little queen*,' Elma said. 'I'm taller than you.'

The assassin chuckled, a cold and cruel sound. 'Unbind my legs, and let's put that to the test.'

Elma clenched her teeth. 'Who sent you to kill me? And why?'

He rolled his head back, sighing as he did. 'Is that all you've got in your repertoire? *Who sent you and why?* My delightful queen, you make me wish you were immortal so I could kill you twice. A thousand times. I'm already bored of you.'

The dagger in Elma's belt, hidden by folds of fabric and fur, seemed to call for her fingers to close around it, for her to jam it once again into the assassin's neck. She stood her ground. 'Answer the question.'

His expression darkened, his grin curling into something more sinister. 'Why should I? What have you offered me in return?'

'I owe you nothing,' Elma said, aware of the rage, the helplessness apparent in her voice. Some part of her had always accepted that her father would die violently, in battle or at the hands of an assassin. Despite his natural death, she felt strangely as if this Slödavan had killed her father. He *would* have, if given the chance. What was the difference? She took a long, shaking breath. 'Tell me who you are, who sent you, and what else they're planning. Are more assassins going to come for me? Is an army on its way across the Frozen Sea?'

'Oh, Elma,' said the assassin, pity painting his features. 'You've never conducted a single interrogation in your life, have you?'

7

Elma was grateful for the ever-howling wind and the chill of the room. Otherwise, the assassin might have heard her shaking intake of breath, seen pink heat rise in her cheeks.

'I have,' she said, realizing that she was losing the upper hand in this conversation. If she'd ever held it to begin with.

'And who did you interrogate, then? I'm dying to know.'

'That's not . . .' Elma slammed her mouth shut, glaring, trying to regain her composure. This man had too much of an effect on her. He made her angry, set her off balance.

He watched her with an ice-blue gaze. She noticed then that his breathing was slightly labored, that every once in a while, he moved his shoulder in an odd way, almost a flinch. She was stupid not to have seen it before. His wound, cleaned and bandaged though it was, still hurt him.

Elma took a step toward the assassin. 'Tell me your name.'

'My name is irrelevant.'

'You know mine,' Elma persisted, not quite knowing why it was so important to her to know his name. But it *was*, the need to understand this creature who had come down from the north to kill her, this man who seemed so unaffected by the thought of her severed head or her rup-tured heart in his hands for the taking.

The assassin watched her for a moment, his expression

unreadable. Then he shrugged. 'Rune,' he said. 'There. Are you happy? Do you feel fulfilled?'

Rune. Somehow it seemed too nice a name, its edges too rounded to belong to him. He was sharp, dangerous. He pierced skin. He reminded Elma of everything she wasn't, of all she'd lost and the few things that were left to her — cold things, dangerous and deadly things. And yet . . .

She took another step toward him. They were close enough now to see one another quite clearly, each nuance of expression, each twitching muscle. 'Rune,' she said. 'Is that all?'

He grinned. 'Maybe. Are you going to use those instruments on me?' He cocked his head, indicating the devices against the wall, the pile of metal things on the table nearby. 'You should try. I might enjoy it. Then you might get something useful out of me, after all.'

Elma ignored the tiny thrill that tickled her skin at the thought. 'How about this,' she said, going on a hunch. 'I'll tell you what I think your motives are, and you can tell me whether or not I'm right.'

Rune snorted. 'I'd prefer the torture devices, but it's your interrogation.'

She swallowed the impulse to lash out, to see what he'd do if she opened up his skin again. 'You want to kill me because I'm the last of the Volta line,' she said. 'Your crown prince sent you here to get me out of the way, leaving him an open throne to claim. You want our foothold at the borders of Mekya and Navenie. You want to protect Rime Ice. Your presence here is a declaration of war.'

Rune nodded sagely. 'Fascinating speculation. Truly sensational. You should write books. Works of fiction, though, obviously – the crown prince of Slödava hasn't told me to do shit. It's his mother who sits on the throne. Or hadn't you heard of a matriarchy?'

Elma's jaw was clenched so tightly it began to ache. She would not let his deflection distract her, as much as it stung. She hadn't known. Her practical knowledge of Slödava was almost nonexistent. 'Why else would you try to kill me,' she said, 'if not to take my throne? To take Rothen?'

The assassin laughed, a spluttering, mocking sound. The movement caused a shock of hair to fall over one eye, and in that moment, he looked truly feral. A beast come down from the snow-capped peaks to hunt Elma.

Unthinking, she pulled her furs tighter.

'What could Slödava possibly want with *Rothen*?' Rune said when he finally finished laughing. 'My prince has no interest in your decrepit throne. I came to kill your father, Elma. I came for King Rafe's head, not yours. But you were all that was left, so . . . I had to settle for the next best thing.'

'You killed my father,' Elma said, almost hoping it was true. She would ride this wave of vengeful ire until it crashed her against a deadly shore. 'Poisoned him on the night of my birthday.'

He blinked. 'Your birthday? Isn't that poetic? Now I wish I *had* poisoned your father. But he died of his own accord, I'm sorry to say. You know, when I found out you were his only heir, that I had to kill you instead . . .' Rune studied her face. 'I was terribly upset.'

'Why?' Elma asked when he didn't elaborate. Her throat tightened.

'Look at you,' he breathed. 'It's like you're carved from ice, frigid and perfect. There are so many things I'd rather do to that body than carve it up, but . . . you being who you are . . .' a predatory gleam lit his eyes.

Elma fought the reflexive urge to back away and held her ground. He had voiced her own darkest, most perverse thoughts. It was impossible not to notice the curve of his neck where his leather jerkin hung open, the enticing angle of his jaw when he grinned, the undeniably athletic body held captive before her.

'Enjoying?' he said.

He saw her too clearly.

'Enjoying what,' she said, 'the brute who failed to kill me? A scarred piece of rubbish blown in from a winter storm?'

Rune lowered his chin, his eyes narrowing slightly. 'Perhaps, but at least this piece of rubbish retains some shred of honor. Unlike your father. Unlike you.'

'You know nothing about me,' Elma said, his words cutting an unseen gouge in her flesh.

His lip curled. 'Don't I? What do you think I see when I look at you? Other than a pincushion for my dagger.'

The interrogation had completely gotten away from Elma. What had she hoped to achieve, she wondered, having never interrogated anyone before in her life? Godwin had taught her techniques, of course. And her father had even demonstrated, once, how some of the implements worked – what parts of the body they were meant to slice or stretch or crush – and when to use them.

But in this room with the assassin, the air so cold and the walls so close, all that knowledge fled from her mind. Theory was one thing, but to do it alone for the first time, and do it well . . .

'What do you think I see?' Rune asked again, tongue pressing against a cut on his lip that had split in the cold. 'Is it the Queen of Rothen?'

Elma turned away, realizing her mistake in coming there. She had shown him nothing but weakness.

'Is it King Rafe's avenger?'

She moved to the door and hammered it once with a fist. The door swung open.

'I see a frightened little girl,' came the assassin's amused words.

The door slammed shut behind her.

Elma stood amongst her guards for a moment, leaning against the door. She caught her breath, pressing the back of a hand to her nose. It had gone numb in dungeon air.

'Throw him back in the cell,' she said at last. 'Don't bother being gentle.'

Cora helped Elma into bed. She had gone straight to her chambers from the dungeon, unable to keep her thoughts or the thrum of her heart under any sort of control.

'I'm out of my depth,' she kept saying to Cora, who sat on the edge of the bed, nodding. 'I don't know how to be queen.'

'You were attacked by an assassin,' said Cora. 'It's only natural you'd feel . . . out of sorts.'

'Out of sorts,' mumbled Elma, pulling the blankets up to her chin. 'My father is dead. The throne is vacant for the next month. And here I lie, an absolute wreck after a botched interrogation.'

'I'm certain you didn't botch it,' said Cora, smiling softly. She had always been good at comforting, at being a rock in the storm of Elma's life.

'How is your family?' Elma asked, half distracted. She couldn't get that cocky grin, that blood-flecked white hair out of her thoughts.

'My brother no longer has a fever,' Cora replied, her eyes downcast. 'My father continues to seek a pardon for the family name.'

'You'll get one,' Elma said, now realizing that she had the power to at least right one wrong in the world. Cora's father had been stripped of his title and land decades earlier, due to some minor indiscretion that even she couldn't keep straight. She had asked King Rafe to make amends with Cora's father more than once. But he had always refused.

Cora's mouth fell open, her eyes wide. 'You . . . you'll pardon him?'

Elma sat up. 'Of course, Cora. You've always been a friend to me. I'll do what I can to reinstate your father's . . . what was it? An earldom?'

Her cheeks on fire, Cora nodded eagerly. She was younger than Elma by almost three years, practically a child, and Elma felt protective of her.

'I'll see it done,' said Elma.

Cora beamed, color high in her cheeks as she drew a hot brick from beside the fire and settled it at Elma's feet, and soon Elma was alone. Sleep did not come easily, and when at last it did, it was tainted with visions of white hair, icy blue eyes, and blades of ice at her throat.

'You're mad if you don't see this as a declaration of war.' Lord Bertram's sharp voice, and the following slam of his fist on the table, cut through the fog of Elma's thoughts.

'Nobody here is mad,' said Godwin, looking as if he'd

been awake since Elma's return to the citadel. Dark shadows hung beneath red-rimmed eyes, and his hair – usually neatly styled – was in utter disarray.

'You will be if you don't get some sleep,' Elma said, pushing a mug of black coffee toward her uncle. 'Drink this, and stop arguing.' She turned to the rest of the advisors, all of whom were in various states of distress. 'Can't this wait until after the coronation?'

Lord Bertram and Lord Ferdinand glanced at one another. Lord Maurice regarded her with a keen eye but was otherwise silent.

'You can't think we ought to just . . . sit here and *take* it,' Lord Bertram said at last.

'Take what, exactly?' Godwin cut in. 'We've questioned the prisoner thoroughly, and he gave us nothing.'

'What I'd like to discuss is Her Majesty's interrogation of the Slödavan prisoner,' said Lord Maurice, speaking for the first time since the start of the meeting. 'If I'm not mistaken, she came away with less than nothing.'

Elma lifted her chin defiantly. 'I did learn something. Rune only came for me because my father was already dead.'

'*Rune*,' Lord Bertram muttered dismissively.

'And that tells us what,' said Lord Maurice, ignoring Bertram, 'that Slödava, or at least this assassin, wants the Rothen monarch dead. Forgive me, but it's hardly a revelation.'

'Speak to your queen with respect,' said Godwin, mug of coffee in his hands so that the steam might warm his face.

'I meant no disrespect,' said Lord Maurice. 'But I rather

69

think we ought to refrain from allowing the queen to reside in rooms alone with her would-be assassin. In the future.'

'Thank you for the input, Lord Maurice,' said Elma, eager for this breakfast to end. 'I realize you're all eager to declare war on Slödava, but I believe it would be a mistake.'

'Rumors are spreading in Frost, Your Majesty,' Lord Ferdinand said, chin resting daintily on his folded hands. 'They say your father was murdered by the assassin, that you single-handedly defended yourself against him. They are angry on behalf of their queen. They see you as a hero at the moment and want to protect you. They're slavering for justice. If you do not send Rothen to war against Slödava, your subjects will see it as weakness.'

'Cowardice,' added Lord Bertram.

'Thank you, Bertram,' Godwin said, shooting a look at the lord.

What do I care if my subjects think I'm weak? Elma wanted to say. *They'd be right.* Instead, she said, 'What good would war do with Rothen in such a precarious position? I need a crown in order to lead an army, and you well know it.' She glanced around at the seated lords, who were listening intently for once. 'After I'm crowned, we'll discuss this war you insist on having. I'll even ride down to Navenie and ask King Alaric for aid, if I must.'

'Months,' said Lord Bertram, slamming his palm against the table again. 'That would take months. The people hunger for justice *now*.'

'And they'll see it carried out,' Elma said. 'In the Death Games. We'll hold a great coronation event, a blood tournament. Put the assassin in the arena with the rest of the common criminals. But let him be the star. Let him die to the fanfare of trumpets and the roar of the crowd.'

The advisors were quiet for a moment. Godwin inclined his head slightly in approval.

'I like it,' said Lord Ferdinand at last, in a tone that suggested he hadn't expected to feel that way. 'The people of Frost will love it. An execution, a Death Game, and a coronation event in one. How could they resist?'

'To rush into war without a queen firmly on the throne *would* be imprudent,' said Lord Bertram, his tone reluctant.

'A fine solution, Your Majesty,' said Lord Maurice, his ever-sharp gaze locked on Elma. 'The Volta blood runs strong in your veins.'

The meeting dispersed soon thereafter, with the advisors satisfied and already planning the events of the Death Games.

Elma walked alone through the halls of the citadel, her retinue of guards trailing behind. She couldn't shake the words that Lord Maurice had said. *The Volta blood runs strong in your veins.* The Volta family had ruled Rothen for hundreds of years, holding off invaders and conquering small townships until the kingdom was vast and the borders strong. But Elma's ancestors were not known for their honor, their mercy, nor their strategic prowess.

The Volta line had always been known, even celebrated, for one thing: a thirst for blood.

8

Elma found Godwin in his study, asleep. His head lay cradled on one bent arm, and a soft snore rumbled through his nose as she approached. She hated to wake him, especially so soon after the advisors' meeting, but she couldn't wait to broach the topic of Cora's father with him.

Before she came to the desk, however, her uncle jolted awake, sitting up and blinking at her in the firelight.

'Sorry,' she said.

'It's all right,' he said thickly, running thick fingers through his hair and rubbing his eyes. 'It's all right, Elma. What is it?'

There was nowhere to sit except at the desk, so Elma remained standing, hands clasped at her waist. 'I have a favor to ask of you. A favor that I thought you might grant the queen.'

He raised an eyebrow. 'Can't the queen simply say the word, and then it is so?'

She wrinkled her nose at his attempted levity. 'I don't know who has the power to . . . to do this,' she said. 'It's a favor for a friend, really.'

Godwin frowned. Elma wondered if he was wracking his brain for evidence of Elma having any friends and coming up empty.

'For my maid,' Elma added helpfully. 'Cora Mannering.'

'Mannering,' said Godwin. 'I know that name.'

'Yes,' said Elma quickly, hoping to avoid any pointed questioning. 'Her father was stripped of his lands and title some years ago. They're struggling to make ends meet. I only came to you because I don't know who issues titles.'

There was an uneasy moment of quiet, in which Godwin studied Elma thoughtfully, and Elma wished she knew what he was thinking. That she was overstepping? That she wasn't being forceful enough?

At last, he spoke. 'I cannot help you in this matter.'

'Then who can?'

'Nobody. I sign the title documents.'

Elma blinked. 'But . . . why not? Cora has been loyal to me, the only woman in the citadel who isn't bound to some horrible man, the only person other than Luca who speaks to me, the –'

Godwin held up a hand to stop her. 'This has nothing to do with your maid. Do you know why Lord Mannering was stripped of his title?'

'No. Some disagreement, or . . .'

He shook his head. 'It was not some disagreement. I won't speak of it. I don't have the time or the desire. I am sorry, Elma. The Mannering name will not have land, it will not be titled ever again. Not while I have the power to keep it that way.'

Elma spent the rest of the afternoon avoiding Cora. She hadn't told her attendant that she would be inquiring about her father's title so soon, but she knew herself. She knew she would give it away with a look the second she saw Cora.

So instead of returning to her rooms, she wandered the citadel aimlessly, feeling less and less a queen with every step she took. She missed the first few years of her life at the citadel, when she had been allowed to clamber down to the training grounds with her father's soldiers, dressed in boys' clothes and swinging a wooden sword in the blowing snow. She even missed her tutor, a stern woman who had never said a kind word to Elma, but who had always brought her sweets from Frost and made certain that Elma knew everything a princess ought to know: geography, mathematics, history, philosophy.

A thought occurred to Elma, pausing in the drafty corridor. Luca had often practiced sword combat techniques with her. They'd been almost indistinguishable then, both lanky and dark-haired and dressed like boys. Elma had even asked her father once if Luca was her bastard brother, but King Rafe had only laughed. 'He is a son of Rothen,' he'd said. 'We are all cut from the same frozen land.' But as the years passed, Luca became increasingly busy with his guard duties, and eventually, they stopped sparring altogether.

Elma turned in the corridor, a mote of levity growing in her chest as she met her guard's gaze. 'Luca,' she said, 'I'm rusty. Would you spar with me, like old times?'

The other guards exchanged glances, but Luca held her gaze steadily. 'Your Majesty, I wish I could, but . . . I can't spar with the queen.'

'What if he hurt you?' said one of the other guards, a light-haired young man called Hugh.

Elma's heart sank. If Luca hurt her, even by accident, he would face punishment. Whipping, at the very least. 'Of course,' she said. 'Silly of me.'

'Cheer up,' said Luca. 'What about that ball tonight? You'll be the star of the show. The Queen's Coronation Ball.'

'How could I forget,' Elma intoned. 'Balls, dinners . . . it feels wrong to celebrate.'

'Your father would want you to embrace your impending reign,' Luca said, his voice low. 'To love Rothen as he did.'

'My father didn't love anything,' Elma replied. 'Not the way he should have. Not even me.'

Balls were never something that Elma had enjoyed. Perhaps when she'd first come to live at the Frost Citadel, they'd held some interest for her, some novelty. Now, they were nothing but responsibilities and expectations for things that did not come naturally to her. She was terrible at dancing, and her partners often didn't know what to do with such a long-legged woman. She had trod on more than one nobleman in her day.

And the men . . . even worse than the dancing. Her father had warned her, of course, and explained where to hurt them most if they took advantage – between the legs, in the eyes, or even a blow to the ears. But even so, Elma hated the way they watched her. Not with the usual lust, though they did that. It was with a burning, cloying hunger. The men who wanted her, it wasn't for her beauty or charm. Men who longed to touch her were longing for the throne.

Elma hated all of it.

'You look miserable,' Cora had said while lacing Elma into her dark green dress. 'At least try to smile. You're the queen now.'

'Almost queen,' Elma said, avoiding Cora's eye.

And now, here she sat, alone on a dais, on a throne that

did not feel like hers. She was flanked by a dozen guards, with Luca at her elbow. Three different men had come to ask her to dance, and she had complied with barely concealed reluctance.

It all felt so empty and meaningless. Leaning her cheek on her hand, she tried to remember the last time she'd felt anything at all. Her time in Rothen had been a vast stretch of unhappiness, and while the gnawing pain in her chest had faded, she still yearned for Orchard House. There were moments of levity, of course. Brief bursts, like sunlight breaking through thick clouds. But they were few and far between and as fleeting as a wisp of fog.

Unbidden, she thought of Rune. He was still held prisoner in the belly of the citadel; she would soon see him die in the great arena. Would it be satisfying, she wondered, watching his body break, his blood gush over the packed snow? Would she feel something at the sight of it?

She inhaled suddenly, remembering goosebumps on her flesh, the thrill of blood on her fingertips, his hot wound in the moonlit wagon.

'Your Majesty.'

The voice brought Elma back to the here and now, though her heart was racing. A man stood at the foot of the dais. He was still bowing, and only the top of his balding head was visible to her.

'Good evening,' she said, holding out her hand. When the man straightened, she recognized his face, but only vaguely.

'What a pleasure it is,' he said, taking her hand and kissing her largest ring.

Elma managed not to grimace. 'The pleasure is mine. How may we serve you tonight, my lord?'

'With a dance, Your Majesty, if . . . if you would be so kind.'

'Of course.' Elma's tone was dry, her words empty of any feeling. She allowed this nameless lord to lead her to the dance floor, knowing Luca's gaze was fixed firmly on her all the while.

They spun and clapped, the man laughing all the while; Elma was barely able to keep pace. The musicians were in their usual form, playing the most popular dances and jigs. This one was a romantic tune, and Elma was sure her dancing partner had waited until just this moment to ask her to join him.

'Condolences on the loss of your father,' said the balding lord. 'We at the Stallard estate sent you a wheel of cheese to show our support.'

'Thank you,' said Elma.

They spun and spun.

'We look forward to the Death Games, of course,' said the lord, whose name was presumably Stallard. 'What a day that will be. The whole family will be coming in to pay respects for the funeral, and we thought, why not attend the Games as well? Quite a way to start your rule, Your Majesty.'

'Thank you,' said Elma.

They spun and spun.

'Perhaps it is imprudent,' said Lord Stallard, 'but I do hope Her Majesty knows how much we look forward to her coronation.'

'Thank you,' said Elma.

The song ended, and Elma felt as if she had curled in on herself or grown a shell. She nodded thoughtlessly as

Lord Stallard bowed, and he disappeared into the crowd. Elma began to return to the dais, to sit once again on her father's throne, and then . . . she stopped. The musicians were starting up another song, a dance that Elma had heard so many times she knew it by heart. It was a dreadful song, repetitive and far too joyous.

'Your Majesty,' someone called to her from the crowd.

Elma was halfway across the ballroom before she realized she had changed direction. She strode toward the exit with a determination that cleared a path through the dancers and revelers, until at last, she was in the corridor. The air there was chill where the ballroom's had been stuffy and smoky. Too many fires and no open windows. Elma breathed deeply, the tension in her shoulders lessening as her head cleared.

Without waiting to see if Luca followed her, Elma made her way through corridors and down curving staircases of stone. She ran her fingers along the cool walls. She listened to her own breath in the quiet, watched fog form at her lips when she exhaled.

Glancing over her shoulder once, she saw Luca and her guards, following respectfully behind. She was glad that they left her alone, that they were nothing more than an armored shadow.

But even alone in these halls, as alone as a queen could be, Elma felt as if the citadel were closing in on her with every breath, with every step she took. How many years would she live in this frostbitten place? How many lords would she dance with, how many *thank you*s and *Your Majesty*s would she endure before, at long last, her mind faded and her body went with it, until she joined her father in the after?

Somehow, she knew, it would be a long reign. The prison of her life would stretch out before her, unending, as if the citadel itself were a coffin.

Elma didn't know how she ended up at the dungeon. She had made no conscious decision, yet here she was. The dungeon guards eyed her curiously but said nothing. Luca and his men hovered in the corridor behind her. She stepped forward, curled her fingers over one of the bars in the dungeon door. Peering down into the depths below, she couldn't see the assassin. She couldn't see anything.

'I would like to go down,' she said, stepping back to let one of the guards unlock the door for her. The same guard held a torch aloft as they made their way down the narrow stone steps.

Luca trailed behind, while the rest of his men waited in the corridor above.

'You wish to see the prisoner, Your Majesty?' asked the guard, squinting at Elma.

She nodded.

The guard carried onward. When they weren't far from the cell, Elma stopped and held up her hand. 'Wait for me here.'

'Pardon, Your Majesty,' said Luca, 'but there's no bloody way I'm letting you near that man without a guard.'

She spun on him, the rage of a life of inertia building in her like a storm cloud. 'You will *wait for me here.*'

Luca had the sense to look abashed. 'Yes, Your Majesty.' He gestured at the other guard, who shrugged.

The cell was not far, only several paces from where Luca and the prison guard waited. But it felt like an eternity before she was there, looking in at him through the bars.

He was exactly as she remembered. A monster, a specter of the north, the man who should have killed her.

He sat just as he had the last time she'd seen him. Knees bent; arms outstretched. This time, he was waiting for her. He must have heard her approach in the quiet. The torch-light carved dark shadows on his face. A bruise bloomed on his bottom lip.

They'd beaten him. There were probably bruises all over his body, in places Elma couldn't see. She regretted that she hadn't been invited to take part. She would have loved to watch him grimace in pain, to carve a little piece out of that tanned flesh.

A slow grin crawled across his features. 'Came to admire, Your Majesty? Didn't get your fill the last time, I see.'

She said nothing.

He watched her with keen bright eyes. 'Or perhaps to gloat, then? I know what you plan to do with me. I suppose you'd like to make sure I'm whole before I die. Wouldn't want to watch an injured Slödavan limping about in the arena, would we? Horrible entertainment. It would curse your rule from the very start.'

Elma was silent. But as he spoke, she leaned forward slightly, until her hands were braced on the cold bars of his cell.

Slowly, almost as if he meant not to alarm her, Rune stood. The chains attached to his legs clanked softly as he did. 'Going to gape at me all night?' he asked, taking a hesitant step forward.

No, Elma thought, but no words came. She swallowed; her mouth so dry she might not have been able to speak even if she tried.

He laughed, cocky and brash. 'No, you didn't come to gloat or gape.' His eyes narrowed. 'You came to entertain yourself.'

Elma's breath caught.

'You came to feel fear. Isn't that what you like? To be afraid? Or maybe it's . . .' he tilted his head, the jagged scar over his eye catching the torchlight. 'Yes, you came to be angry. I see it in your eyes. If only I'd come a day sooner . . . I'd have slit your father's corrupt throat with my blade, and you could have watched me do it. I would have slit yours too if you asked me.'

Her fingers tightened on the metal bars. She wanted to say something, to cut him with words. But . . .

'Look how your cheeks redden when I talk about *killing* you,' murmured Rune, almost as if he couldn't believe it himself. 'And your eyes . . . your pupils are enormous. What are they doing to you in this place?'

He moved closer, and Elma's heart hammered in her chest. She could smell him properly now. Not just blood and filth but another scent, something deeper and wilder.

Then he shifted slightly, a small, subtle movement. And before she understood what it was, what he was doing, he lunged for her. Somehow his arm was free, and his body was against the bars, his arm reaching through and grabbing her by the waist, pulling her into the bars.

She knew then what he was after – the dagger in her belt. His hand was deft, as if he knew exactly where to tuck his fingers in and pull. In the work of half a breath, the dagger was in his hand.

A half second longer, and Elma would have been dead.

But strong arms grasped her, and Luca hauled her away

82

from the cell bars at the same time Rune slashed out with her dagger. She felt the displacement of air against her throat. Stumbling back against Luca, she lifted her hand to her neck. It came away clean, but for a tiny droplet of red.

If Luca hadn't seen what was happening . . .

'Get the queen to safety,' Luca said, his words clipped, authoritative. 'Bring her to her rooms, and do not let her leave without my order. I'll deal with him.'

Elma stared at Luca, her hand still hovering at her neck. 'Thank —'

'Just doing my job,' he snapped, holding out her knife. 'Take better care of this.'

Several more guards had gathered at the cell and were clearly waiting for Elma to leave before they exacted punishment. Luca joined them as Elma watched, unable to turn away until the prison guard with the torch was forced to take her arm and drag her out of the dungeon.

The last glimpse Elma caught of Rune, just before Luca's fist met his face, was a wicked grin.

9

Gray-blue sky cut through the overhang of clouds, glazing the great arena in a frozen shimmer. Elma's reign had been blessed with little snow on the morning of the Death Games. At least, this was what the courtiers told her when they came to pay respects at the arena, bowing low and offering her skins of wine and herbal concoctions, gifts of good luck to wish her an auspicious life on the throne.

She accepted each gift with a strained smile. If it had been snowing, she might not have been so cold. As it was, the chill air cut through her furs and thick woolen layers. Elma could not seem to stop shivering, even with a hot brick in her lap and a goblet of steaming wine cupped in her hands.

A roar rose up from the arena's crowd, a deafening cacophony, as the first set of warriors strode onto the packed snow. They bristled with weaponry, though their armor was minimal. These were the Death Games, after all. Bloodshed was the attraction.

'Try not to look so miserable,' said Godwin, similarly swathed in furs. He leaned toward Elma, resting his bearded chin on his fist. 'There's no danger here. All entrances are fortified. The assassin is being watched. He'll be gone soon enough.'

There shouldn't have been danger in the dungeon, she thought, gripping her wine with half-frozen fingers. 'I know,' was all she said.

She and Godwin were alone in the royal box. Courtiers and nobles were permitted to pay respects, and then quickly ushered away. Elma's safety was paramount, and only Godwin was trusted enough to sit with her. The other advisors had their own seats nearby, where they huddled looking dire. Only Lord Ferdinand seemed interested in the Death Games, an eagerness about his countenance that seemed out of place in the wake of Elma's second brush with death.

'Try to enjoy it,' said Godwin.

But Elma wouldn't enjoy anything until her father's would-be killer, *her* would-be killer, was dead. Until he was crumpled on the snow below in a pool of his own blood.

Trumpets blared a fanfare, announcing the start of the Games. The warriors below were arranged in two lines, facing each other across the arena. And as the trumpets sounded, the warriors rushed forward. Almost immediately one of them fell, a hand severed, another warrior's sword buried in his gut.

Elma knew these were criminals, thieves or rapists or murderers. Yet a vague unease curdled in her belly as she watched them brutalize one another. And as she watched one man take hold of another and draw a blade roughly across his throat, watched the red gush down his body and onto the white snow, her chest tightened.

That blood could have been hers, in the wagon in the dark. Or it could have been hers last night, in the torchlit dungeon.

Luca hadn't spoken to her since the incident. She had tried to apologize for her own lack of caution, but he wouldn't hear it. He blamed himself. She thought if he'd had his way, he might have ordered himself whipped in the training grounds.

As Elma watched the slaughter unfold below, she couldn't keep her thoughts from drifting back to the dungeon. To the assassin's fingers in her dress, deftly lifting her dagger as if she were nothing but a game to him. No one could understand how he'd freed himself from his chains. Had he dislocated a thumb? Picked the lock? Or, Elma wondered, had he turned to snow and fog and simply let the shackles fall?

As if summoned by her thoughts, a deep horn blew in the arena, signaling the arrival of the next tournament contestant. Elma had barely noticed the first batch of warriors falling, one by one, until only one was left – a tall man wielding a blood-stained flail. He seemed to be all muscle, rippling with each movement. From this distance it was hard to tell, but Elma thought his beard dripped with red as if he'd bitten living flesh.

But her attention was only on him for a moment. From a black, arched doorway on the far side of the arena came Rune. He carried a sword in one hand, a wicked dagger in the other. And despite his imminent demise, he strode toward the other warrior with a cocky arrogance that made Elma's blood boil.

After everything, he still thought himself a hero.

Elma set down her wine, gripping the arms of her chair as she leaned forward to watch.

'Five silvers says he's dead in under a minute,' said Godwin, pulling thoughtfully at his beard.

Rune twirled his blades, an effortless boast. The crowd's jeers rose up in a wild roar – the city of Frost knew well

87

what he'd tried to do to their queen. Just as the advisors had claimed, Elma's subjects hungered for justice.

'I think he'll win this,' Elma said, knuckles white and teeth clenched. 'Easily.'

Godwin raised his eyebrows but said nothing.

The fight was over as suddenly as it began. Rune circled the bigger man, grinning, and obviously taunting him, though Elma couldn't hear over the roars of the crowd. And when the bearded warrior lunged, flail swinging, he was as good as dead.

Rune darted beneath the weapon, moving like quicksilver, his sword slicing across the other man's stomach. His dagger found its home in the man's kidney, a clean kill. There was a moment of shocked silence as the warrior fell, and when his body hit the packed snow, a deafening thunder of protest rose up from the crowd.

'Luck,' Godwin muttered. 'Double it for the next fight.'

'Done,' said Elma.

Three more opponents fell to the assassin's blade. He seemed almost lazy, casually dispensing the arena's most brutal criminals as if it were a waste of his time.

'You owe me an immense amount of gold,' Elma said, shooting a playful look at her uncle, whose frown deepened with every one of Rune's wins.

'They'll be bringing out the Fang in a moment,' Godwin mused.

Elma raised a brow. The Fang was the reigning champion of the arena and rarely came out to fight anymore except for ceremonies. 'Five gold pieces says they don't,' Elma said.

But she didn't hear Godwin's reply; she was already focused on the next battle, Rune against the Twins, a pair of swift fighters who excelled at disorienting their opponents. Yet, even they fell before the Slödavan assassin as if their deaths were inevitable.

A strange fire ignited in Elma's chest, at the beautiful, efficient slaughter. The way Rune's body moved; it was . . . unreal. He wasn't strikingly tall, nor was he heavily muscled like most of the arena's successful warriors. But he was fit, athletic, and flowed like water. What else could such a body accomplish if given the right opportunity?

And then Elma's attention snapped away as a goblet of wine toppled into her lap, soaking her furs and gown in spiced burgundy.

'*Shit*,' Cora gasped, scrabbling for the dropped goblet. 'Forgive me, Your Majesty, I lost my balance. The ice on the steps –'

'It's all right,' Elma said, silently glad for the distraction. She stood, shaking her clothes. Hot droplets sprayed everywhere.

'Let me help you,' Cora said, obviously flustered. Elma had never punished her maid for anything, let alone a simple spill. But Elma was queen now, and Queens of Rothen were known to be ruthless.

Elma swallowed and held out a hand, preventing Cora from assisting her. 'I have spare gowns in one of the dressing rooms. I'll go and change.'

'I'll come with you,' said Godwin, half rising from his chair. 'You shouldn't go anywhere alone.'

'I'll be *fine*,' Elma replied, turning to hold her uncle's gaze. 'The assassin is in the arena, in full view. As you said, there's no danger here.'

Godwin hesitated.

'It will take no more than a few minutes. And . . .' Elma hesitated, vulnerability never having been part of her relationship with Godwin. 'I need a moment alone.' She hoped he would assume she meant a moment away from the horrors of the arena, the sight of her almost-killer.

'If you're not back in ten minutes,' said her uncle, 'I'm coming to fetch you.'

When Cora offered to attend to Elma, she shook her head in refusal. She could dress herself; she was a grown woman. Queen or not, she wasn't helpless.

Nobody stopped or questioned Elma as she made her way up a short set of icy stairs to a narrow corridor manned by silent guards. Someone had laid carpet for the benefit of women's dainty slippers. The crowd's bellowing was muffled in here, softer, almost like the sound of a distant seashore.

Passing an open doorway, Elma caught sight of colorful fabric, of bearded faces. She stepped quickly backward, hoping the men inside hadn't seen her. It was Lord Ferdinand and Lord Bertram, obviously taking advantage of the warmth and the casks of wine that Elma knew lay within. She knew the arena as well as the citadel and had mapped every room and corridor.

The last thing she wanted was reprisal from the advisors, or worse, discussion of politics. She'd had more than enough of that. All she wanted was solitude.

Elma gathered her skirts in her hands, preparing to dart past the doorway as quickly and quietly as she could, until a few choice words caught her ear, freezing her in place.

'. . . not equipped to wear the crown, blood be damned. She's never had the guts.' She recognized Lord Bertram's usual bluster.

'But even if she were,' said Ferdinand, his voice more difficult to hear – he must be facing away from the door. 'She'll never call for war. She deflects. Delays. If I'm to be frank, it's a great pity the assassin botched the job.'

Elma's blood ran cold. Had she heard them correctly? Had she understood? The way Ferdinand had spoken, it sounded as if . . . as if the assassin had been hired by him and Bertram. It wouldn't be such a shocking revelation. If they didn't believe in her ability to rule Rothen, Elma knew these men would stoop to any level to get what they wanted. And she knew what they wanted – war with Slödava, a thing she had no interest in supporting.

What else could he have meant by *botched the job*?

Her ears rang as she stood, back pressed against the wall, waiting for something more. Something to confirm the advisors' involvement in her attempted assassination. But their talk turned to more banal topics, money and women and the Games.

Afraid of being caught spying, Elma took a different route to her dressing room and changed, grateful that one of her spare gowns was easy to put on and lace. Her fingers would not stop shaking. *The conversation was out of context,* she thought. *They were joking. Drinking wine. It meant nothing.* And yet fear would not relinquish her heart.

They did not trust her to rule. They did not believe she was equipped.

And these were not men whose opinions could be ignored. Elma had seen who they really were, had heard them at feasts and at the Death Games when they thought no one was listening. She had heard Bertram speak of his eldest daughter like a prize horse, hoping to sell her to the highest bidder. She had seen Ferdinand fondle servant girls and warned them not to tell.

They were vicious, selfish men, and she was right to be afraid.

Elma was halfway back to the royal box when Godwin found her, his face set in grim lines.

'For god's sake, Elma, I said *ten* minutes.'

She crossed her arms to hide her shaking. 'I lost track of time.'

'It doesn't matter,' Godwin said, offering his arm. 'Take better care of your own life,' he said as they made their way back to their seats. 'You're not a princess anymore. Your father is gone. You are all we have.'

'You needn't remind me,' Elma said.

'I'm sorry.'

'I know that too.'

If there was one man Elma could not come to with her suspicions about Bertram and Ferdinand, it was her uncle. She loved him almost as much as she had loved her father, in the way one loves their armor in the midst of battle. But she did not *know* him. And while she hoped she could trust him, hoped he would stand his ground with her no matter the danger, there was no proof of it. He, like the other lords, was a man adjacent to power. Elma was the only obstacle in their way, and any manner of weakness might push a man like him to betrayal.

But Elma didn't have time to think or mull on what she should do. The next fight was beginning, and the horns blared, announcing Rune's next opponent.

'You see,' said Godwin, slapping his knee. 'I knew it.'

Because the man that Rune would fight next was the Fang.

10

Elma found it hard to breathe as the gates were opened, as the challenging warrior emerged from the shadows and onto the blood-soaked snow. He was almost unnaturally tall, with long corded limbs and a sharp toothy grin. A wolf pelt was draped over his shoulders, and he held no weapon.

But it wasn't the Fang himself that made Elma tremble with anticipation. It was the wolves that flanked him. There were two, one black and one snow white. Red ribbons were tied in their fur, one for each of their slain foes. Elma had once tried to count the ribbons, but it was impossible – there were so many, and more were added all the time.

'Too soon,' Elma murmured. She didn't want Rune to die so soon. Not when she'd only gotten a taste, a hint of what he could do in battle, the extent to which he might draw out this punishment. She wanted to see him fight and win, to battle until he couldn't, until he was exhausted and bleeding. She wanted to see him suffer. She was realizing belatedly that the Death Games were far too quick a death.

Godwin glanced at her. 'You think he's outmatched?'

An icy wind ruffled the fur at her neck. 'He's been injured,' she said. 'My guards brutalized him. Do you see his face?' *They marred him.*

Her uncle squinted. 'Care to bet on it?'

'Fine, we'll add to the pot. Ten gold coins says he wins.'

'Is this confidence or wishful thinking?'

She shrugged. 'Does it matter?'

Her uncle chuckled.

It *was* wishful thinking. A pathetic hope that Rune's suffering might be drawn out if Elma hoped hard enough, if enough gold was on the line. That she might watch as he defeated champion after champion, as blood began to stain his lithe and competent body, as his graceful movements grew staggered and slow. She wasn't ready for it to end. The Fang couldn't reign over the arena forever.

But as the two men circled each other, their feet kicking white snow over patches of red, her heart sank. The wolves alone would likely rip Rune's gullet from his throat in a second. She had seen the Fang fight many times, and each battle had been different. Sometimes he used his limbs to hold his opponents, spider-like, until his wolves dealt the killing blow. Sometimes the Fang did it himself, with a snap of the neck or a crushed windpipe. But he never fought with weapons. The Fang with a sword would have been almost unfair.

Even so, Rune appeared just as confident as he had in his last fight. He twirled his weapons, their blades catching the pale sun and glinting. He was like a dancer, all controlled muscle and graceful movements.

The Fang and his wolves bared their teeth, threw back their heads, howled in unison, and attacked.

Elma watched, tense with anticipation. Every time one of the wolves lunged for the assassin, she was certain it would be the end. Yet every time, he managed to roll away or leap sideways at the last moment, snow flying up in great bouts as the fight wore on.

For a while, it seemed that he and the Fang – miraculously – were evenly matched.

Until the Fang managed to swipe at Rune's ankle as he dodged the white wolf, sending Rune crashing to the packed snow. It was the first time Elma had seen him falter, let alone lose an upper hand.

The crowd roared for blood.

But the assassin leapt to his feet with ease, backing quickly away from the lumbering opponent. As he did, the two wolves closed in on him. And when they fell upon him, he managed to avoid a gutting, but just barely. One of the wolves bit him in the side, the other in the delicate flesh of his underarm.

Rune staggered, trailing blood as he sidled away from the Fang and his wolves.

The crowd bellowed its approval.

'You'll be buying my drinks tonight,' said Godwin.

Not yet, thought Elma.

But as more and more of Rune's blood graced the snow, Elma began to realize her uncle was right. The Fang was going to win. Rune was fighting for his life now, his weapons used as defense rather than attack.

Again and again, the wolves darted in to attack. And each time, Rune deflected their dagger-sharp teeth. The Fang himself hung back as if waiting for the right moment to join in.

The assassin should have been dead by now. Any other man would have succumbed, might have been killed with the first of Fang's blows. Elma's teeth pressed against her lip as he took hit after hit, his face a grimace of pain and rage.

And then the fight was over. Almost lazily, the Fang strode past his wolves. With a movement so quick that Elma couldn't follow it, he fastened his overlarge hand around Rune's throat, lifting the assassin off his feet.

Elma watched, heart in her throat, as the assassin kicked out at the much taller man. But the Fang's arms were too long, and Rune was bleeding from several wounds.

He's going to break his neck, Elma thought. *That brute is going to snap him in half as if he were nothing.*

Something occurred to her, then. An idea. A thought. A dark, wriggling notion that came from seemingly nowhere. The sort of thought her father might have had. The Volta blood ran strong in her, and there was no time for doubt.

'Stop the Games,' she said. Her voice was steady, forceful, a queen's voice.

Godwin swung his head to stare at her. 'Wh –'

'*Stop the Games, now.*'

The Fang was gloating, holding Rune aloft as the crowd jeered and cried out for blood.

Frowning deeply, Godwin gestured to a nearby box where the master of ceremonies sat. A moment later, a deep horn sounded, reverberating through the stone of the arena.

'I want him alive,' said Elma. 'See that he's brought to one of the warrior's cells below. I'm going to speak with him.'

She spun on her uncle, his protests catching in his throat. She spoke as she'd heard her father do so many times when he gave orders that were not to be disobeyed on pain of death. 'Do *not*,' she said, holding Godwin's gaze until she knew he understood, 'follow me.'

*

Miraculously, Godwin did as he was told. He did not follow Elma, nor did he send anyone to trail her. She had half-expected Luca to appear in the shadows behind her, but no one did. When she came at last to the belly of the arena, she was hit by a wall of stench. Sweat, blood, leather, and the stink of men all combined to make her gag.

'Your Majesty,' said one of the guards, clearly taken aback by the queen's sudden arrival at the last place she ought to be. 'Are you lost?'

'Of course, I'm not lost,' Elma snapped, sweeping past the guard. 'I grew up in this filth. Where is the assassin?'

'Forgive me, Your Majesty,' spluttered the guard. He and two others clustered around her as if to protect her from the scenes unfolding as she strode through the dank corridor. She passed rooms full of death, injured men, bloody armor, discarded weaponry. 'You shouldn't be down here. My orders –'

'Your *orders*,' Elma said, turning on the guard, 'come from your queen and your queen alone. I wish to speak to the assassin, and you will take me to him.'

The guards shared a glance.

'He may not be up to much talking,' one of them said.

Elma raised her eyebrows. 'Did I ask for an opinion?'

'No, but –'

'Take Her Majesty to the prisoner,' said the first guard, interrupting hurriedly. 'Apologies, my queen, we're not . . . accustomed to royalty down here.'

Elma regarded him coolly. 'See that you become accustomed to me.'

By the time they came to Rune's cell, Elma's heart was fluttering in her throat, blood racing in her veins. This was reckless, ill-informed, *mad*. But she didn't allow herself time to think, to wonder, to doubt.

'He's been patched up a bit,' said the guard who had accompanied her, 'and he'll live, but he looks like the Fang chewed him up and shit him out. Pardon my language.'

'Leave me,' said Elma, and the guard departed.

She fixed her gaze on the assassin. He wasn't unconscious, he wasn't on his deathbed. He sat in a tiny cell, even smaller than the one in the dungeon, his head in his hands. He wore only trousers and a bloody shirt, his leathers nowhere to be seen. Bloodstained sawdust carpeted the floor, and there was a tang of vomit in the air. She could hardly believe it.

Lost for words, Elma gaped at the man until he lifted his head slowly. This time, he didn't smile. 'You again,' he croaked. Angry red-purple bruises marred his neck where the Fang had squeezed. He was bandaged in several places. His face was cut and swollen.

'You should be dead,' Elma said, unthinking.

He leveled a long, steady look at her. One of his ice-blue eyes was half-closed from swelling. 'Want to finish me off?' He almost smiled then, a pained, pathetic curl of the lips. He was clearly suffering, though a lesser man would have been dead. *Should* have been.

'On the contrary,' Elma said. 'I have a proposition for you.'

Rune's eyes brightened with interest. 'I'm a bit worse for wear, but if Her Majesty doesn't mind a lackluster lay . . .'

'Don't make me change my mind,' Elma snapped in disgust. 'I can put you back in the arena right now.'

He laughed briefly, a hacking choke. 'What's the proposition?'

You're being a fool, thought Elma. *You're signing your own death warrant.* But she ignored her better judgment and leaned into her birthright. Mistrust, bloodlust, and by any means the upper hand. 'I need a bodyguard.'

'Congratulations.' He coughed, blood flecking his sleeve. 'Where do I come in?'

'You're the bodyguard.'

Slowly, he leaned back against the wall, crossing his arms over his chest. 'You're kidding, right? This is your adorable way of playing with me like a cat with its mouse?'

'I wouldn't do that.'

'Yes, you would.' He grinned lopsidedly. 'Your father would.'

How did he always manage to derail her like this? Elma set her jaw. 'I'm deadly serious. In a few minutes, my uncle and guards will come swarming in, and this time I'll let them kill you. Unless you agree to my deal.'

'You want me to be . . . your bodyguard.' Rune licked cracked lips and frowned. 'Why?'

Elma had no choice – he wouldn't believe that she was genuine unless she showed him her hand. 'I know my advisors hired you to kill me. I overheard them discussing it, so there's no point in denying it. You failed, and now you're going to die. But it doesn't have to be that way. They won't stop until I'm dead. And the only person I know who won't benefit in any way from my death is you.'

'Except, of course, whatever payment they've hypothetically promised to me.'

'I'll pay you five times as much. Ten. I don't care.'

'I don't want your money.'

There was a long moment in which Elma considered

killing him after all. There were plenty of weapons available in the bowels of the arena. No one would blame her. And perhaps Luca would relax a bit if the assassin was finally dead.

But she knew in her gut that this wouldn't end with Rune. If her advisors were determined to remove her, they would keep trying until they succeeded. Until they were free to declare war on . . .

'Slödava,' Elma said aloud.

'So, you *are* mad,' said Rune, sighing.

'This is what I propose,' said Elma, impatient. 'You keep me alive until my coronation, a month from now. And when I'm crowned queen, not only will you be set free and pardoned, but I will broker a peace treaty with Slödava. Rothen will never come for you or your Rime Ice again, at least not while I live. You have my word.'

'The word of a Volta . . . how enticing.'

Elma lifted her chin. 'It's all I have.'

'Peace with Rothen.' The assassin tilted his head. 'What makes you think I care about that?'

'Because when you spoke of your crown prince . . .' Elma hesitated, knowing this was a gamble. 'There was honesty in your voice. You *did* want to present my heart to him on a platter. You love your home and don't want to see it fall to Rothen. You're not just killing for money. You're a man of honor and principle. If my advisors hired you, and I believe that they did, you should know it's because they want a war with Slödava.'

'And you don't?'

'I don't.' Elma knelt then, her knees on the bloodstained stone so she could look him in the eye. 'I am the only one in the court of Frost who doesn't thirst for war. I want the people of Rothen to be well-fed and to live their lives as they see fit. That's all.'

'Interesting.' Rune narrowed his eyes. 'And what happens after the coronation? You take me into some back alley and finish the job that filthy wolf-man started? There's nothing to stop you from betraying me.'

Filthy wolf-man. Elma bit back the mad impulse to laugh. 'All I have is my word. If I was to kill you, what would I gain?'

He huffed. 'A sadistic sense of satisfaction?'

Elma scrambled to her feet again and brushed sawdust from her furs. 'I'm the one thing standing between Slödava and a long, drawn-out war with Rothen. If at any moment you doubt me on this, between now and my coronation, cut my throat. Otherwise, accept the deal.'

Rune let out a long and dramatic sigh. He rubbed his chin with blood-stained fingers. At last, he met her stony gaze with icy blue. 'After much thought and deliberation, I've decided I'll do it,' he said. 'And if for one second I believe you've broken your word, or that you're about to break it, or are in the act of breaking it, I will, as you've suggested, kill you.' He smiled.

Relief and something like excited, fizzing fear raced through Elma's veins. 'Deal,' she said and summoned the guards to release her assassin.

I I

'You cannot be serious,' Godwin said for what seemed like the hundredth time that evening, each with increasing desperation. After Elma announced her decision to take the assassin on as her personal bodyguard, she'd been met with outrage and protests from the advisors and icy disapproval from Luca. Through it all she held her head high, never bending. She would have her bodyguard, and no one had the power to stop her.

She had gone straight to the citadel from the arena, her uncle and advisors in tow, to draw up the necessary paperwork. A Slödavan assassin could not simply be allowed to wander the citadel as he pleased; a contract must be written. Elma dictated, and one of her father's scribes – her scribe now, she must remember – had drawn it up.

Only a few hours had passed since her meeting with Rune in the arena, but it felt as if days had gone by. Weeks. Everything seemed different now. Her advisors no longer gave her comfort but hovered at her back like shadows. And Rune . . . he was something else altogether.

Sighing, Elma looked up from the pile of parchments spread out before her on the desk. Her father's old study had been the perfect place for her to finalize the paperwork. As long as everything was legal and above board, no one could fault her.

'You can see very well that I *am* serious,' she said. 'You

read the document yourself. Signed and stamped it. What more do you need?'

'I need you to remember who you are,' Godwin said, bracing his hands on the desk until his eyes were level with Elma's. 'Whatever madness has overtaken you, whatever infatuation . . .'

Elma raised her brows. 'I'm choosing to ignore that insult. This is about my safety. The assassin has agreed to protect me until I'm officially crowned, and then you can do whatever you like to him. I saw him in the arena. He's too talented a fighter to throw away like that. And better he be on my side than not.'

'He'll kill you in your sleep.' Godwin's brows were deeply furrowed, the lines of his face tight. He couldn't understand, Elma knew. She imagined what she must look like to him, a young woman on the cusp of power, throwing her lot in with the very man who had tried to kill her. Twice.

'I made a personal pact with him,' she replied coolly. 'You needn't know the details, but I trust he won't betray me. Not unless I betray him first.' She set down her quill and slid the parchment across the desk. 'Read the official terms again, if you must. The Slödavan assassin has sworn an oath to protect the Queen of Rothen, and so on, to be her official bodyguard, given leave to make such decisions as would affect the queen's safety, and so on, and so forth. You *signed* it.'

'I know I did,' said Godwin, shaking his head. 'I seem to remember you ordering me to.'

'You know it needs to be official.'

'Just . . .' Her uncle looked tired then, more man than general, slumped as if a great weight sat on his shoulders. 'Remember who your father was.'

Elma sat back in her father's chair and crossed her arms. 'It's impossible to forget.'

It wasn't until the next day that Elma saw her bodyguard, in an official capacity, for the first time. She waited in her firelit parlor, a small room where she often read or napped during the long winter dark. Snow fell beyond an arched window, and though it was morning, no sunlight made its way through the thick cloud cover. It might have still been night, for how dark it was.

'Your Majesty,' said a servant, appearing at the door. 'Your bodyguard, Rune.'

Elma stood, hands folded in front of her, conscious of how cold her skin was. Everything was cold in the citadel, no matter how many fires burned in soot-blackened hearths. Drawing a shaky breath, she nodded curtly. 'Send him in.'

Luca came in first, bowing low. A chain, delicate in his broad hands, dangled from his grip. And at the end of it was Rune, his wrists bound before him. His head was held high, despite his leash in Luca's hand. He wore the black leather he had worn in the arena, though it had been cleaned and mended, and a tunic of the Volta colors, red and black, clung to his chest. A sword belt hung from his waist.

He looks good in my colors. Elma couldn't help the thought that flitted through her mind, then tamped it down with impatience.

'Why is he bound?' she asked pointedly, addressing Luca.

'For Her Majesty's safety,' said Luca.

'And how is he expected to protect me if he's in chains?'

Luca colored slightly. 'Your Majesty . . . please. Forgive my boldness, but this is a mistake. This man has no honor, no sense of morality. He'll gut you the first chance he gets. And . . .' he swallowed, uneasy. 'Have I not served you well, my queen? I have been at your side for so many years.'

Regret gnawed at Elma. She had known this would hurt Luca. 'You've always kept me safe,' she said, softening. 'And I know you will continue to prioritize my life, as you have since we were both children. But in a month, I'll be crowned queen. I need more than just a retinue of guards. I need the most dangerous men in the north on *my* side.'

The guard nodded stiffly.

'Luca,' Elma said, 'I need you to trust me.'

The assassin glanced between them with sharp eyes. 'I'm touched,' he said, holding up his hands. 'Truly, a lovely moment of vulnerability between lifelong colleagues. Now, won't someone deign to unchain me?'

'He's an ass,' Luca said, with raised brows.

Elma closed her eyes for a long moment, gathering her patience. Whatever partnership this was going to be, it would not be easy. 'I'm aware of that. Unbind him.'

Shaking his head with disapproval, Luca obeyed. He gathered the chain in a bundle and dropped a bow. 'Your Majesty,' he said and left her there alone with Rune.

The two stood watching one another in silence, assessing. As if both were performing calculations, making lists, trying to sketch an image of a person who, until now, had existed only as some caricatured villain in their minds.

Elma noted that Rune was, for the first time since she'd met him, not covered in filth. His hair, so matted with blood and dirt before, now shone brightly in the firelight.

It was cropped shorter than hers, barely brushing the nape of his neck and falling longer over his forehead. The bruises and cuts on his face were clean, and the swelling had faded – the citadel physicians had cared for him properly, as she'd ordered. His knuckles, though, were raw and red. A purple bruise still marred his eye. And that scar . . . it gave him a wild look, even dressed in her family's colors.

'You *do* like looking at me, don't you,' Rune said, shifting his weight.

Elma bristled. 'Don't flatter yourself. I was only wondering why you are so . . . short.'

His eyes widened for an instant, a breath of true surprise beneath that haughty veneer. 'Short?' he said, placing a hand on his chest. 'On the contrary, look at *you*.' He eyed the length of her body, not bothering to hide a lustful smirk. 'They say the Volta family descended from giants, and I'm starting to believe it.'

'You remind me of one of my great aunt's little lapdogs,' Elma said, smiling a little. 'It had the same hair.'

Rune took two long strides toward her, crossing the distance between them easily. He was so close all of a sudden, too close. He smelled of soap and leather. Elma froze, breath catching. Was he going to attack her?

'Look at me,' he said, 'In the eye.'

Elma tilted her chin up, grudgingly, and met his gaze. His eyes were strikingly blue, like mountain waterfalls after a snap freeze.

A slow grin spread across his face. 'I *am* taller than you.'

'You'll address me as Your Majesty,' Elma said, backing away.

'That's your first lesson, *Your Majesty*,' said Rune, crossing his arms. 'The bodyguard is always right. Suppose your life depended on knowing our height discrepancy. What then?'

'You *are* an ass,' she muttered. She took a moment to breathe, to let her heart slow its speeding gait. Rune waited, expectant, a half-smile still catching at his lips. 'I didn't summon you here to compare heights,' she said at last. 'I want to discuss my schedule, the events leading up to my coronation. Beginning with tonight. A feast is being held in honor of my father, a family affair. I'm not particularly concerned for my safety. The advisors will not be in attendance, except for my uncle Godwin. But . . . *What?*'

Rune blinked. 'Oh, nothing, Your Majesty.'

'You made a face.'

'Did I?'

'You don't trust my uncle?'

'Nothing like that, Majesty, it's just . . .' Rune shrugged. 'Sometimes, these family events can get rather bloody if you're not careful. Things happen. Comments are made, blades are drawn. All of a sudden, your dinner party is a slaughterhouse. Do you trust them? Every last one of your kin?'

'It's the advisors who –'

Rune moved toward her again, lifting one finger and pressing it gently to her lips. She wanted to bite it and draw blood.

'Your Majesty,' he said, as if telling off a child, 'answer a question for me. Which of us is the bodyguard?'

Resisting the urge to draw her dagger and sever his hand, Elma swatted it away with a curse. 'Fuck you,' she spat. 'Touch me again, and I'll have you drawn and quartered in the Frost square. Understand?'

'Completely.' He tilted his head, never removing his icy gaze from hers. And even though he was no longer in her personal space, he seemed still to envelop her, to wash over her like a snowstorm. 'Answer my question.'

She glowered. 'You are.'

Rune smiled. 'Very good. Then you won't mind if I make the call, going forward, on whether or not an event is worthy of *particular concern*. Understood?'

Elma was not deluded enough to think that her royal status would control this man, least of all, protect her from him. For a moment, she felt truly unsafe, if only for a breath. She was alone in a room with the most skilled fighter she had ever seen in action, a man who would have killed her if it weren't for . . .

Something came to her, a memory of Rune's shape in the darkened wagon, the glint of a wicked blade in the moonlight. 'In the wagon that night,' she said. 'You could have killed me while I slept. And again, while we talked. I sensed . . . I thought you might have . . .' she swallowed dryly. 'You had every opportunity.'

The assassin's expression was unreadable. 'I don't kill sleeping women. And in the spirit of honesty, well . . . I wanted you to look me in the eye before I killed you. Before you bled out all over me. Makes for a far more enjoyable experience.'

'A man of principle,' Elma said, unable to hide the disgust in her voice. She gestured to a chair and sat across from it in one of her own. This was a business arrangement and nothing more. A truce between enemies. There would be no understanding him and no peace between them as individuals. 'Never mind,' she said. 'Let's discuss where you'll be needed, and when. And most importantly, I'd like to remind you that you are not to speak at any of these events.'

Rune settled in his chair, one leg bent so his foot balanced on the opposite knee. He looked more lazily relaxed than Elma thought she'd ever been in her life. 'Not even to compliment my queen on her dedication to the Volta family legacy of blood and cruelty?'

Elma stared into the flames, her lips pressed together. This was going to be a long month.

I2

'I find it worrying,' said Lady Devereaux, popping a hunk of sharp cheese into her thin mouth, 'that you've adopted a Slödavan as your personal lapdog. You could have had any number of bed slaves, but you've gone and given this one a *sword.*' Flecks of cheese and spittle flew out of her mouth as she spoke. Her age was impossible to tell, her features as craggy and cruel as the mountains of Rothen. Lady Devereaux was Elma's third cousin by marriage, a woman whom Elma saw very seldomly but for major family occasions.

King Rafe's death and Elma's subsequent upcoming coronation had been deemed worthy enough, it seemed, of Lady Devereaux's attendance.

Elma smiled wanly in reply. The feast was well underway, though Elma felt wholly separate from it. She sat in her father's chair at the head of the table. It felt far too big for her despite her height – too heavy, wide, and dark. As if the memory of him clung to it, a ghost of a man whose shoes Elma would never fill.

These and other gloomy thoughts invaded her mind as she picked at her food, letting the meaningless drone of conversation fill her ears, none of the words taking shape. And though she made every effort to keep her attention on her guests, on the food in front of her . . . Elma couldn't help but let her thoughts drift over to the shadow that lurked behind her.

Rune was not inconspicuous, though he had tried his best to be. The room was dim enough that he should have blended into the shadows, a silent specter of warning to anyone who might attempt to harm the queen that night. But his eyes and hair gave him away – bright beacons of strangeness, reminding everyone present exactly who he was and why he was there.

'Are you listening, my dear?' Lady Devereaux insisted, laying a gnarled hand on Elma's arm. 'It's *unseemly*.'

The moment Elma's cousin reached out to touch her, Rune was there at her side. With the practiced grace of a dancer, he bowed, lifted Lady Devereaux's hand from Elma's arm, set it on the table, and said, 'Don't touch her.'

A breath later and he was back in the shadows.

Lady Devereaux's eyes threatened to pop out of her head. 'He dared lay hands on me,' she croaked, her voice cutting through the general din of conversation. 'I want him whipped! I want him –'

'Please, Your Grace,' Godwin cut in from Elma's left, his tone calm but forceful. 'The northerner is overly cautious but means nothing by it.'

'Am I not to touch my own kin?' Lady Devereaux demanded.

'No,' came Rune's low voice from the shadows.

Elma bit her lip to stop a bark of shocked laughter from bursting forth. The bastard – she had never been so out of her element. And yet, twice in a week, she'd almost laughed. Perhaps she *was* going mad. She turned around in her chair to glare at Rune. He stared back, one eyebrow cocked.

'Allow my cousin to touch my arm if she so wishes,' she said.

'Yes, Your Majesty,' Rune intoned.

Elma turned back to her guests, many of whom had stopped their own conversations to watch hers with great interest. Her cheeks burned.

'I, too, wonder what benefits one might possibly see in welcoming an enemy so readily into the bosom of the citadel?' said another of Elma's somewhat distant cousins, Lord Churnley. He sipped thoughtfully from a goblet. He had always played the picture of rationality, a man who looked as bland as his opinions and wasn't afraid to voice them.

Elma glanced at Godwin, who had clearly been about to speak on her behalf. She shook her head slightly to stop him. She had put herself in this situation and she would address it herself. If she allowed her family to walk all over her, it wouldn't stop there – her weakness would be laid bare for all the court to see. She needed them to see that her safety was paramount, that her decision was good – not because it was logical, but because she, the queen, had made it.

'Good evening, Lord Churnley,' Elma said, raising her goblet.

He raised his in turn, lowering his chin in deference.

'I hear your concerns,' she went on, returning her goblet to the table, untouched. 'And because I'm feeling generous, I'll address them. Once. You ask the purpose of my bodyguard's presence. The purpose is to protect me, cousin. Or have you guzzled too much wine tonight?'

Laughter rumbled through those seated at the great table.

Elma remained stern. 'I believe you're aware that assassins generally work for payment. I saw this one in the arena and was taken by his technique. And because I value things that kill with great efficiency, I wanted him for my own.' She smiled coldly. 'So that if anyone asked me such pointless questions as yours, they might be easily dealt with.'

Godwin radiated approval, though his mouth remained tightly shut. Even Lady Devereaux seemed to curl in on herself, retreating like a burrowing spider into its hole. The Volta heir had spoken in a language they all understood.

'If I hear rumblings again of my choice in bodyguard,' said Elma, catching each of her guests' eyes one by one, 'I will personally see to it that you're silenced.'

Rune stepped forward into the light and leaned arrogantly over her chair, practically draping himself across it, smiling viciously. 'She means I'll cut out your tongue.'

The room was dead quiet. Elma thought she heard someone swallowing uneasily.

Then Godwin lifted his own goblet, claret wine sloshing from its sides and spattering the table with red. 'To the Queen of Rothen!'

As one, the rest of the guests raised their glasses.

'To the Queen!'

'May she rot,' Rune murmured, his breath hot in her ear, before drifting back into shadow.

A week before her father's funeral, Elma sat in her parlor, legs curled under her in a chair facing the fire. Its flames guttered in an unseen draft. In a shower of embers, another log landed on the blaze.

Starting, Elma tore her gaze away from the flames. 'Cora, I didn't see you there,' she said, embarrassed by the hammering in her chest.

Her maid curtseyed. 'Forgive me, Majesty. Your thoughts must have been far away.'

'Elma,' said the queen. 'It's Elma when we're alone.'

'Elma, then,' repeated Cora, smiling.

But there was hesitancy in her maid's expression, uncertainty. And something else that Elma couldn't quite read. She supposed that anyone in Cora's position would be afraid. Afraid of being caught up in an attempt on Elma's life, of ending up as a casualty in a murder not meant for them.

'Your safety is assured,' Elma said, adopting a tone she thought was queenly and reassuring. 'So long as you're with me. My bodyguard will see to it.'

Finished stoking the fire, Cora wiped her hands on a cloth before tucking it into her pockets. 'That is magnanimous.'

A prickle of unease ran up Elma's spine. 'I'm not trying to be magnanimous. You're my friend.'

'Of course.' Cora's smile tensed.

Elma stood then, made uneasy by the distance between them, dancing shadows on Cora's face. 'Cora,' she said, hesitant despite herself, 'I thought you might do something for me. If you're able.'

'Anything, Majesty,' said her maid, an automatic response.

Something about Cora's eagerness unsettled Elma; she was about to ask her maid to put herself in potential danger, yet she had agreed without question. Without knowing the stakes. 'Wonderful,' she said, trying to smile. 'All I need is a little information. I suspect two of my advisors, Lords Bertram and Ferdinand, may be . . . acting against the best interests of the kingdom.' She chose her words carefully, hoping her maid would understand. 'If you happen to find yourself in the room with them more often than usual, if you overhear anything strange, or . . . questionable, I only ask that you take note of it.'

Cora's gaze was cautious. 'You want me to spy.'

'I want you to listen and observe, nothing more.'

'I won't disappoint my queen,' Cora said, tense but earnest in her loyalty.

Elma's heart began to fracture. And then it came to her, all at once. She'd been so distracted, so overwhelmed by her duties and the low-hanging cloud of danger. She'd forgotten.

'Oh, Cora,' Elma breathed, 'I'm sorry. I meant to tell you. I spoke to Godwin about your father's title.'

Any remaining tension in Cora's face melted, her eyes brightening with eagerness. 'You *did*,' she said, an exhalation of relief. 'I thought . . . I mean, I thought you weren't going to . . .'

'Of course, I was going to,' Elma said, almost harshly. 'But I'm afraid I don't have news you'll want to hear. My uncle refuses to relinquish the Mannering estate. He will not grant your father his title.'

Cora's face crumpled into disbelief. 'But I already told them. I told my family that you were going to take care of it.'

Hot shame bubbled in Elma's chest. 'Well, you should have waited to –'

'You said you'd do it.'

'I *tried*.'

'You're the queen,' said Cora, her eyes bright with unshed tears. 'What use is that if you have to ask permission from your *uncle*?'

Elma lifted her chin; Cora's words lodged like a glass shard in her chest. 'The queen must heed the law, and advice given to her by others,' she said. 'Otherwise, she is nothing more than a tyrant.'

A horrible silence hung between them, Cora worrying her lips between agitated teeth. Then the maid set her shoulders, and her gaze grew distant, cold.

'As you say, Your Majesty.' In a sweep of her skirts, Cora fled the room, leaving Elma alone in the firelight.

'What a delightful little drama,' said Rune, peeling away from the far wall where he had been lurking in the shadows. 'You should put on a show for the citadel. Call it *Queen Elma, The Raging Bi* –'

'Where in your contract,' Elma cut in, 'does it state that you are to make obnoxious commentary in addition to your physical services?'

Rune chuckled, settling himself into Elma's chair. '*Physical services*. Don't give me arrows if you don't want them loosed upon you.'

'You're a boor.'

'I know.' A grin split his handsome features. No longer bruised or swollen, his face bore no evidence of the brutalities inflicted only days before. Elma was free to study the curve of his arched nose, the slight divot below his bottom lip. 'You know,' he continued, 'your maid has a point.'

Elma scoffed. 'Get out of my chair.'

'It's cold in the shadows, Your Majesty. Please . . . allow a poor fellow some time by the fire. Or do you need to ask your uncle's permission first?'

The glee in Rune's voice made Elma's blood boil. 'You know nothing of it.'

'Don't I?' The assassin stared into the fire, hair falling so that Elma saw only his nose and chin, his expression veiled from her. 'I know what kings and queens are like. I know that those who hold power are loath to risk it. That should one finger slip, they might lose their grip and let it fall from their grasp. It's easy to cast blame, to playact duty, and *should this* and *should that*. But if you won't risk lifting a finger to help a friend, soon you'll be all alone in your frosty tower, clutching a heap of power with no one to help you catch it when you inevitably lose your grip.'

Elma hated that she understood him. Even more, she hated that he had not taken her side. The fire was suddenly too hot, the room too small. Anger and regret closed steely fingers around her throat.

'I need fresh air,' she announced. 'A walk in the courtyard.'

Rune sighed. 'I suppose you're aware that I'm unable to protect you from death by freezing.'

'One more joke,' said Elma, 'and I'll have an addendum put in your contract: no sarcastic remarks on pain of death.'

'Don't be silly,' said Rune, rising from his chair, 'you adore my japes. One day you'll outright laugh at something I say and hate yourself for it.' His eyes shone. 'I can't wait.'

13

There were several courtyards in the Frost Citadel, but Elma had a favorite. It was the largest of them and the only one in which someone had, long ago, attempted to grow hedges and trees. But the winters in Rothen were too harsh, the summers too brief and pale. So now, only black shapes rose up where trees had been planted, a stark reminder of Elma's birthright. But they were still trees, dead or not, and their silhouettes against the snow gave her some small measure of peace.

Statues also graced this courtyard. Statuary was rare in Rothen; art was deemed a frivolous pursuit. Yet one of her ancestors had ordered these marble works from Mekya, had them hauled all the way up that treacherous road, and installed them in the courtyard.

Elma was glad they had. This courtyard, with its sad attempts to break away from the relentless bleakness of Rothen, comforted her. It reminded her that somewhere, art was being made for the sake of it. Trees were reaching up to the sun, and flowers were blooming. Even though she couldn't see it, might never see it again, it eased the heaviness in her heart.

Snow crunched under her feet as she went to her favorite statue, a woman draped in a filmy dress with tree boughs in her hair. There was an echoing crunch as Rune followed.

Not caring what the assassin thought of her, Elma

reached out to touch the statue. Snow clung to its divots, and she brushed it away to free the woman's feet.

'Mekyan marble,' Rune said, coming up to stand beside her. 'I didn't realize your kind had any concept of art.'

Elma bit her tongue. He would prick her with a thousand needles, but she refused to grant him the satisfaction of reacting.

'Indeed, we do,' she said evenly. 'My great-great-great-grandfather commissioned these statues from Dagomari De Rixiis himself. The cost was exorbitant. There are twelve in total, most in this courtyard. I used to love coming here in the summer when I first returned to Rothen. Sometimes, the snow even melted, and there was green underneath. It reminded me of Mekya. My father always hated the statues but never got around to removing them. I suppose he saw how much I . . .' she stopped herself. The tense conversation with Cora had set her off balance; she had not meant to share so much.

'Didn't you grow up in Rothen?' Rune asked.

Elma turned to face him, ready to make some biting retort. But his gaze was clear; no cruel joke threatened there. A chill breeze ruffled the fur of his cloak, brushing white hair over his forehead.

'I was born here in the citadel,' Elma said, 'and the next day, I was sent with a wet nurse to the city of Lothyn. My father wasn't a trusting man. He had many enemies. I was born after years of failing to produce an heir. He didn't want to lose me.'

'So, he banished you to Mekya.'

'It wasn't a banishment.' If Elma closed her eyes, she might be able to feel the hot sun on her skin, hear the rustle of thick green leaves in the Orchard House courtyards. 'I loved Mekya.'

'Then go back,' Rune said.

'I can't just *go*,' said Elma, and the admission hurt to voice aloud. 'I'm the Queen of Rothen.'

He leaned against the statue, arms crossed. 'Why not? I don't see a crown on your head.' His eyes flashed, perhaps realizing that he had found a weakness in Elma's armor, that if he prodded and chipped away at it enough, she might strike back.

The answer caught in her throat. *Why not?* There had never been a choice for her. She was Elma Volta, her fate laid out before her since the first Volta placed a crown upon his head and called himself King. Her blood was tied forever to Rothen.

The crown was nothing to Elma but a cage.

She closed her eyes briefly to hide the sting of rising grief. Would she ever see a clear blue sky again? Or walk barefoot through a garden? Or feel the heat of a summer wind in her hair? The thought nearly broke her, and she might have fled the citadel there and then if it weren't for the fact that she had nowhere to go. Godwin would stop her; she would be dragged back to Rothen and placed on the throne like a doll. That was her destiny.

'It is my duty to reign,' Elma said at last. 'Though I don't expect you'd understand duty on such a scale.'

'You'd be surprised.'

'How could I forget. A hired killer with a sense of duty.'

He shifted, leather creaking in the quiet courtyard. 'A *Volta* with a sense of duty, on the other hand . . . Shocking. Your bloodline is rife with liars, tyrants, murderers, and traitors.'

'You know nothing about me,' Elma said, moving in on the assassin, cornering him against the statue. 'You can't begin to *fathom* that there might be a person behind my name. That I'm flesh and blood.'

Rune allowed her to crowd him, to fill up his space. He never turned his gaze from hers. 'On the contrary,' he said, his voice low and intimate. 'I know more of the Volta character than even you. What do you really know of your father's cruelty? Your uncle's, or even your mother's?'

The knife was in her hand before she realized she'd reached for it, and in half a breath, she was pressing it to Rune's throat. A rage pulsated in her chest, an uncaged thing.

'How dare you speak of my family,' she growled, and she watched with satisfaction as a thin line of blood unfurled along the assassin's neck. 'I, more than anyone, understand my father's thirst for pain and cruelty. You think I'm so sheltered, so ignorant, that I never once sat at King Rafe's feet as he chattered gleefully of all the men he'd slaughtered? That I never watched him at the Death Games, laughing uproariously whenever someone's guts spilled on the snow? That I never saw him kill?'

Rune chuckled, a strangled sound. The line of red down his neck thickened. 'Is that all?'

'Compared to you,' Elma said, 'my father was a gentle and forgiving man.'

'How lucky you are to believe in such fairytales.'

That was enough. Elma's frustration, her grief at the loss of her father and the ongoing loss of Mekya, her claustrophobia in the dark stone prison that rose up around her and threatened to choke the life from her at every moment . . . she couldn't contain herself. She ached so desperately for release, for a deep breath of clear air.

But all she had was Rune.

She twisted the knife, just slightly, her breaths shaking and shallow with rage. Another thick drop of red pearled at the point of her blade and ran down the assassin's neck.

Slowly, defiantly, he lifted his chin so that his muscle flexed against her blade. The trickle of blood had reached the collar of his jerkin. Soon, it would pool at the dip of his collarbone. Elma wondered if he felt pain the same way she did, whether his breaths were harsh and fast because of the pain or something else entirely.

Rune smiled, slow like honey. 'Are you having fun, Your Majesty?' he purred. 'I wonder how many other women at court grow excited at the sight of blood. Your pulse is thrumming like a snow rabbit's. You're *hungry.*'

Elma refused to remove the blade, refused to let him get under her skin. But the sight of him like this, backed against the statue, neck laid bare to her . . . she ached. She *did* hunger. And he only watched her with steady blue eyes as if daring her to try it.

'Open your collar,' she said.

The assassin's blue eyes widened just slightly. But instead of laughing, or refusing, or calling her as mad as she felt, he reached up, ever so slowly. And with deft fingers, he undid the silver clasp at the top of his leather collar. Then the second one, and the third.

His jerkin fell open to reveal the curve of his tan neck and the soft white linen of his undershirt. His blood was still flowing, though the wound was small.

'Your undershirt,' she said.

Rune opened his mouth as if to speak, then thought better of it. Perhaps he saw the same animal rage in her that she had seen in her father and knew to keep quiet lest she snap. *Always a moment away from snapping,* she thought distantly. *A moment away from becoming my father.*

Yet even as she warred with herself in an attempt to quiet her emotions, Rune began to painstakingly unlace his undershirt until his entire neck and the delicate bones that framed it were open to view. Gooseflesh dotted his skin. His breaths were quick and shallow.

'You'll want to go a little deeper,' he said, 'to quench your thirst.'

Unwanted heat coiled in Elma's belly. With a slow exhale, she pressed the blade further into the assassin's flesh, just enough to send another thick droplet cascading down to join the rest. And as she watched, the blood caressed his collarbone and at last came to rest, pooling into the center divot.

'When they said the Volta thirst for blood,' Rune breathed, 'they weren't lying.'

Elma leaned forward, still holding the knife to his throat. She was entranced by it, the contrast of red against his skin, the way he submitted to it, allowed it. His own fingers laying himself bare to her.

She wanted to close her eyes and lick the thick red from his skin, taste the metallic salt of it. She imagined him fighting back, drawing a steel edge delicately across her own bare flesh. She wondered if it might feel like the caress of a lover. Hatred, helplessness, and an insidious lust warred for dominance in her chest.

And somewhere in the recesses of her mind, Elma felt vividly *alive.*

All at once the world snapped into focus. Elma saw herself in that moment, knife to the throat of her own assassin, his shirt undone, both of them breathing hard. The heat in her belly turned to ice.

Elma stepped back. Dropped the knife. Nausea rose up to replace her hungry rage. She glanced around, horrified that someone might have been watching, might have *seen* . . . seen what? A queen punishing her lackey for his impertinence?

No, thought Elma. *A woman becoming a monster.*

'All done?' Rune asked, already lacing up his shirt. 'I thought we were getting somewhere.'

Elma opened her mouth to speak and found no words. Her face heated.

The assassin grinned, fastening his jerkin until his neck was once more obscured by leather and linen. 'You *are* your father's daughter.'

Elma's throat constricted, the ice in her gut rising up to choke her. *I want to be alone*, she thought. She wanted to be alone in the vast tundra, a speck of color against a white-gray expanse. Nobody, forgotten, a lost soul in the frozen nothing. She could not breathe here. She could not think.

Rune knelt, felt around in the snow, then stood again. He held out her dagger. 'You dropped this.' His expression was contrite, though a haughtiness burned behind his eyes.

'The next time you speak ill of my family,' Elma said, returning the blade to its place in her belt, 'will be your last.'

She could have sworn she saw a flash of eagerness in

the assassin's eyes, but it passed in an instant, replaced by a cocky smirk. 'Understood, Your Majesty.'

No matter how hard Elma scrubbed her dagger that night, no matter how thoroughly she polished it, she could not stop seeing blood.

The next day, she put a new blade in her belt.

14

King Rafe Volta's funeral was held high in the mountains, where all his ancestors had been laid to rest. Reaching the hallowed place required a long hike up a narrow path that wound between walls of sheer ice and stone until it opened up on a flat valley. Rafe's body lay on a tower of black wood, oiled and ready to be lit.

'I don't seem to recall mountaineering in the list of my duties,' Rune practically shouted into Elma's ear.

Even then, she hardly heard him. The winds were fierce that high in the mountains, far above Frost Citadel. The air was thick with snow that fell from a blue-black sky and picked up from the ground, pummeling her face like tiny frozen blades. Their company was primarily made up of those who had been present at the family feast. A few additional lords and ladies attended, though Elma could have counted them on one hand.

They numbered two dozen in total. Elma had known her father was not widely loved. But so few to see off a kingdom's ruler . . . she shook the thought from her mind. There were more pressing matters than her father's legacy, even on the day of his funeral. Rune had warned her that the threat of attack would be high that day, despite the remote location. Anyone who knew it was King Rafe's funeral would also know that Elma would attend; the deep mountain shadows and the howling weather made for effective hiding.

As Elma made her way toward the funeral pyre, Rune held out a hand to stop her. 'Careful,' he said, his lips against her ear. 'Let someone else go first.'

Elma glared back incredulously, unwilling to shout to be heard over the howling wind. If an assassin was already waiting from some vantage point, no arrow would fly true in this weather.

They had not discussed that day in the courtyard. It was as if it had never happened, as if Elma had not imagined the taste of Rune's blood on her lips. She almost wished he would taunt her about it, make some cruel joke. She was beginning to think it had been a figment of her imagination, evidence of true madness taking hold.

Elma and Rune continued as they had since the day of their deal, with a taut animosity humming between them, setting Elma's skin ablaze. Only two weeks remained until her coronation. The time had swept by, and she didn't feel remotely ready.

Elma took her place by the pyre, shoulder to shoulder with Godwin. Rune remained behind her, a respectful distance away. The remaining attendees gathered around the pyre, watching. No words were spoken. It would have been pointless, in that wind. But when a servant came to hand Elma her torch, a massive lance-like thing with a flickering flame at its end, Godwin laid a hand over hers. Just for a moment. It was all she needed from him – reassurance, loyalty, support.

Horns rang out over the wind. They were carved from the horns of mountain sheep and had been passed down for thousands of years. It was an eerie sound.

As the horns rang out, a lump rose in Elma's throat.

Carrying the torch aloft, she lit the pyre. At once great flames licked upward, hungry for the dry wood, and soon enough, the king was engulfed.

Elma imagined her own body on the pyre, flames dancing on her corpse. Would she be mourned? Would citizens line the paths to the mountaintop, carrying herbs and gifts for the dead? She couldn't see it; she had done nothing to deserve such a thing. She was her father's daughter, and that was all. Queen Elma was a stranger to her.

'You must accept in your gut that you are better,' her father had always told her. 'A king is not made. He is born. You were born a queen, imbued with power. Chosen by the earth, the sky, the snow. When the time comes, Elma, it will feel right.'

But as King Rafe burned on the pyre, Elma stood below, watching, feeling as if she were a teenager again. Nothing felt right. Least of all, the man whose presence lurked ever in her peripheral, a white-haired shadow. What would her father have thought of her working with a Slödavan assassin? Putting herself at risk in the hope that a wild thing might prove loyal?

Perhaps she was delusional, but Elma hoped that her father would have been proud, in his way. He knew that effective queens took risks for the greater good. But was her life worth all that, she wondered. Was she good for the people of Rothen? Or would she sit impotently on the throne, letting others make decisions for her, time and inaction washing over her until she was gone and lost to memory?

Elma watched until the pyre was burnt to nothing, a pile of black cinders in the snow. Most of the other attendees had gone, peeling away and heading down the mountain pass, eager not to miss the remaining daylight. The wind had died down, and an evening chill began to seep into Elma's bones. Only Godwin and Rune remained with her.

'Your father was a great man,' Godwin said, turning to take Elma's hands in his. 'You'll be an even greater queen.'

She thought she heard Rune scoff behind her and wished he would miss a step and fall off the mountain. 'Thank you, Uncle,' she said. 'I hope you're right.'

The mutual hatred became almost like a game. Elma would toss out an insult, and Rune would return it in kind, with a twist of his own. They might sidestep one another, avoiding the barb. But with each passing day, the game became more engaging, and Elma found herself enjoying it in some distant, perverse way.

'You'll never rule a kingdom if you can't even control a roomful of fools with shriveled balls,' Rune said to Elma, only days after her father's funeral.

Elma had just swept from a meeting with her advisors in a foul mood, her thoughts a tangled mess. The usual retinue of guards traipsed several paces in her wake while Rune strode easily beside her, one hand on his sword pommel. She turned to glare at the assassin. 'And how might you be aware of the state of their *balls*?'

'I have many secrets.'

'All of them repulsive, I'm sure.'

His eyes danced. 'Naturally.'

'My advisors constantly push me,' Elma said, turning to gaze out a tall window at swirling snow beyond, her guards hovering at a respectful distance. She couldn't focus on the banter, the indulgence of verbally sparring with Rune. 'They demand that rations go to the army when there is no war. I suggest other uses for the rations, they refuse. They plan for my journey to Navenie after I'm crowned; little good it will do. And all the while, I'm forced to endure Ferdinand and Bertram watching me like ravenous hogs.'

'A queen doesn't *suggest*, she orders,' Rune said, coming up beside her. 'You balance on a knife's edge. With those clumsy long limbs, you're bound to fall.'

She turned to glance at him sidelong. 'Do you stay up late at night practicing these jabs?'

He laughed, a short quick exhalation through the nose. 'If that's the sort of thing you imagine I do alone in my rooms, then you don't know me at all.'

Their hands were close enough to touch, if Elma were to extend a finger, to brush her cold skin against his. The storm outside seemed almost lovely, a symphony of blue-gray and white, so removed from her, and yet, only glass and stone stood between her and an icy death. She had never noticed it before, the beauty in the storms.

'Let's keep it that way,' she said.

'Why not have them executed?' Rune asked, his tone lacking its characteristically sharp edge. 'It would send a message.'

Elma regarded him with a raised brow. 'And you'd be free of your bargain.'

He turned to face her, arms crossed. 'Isn't it what your father would do?'

Uneasiness curdled in Elma's gut. It was exactly what her father would do. But she wasn't Rafe. She didn't want to be. 'I'd rather not show my hand just yet. There might be others plotting against me. It's better if I look ignorant. Weak.'

'And how do you suppose that game plays out?' Rune asked. 'You're crowned queen, and suddenly nobody wants to kill you anymore?'

'No,' Elma said, the unease in her belly souring to anger. 'As queen, I will have power at my disposal, with the laws of the land on my side. More resources.'

'You'll end up doing exactly what King Rafe would have. You stay your hand now, but in less than two weeks, you'll be calling for blood. And the people of Rothen will be reminded that they exist at the whim of a cruel tyrant.'

'If I call for blood,' Elma said through clenched teeth, 'it will be yours, first and foremost.'

'Now, now,' said Rune, taking a step toward her. 'That's not what we agreed. But if you play nice, I might let you sample my wares before I go.'

Elma almost turned away, but the assassin's gaze caught at her like an irresistible web. 'Your wares,' she scoffed, glancing over her shoulder to ensure her guards weren't within earshot, that the corridor was empty. 'What's that supposed to mean?'

His grin turned to a lecherous smirk. 'Oh, I think you know. The conclusion to our prelude in the courtyard, Majesty. Don't pretend you haven't thought about it. Using me, playing out your sadistic fantasies.'

Embarrassed heat fluttered in Elma's chest, coloring her cheeks. 'I don't have fantasies.'

'Your body's response to me tells a different story. I wouldn't mind it, you know.'

Where her skin had been cold before, Elma now felt hot, itchy in her woolen stockings and heavy gown. She couldn't meet Rune's gaze. 'There's something deeply wrong with you,' she said, turning to go.

'The offer stands,' he said, keeping up with her easily, their gaits evenly matched. 'I'm not above fucking my enemies. And you could use a distraction.'

Elma said nothing, clutching her skirts in her hands like some kind of scandalized maiden. She knew it was all a game, another attempt to set her off balance. Because when Rune spoke like that, she couldn't think. Couldn't breathe.

He spoke of her body's reaction, her pupils, the way her breaths came shallow in her tight bodice. But that was only what he saw. When he said things like that, her thoughts blazed with him. He was the only bright thing in a world of frostbitten death. And with each shaking breath Elma took, she proved herself a traitor – to her kingdom, her father, the crown, and most of all, herself.

Because she yearned to kill this man, but with every passing day, he embedded deeper within her like a thorn. She could not extract him.

15

Elma had practiced smiling in the mirror that morning. It wouldn't do to ride through the city of Frost with her brows furrowed and her mouth a thin line. But her practicing had done little good. What was there to smile about? She rode on horseback, Rune and Luca at her flanks. They rode slowly through the streets of Frost to the sound of flutes and drums and lyres, while brightly colored pennants flapped in the cold wind. It was a coronation parade, and Elma was its star.

She hated every moment of it. It had been years since Elma rode through Frost like this. The act seemed ostentatious, brash, almost boastful. *Look at your soon-to-be queen, look how splendid her garments. Look how shiny her horse, how heavy her shoulders under so much finery.*

And so, the smile, plastered on her face at first like a rictus grin, quickly gave way to her usual grim expression.

'They will think you hate them,' said Luca, glancing sidelong at the crowd that had come out to watch them parade through the city.

The streets were hardly packed with bodies, but Elma found it to be a shockingly large turnout. Children darted in and out of the road, goggling up at the horses and bright-armored guards, gazing in wonderment at the gilded royal carriages. A ballista, for some unknown reason, had been brought out for the occasion, was draped in brightly colored flags, and was being wheeled along with the procession. Elma couldn't imagine what might impress these people about a ballista, but she didn't care enough to question.

'I meant that you should smile,' Luca added, and had the grace to sound apologetic.

'Why?' Elma said. 'What good will my happiness do them?'

'The monarch's joy raises the spirits of her people,' her guard said, almost sing-song, as if it was something he'd heard repeated over and over. 'This parade is for them as much as it is for you, Majesty.'

Poor things, Elma thought, turning to gaze out at the people watching, their upturned faces all blurring together like smeared paint. *I am not the one to raise your spirits.*

'Queen Elma!'

The voice was small, but it rose above the music and the horses, the loud rumble of the ballista on cobblestones.

Elma looked for the source of the voice but saw only a blur of faces, gray and cold.

'Queen Elma!'

This time there was movement – a pennant, waving wildly and brightly. A small hand held it up, and a bright-eyed smiling face gazed up at her . . . a little girl. Elma had never been around children and did not understand their ages. The child could have been five or twelve. But her eyes were shining, and as Elma watched, she pushed her way to the front of the crowd, accompanied by a harried-looking man. Her father, no doubt.

'Queen Elma!' the girl shouted again, jumping up and down. She held her pennant aloft as if it were a holy thing or possessed of some magic. As if, upon waving it enough, she might summon forth her queen's attention.

'What's wrong with you?' Rune asked, riding up beside her. 'You look ill.'

But she ignored him, an ache rising in her chest. Why was this child so eager to see her? What did Elma know of the world, of sadness and pain? *I am nothing to her. I'm a symbol. I will sit on the throne of her kingdom as it rots below me.*

The parade rode slowly past, and as they drew closer, Elma could now see the girl's face in full. She was smiling, but her cheeks were gaunt, her skin wan. Her father watched the parade with hollow eyes, and all at once the faces in the crowd became clear to Elma, no longer a smear of formless souls who expected too much of her. Instead, they were suddenly, painfully human. Many watched Elma with obvious resentment, while others gazed up at her with something like hope. Yet every one of them appeared to be unwell, their clothes were old and drab, their bodies sickly.

She turned in the saddle, seeking out Godwin. He rode not far behind her, dressed in his finest raiment, his beard full and dark, his eyes keen. Elma thought of the feast that had been held in her name, the food she had only picked at.

'Queen Elma!' came the girl's voice again, though now Elma thought she heard a hint of disappointment, as the pennant's waving slackened.

A hand seemed to tighten on Elma's throat. Was this her legacy? Would this be how she carried out her years, watching these faces gaze up at her from below, and doing nothing to help them?

Elma pulled back on her horse's reins, coming to a stop.

There were shouts as the guards, and the rest of the parade behind her, warned of a sudden halt.

'Your Majesty,' said Luca, 'What –'

But Elma was already swinging her leg over the saddle, her feet landing hard on the cobblestones. She wasn't dressed for walking, but she didn't care. Gathering her heavy skirts in one hand, she strode around the horses and the trumpeters, the guards and all their pomp, and went to stand before the little girl.

Rune followed without a word, Luca not far behind him, Elma's shadows.

'Queen Elma,' said the girl, her pennant now hanging motionless, her eyes wide, and her mouth hanging open in surprise.

Elma hesitated. She had never spoken to a child like this, let alone a strange one from the city. Her heart hammered in her chest. *What would my mothers have done?* They had always treated Elma as an equal, a girl whose voice deserved to be heard.

'Your Majesty,' Luca said, his tone urgent. 'You cannot . . . you must return to your –'

But she only held up a hand to silence him and lowered herself to one knee until she was eye-to-eye with the girl. She held out a hand to the pennant, which was hanging limp at the girl's side now. 'May I see?'

The girl's face lit up as she held out the pennant, and Elma saw that it was handmade, a patchwork of many smaller bits of fabric all sewn together with twine. It was black and red, the Volta colors, and in the center of it were a trio of letters: E.V.I.

'Elma Volta the First,' Elma breathed, brushing a finger

over the rough cloth. She looked up at the girl, who was vibrating with barely contained excitement. 'Did you make this?'

'Yes,' gasped the girl, as if she'd been waiting for this very question. 'I've never had a queen before. Papa says –'

The man standing behind her, presumably her father, laid a hand on his daughter's shoulder. 'Remember your manners,' he murmured.

'Oh,' said the girl, 'sorry.' Then she dipped a curtsey and said, '*Your Majesty*, Papa says your reign will be . . . oss . . . ospi . . .'

'Auspicious, Your Majesty,' said her father, bowing his head in deference.

The girl only grinned, her nose and cheeks pink in the cold.

Elma realized then that the city seemed to have gone quiet. The parade stood unmoving, waiting for her to rejoin its ranks. Luca and Rune stood just behind her, tension radiating from them – they were ready to strike at anyone, even, presumably, children. There was no music, and even the crowd along the street was silent, watching this exchange with something like frightened awe.

King Rafe had never done this, Elma realized with a sudden certainty. He had never spoken to his subjects, let alone stopped a parade to do so.

She glanced up at Rune, expecting to see disapproval in his gaze or amusement at her gaffe. But he was watching the girl, a soft smile playing at the edge of his mouth. And when his eyes found hers, he only held her gaze with an air of anticipation, as if to say, *your move*.

Elma turned back to the girl, who was still watching

her with wide-eyed awe. Elma's heart twisted. 'What's your name?' she said.

'Winifred,' said the girl, her excited smile returning. 'You can call me Winny, though.'

'Winny,' said Elma, and it was shockingly easy to return the girl's smile. She returned the pennant to the girl's eager hands. 'Thank you for your confidence in me. I will do my utmost to live up to it.'

She returned to her horse under the stormy gaze of Luca, and Rune's unreadable expression. As the parade started up again, the assassin drew closer to her, their feet almost colliding as they rode.

'You think I'm an idealistic fool,' Elma said, not waiting for her bodyguard to speak.

'I don't know what I think,' said Rune. 'But if you pull something like that again, Luca might burst into flames.'

'I can hear you,' Luca said.

Elma couldn't help the snort of laughter that bubbled forth, and she covered her mouth with a gloved hand.

That evening, Elma wrote up an order for her uncle to sign: the Frost Citadel's rations would be divided up and distributed to the people of the city, each household receiving enough to feed them well for months. There would be plenty of time after her coronation, Elma insisted, to trade with Mekya for more.

Rune was uncharacteristically quiet as they made their way back to Elma's rooms for the night. He had been seemingly morose all day, his usual sharp witticisms strangely lacking. Elma should have been relieved, but instead, she found herself set off balance by the assassin's reticence.

'Well?' she said at last. 'Out with it.'

'Out with what?' Rune asked.

'Whatever scathing commentary you've been sitting on all day. Don't hold back on my account. I'd rather you flay me verbally than put up with this silent brooding.'

Rune paused in the cold corridor, turning to face her. Like clockwork, her guard retinue, several paces behind, paused as well. 'I don't brood,' Rune said. 'I'm simply . . . thinking.'

'About?'

'The parade. I didn't know the Volta had it in you.'

Elma bristled. Here came the insult. 'Had what in us?' she asked when her assassin wasn't forthcoming.

Rune moved toward her, his voice low so no one else could hear. 'Humanity,' he said.

Elma opened her mouth to protest, to shoot back some barb. But the words caught in her throat. 'Neither did I,' she said, unable to meet the assassin's gaze. 'I didn't expect . . . I thought perhaps my father was right.'

'Right about what?'

'That we are all bloodthirsty in Rothen.' Elma crossed her arms. 'But I'm finding that my father was wrong about many things.'

'Interesting,' said Rune.

She frowned. 'What is?'

The assassin's mouth quirked. 'You.'

'Right,' said Elma, turning on her heel and striding off again, toward her room. 'Of course. Keep your insults to yourself, then.'

But Rune said nothing as he accompanied her to her chambers, and when she shot him a glower as she closed the door in his face, he only blinked, as if distracted, his gaze far away.

16

Ten days before the coronation, Elma had almost begun to feel safe. Her days were busy with meetings and events, her nights quiet and lonely. And while she never once relaxed, no attempts were made on her life. Perhaps, she thought, they had given up. Maybe Rune had been her advisors' first and only grasp at power, and after his failure, they had accepted defeat.

Elma took dinner in one of the smallest citadel dining rooms. She was joined by Godwin, Bertram, Maurice, and her cousin Lady Devereaux. As ever, Rune waited in the shadows, only his edges illuminated by firelight.

Conversation was sparse; the hour was late, and everyone was in a foul mood. Elma's advisors had complained of everything – the gown she planned to wear on her coronation, the food to be served. They had been markedly more irritable since Rune's introduction to the court, yet further proof to Elma that she'd made the correct choice in employing the assassin.

Tureens of thick stew and jugs of wine were brought out. A servant poured Elma's wine, and she lifted it to her lips.

A scream cut through the night.

'Your Majesty!' came the panicked shout, shrill and trembling. Elma spun to see Cora struggling to enter the room. She was dragging something heavy, something large . . .

Before Elma could react, Rune was at her side. He

wrenched the goblet from her fingers, sniffed it once, and cast it violently to the floor.

'Poison,' he spat.

But Elma was still catching up. She stared at Cora, whose face was wet with tears. And then she saw what her maid was clutching at, dragging forward – the body of Elma's taster.

Elma stood, her chair nearly clattering to the floor as she pushed it back roughly. She made to rush to Cora's side, but Rune's arm curved firmly around her middle, holding her in place.

Godwin and the advisors collected themselves almost immediately and began to gather around Cora, demanding explanations. Luca stood at the door, his face a mask of grief and rage.

He should have stopped this, Elma thought. *Rune should have stopped this.*

'Your Majesty,' Rune murmured in her ear, 'please stop struggling. You're safe. But I need you to stay here, with me, until I understand exactly what happened.'

Turning away from the others, Godwin locked eyes with Elma. She had rarely seen him so visibly frightened. 'Did you drink the wine?' he asked.

Elma opened her mouth and found it was too dry to speak. She shook her head.

Her uncle sighed, running a hand over his face. 'Good. It might be in the food, too. Don't eat anything, Lady Devereaux.' This last was directed at the table where Elma's third cousin still sat.

'Would never have happened at *my* stronghold,' Lady Devereaux muttered, glancing around wildly. 'Poison . . . in the *wine* . . .'

'Stay here,' Rune said, taking Elma by the shoulders and holding her gaze. There was nothing cruel or humorous in his eyes. She nodded once. Seemingly satisfied, he turned and made his way across the room to the cluster of advisors and Cora and the partially obscured body of Elma's taster.

Elma had seen tasters killed before. Her father had gone through at least four while she'd been at the citadel, maybe more. And each time, his avoidance of a sure death had been celebrated. *Poison cannot touch the King of Rothen.*

But now, seeing it first-hand, the crumpled body . . . knowing that the poison had been meant for her, that the only reason this man lay dead was because of *her* . . . Elma braced a hand against the table for support.

All at once, the men turned away from the body, leaving Cora where she knelt, still sobbing gently. They watched Elma with the same sort of sad, apologetic expression that meant bad news was about to be delivered. As if Elma hadn't seen, as if she wasn't right there.

Godwin spoke first. 'Your Majesty, an attempt has been made on your life. There is poison in the wine and the food. Do not eat or drink anything but water tonight, taken directly from the well and tested in advance. Until someone is chosen to replace your taster, we will make do with one of the others.'

'Others,' Elma said, trying desperately to focus on her uncle's words.

'The other tasters,' Bertram interjected. 'There are several employed at the citadel, Majesty. Should we lose one, we need *someone* to . . .'

'I understand,' Elma bit out. 'And who is going to pay for this offense?'

'Your Majesty,' said Ferdinand, stepping forward, 'Luca and his men have gone to search for the responsible parties. But it may take hours to launch a proper investigation.'

'Hours?' said Elma, regaining her composure as she spoke. 'More could be harmed in that time. Launch your investigation immediately. Or would you have another assassin roaming the Frost Citadel freely?'

'Perhaps you could start a collection of mercenaries,' said Lady Devereaux, apparently having collected herself enough to make jabs.

'Be quiet, cousin,' Elma said, vibrating with pent-up emotion, 'or I'll sic him on you.'

Rune caught her eye, and she thought she saw a predatory glint there. 'Your Majesty,' he said, 'I am a shield, not your attack dog.'

'You are what I say you are. And right now, I need you to find the person who did this and bring me their head.'

Godwin frowned but said nothing.

Despite the bubbling nausea in her gut, Elma gathered herself and strode forward, pushing past the men, and knelt beside Cora. She couldn't hide from this; she had to look it in the face, this death. This loss that was meant for her.

Cora's sobs had quieted, but tears still slid down her face and dripped from her chin. Elma laid a hand on her maid's shoulder. 'Cora,' she said, 'you're safe. It's all right.'

The other woman said nothing.

At last, Elma turned her gaze to the taster. He had been young, a boy from the city. She'd never learned his name. After all, why should she have? The thought was bitter in Elma's gut. Why should she have met him, or cared for him, when her father had never done the same? Such a thing had never been shown to her. And some selfish, scared part of her was glad she hadn't known him – why submit herself to the pain of knowing a man whose purpose was to be expendable?

'I'm sorry,' Elma murmured.

Cora sniffed and turned to look at Elma. Her eyes were swollen, her nose bright red. Snot clung to her nostril. 'You didn't drink it?'

'No,' said Elma gently. 'No one did. Except . . .' She swallowed. 'Cora, did you see it happen? Did you see anyone in the kitchens or the corridors who shouldn't have been there?'

Rune, who had still not left despite Elma's order, moved toward them. 'It's just as likely your maid poisoned the wine.'

The advisors muttered half-hearted assent.

Elma leapt to her feet. She wouldn't have that. 'Cora has been my maid for as long as I've been in Rothen,' she said, her voice ringing through the room. 'I trust her. This wasn't her doing.'

Cora coughed and slowly rose to her feet to join Elma. She brushed away her tears with a hasty hand. 'I think . . . I did see someone.'

All eyes in the room turned to her.

'You said nothing of it a moment ago,' Godwin said, suspicion and frustration warring in his expression.

'I was frightened,' Cora said, glancing at Elma. 'Confused. I didn't think you'd believe me.'

'Of *course*, we'd believe you, foolish girl,' Lord Ferdinand cut in, sounding very much like he meant the opposite.

'You simply cannot keep secrets when the queen's life is at stake.'

Elma ground her teeth but ignored the lord's outburst. He and Bertram were likely behind this, though they would never have dirtied their own hands. They would have used someone else, a hired goon, or someone who shared their distaste for Queen Elma of Rothen.

'Who did you see?' Elma urged, taking Cora's hand. 'You're in no danger. I'll ask Luca to station a guard at your door tonight to see that you sleep safely.'

Cora glanced at the advisors, then back at Elma, her brows knitted together. 'I *thought* I saw, darting through the shadows . . . well, I know it sounds mad, but I saw a Slödavan.'

Every head in the room turned to Rune.

'It wasn't *me*,' he said, indignant.

'It wasn't,' Elma added quickly. 'He's been with me all day. Cora, are you sure?'

Her maid nodded. 'He had white hair and blue eyes. And . . . a blade of ice.'

'Well, there you are, Your Majesty,' Lord Bertram exclaimed, his face wobbling and bright red with suppressed anger. 'What else could it be but another Slödavan assassin? They would have our kingdom fall to rubble around our feet!'

'Stop trying to be poetic, Bertram,' Godwin said. 'You sound ridiculous. I hate to say it, but he's right. I don't know any members of court who look like that, do you?'

The question was for Elma. He was passing the matter to her, their monarch, and she could not have wanted it less. Another Slödavan assassin sent to kill her. Perhaps she *should* start a collection. 'You know I don't,' she said. 'We must proceed as if there's an assassin in the citadel.'

Godwin doled out orders swiftly and efficiently, and Elma nodded as if the orders had been hers. Cora was sent to her room with an armed escort. And at last, Elma departed with Godwin, Rune in her wake.

'Rune,' Elma said, turning to him, 'why are you still here? I'm waiting for a head on a platter.'

The assassin cleared his throat. 'May I speak with you alone, Majesty?'

Godwin's frown deepened, and he stopped walking, turning to face the assassin. 'You would choose pertinence at a time like this?'

Elma laid a hand on her uncle's arm. 'It's all right,' she said.

'Do not wander,' said Godwin, his gaze steely. 'Go straight to your chambers. Luca's men will already be there. It's the safest place.'

'Thank you, Uncle,' Elma said.

Godwin turned on his heel and left them alone in the corridor, the queen and her assassin.

Elma turned to Rune. He seemed more drawn than usual, almost unsteady. 'What is it?'

He glanced around as if someone might be listening. But only the usual guards stood at their stations along the corridor, none close enough to hear a quiet conversation. 'I don't like this,' he said at last, a muscle working in his jaw. 'There is something rotten here.'

'Your murderous countryman, perhaps?'

She expected him to snipe back, but he only shook his head. 'If another assassin were coming to kill you, I would have . . . *should* have known about it.'

Elma frowned. 'Why? You've been away for weeks, at least. While you were crossing the Frozen Sea, perhaps they hired another, in case you failed.'

Rune ran a hand through his white hair. 'No. I would have known.'

'You keep saying that. How? Are you in some sort of assassin's guild? Is there a schedule of the month's killings posted on the wall?'

He huffed impatiently. 'Not quite. Not . . . like that.'

Elma's thoughts slid away from Rune and back to the taster, his twisted face. Cora's red-rimmed, tearful gaze. *A death meant for me*, thought Elma, again and again. She heard Rune's voice talking to her but didn't care to listen. Too many bodies, too much blood, and an unyielding citadel all around her.

Rune's face appeared in her line of vision, his brows drawn. 'Your *Majesty*,' he said, his voice low. 'Are you . . .'

'I'm fine,' Elma said, coming back to the present in a rush. Her stomach rumbled from lack of food. Somewhere in the near distance, she heard the forceful sound of guards' voices and the clatter of arms and armor as the search for the Slödavan assassin began.

'Normally, I'd let you get away with that lie,' said Rune, 'but I'd rather you be at your mental best just now. I can't have you wandering straight into the clutches of your would-be killer just because you're . . .' he squinted at her, then frowned more deeply, 'unwell.'

'I'm not unwell,' she lied again.

But Rune wasn't so easily dislodged. He pursed his lips, then his expression lit up as though a thought had come to him. 'I know just what will lift your spirits. A tasty morsel of information about me. I haven't told anyone, not even Godwin. It's a terrible secret.'

Elma couldn't help but react, the faint urge to laugh at Rune bubbling up from deep down. 'I don't need a distraction, nor do I need cheering up. Let's –'

Rune shook a finger. 'Now, now, Majesty. I don't see you smiling yet. Haven't you ever wondered what sort of life I lead back in Slödava?'

She had, but she'd never admit it to him. Elma shrugged.

He grinned. 'In the city, I'm known for my taste in fashion.'

Elma stared.

His grin widened, and he struck a casual pose, hand draped over the pommel of his sword. 'Are you imagining it? Whatever you're envisioning, add at least a dozen more silver buttons, a handful of tassels, and – *yes*, velvet. Scads of it.'

'Fashion,' Elma managed at last, looking him up and down. This was not at all the sort of *terrible secret* she'd imagined he was about to reveal. 'But you're . . .'

'Dressed as a bodyguard, I'm aware. Do you imagine I lounge around at home, or at feasts and parties, dressed in full leather armor? With my outside boots dirtying the carpets? I think not.'

The mental image of Rune, scarred and glowering, dressed in the finest silks and velvets of a lord with a delicate decorative blade at his hip, his sleeves comically puffy and dangling with tassels, made the urge to laugh even stronger. 'I'm sorry, I . . .' she bit her lip.

'There,' Rune said, his eyes lighting, 'don't you feel better?'

He had sharpened in her vision as if everything around her was only a dream, and he was the only thing that mattered. As if he were a sun and she were a pale flower in early spring. As if she were a snowfall and he, the mountaintop she yearned to fall on. *I'm going mad*, she thought, saying nothing. Instead, she raised her eyebrows expectantly.

'Good,' said Rune, his expression turning serious again. 'I need you here, with me. You're in considerable danger.'

'I thought that was a given,' Elma said. 'Are you so uneasy because one of your own kind tried to poison me?' she asked, unable to keep the bitterness from her tongue. 'It shouldn't make a difference.'

'There is more to this,' said Rune. The light from a nearby window cast cold illumination across his face, causing his scar and blue eyes to stand out, harsh and ethereal. 'You're not safe unless you're with me and alert.'

'Then escort me back to my chambers and allow Luca's men to do their jobs while you seek out the assassin.'

'Luca's men are not adequate.'

Elma bristled. 'Not adequate for fending off one Slödavan?'

Rune's lip curled. 'If you think I'm the best that my kingdom has to offer, you're terribly mistaken.'

Elma raised her chin, fixing Rune with a deadly gaze. 'It is not up to you. You are mine. I am the queen. And as such, when I tell you to escort me to my chambers,' she said, enunciating slowly and clearly as if speaking to a foolish child, 'you obey. And when I tell you to bring me a head *on a platter*, you obey. Is that clear?'

A storm continued to rage behind Rune's eyes. But at last, he said stiffly, 'Yes, Your Majesty.'

17

Elma could not stay still. Pacing the length of her room, her heartbeat was a staccato of impatience against her ribs. Rune was out there, alone. And while she had no doubt that the assassin could fend for himself, she found that once he had gone, she didn't savor his absence. Perhaps it was the familiarity of a constant shadow, someone Elma was not afraid to speak her mind to and who was not afraid to speak his in return.

Luca and Cora were as close to friendship as Elma had ever come, but somehow, Rune had become something different. Something more. No pane of royal glass hung between them. They had cut one another, hated one another. They yearned to bathe in each other's blood.

Perhaps Rune, more than anyone, understood what it was to be Elma.

And she had sent him out alone, perhaps to die. Suddenly, the thought of losing him became too much to take. Her thrumming heart became an ache. It frightened her how desperately she feared for him, that he might die before she had a chance to properly hate him.

It was just past midnight when Elma decided she couldn't bear to wait. Her fire, untended by Cora, had burnt down to embers. No news had come from Luca, Godwin, or Rune. And if Rune's words were true, if he truly wasn't the best Slödava had to offer, then another assassin might be the end of him. Yet perhaps if she were there to help him . . .

Not allowing herself to consider the consequences, Elma went to her chamber door and threw it open. Five of Luca's men were stationed outside in the corridor. When she emerged from her room, the closest two spun to greet her.

'Your Majesty,' said Hugh, eyes wide, 'you must go back inside. The assassin could be anywhere.'

'In a moment,' said Elma. 'I only wish to see Cora. Send a man to fetch and escort her to my room, please.'

Hugh's expression was doubtful. 'Luca said . . .'

'I don't care what Luca said,' Elma cut him off. 'You can spare one man for a few minutes. I require my attendant.'

Hugh and the other guard exchanged a glance.

'That's an order from your queen,' said Elma.

'Yes, Your Majesty,' Hugh said, words heavy with reluctance. 'Go back inside, now. I'll summon you when Cora is here.'

Elma didn't have to wait long. She had paced the room only a few times when a soft knock came from her door. Rushing to it, she threw open the door to reveal her attendant looking worse than she'd ever seen her. Cora's eyes were swollen and red-rimmed, her face pale as snow. She gave Elma a weak smile.

Elma's heart clenched. 'Cora,' she breathed, 'come in. Sit by the fire.'

'It's burnt out,' Cora said, turning to stare at the hearth.

'Never mind,' said Elma, once again pacing. 'I need your help. It will only take a moment. I need to get past my guards without their knowledge. And I need you to distract them.'

The attendant's face grew whiter, her mouth falling open. 'Majesty . . . you can't be serious. There's a killer on the loose.'

'I can't just sit here and *wait*,' Elma burst out, finally ceasing her endless pacing and turning to Cora. 'I didn't realize . . . I don't like waiting, Cora. My bodyguard wanders the halls alone; what if he needs assistance? What if Luca and the others . . . I don't like not *knowing*. There are more lives at stake than just the taster's. I didn't even know his name, and he died for me.' She looked about wildly as if for some answer, some escape. How had her father lived like this? He may have been carved of ice, but Elma was flesh and bone. 'Cora, the walls are closing in around me.'

The attendant listened with a slight frown. She looked as if she might protest, but then furrowed her brows in thought. 'I might have an idea.'

Elma stood in the deepest shadow she could find, breathing hard. She was alone, utterly alone. The corridor was empty. Now that the queen was reportedly safe in her room under guard, every other guard in the citadel was on the hunt for the assassin. In the distance, she heard the clang of metal echoing against stone – guards patrolling the halls.

Cora's idea had worked flawlessly, the exchange of clothes, Cora devising a distraction to allow Elma to dart away, out of her room and into the corridors.

Elma couldn't risk being seen. Even in Cora's too-short dress and plain cloak, Elma stood out as the only person creeping from shadow to shadow. But it was too late to turn back. She would find her bodyguard and stay by his side. He would not die without her permission.

Following her instincts, Elma made her way deeper and higher up into the citadel. If she were an enemy assassin, out of her element in a strange palace, she would go for one of the tallest spires, get a look at her surroundings, and orient herself. And Elma knew enough of Rune to know that he would do the same. The journey was almost unsettlingly easy. Elma knew the citadel inside and out. She had grown up playing in servants' passages, hiding in abandoned rooms, and inventing stories. Every time she came across a guard patrol, she found it too easy to duck inside a well-hidden door or a heavy shadow.

When she at last came to one of the tallest spires of the citadel, Elma was thrumming with eagerness and no small amount of fear. The longer she went without coming across Rune or the enemy assassin, the surer she felt that she was drawing near one of them. The wind's howl was unearthly at this height, as if fabled beasts circled the citadel on leathery wings, clawing at its walls with curved talons.

Elma almost thought she could hear voices in the wind.

But no . . . those were voices in the corridor. Low, unintelligible above the wind, and very close. Pressing her back against the wall, Elma edged toward its edge, where another corridor cut across her path. When she came to the turning, she peered around the wall as slowly as she could manage.

The sight struck her in the chest. Not far down the other corridor, illuminated starkly in the moonlight, stood two figures. Both were lithe, armed to the teeth, with gleaming white hair. Rune was angled away from Elma, and the other man facing him bared his teeth in a glare.

She held her breath, waiting for Rune's killing blow, but none came. The two Slödavans were just . . . talking.

Kill him, thought Elma.

But Rune did not. He said something harsh, but even with his voice raised, Elma couldn't make it out over the wind. The other man seemed to laugh, shaking his head. There were no guard patrols here; nothing to distract Rune from killing his mark.

It struck Elma that there was no reason Rune should not befriend this assassin and turn on her. They were countrymen. And with the two of them together, surely they would make easy work of Elma's death. A sickly cold filled her chest. She was a fool. A naive girl. In a matter of days, she was set to be crowned as Queen of Rothen. Yet here she cowered, huddled against a wall like some child seeking adventure. If either of the men sensed her there, she would be dead in an instant.

And why? Because she had feared for Rune. This ruthless killer, her enemy, her father's enemy. A man who stood by her side only under duress. And while their bargain had felt true to her, and she believed that Rune had every reason to stand by it . . . here, in a swaying tower with the sound of phantom monsters bellowing in the wind, Elma doubted everything.

I need to go, she thought, clutching her skirts with trembling fingers. *I should not have come here.*

Just then, both figures in the corridor turned, their gazes directed at Elma. Their eyes seemed to glow blue-white in the moonlight. A spike of cold fear thrust through Elma's heart. Before they had time to call out or attack, she turned and ran. Frozen fingers of fear choked her as she made her way back to her room, shadow to shadow, until she was safe again under Hugh's furious gaze.

Elma started awake to the sound of her bedroom door opening. She sat up, heart pounding, feeling as if she had only just fallen asleep. It had been early morning by the time she was able to drift into oblivion, though her dreams had been sharp and strange.

Blinking, Elma pulled her blankets up to cover herself. A figure stood in the doorway, dressed all in black. Rune. And dangling from his outstretched hand, his fingers tangled in its white hair, was the dripping head of the enemy assassin.

Elma opened her mouth, her brain still catching up. Rune had done it. He'd killed the other Slödavan. He had not betrayed her. An unfamiliar feeling crept along her nerves, thick and honeyed.

'You did it,' she breathed.

Rune raised his eyebrows. 'What did I say? Something rotten.' He let go of the head. It fell with a horrible thunk, rolling twice before it lay still. Its eyes stared at Elma, unseeing.

'What do you mean?' she asked, scrambling out of bed. Her pulse was thrumming; she had never seen a severed head up close. She knelt to peer at it. Its skin was paler than Rune's, its white hair duller, but it was obviously Slödavan. Even the eyes were blue.

'Where's his Rime Ice blade?' Elma asked, unable to take her eyes off the thing despite the roil of nausea in her belly.

'Fascinatingly, there wasn't one.' Rune came to kneel at her side, his movements stiff and impatient. 'Look,' he said, using one finger to pull down one of the severed head's lower eyelids. 'Those are not Slödavan eyes.'

Elma frowned, leaning forward. 'They look blue to me.'

Rune took her chin in his hand, firm but not rough, and turned her head to face him. His gaze was fierce, almost violent in its intensity, his scar craggy bright in the morning light. 'Look at my eyes.'

She had done it countless times, in anger or frustration or even bursts of lust. But he was so close, and unlike all those other times, his gaze was icy clear. Her stomach in knots and her heart pounding, Elma studied the assassin's eyes. They were bright blue, the bluest she'd ever seen. Ethereal, almost frightening in their strangeness, as if they harbored a magic all their own.

'I know they're pretty,' Rune said, 'but you needn't take all day. Now look at his.'

Reddening, Elma turned back to the severed head. Its eyes *were* blue, but she saw it now – they were ordinary blue, a dull, muddy color that was almost gray. If all Slödavan eyes were like Rune's, then this was no Slödavan.

Elma turned to her assassin, questioning. 'But . . . his hair.'

'Look at it,' Rune said, disgust in his words. 'It's been dyed, the color bleached out. And don't worry, I took the liberty of checking the hair between his legs before I turned his body over to your men. It didn't match.'

'You mean you have white –' Elma said, then bit her tongue.

'Yes,' Rune said impatiently. 'I'll show you later, you depraved thing. But first, care to shed any light on these events? Any idea why a man might be traipsing through your citadel disguised as a Slödavan? I can think of at least one reason.'

He wasn't the only one. Elma knew exactly why another Slödavan might be here, coming for her throat. Bertram and Ferdinand would not give up on their coveted war. She stood, and as she did, realized suddenly she was wearing only her nightgown. 'Where is Luca?' she demanded, crossing her arms tightly across her chest. 'My uncle should be informed. We ought to convene –'

Rune leapt to his feet, cutting her off. 'Whatever you were going to say, don't. You and I are the only ones who know of this ruse. I spoke to your men already and gave my full report. I confirmed that the assassin was Slödavan, that he was the one who tried to poison you. They allowed me to come in here alone to present my gift to you.' He nudged the head with the toe of his boot. 'As I said before, when you so frustratingly refused to listen,' he took a step toward her, 'Something is *wrong* here. All of your men, even Lord Godwin, saw this creature and his lank, dreary hair and said, *that's a man of Slödava.*'

'If you're suggesting that my uncle is in on the lords' plotting,' Elma said, 'you're mistaken. It's not so obvious this man is in disguise. Seen in the dark, from a distance, or already dead . . .'

Rune raised an incredulous brow.

Elma scowled. 'They wouldn't be looking for *dyed hair,*' she finished. 'It's another one of Bertram and Ferdinand's attempts to start a war. Perhaps they were unable to summon another Slödavan assassin and . . . went for something more readily available.' Suddenly, the sight of that head made her feel dizzy and sick. As if she were fourteen again, seated by her father at her first Death Games. At last, she let out a resigned sigh. 'My own advisors are so vile that they would knowingly sentence their own men, men of Rothen, to death. Just to steal a throne, or to make a reckless attempt to obtain your cursed Rime Ice.'

'Good luck to them in their endeavor,' Rune said cuttingly. 'I've only seen true Rime Ice wielded twice in my life. If anyone in Rothen has seen it in battle and lived to tell the tale . . . well, I'd owe your men an apology for severely underestimating them. It's rare, and not every Slödavan has the ability to use it. We don't just swing Rime Ice around like a dick in the hand. I knew something was wrong when your attendant claimed to have seen a man wielding an ice blade here, at the Frost Citadel.'

'Cora wasn't lying,' Elma said defensively. 'She was frightened and confused. Any blade could glint in the light and look like ice.'

'No need to lose your head,' said the assassin. He smirked, glancing at the severed head. 'Yet.'

'This is both of our lives at stake,' Elma said, hugging herself. The room was cold, and her feet were bare. 'If I die, so do you. And best of luck to your darling kingdom when the might of Rothen is at its doorstep.'

'Mmm, so you say.' Rune tilted his head and ran his gaze languidly from her feet to her face. 'You can stop looking so uncomfortable, Majesty,' he said. 'Yes, your nightgown is very thin, but I've already seen everything. Relax.'

Elma inhaled sharply, squeezing her arms even tighter around her midsection. Marching to her wardrobe, she shrugged on a robe, knotting its belt tightly around her. She took a long, steadying breath, then turned back to the assassin. Ice crackled in her gaze. 'I can't talk about this here. You're dressed, and I'm not. There is a head lying on my floor.'

'Then where do you suggest we discuss the matter?' Rune asked, frowning deeply as he nudged the head around in a circle with his boot.

'Stop doing that,' Elma said. 'You're going to get blood everywhere. I need to clear my head.' She paused, collecting her thoughts. She needed fresh air, the sky, to move her body. She glanced at Rune, wondering if it was too much to ask, if such a thing might cross a line. But she was exhausted, confused, and most of all she wanted to get out of her room. 'Would you . . . spar with me?'

The assassin blinked, his eyebrows slightly raised. 'As in . . .'

'Spar with me,' Elma repeated. 'Nothing *lewd*. Swords. Sparring.'

A slow grin spread across his face, fingers flexing on the pommel of his sword. 'Your Majesty, I thought you'd never ask.'

18

'I'll go easy on you, Your Majesty.'

Rune's wide smile cut through something rigid yet fragile in Elma, and she tightened her grip on her sword pommel. The day was oddly quiet, the gray sky still and low. Sunlight bounced between the clouds and the citadel, so bright that Elma had to squint to see properly. Rune's hair shone in contrast to his skin, his dark leathers. He seemed kinetic in his movements, where he stood waiting across from Elma in the sparring ring, unable to keep still.

Elma patted her chest, the feeling of it dulled by her reinforced fencing doublet. It would not protect her from a proper blow from Rune's sword, but she trusted – perhaps foolishly – in her ability to block him and his reluctance to kill her. Yet.

'No points below the waist or above the neck,' she said, rolling her shoulders to loosen them. It had been so long since she'd sparred properly. And despite it all; the poison in her wine, the head on her floor . . . standing there in the courtyard, sword in her gloved hand, she felt *vivid*. As if nothing existed but this moment, the cool air in her lungs, the strain of her muscles as she lifted her weapon.

'Ready?' Rune asked.

Elma lifted her blade in salute, and Rune mirrored her.

'Ready,' said Elma, allowing a small smile to creep across her lips. 'Begin.'

He moved like a specter. Elma had never seen anything like it. He first came at her with a sweeping blow, which she barely deflected. Her lungs burned, her nerves sang, and she almost laughed as she spun and parried, lunged, ducked, dodged, and spun again. It was a dance, a deadly one, but she couldn't deny the freedom in it. The way her hair flew around her ears and clung to her forehead. The unselfconscious grunts she made with every block, every sweeping attack. This was not a queenly activity; this was raw and breathless. It was *fun*.

'Had enough?' Rune asked, circling her slowly with a predatory smile. 'I see you're tiring. Swordplay isn't for the weak.'

Elma scoffed. 'Tiring? I'm just getting started.'

She lunged, curving her blade in an arc. Rune parried her easily, bouncing back on his heels. He was smiling brightly, and as Elma circled him, he appeared almost boyish. A young man enjoying the air and a fight.

'I saw you last night,' Elma said, cutting through the air and missing Rune's belly by an inch as he leapt backward. She twirled her sword once, a boast. 'In the high tower.'

Rune feinted right, then swung at her from the left. 'So, it *was* you. Make a habit of creeping about the citadel in your maid's clothes, do you?'

Elma blocked the blow at the last second, stumbling slightly. Of *course*, he'd seen her. 'Only when I don't know who to trust.'

'You can trust me,' Rune said. He was breathing hard, a strand of white hair plastered to his cheekbone. 'In this matter, at least.'

Elma felt the wild urge to lift the hair and tuck it behind

164

his ear. Instead, she swung low, forcing Rune to jump over her blade as it cut a wide arc across the ground. While he was still unsteady from the jump, she made to swing high. And when he moved to block it, she sidled into his personal space and tapped her blade deftly against his chest.

It was a series of moves that took less than two breaths. But to Elma, moving between Rune's limbs like water, predicting his next attack, his next dodge . . . it was clear and methodical.

'Point to me,' she said, unable to keep the smile from lighting her face. 'That's one to none.'

'You're actually quite good,' he said, leaning jauntily on his sword as if it were a walking stick. 'I had no idea Frost was hiding such . . .' he trailed off, clearing his throat.

'Such what?' Elma asked. 'Or maybe I don't want to know.'

'Oh, you do,' he replied, 'but I don't want to say, or you'll get a big head.'

'What were you talking about?' Elma asked, thinking she might catch him off guard with a return to the subject. She found herself entranced by a droplet of sweat as it made its way down Rune's neck.

'When?'

'In the tower last night.'

'Stop leering at me, and I'll tell you.'

Elma's gaze snapped to Rune's, her pulse speeding. Since when was she so easily distracted by *sweat*? This man was her enemy. She shouldn't be losing her head. Especially not while they were both armed. 'I wasn't leering.'

He grinned. 'There's no point in denying it. It's only fair, after my glimpse through the nightgown.'

She glared. '*Tell* me.'

'All right, all right,' Rune said, feigning indignity. 'No need to be angry. I was only questioning him. What else do you think I'd be doing?' He took a step toward her. 'Plotting against you?'

Elma swallowed. She could smell the tang of his sweat, feel the heat of his body, even through her thick doublet. 'Obviously,' she said, betrayed when the word caught slightly in her throat. 'I'd be a fool not to doubt you.'

'And I, a fool not to find out who's behind the poisoning. Unfortunately for both of us, the assassin wouldn't talk. And he was *such* a dullard, I couldn't listen to his pleading for another second. It wasn't long after you ran off that I gutted him and claimed his head. Oh, by the way,' he added, smiling, 'you may want to practice breathing more quietly. You sounded like a bellows in that hallway.'

'Then we're back where we were before the poisoning,' Elma said, ignoring his dig. A sliver of hopelessness began to wriggle its way into her skin. And alongside it, her closeness to Rune was making her almost dizzy.

'Exactly where we want to be,' said Rune. 'The coronation is days away. Your men are grasping. No one in Rothen could possibly best me in a fight. Your safety is all but secured.'

Then why does my throat constrict? Why can't I breathe? Elma wondered desperately. She stepped back, putting much-needed distance between herself and the assassin. He was becoming a sickly drug, a strong one, and the sooner he was gone, the better.

'We're not done sparring,' she said, forcing a jovial tone. 'Best of three?'

Her assassin smiled wickedly. 'Let's make it a little more fun. To the blood.'

A traitorous heat bloomed in Elma's chest. To the blood was riskier, with more chance of true injury or infection. Godwin would have forbade it. But Rune was as skilled with a blade as any man she'd fought against. Elma knew he would not cut too deep. And to see him bleed again . . .

'To the blood,' she breathed.

Rune didn't wait to lunge, his blade flashing. Elma was only just able to drop and roll away, breathing hard. Not missing a beat, she leapt to her feet and returned the favor, cursing as her sword sliced air. The assassin was liquid, ever-moving, and impossible to predict. Elma's vision zeroed in on him as the fight became a breathless staccato of steel against steel, hearts against ribs.

And then, just as Elma was beginning to enjoy herself, she misjudged an attack from Rune. In the next breath, her sword was clattering to the ground as the assassin pulled her against him, her back to his chest, his blade at her throat.

But he did not draw blood, not yet.

Her lungs heaved. Uncomfortable sweat soaked her back and the dip between her breasts. 'Well?' she gasped, not daring to move with Rune's steel against her skin. She wondered if he was contemplating killing her, whether it might solve more problems for him than it would cause.

'It would be a shame,' Rune said, almost crooning in her ear, 'to mar your lovely neck. Let's say I've won and leave it there.'

'A Slödavan, reluctant to draw blood?' Elma said, keenly aware of how close she was to Rune, noting every breath he took, every place where their bodies touched. She felt him as bright as a star, a fire burning through winter's chill. His breath ruffled her hair.

'Reluctance has nothing to do with it,' Rune murmured. His voice sent shivers down Elma's spine. 'As much as I'd happily . . .' he paused, a shaky-hot exhale warming Elma's skin. 'I'd *prefer* not to explain myself to your men when you greet them with a bandaged neck. But I urge you to remember, Queen of Rothen, that you are alive only because I allow it.'

A wash of incomprehensible emotion filled Elma to the brim. Something like fear or rage or lust, perhaps a mixture of the three, pulsed through her veins. She wanted to rip the sword from his grip and gut him with it. She wanted to watch him writhe and bleed on the flagstones, begging for mercy. She wanted to feel his hands on her, to know what else he might elicit, what mad, hateful ardor he could summon forth.

And then he dropped his hand, the blade no longer at her throat. She took a long, shaking breath, and moved to separate herself from him. But his left arm remained crooked around her shoulders from behind, holding her in place.

His words were low, his lips faintly brushing her hair as he spoke. 'One day, you'll let me in on those twisted thoughts of yours.'

Elma's elbow caught him in the ribs, and he gasped, releasing his grip. She spun on him, hating herself for the way she drank in the sight. He stood so casually there in the courtyard, lazily sliding his blade back into its scabbard as he chuckled, his gaze caught on hers.

'Rude,' he said, rubbing his chest where she'd elbowed him. 'I thought we weren't playing dirty.'

'I said nothing about that,' Elma replied, fixing him with a pointed glare. 'We only set parameters for points. I'll play as dirty as I like.'

The assassin grinned. 'You always know exactly what to say.'

Elma was so caught up in Rune, his jagged smile and impenetrable armor, that she didn't notice Godwin approaching them until he spoke.

'Your Majesty,' he said, his mouth tight in a disapproving frown. He wore his armor, no longer dressed as a lord but as a warrior. 'I beg a moment of your time.'

Elma bent to pick up her sword and sheathed it, consciously ignoring Rune. Ignoring the way her heart still hammered in her chest. 'Of course, Uncle,' she said. 'What is it?'

'Alone,' Godwin said, his gaze shifting to the assassin.

'He's my bodyguard.'

'And he'll give us a moment alone,' Godwin said, 'by your order.'

Turning, Elma caught Rune's eye and nodded. The assassin bowed stiffly at the waist in capitulation, then strolled across the courtyard until he was well out of earshot.

Godwin gave Elma a long look. 'Sparring with the enemy,' he said at last, the fingers of one hand flexing and unflexing, the other braced on his sword pommel. 'Have I taught you nothing?'

'I'm unharmed,' Elma said, defiant in the face of child-like scolding. 'I needed an outlet, fresh air, to move my body. Or would you rather I rot in my rooms until I'm utterly useless to anyone?'

'Cease with the dramatics,' said Godwin. 'Have you

not considered your own safety? If not that, have you not considered how this *looks*? A Slödavan assassin infiltrated the Frost Citadel, managed to poison your food without obstruction, and evaded guards for hours before his capture. This wasn't the work of a lone man. Someone let him in. Assisted him. Who's to say it wasn't your very own lapdog?' Godwin's eyes were dark, his words bit out through clenched teeth.

'My *lapdog* is the one who divested the assassin of his head,' Elma said, frustrated and defensive. As if her uncle truly believed she would be so oblivious, so silly as to blindly employ her own enemy without precautions. Without using her brain.

Yet some small part of her wondered if Godwin was right. *Do you know what you're doing, Elma?* she thought.

Godwin's expression only grew darker, sterner. 'I suppose it hadn't occurred to you that your *Rune* might have turned on his co-conspirator when the poisoning didn't work. He's far more useful to Slödava at your side. You've let a wolf in among the sheep, and –'

'I am not a paddock of *sheep*,' Elma snapped, lifting her chin. 'You forget yourself, Uncle. I'm not your wayward niece, not anymore.'

Godwin's brows drew together in frustration. At last, he sighed and drew a hand across his face. 'Elma,' he said, his voice softer now. 'At least until you wear the crown . . . be deadly cautious. This bodyguard of yours might save your life, or he might prove to be the very knife in your back. There is always more to a person than what one sees. To trust wholly is to embrace weakness.'

Elma swallowed. She could still feel Rune's blade, cold

against her throat. 'Thank you, Godwin. I'm well aware.'

He knew a dismissal when he was given one. Bowing once, Godwin spun on his heel and left the courtyard. Elma watched him go, a yawning gulf opening between them. And as Rune made his way toward her, her protector returning, an indescribable loneliness opened up in her chest.

19

Elma returned to her rooms with her gut in knots; Rune followed in her wake. Her thoughts were in a worse state, her uncle's words of warning ringing in her ears. *To trust wholly is to embrace weakness.* But how could a person function, live day to day, let alone rule a kingdom, without trust?

No, Elma did not trust Rune. There were very few people in her life that she did trust, and her assassin was not one of them. But she trusted in his loyalty to Slödava, his desire for peace. She trusted in his depravity. She trusted in his cutting words, his lopsided grin. He was an amalgamation of sureties, known bits that made up an enigmatic whole.

Pain expanded in her chest as they walked together through the citadel. A pain so fierce that she couldn't hold it in, no matter how desperately she fought it. She wanted so badly to trust Rune if only for the peace it would bring her. To believe that he could save her – from death, from the crown, from dangers unimagined.

But he was her enemy. He had tried to kill her. And the ache of loneliness overtook her.

The fire was built high in her rooms as Elma went to change out of her sweaty dueling gear. The blood on the floor was gone. Only the faint smell of vinegar remained to indicate that an assassin's head had recently been rolling about on it. Elma had a wild fancy that the head had all been some kind of dream, that Rune and her life in Rothen had been a dream, and she would wake up suddenly in her room at Orchard House, the sun streaming in.

'Your Majesty?'

The voice startled her back to reality. Elma turned to see Cora standing in the doorway. 'Cora,' Elma said, 'you startled me.'

'I knocked,' said Cora, apologetically. 'You didn't hear.'

Distracted, Elma began unbuckling her sword belt. 'I'm sorry, I've . . . I didn't sleep well. The assassin. And I'm sure you . . .' she trailed off, unsure how to continue, whether she should discuss the taster or the Slödavan in the corridors. Instead, Elma moved the subject to safer topics. 'Is there anything you need, other than . . . I mean, is there anything I can give you? It's been a while since I sent any food, and my dowry won't miss a few items if you need them.' She laid the belt on her bed while Cora came forward and set about unbuckling Elma's doublet.

'No,' said Cora, her fingers working nimbly. 'Thank you. My brother's apprenticeship ended at last. He's working as a blacksmith now. It's honest, and it keeps us fed and clothed.'

Elma hesitated while Cora was in the middle of pulling off Elma's doublet and turned to face her maid. Cora's cheeks were pink, her smile hesitant. 'That's wonderful news,' said Elma. 'But you know I always –'

'I know,' said Cora, shaking her head. 'It's all right. We're doing all right, now. On our own.'

'I'm glad,' said Elma, frowning slightly.

'You have a letter,' the maid said, after putting away

Elma's doublet in a strained sort of silence. She held up a roll of parchment, sealed with blue wax. 'I'll leave it here, Your Majesty.' Bowing deeply, Cora laid the letter on a table by the door and took her leave.

Elma's heart leapt at the sight of the blue wax. Even Cora's abrupt departure could not lessen her excitement. This was a letter from her mothers, from Orchard House. This was a letter from home.

Pigeons could not easily make the flight from Lothyn to Frost. It was a few days' journey, even in the summer, and often birds returned home when the winds were too fierce and the cold cut too deep. Thus, Elma didn't often hear from her mothers, nor did she often write to them. It was easier that way, after all – she could pretend that there *was* no other home, no mothers far away who loved her.

Even the act of rubbing her thumb across the seal, of unrolling the letter, opened badly healed cracks in Elma's heart. She needed her mothers now more than ever. After King Rafe's death, she had written to them, alone and desperate, begging for help. For wisdom. For *anything*.

And Dae, at last, had responded. She wrote on behalf of the three women, the only women in the world Elma trusted with every cell of herself. She read the letter, first quickly and then again more slowly, savoring each word. It was filled with love, as if the paper itself were imbued with her mothers' embraces. But even though the words were kind and encouraging, Elma's sadness grew as she read it.

Because there was no answer to her pain. Her mothers had not sent a needle and thread with which to stitch up Elma's broken heart. They had not gifted her a new kingdom, one made of long summers and birdsong. Instead, they only urged her to be brave. To believe in herself. To stay strong, fight, and persevere.

Elma crumpled to the floor, holding the paper in shaking hands. Wear your heart like armor, they had said. Grow a craggy, hard shell. Open up for no one. You are loved. You are ready. You are Queen of Rothen.

A hot tear ran down her face. She didn't want any of that. She ached to be soft again. She yearned to open up like a bloom, to trust, to be vulnerable.

This wasn't the letter Elma wanted. There was nothing she wanted but escape from the harshness of her life, and only death would bring it.

Gritting her teeth, Elma crumpled the letter in her fist and hurled it into the fire. And then she allowed herself to truly weep, a guttural, despairing, lonely act.

You are loved, her mothers had said. *You are ready. You are Queen of Rothen.*

But Elma didn't feel any of those things. She was alone, and death waited at her doorstep.

She sat on the floor, sobbing gently, losing track of time. When she finally wiped her tears on her sweat-stained sleeve, watching as the fire licked the air, it occurred to her how childishly she was behaving. She was a queen, not an infant.

Elma stood, her legs stiff from being curled under her. She changed out of her sweat-stiffened shirt and leggings, washed herself hastily, splashing her face with cold water from the basin. Then she donned a simple gown of wool with a silk overdress and a corded belt. And taking a deep breath, she decided that it was time to return to old comforts, to do what her mothers would have done in her place. She would light a candle and pray.

Elma hadn't turned her thoughts to the heavens since leaving Mekya. Not in the way that her mothers had taught her. They spoke not to any deity, but to the heavens themselves – the wheeling stars, the sky, souls who had passed and waited in the after. The ritual had comforted Elma, once. In Rothen, it had only served to feed her isolation.

But she still had her candles, tucked away in a drawer, wrapped in colorful cloth, and bound with soft twine. Reverently, she unwrapped them and tucked each one into its clay holder. Going to the fire, she lit one candle and used it to light the rest.

When she was done, she knelt before all seven candles. She had arranged them on the floor, near the fire where it was warm. Taking a long, deep breath, she closed her eyes and murmured the prayer that would open her mind to the beyond, allowing her to listen to the sky and understand. As her breathing grew slower, her thoughts moved inward until even the crackle of the fire was barely audible to her. She existed in the quiet of her mind, in candlelight, and between the stars.

Am I on the right path? The question was hesitant, unclear. She sank deeper into the dark of her thoughts. *Will I be a good queen?* No, that wasn't the right question either. Without knowing what to ask, the heavens couldn't guide her. It had been so long since she'd done this.

What was it that she truly wanted, needed? *Softness. Trust. To bloom unharmed in a frozen waste.* She breathed deeply. The candle flames popped, their wicks thick and dark.

Show me the way to trust. Show me which path to follow if I am to rule with love instead of fear.

Elma opened her eyes. She blinked in the sudden brightness, the sputter of the candles. Smoke swirled before her, painting rivers of soft gray-white in the air. When she had done this in Mekya, or alone in the courtyard, or in the cool breezes of her room with an open window, shapes resolved in the smoke. Questions became answers. But now, only abstract swirls remained of the candle smoke.

She sat unmoving for several minutes, watching hot wax drip down the candle sides, peering at the smoke, hoping some image or message might appear to guide her. But she felt in her stomach that nothing would come to her that day. Or, perhaps, ever again.

Leaning forward, Elma blew out the candles.

Very well, then. If the heavens would not show her a sign, or illuminate the path to tread, then she would find it herself.

20

Days passed one after the other, fading together like winter clouds before a snowstorm. Elma carried out her duties as was expected of her. She rose in the morning and took her breakfast, dressed in queenly raiments, and met with her advisors. She made last-minute decisions about the coronation, listened to her uncle's repeated warnings of danger, his insistence that he saw things in the faraway snow – that an attack from Slödava was not to be dismissed as impossible.

And through it all, Elma drifted as a ghost.

'You look unwell,' Godwin said, five days before coronation. 'Have you been eating?'

Three days before the coronation, a heavy snow fell. There could be no travel to or from the Frost Citadel, and Godwin was so agitated that he returned to his duties on the citadel battlements, appearing at evening dinners with ice in his beard.

'There's nothing to worry about,' Rune said when only two days remained. 'Reigning is easy. The hard part is determining who wants to kill you and killing them first.'

On the night before her coronation, Elma undressed slowly. It was late, and the moonlight reflected on the snow outside her window, illuminating the room in pale blue. There had been a feast that evening, small but celebratory, though Elma felt none of her family or advisors' anticipation, let alone excitement. A heavy rock had settled in her stomach and showed no signs of leaving.

Tomorrow, she would be Queen Elma. And with that crown would come stability, power, and the ability to declare lasting peace . . . or war. When her fingers tightened, the realm would feel it. With a crown on her head, the rest of the world would have no choice but to recognize her place, her influence.

And she'd be free, at last, to rid herself of Rune.

The stone settled deeper in her gut. She ought to have been eager for the power, the freedom this queenhood would bring. But all she saw stretching out before her was a vast emptiness, a frozen waste, a long and joyless reign.

He makes me laugh, she thought, unlacing the sides of her overdress before pulling it over her head. *No one else makes me laugh*.

Pressing her lips together tightly, Elma shrugged off her woolen underdress and hung it in the wardrobe. She shivered with only her thin undergarments to protect her from the room's chill. The fire had died down during dinner, and Cora had not tended to it.

'Laughing is overrated,' Elma muttered, pulling her nightgown from the wardrobe.

'Couldn't agree more.'

Elma spun, heart hammering, her throat constricted. The voice had come from within the room. And as she stumbled backward, shocked into inaction, a figure emerged from the shadows. As if he'd been there forever, waiting for just this moment.

He was tall and lithe, dressed all in black. His hair was cut short, close to the curve of his skull. But even in the dim light, Elma saw that it was white. The man smiled, a ruthless, predatory glimmer of teeth. Firelight danced in his blue eyes as if he were gazing hungrily out at Elma from the underworld.

Cold realization settled in Elma's chest, painful and sharp. This was no imitation Slödavan. She was about to die.

As she watched, still frozen in horror, the man stepped toward her. His movements were like Rune's – smooth and controlled, as much a dancer as a killer. He licked his lips.

'You're looking lovely tonight, Elma Volta. Ripe and ready for the picking.'

She opened her mouth to speak but found her throat and tongue were utterly dry. Only a strangled sort of whimper came forth. She knew she ought to do something, call out, defend herself. But the Slödavan was so close, so real and horrifying in the night, and his presence overwhelmed her.

How did he get in? her thoughts demanded.

'Not a word of welcome,' he said. Like Rune, his skin was tan, his features nothing short of beautiful. But a feral cruelty glimmered in his gaze, a cruelty Elma realized she hadn't seen in Rune's face for days. Weeks, even.

As he spoke, the assassin drew his weapon, a gorgeous silver blade that rivaled Elma's own queenly sword. Grinning with satisfaction, no doubt thinking her an easy mark, he lifted the blade, ready to swing. His eyes had darkened to the color of the mountain itself, granite and unyielding.

Elma threw herself to one side in unthinking panic. There was no strategy here, no plan. No defense. She knew what Slödavan assassins were capable of; she had seen Rune in battle. Here, unarmed in her flimsy under-garments, she was no better than dead.

She landed hard on the floor, shuffling backwards until her back hit the far wall. She bent her knees up to protect herself. The air in her room had turned to ice as if the frozen sky itself had come to swallow her up.

The assassin stalked toward her. He was silent now, his prey laid out and ready to be slain. Unlike Rune, he did not seem the talkative type. Then a sound permeated the haze of Elma's terror. A small thing, the faint slide of metal against wood.

And as the assassin's blade came slicing toward her throat, she recognized the sound as her bedroom door opening.

Had she not sensed that there might be some escape, that someone had come to her aid, Elma might have simply let the Slödavan kill her. Perhaps, for an instant, just before the infinite darkness fell, she might know peace.

Instead, she rolled sideways along the wall toward her bed. But too late, she realized there was nowhere else to go, and in the next moment, he would have her.

'Well, well,' said a voice from the doorway, 'what have we here?'

Elma froze, blood thrumming in her ears. *Rune*. She was shaken by how calm he sounded, how unsurprised to find a killer in her room.

Her attacker spun away to face the door, and all at once, he seemed to relax. His shoulders eased, and with an almost careless movement, sheathed his weapon. 'Rune. I thought . . . we weren't sure . . .'

'That I was coming back?' Rune scoffed. 'Please.'

They know each other. The realization hit her like a blunt force to the chest.

Needing to see what was going on, Elma struggled to a kneeling position, using her bed as support until she could see over it to the far side of the room. There stood Rune, eyeing the other Slödavan with a look she couldn't quite read. His stance was casual, friendly even, but something about his expression remained stiff. Guarded.

A small, pathetic glimmer of hope remained in Elma's heart that he might defend her. That even if this stranger was Rune's comrade in arms, the deal they made was stronger than loyalty to a countryman. That Rune's desire for peace between their nations might win out, above all.

And some even smaller, even more hopeless part of her wished that he might take her side for some other, more personal reason.

'Word came that you'd been captured by the Rothen filth,' said the intruder, still facing Rune, his back to Elma. His tone was contrite, apologetic. 'I came to retrieve you if you lived. And, well. King Rafe may be dead, but his daughter remains.'

'And you've decided to clumsily bludgeon two birds with a single stone, I see. Might it have occurred to you that I had the situation under control?' Rune tilted his head, falcon-like in his keen intensity. 'The girl has been firmly leashed since the moment I arrived in Rothen. Whose idea was it to send *you*, anyway?'

Elma's fear and uncertainty curdled into something darker, something worse. Her fingers curled in on themselves, her fingernails digging into the soft skin of her palms. *Firmly leashed.*

The taller assassin shifted in obvious discomfort. 'Word

came from an anonymous source in Rothen. Someone needing a job done. And your mother –'

'Isn't a fool, so whose idea was it?' Rune interrupted. 'You're really starting to annoy me, Edvin. In no world would anyone in their right mind send you to buy a loaf of bread, let alone assassinate the Queen of Rothen.'

'But I *had* her,' Edvin protested.

'Then why is she still alive?' Rune asked, gesturing toward Elma.

It was as if the floor dropped out from under her. She had been betrayed. The revelation of someone within Rothen – that wasn't a shock, though it felt like a knife turning slowly in her gut. But Rune – his betrayal hung in her mind like a mote of dust, as if, were she to touch it, it might become true. Real. Faced with a real Slödavan, his *friend* no less . . . Rune could have killed the other assassin at any time. He could have shown his loyalty from the instant he entered the room.

But his loyalty did not lie with Elma.

'I was about to,' said Edvin, his words growing distant in Elma's ears. 'Until you barged in.'

'I don't *barge*,' protested Rune. 'I've never barged in my life.'

As the two bickered, their obvious familiarity driving a wedge of ice deeper into Elma's heart, she reached under the bed. Upon her arrival in Frost, she had hidden knives all about her rooms. She had no chance against two Slödavan assassins, but she refused to go out whimpering and unarmed.

'How on earth did you manage to get inside the citadel, anyway,' Rune asked, 'let alone the queen's rooms?'

Elma dragged her shaking fingers along the bottom of the bed, but there was no knife.

'She's not the queen yet.'

'Semantics.'

There. Elma's finger brushed against metal. The knife was still here, wedged between the mattress and her bed's frame, exactly where she had left it. Knowing that she wouldn't be able to wrench the knife free without making noise, Elma braced herself. There would be no time to hesitate. If she could move quickly enough, from her position on the floor she might be able to bury the blade in Edvin's knee. And when he stumbled to her level, she would drive it into his eye, piercing the brain.

Rune would be dealt with afterward.

'I suppose I ought to let you do the honors,' said Edvin grudgingly.

'Not at all,' Rune said. 'We're both here now. What if we took turns?'

Bile rose in Elma's throat. In a moment, they'd turn their attention to her, and her chance would be lost. Her heart beating so fast she thought it might burst, she wrenched the knife out from under the bed.

She leapt to her feet and rushed at Edvin.

'What –' Edvin said, turning as she charged him. Almost lazily, but with uncanny speed, the tall assassin extended his arm and slammed a fist into Elma's side before she could reach him.

Her knife clattered to the floor as she tumbled sideways toward the far wall, choking for breath, her lungs emptied of air.

'A fighty bitch,' said Edvin, leaning over her. 'I see why

Rune likes you.' There was a metallic ring as he drew his sword.

Elma tried to speak, to curse him, tell him to go back to the frostbitten hellhole he had crawled down from, but she struggled to breathe. Her lungs were compressed by both the blow to her ribs and the knowledge that she was about to die. She only managed to cough weakly.

Edvin paused to glance over his shoulder at the other Slödavan. Rune stood motionless, his gaze fixed on Elma.

'Well?' said Edvin. 'Want to have some fun?'

Before Rune had a chance to respond, Edvin thrust out his free hand, grabbing Elma by the throat. His fingers were long and deft, his grip strong. Slowly, almost playfully, he lifted her up by the throat, until her feet were dangling above the floor.

Her neck burned, her lungs screaming for air. Scrabbling weakly at his hand, she kicked out with her feet, trying to catch the assassin in the groin. But he was far too nimble. And she was losing consciousness.

Through the fog of her vision, Elma watched as Rune strolled forward to stand next to his countryman. 'Enough,' he said.

'You'll have your turn,' Edvin growled, his fingers tightening on Elma's throat, his eyes bright with bloodlust, 'when she's dead.'

The edges of her vision were darkening. Her lungs screamed in pain. Death knocked, but she would not open to it willingly.

'I said, *enough*.'

'It's not your call to make,' said Edvin. 'Not anymore.' His gaze was locked on Elma's.

Elma's vision fled at last. She hated that the last thing she would see in this world was Edvin's cruel face, gleeful at the sight of her death.

I'll never see home again.

The thought drifted into her mind unbidden, a painful reminder of who she was, what she had given up, even in death.

I'll never have a chance to be a good queen.

A single tear welled in her eye, ran down her cheek.

'Oh, Edvin,' came Rune's voice from so far away. 'I wish you hadn't said that.'

The bright sound of steel rang in the darkness. There was a horrible squelching noise, a grunt, and then the fingers loosened around Elma's neck, and she was falling, crumpling to the ground in a heap. She coughed violently, gasping, clutching at her throat as her lungs filled with precious oxygen.

There was another horrible, wet grunt, and then a *thud* as something heavy hit the floor. Then, nothing but silence and pain.

'Elma.'

The voice was close, inches from her. She choked again, useless in her agony, her gasping lungs. And as her vision swam slowly back into focus, the darkness giving way to light and shadow and shape, a pair of hands grasped her face.

'Are you hurt?'

She let out a small, frightened sob. That was Rune's voice. Were those his hands? Or Edvin's, ready to strangle the life out of her for good?

The hands left her face, moving down her neck,

shoulders, arms. They were seeking but gentle, roving over the whole of her body with quick efficiency. 'Elma, are you *hurt*,' came the voice again. 'If he hurt you . . .'

Elma blinked, squeezing her eyes closed and opening them again. She could see more clearly now, though details were blurry. Rune was kneeling over her, lit by the dying fire, his face half in shadow. But even in shadow, his crumpled expression opened a chasm in her chest. She had never seen him look like that. *Frightened.*

His hands found her face again, rough but warm.

'Elma,' he murmured, 'You're safe. You're safe.' It sounded as much a reassurance as a prayer on his lips.

'Rune . . .' Elma croaked. Out of the corner of her eye, she saw something dark, thick, and red pooling across the floor. With the gradual return of air to her lungs came clearer thoughts, and all at once, it hit her. 'You killed him.'

Rune said nothing. They stared at one another, breathless, both pale with fear. Elma could not bring herself to look away. Rune, the man who should have killed her. The man she had thought betrayed her. Instead, Rune's own countryman lay dead, his blood spreading across the floor.

Elma felt achingly, blindingly alive. She had felt death coming, had *known* it was on its way to claim her. But here she lay, her lungs heaving and heart hammering. Suddenly aching to see him, the man who'd saved her life yet again, Elma drew herself up to her elbows until her nose was only inches away from Rune's. His blue eyes were bright like a fresh lake freeze, his lips slightly parted. In that breathless moment, she almost felt like his heart was beating in tandem with hers.

She glanced at Edvin's body where it lay nearby. His gut

where Rune had opened it, his head several feet away. The confusion on his frozen expression, the sheer shock of it, made Elma's breath catch in her throat.

'You killed him,' she murmured again.

And when she turned her gaze back to her assassin, the relief in his eyes nearly drowned her.

'He deserved it,' Rune breathed.

For a moment they were frozen in time, gazing at one another in mirrored wonder, as if discovering each other at long last. And then they collided.

21

Elma reached for Rune at the same moment he pulled her into his arms, crushing his lips to hers. He smelled of blood and leather and salt.

No . . . he was *better*.

Rune was real, solid, and true. Elma had accepted death, yet here was this beautiful, deadly creature returning her to life. He offered the release that Elma desperately needed. And with every sweep of his tongue, every frantic bite at her lips, he began to fill a deep, dry well within her.

Kissing him was like the first mild breeze after a long winter. It was a dam breaking, a glacial river pouring forth over her landscape. With teeth and tongues, hands grasping desperately, her body on fire, she yielded gladly to him.

And he surrendered in kind, allowing her to pull him closer. To thread her fingers in the hair at his nape. To bury her teeth in his bottom lip until she tasted blood.

With every kiss, every hungry sound he made deep in his throat, Elma returned to life. Her world crackled with desire and the taste of him. She could not have enough.

Not enough skin, not enough stifled moans, hands on her body, hands in her hair. She wanted him. There was blood on the floor, a body within reach, but . . . she *needed* him. Now. She had wanted him since, perhaps, the moment she first saw his shape in the darkness of her carriage, death come to claim her.

Too soon, he broke the kiss, pressing his forehead to hers, his hair tickling her nose. Their hot breaths and a thousand unsaid words tangled between them.

But words would come later. Elma saw two possible moments extending outward from this one – Rune moving away from her, standing, helping her to her feet. And one where he didn't. She wasn't ready to stop the rising flood inside her; she needed the white-hot moment of release, and she needed it from *him*.

Twisting her fingers in her assassin's hair, Elma held him firmly at the nape, her lips brushing his as she spoke. 'I need you to make me come.'

Rune's gaze caught hers, and the hazy lust she saw there almost brought her to the brink.

'*Now*,' she said, her skin on fire, her thighs tightening with an unspent ache.

He did not hesitate. One arm wrapped tightly around her, he lowered her almost roughly to the cold floor and crawled over her, his hands braced on either side of her. His body was too far away; there was too much distance between them.

Elma's hips lifted up to meet him, and he exhaled a shaky breath.

'Is it blood that makes you want me?' he murmured breathlessly, pulling the neckline of her undergarment down until her hardened nipple was exposed. Slowly, almost rapturously, he lowered his head until he covered her breast with his hot mouth, licking circles around her nipple.

She drew up her leg to frame his hips and bucked beneath him, gasping, one hand still buried in his hair. Her desire was heavy and eager between her thighs, pulsating with every sweep of his tongue. The burning ache flared as his teeth grazed her nipple, and she knew he was playing with her now. He would be her undoing, one way or another.

'I said *now*,' she managed, her breaths coming in quick gasps. The need for release was overwhelming. The knowledge that this was her assassin, the man who'd tried to kill her, whose blood she so yearned to spill, only sharpened her desire.

Rune chuckled, moving his mouth down her belly, leaving wet marks on her flimsy underclothes where he kissed her.

'Or is it the danger that you like?' he asked, nuzzling the inside of her thigh. 'The brush with death that makes you wet?'

Both, she thought, or said aloud – she couldn't tell. She *needed* . . .

But as he spoke, almost casually, Rune pulled her underclothes aside and buried two fingers deep inside her.

The surprise of it drew a moan from Elma's lips, and she couldn't help but angle her hips to take his fingers deeper. They were long and deft, stroking the inside of her until she could hardly think.

'God, you're soaking,' he murmured, dragging his teeth along her thigh where he'd kissed her. 'Sweet, depraved creature. I've never met anyone with such bloodlust.'

Slowly, he eased another finger inside her. She bit her own lip until tears came to her eyes, desperate for more. She had never needed anything as badly as she needed this. Needed *him*.

'I ordered you to make me come,' she said, surprising

herself by how steady her voice sounded, even with three fingers deep inside her. 'Not tease me.' *Please.*

'The danger *and* the blood, then,' he breathed, easing his fingers in slowly, deeper, then out again. So softly it was tantamount to a breath of air, Rune's thumb brushed her clit.

Elma's back arched with pleasure. Even the softest touch from him was ready to undo her. 'No,' she said, needing more. Needing to know that he was hers, utterly, in this moment. She needed him to worship her. 'With your *mouth*.'

Rune seemed unable to contain the groan he let loose. 'Elma,' he said, his breath hot on her thigh. He stayed there for a moment, breathing hard. At last, he said, 'I want . . . But you nearly died. If I hadn't been . . . And tomorrow, you . . . There's blood every . . . I –'

She raised herself up on her elbows to look at him. He looked absolutely wrecked, his cheek pressed to the inside of her leg, his expression both desperate and so full of *want* that it nearly overwhelmed her.

And all the while, his fingers continued their slow, rapturous stroke inside her, bringing her too close to the edge. And those two words rang in Elma's ears: *I want.*

'Stop talking,' she said, 'and do something useful with that tongue.'

It was all the encouragement he needed. He seemed to collect himself, and a smile curled his eager lips. 'Yes, Your Majesty.'

He removed his fingers from her slowly, leaving her bereft. But it was only for a moment. Gripping her thighs with strong fingers, Rune wasted no time in opening her legs, lowering himself until he was practically groveling before her. *Exactly where he belonged.* From where Elma lay writhing in anticipation, she was almost certain that the blood had spread across the floor, that Rune was half-kneeling in it. She wondered if it was still warm. If he could feel it seeping through the knees of his armor.

And then he pressed his mouth to her, a gentle yet insistent kiss, and she was overcome with him. He moved slowly at first, a rhythmic press of lips and tongue, drawing pleasure from her like a ribbon from a spool.

Elma rocked her hips against his mouth, the ache ever building in her belly. She couldn't believe that this insistent mouth of Rune's, unspeakably intimate, belonged to her assassin. Her protector. Her enemy.

Hers.

And then his tongue, at last, wiped her mind clean of all conscious thought. He licked her opening long and slow, and when she thought she might combust with the pleasure of it, he plunged his tongue deep inside her.

The perfect, full sensation almost brought tears to her eyes.

'Fuck,' she bit out, slamming her palm against the wall behind her to brace herself.

'That's the idea,' Rune chuckled before circling her clit with his tongue and sucking hard.

There was nothing left but pleasure after that. Elma could not think, could hardly breathe. It was as if she were dying again and again, losing herself in the fog of the tightness building between her legs. Losing herself in Rune. And as Elma's movements became more insistent, more erratic, he held her hips with firm hands, his mouth and tongue urging her, drawing her forth.

When at last she reached the apex of her orgasm, waves of hot, vibrating sensation rippling inward to a euphoric release, Rune held her. He kissed her hot skin. Murmured meaningless syllables into her thighs until she stopped crying out, until her gasps subsided.

Then Rune sat up, his eyes bright. He eyed her intently, his own pupils blown wide, chest heaving.

He opened his mouth as if to say something, but before he could speak, a knock sounded at the door.

Elma and Rune's eyes met in mute horror.

'One moment,' Elma called, wondering who could be at the door at this hour.

'I'm not exactly in a state for visitors,' Rune said, already on his feet, taking Elma's hand and lifting her easily to join him. She clung to him for a breath, unsteady on her legs. And then she backed away quickly, hating herself for how much she enjoyed touching him. How all she wanted to do, just then, was tumble into bed with him and see if she could make him beg.

The knock sounded again.

Glancing down, Elma realized she was still only in her undergarments. Dark blood pooled only inches from her bare feet. She ought to have retched or recoiled, but at that moment, she felt only a distant humiliation. Had she lost her *mind*? Letting her assassin lick her senseless with a body only inches away? And the worst of it was, she had liked it. She wanted to do it again, as much as possible.

While Elma's thoughts threatened to undo her, Rune was already at Elma's wardrobe, fetching her a robe. He held it out for her while she shoved her still-shaking arms into its sleeves.

'There's blood on your clothes,' he said, wrapping the robe tightly and securing it at Elma's waist. His movements were professional, distant. As if he hadn't just murmured nonsensically into the skin of her inner thigh moments before. 'Don't want anyone asking why you've been rolling around in gore, do we?'

'Good god,' Elma breathed, moving to the door. 'Nothing happened. If you say anything . . .' she swallowed dryly.

He cocked an eyebrow. 'Say anything about what? How good you taste? The sound you make when you come? How much I want to kill whoever's outside your door and lay you out on the bed just so I can hear that sound again?' He smiled serenely. 'I won't say a word.'

Renewed heat flared between Elma's legs, and she took a long, steadying breath, leaning against the doorjamb. 'Just keep your mouth shut,' she muttered. This would not happen again. *Could* not happen again.

At last, she threw open the door to her chambers. Luca and Godwin's concerned gazes met her in the corridor, and the guard wasted no time in shoving past her into her receiving room.

'Where's your blasted assassin?' he spat, his expression dark. 'We heard you might be in trouble. Cora came to warn us of a disturbance.'

Heat flushed Elma's face. What had Cora heard? Edvin attacking the queen, or Rune pleasuring her?

'Right here,' said Rune, coming to lean on the doorframe to Elma's bedroom. His leather trousers were dark with blood where he'd knelt in it.

Luca's gaze turned to ice, and he made to lunge at the

assassin, but Elma put out an arm to stop him. 'He *saved* me,' she said. 'Only moments ago. If he hadn't been here, I might be . . .' the words wouldn't come.

But it didn't matter that she couldn't speak, that the events of the night were forming in her memory with increasing clarity, filling her with an unspeakable dread. Godwin and Luca were already pushing past her into the bedroom and then cursing loudly and vehemently – they'd just seen the dead Slödavan.

Rune joined them, the three men conversing in sharp tones. They spoke of Slödava and blood and death.

But Elma stayed in the other room, their voices a distant hum. Edvin had not come out of thin air. He had been waiting for her. And while the citadel walls were technically scalable, Elma's window did not open to the outside. And she was always surrounded by guards, by Rune.

Someone had let him in.

'Godwin,' she said so quietly she hardly heard herself. She went into her bedroom at last, once again met with the small sea of blood, the assassin's guts opened wide, red and death and gore. 'Godwin.'

Her uncle turned to her, frowning deeply. 'What is it, Elma? This is grave indeed –'

'Someone let him in,' she said.

'That's been established,' Luca said.

Elma wanted to hit something. She was so tired of feeling lost and alone, isolated in her distrust; of being treated like a girl when tomorrow she'd be queen. She knew who had done this, who had sent for Edvin – the same advisors who had tried to poison her. But she couldn't name them, couldn't risk anyone knowing that she suspected. Not even

Godwin or Luca. Not yet, not until she was lawfully queen.

'I've been *betrayed*,' she said, her voice at last finding its footing, firm and commanding. 'Again. And the three of you are, what . . . Dawdling? I want this *thing* out of my room immediately. I want the traitors found and executed.'

Godwin and Luca exchanged looks. 'Majesty,' Luca said, his gaze flitting to Rune, 'it's just as likely that whoever snuck in the other one . . .'

'It was not my bodyguard,' Elma said. 'He killed this man just as he killed the other one. I'm beginning to wonder, Luca, if you have full control of your guards. I am to be crowned queen tomorrow, and a man lies dead in my chambers.'

'Majesty,' Godwin said, 'this is Slödava's doing. If there is ever a time to –'

'It's always *war* with you!' Elma roared; all that pent-up pain of betrayal, the fear of her crown, rising in her like a gale. Her throat was raw with the force of her words. 'Godwin, Luca. Get out of my room. Bring the body with you. And if either of you bring up war with Slödava again, I will take your eyes out.'

Rune watched her with something like lustful awe, his mouth falling open slightly.

'Yes, Majesty,' Luca murmured. Godwin was silent, but Elma saw in his eyes that he would obey.

'With me,' Elma said, gesturing for Rune to follow her. 'I need to breathe.'

22

Soft gray filled Elma's vision. Cold flakes fell on her cheeks as she closed her eyes, breathing in the fresh and frigid air of the citadel courtyard at night. She reveled in the icy cut of it inside her lungs, the warm release as she exhaled. She hadn't laid in the snow like this for years. For some time in her youth, it had been a refuge, a quiet place where the world was muffled, the harsh winds of Rothen kept out by the thick walls of snow all around her.

Despite the years that had passed since her escapes to the snow, Elma's thoughts were much the same now as they had been the last time she lay supine in the courtyard, slowly being buried alive in the powder. Her mind was bright with fear – of being queen, her duties as a monarch, the life that lay ahead of her in Rothen. But she was also afire with new thoughts, new anxieties. Rune, chief among them. Would she survive long enough to wear the crown? And even if she did, would she wear it for long? Or would her reign be short and bitter?

There had been so much death. So much blood, for so many years. And soon, the only person who seemed to see her as she was . . . would be gone.

A steady crunching approached, footsteps in the snow, until Rune was standing over her.

Elma peered up at him through the snowflakes trapped in her eyelashes. He looked like a dream, a creature of the winter. Had he ever been real? Been solid? Would Rune the man ever make sense to her? Or would he disappear without explanation when the crown was on her head, such a force in her life, but for only a breath?

'Are you going to lie there until you're dead?' Rune asked, leaning down. Snowflakes shimmered in his white hair, making him glow in the pale moonlight.

'As if you care,' said Elma. With her father gone, she supposed, only her mothers in Mekya would grieve her. And Godwin, though she knew him better than to think he'd wail and sob. He might sigh deeply, drink slowly from a goblet, and move on.

'Stop self-flagellating,' Rune said, kneeling down beside her. 'You're going to be Queen of Rothen tomorrow. You can't very well freeze to death moments before the coronation. And I hate to admit it, but I'm not particularly fond of the idea of you dying so soon. Though I suppose you've guessed as much, considering Edvin's current state.'

Elma's heart skipped a beat. She took him in, the ice-fine features, cruelly full lips, the scar that marred his tanned face. She sat up and brushed snow from her hair. 'Who was Edvin to you?' she asked, the question strangely vulnerable, hesitant.

Rune glanced away. 'Someone from home.'

'A friend?'

'Not exactly.'

'But you knew him.'

'We were . . .' Rune sighed, still not meeting her gaze. 'Colleagues, I suppose. Peers. We grew up in proximity and not by choice. I never liked him much. A brute, as you saw. Unworthy of spilling your blood.'

Elma swallowed. Rune hadn't hesitated. He had gutted the man, removed the head from his body. It had been a violent, angry kill. 'Do you regret . . .'

His gaze shot to hers, sharp and steady. 'I made a deal. I don't renege.'

Trying to ignore the sinking in her heart, Elma closed her eyes against the soft fall of snow. 'Of course.'

'Don't be like that,' Rune said. 'I meant what I said. I don't like the idea of you leaving me so soon, not yet. And I suppose, if you must die, I'd prefer to be the one to kill you.'

'How poetic,' Elma said.

'Not to mention,' he said, the corner of his mouth curling. 'I revile the idea of that sweet, wet pussy going forever unplowed.'

'For god's sake,' Elma spat, scrambling to her feet in annoyance. 'I hate you.'

'As you should.' Rune moved toward her, and the air between them seemed to electrify. 'But strangely, I don't hate *you*. Isn't that interesting?'

'You . . .' Elma said, her mouth dry. 'You don't?'

He was so close she could feel his heat. His chest rose and fell in the cold, steam forming at his lips.

'I wish I hated you,' he said softly. 'It would be easier. But . . . you're not like your father. You've made that painfully clear. And even if you were, I . . .' he paused, shaking his head. Then he reached out and took her chin in his fingers, delicately, as if he were about to kiss her. 'You don't take your impending rule lightly. I see it in you. Only a dedicated woman would go and lie in the snow like this.'

Elma made a derisive sound. She couldn't be hearing him right.

'Don't give me that *look*,' Rune continued, his mouth quirking in a smile. He dropped his hand, moving back just a fraction. Elma wanted to pull him back, to bury herself in him. Instead, she remained silent, breathless, as if any sudden movements might scare this honesty back into him, never to be seen again.

'I'm being completely serious,' Rune said. 'Your father was an effective king. His people feared him, and he defended his walls mercilessly. Rothen stands on the foundations that your father and his ancestors created, blood-soaked as they are. But you . . .' Rune looked at Elma as if she were the only thing that existed in that moment. 'You could be loved, Elma Volta. You could grow a garden.'

Any remaining animosity she had toward Rune, stubbornly as she wanted to cling to it, evaporated. Before her, just for that moment, stood an ally, a man who would see her be a great ruler. And if she could live up to the hope that shone in his eyes, perhaps she would be a worthy queen after all.

Elma could hardly move under the weight of her coronation garments. She had unthinkingly worn her usual woolen underclothes, not considering the layers of fabric that would be draped around her for the next several hours. Over her gown was a surcoat of silk and embroidery, and draped over her hips was a belt of golden discs that must have weighed ten pounds on its own. Over that, she wore a flowing robe in gold and black, and finally, the fur-lined coronation robe.

She placed the back of her hand on her cheek in an attempt to cool it. She considered asking someone to do something with the fire, but if she could not endure a little heat in a too-warm room, how could she hope to rule a kingdom?

The room was quiet. She, Rune, and Godwin waited in a small antechamber attached to the throne room, where the denizens of the citadel gathered to watch the coronation ceremony. The advisors were already seated, no doubt, as was Elma's extended family. She wondered if Cora's family had managed to come – she had extended an invitation, of course, but the day-to-day lives of those in the city of Frost were as vague and unknown to Elma as those in Ordellun-by-the-Sea.

As if Elma's thoughts had summoned her, a door opened, and Cora's head peered through. 'May I come in?' she asked.

'Please,' Elma said, holding out her hands, desperate for friendship. A steady presence, someone familiar.

Cora approached and curtseyed but did not take Elma's hands. Instead, she bowed her head and said, 'I have what you requested, Majesty,' and held out a rolled-up scroll of paper.

Trying not to dwell on the sinking of her heart, Elma took it and forced a smile. 'Thank you,' she said. 'I won't need you during the coronation. You may go and sit with your family if they're present.'

Her maid curtseyed again and fled the room.

Godwin caught Elma's eye, nursing a goblet of spiced wine and staring out at the snow. He raised one gray-flecked eyebrow.

'You may go, Uncle,' Elma said, standing firm. She knew he wanted to ask what the scroll was but was too proud to ask. And she could not tell him, as much as she loved him.

As much as she wanted to trust him. He was too entwined with the advisors, too much a part of their web.

Only Rune could be trusted. And even then, only with her life.

'You've memorized the words?' Godwin said, holding Elma's gaze.

'Yes, Uncle.'

'And you know the –'

'I *know*, Godwin. I'm ready.'

He stepped toward her, gripping her arms in his large, rough hands. Even in his finest raiments, Godwin still looked as if he had just come in from the citadel battlements – jagged and frosted, the wrinkles at the corners of his eyes deep and constant. 'You are your father's daughter,' he said. 'You are strong, unbending, unyielding. You were born for this.'

And just like that, he was gone.

Firelight danced in the grate. A terrible itch grew on Elma's back, between her shoulder blades. She could hear the trumpet fanfare in the throne room, the shuffle of feet finding their seats. The coronation raiment hung heavy, so heavy on her shoulders.

Rune shifted where he stood. 'Are you going to open it?'

Elma sighed. 'I feel as if . . . if I open it, whatever I see inside will become real.'

'And it's not real now?'

'No.'

The assassin held out his hand, his gaze soft in the snow-muffled light. 'Give it to me.'

Wordlessly, she handed him the scroll. He unfurled it without fanfare or pause and scanned it with a slightly furrowed brow. Then he folded it several times and handed it back to her.

She read it slowly, the words barely registering as she did. It was a list of conversations overheard, of monetary transactions between Rothen and Slödava and where to find them. A promise of more, should Elma ask for it.

'It's clear evidence,' Rune said, bringing voice to Elma's thoughts. 'Bertram and Ferdinand won't have a chance of contesting it. Cora has more hidden away. After the coronation, with that evidence . . . no one will be able to contest an arrest.'

'An execution,' Elma said, staring into the flames.

'If that's what my bloodthirsty queen so desires.'

She glanced at Rune sidelong. 'I am anything but *yours*.'

He grinned, but something tugged on the corners of it, weighing it down. 'If it makes you feel any better, Majesty, I am nothing if not yours.'

The coronation ceremony drifted past Elma like a dream. It was as solemn as a tomb, only the opening fanfare of trumpets serving to indicate this was an event worth celebrating. Incense choked the room, and Elma breathed deeply until her lungs burned. Then there were the prayers, the chanting everyone knew by heart. Elma's slow procession to the throne.

There, she spoke the words of the ruler in the language known only by those descended from the line of kings. It was a strange language, its origins having come from the people who lived on the ice thousands and thousands of years ago. And before that, it came, her father had said, from the stars.

Finally, Elma knelt before her uncle, Lord Godwin, brother of the late Rafe III, King of Rothen. He placed the coronation crown upon her head. It was heavy and black, with sharp spires of metal inlaid with rubies. It dug painfully into Elma's skull, her neck aching under the weight.

'Stand, Elma Volta, Queen of Rothen,' her uncle intoned.

She stood.

At last, there was applause, small and scattered.

And then the ceremony was over. Elma I, Queen of Rothen, took her leave with a lump in her throat. None of it felt right. Her mothers should have been there. Her father shouldn't even be dead. She should not be wearing his crown, draped in his furs, applauded by a throne room of subjects she hardly knew.

The antechamber door slammed behind her. She leaned against it, breathing hard, relieved to be out of the throne room. She had hardly noticed Rune following her in, always her shadow.

'I want to be alone,' she said. All she wanted to do was rip off all these layers of finery, get that horrible crown off her head, and go to bed.

But she was *queen* now.

She closed her eyes for a moment, willing herself not to cry. *I am strong enough*, she thought. *I was born for this.*

Rune said nothing. It was then that Elma realized he had no reason to be here. She had been crowned; she was Queen Elma, alive and breathing. Rune had fulfilled his half of the deal.

'You can go,' she said, spitting the words even though it hurt. 'You're pardoned. I'll uphold my end, sign the papers. I'll make peace with Slödava.'

Rune tilted his head. 'That's not why I'm hovering at your shoulder if that's what you're wondering. I can't leave you here alone yet, a ripe fruit ready to be plucked from the tree.'

'What a metaphor,' Elma said, trying to ignore the relief she felt at his words.

A growing storm howled outside the Frost Citadel, rattling the windows. And as the reality of Elma's coronation sunk in, as the rest of her life extended before her, she felt as if her chest were crumpling inward. Even after all these years, her heart was still in Mekya, in that beautiful garden kingdom, with her mothers at Orchard House. Yet today, she had tied herself inextricably to Rothen. She could never truly leave. And Rune would soon be gone. The storms would forever envelop her.

Rune moved to her then, wordlessly reaching up, and lifted the crown from her head. It was a quiet gesture, kind, as if he had known exactly where her pain was. And if it was just a distraction, if he planned to kill her now, then she wouldn't fight it.

But he only set the crown aside. And when Elma made no move to protest, his deft fingers unhooked the coronation robe from her shoulders and draped it gently across the back of a chair. She watched as if from far away, these simple movements, the intimate closeness of him. The gestures of a friend.

'I know what it's like,' he said, running one hand down the soft, furred edge of the coronation robe. He was half-turned away from her, his face obscured behind a fall of white hair. 'To be overwhelmed by one's duty. To wish for something different.'

When he turned back to Elma, his gaze was open. There was sadness in his eyes, reflecting back at her. She saw her mothers there, the blue sky, the fruit trees, and the symphonies. She wondered what he saw in her own eyes, what it was that he wished for. And she wondered, a crack opening in her frozen heart like spring's first thaw, if she would miss him when he was dead.

You'll miss him like a vital organ. And there's nothing you can do about it.

Something in Rune's expression changed then, like a fire burning out. And Elma knew, somehow, that he had been thinking the same. That there could be no homecoming between them. Not in that lifetime.

23

An hour had been set aside for Queen Elma I of Rothen, for her to reflect. To be alone. To be pious and quiet and solemn. Elma, the woman, could not have wanted anything less. She had few things to cling to, few comforts in that life, and her enemy had become – inexplicably, achingly – one of them.

'Rune . . .' she spoke his name softly, that single syllable laden heavy with a question.

'Come here,' he growled and pulled her into him.

She bent to him like an aspen in a gale. He was eager, forceful, rough. Exactly what she needed in that moment. To give way, succumb, to melt into pleasure. Rune seemed all too ready to please her without being asked. He kissed her deeply, pulling at her hair as he did. His other hand braced against her back, holding her body flush with his while his lips explored hers.

His mouth alone nearly undid her. It was so easy to give in to Rune. He knew how to nip her lips, when to lower his mouth to her jaw, to scrape his teeth along her flesh. When to kiss her neck, softly sucking. He knew exactly how to make her moan.

Everything he did was planned, immaculate. As if in the throes of pleasure, just like in taking a life, one need only apply the right pressure to the right plane of skin. To elicit the right response. To cause Elma's breath to catch in her throat, her hips to roll against his.

As the ache between her thighs grew into a desperate need, Rune lifted her effortlessly in his arms. She wrapped her legs around his waist and felt his hardness there. She arched her back to press herself against him, the heady feel of it eliciting a soft moan from his throat.

He backed her against a wall, legs still tight around him. He kissed her deeply. Slowly. Unlike the night before, when she'd been desperate to command, to control, this was all surrender.

The fingers of Rune's free hand shoved the layers of her skirts higher, exposing bare thigh above her stockings. And then she felt him fumble at his own belt, the buttons of his breeches. With a distant satisfaction, she realized even he was shaking.

'I want you to lose yourself in me,' she breathed. Her hair had come undone; a loose wave fell over her face, tickling her nose when she spoke.

Rune paused and met her gaze. He was breathing hard, his chest rising and falling in tandem with Elma's. They were both fully dressed, other than Rune's unfastened breeches and Elma's rucked-up skirts. But in that moment, she felt fully exposed to him, laid bare to see, all her flaws on display.

His gaze held hers like a gentle embrace. 'I already have,' he said.

In one deft motion, he reached between them and freed his hard length; in the next moment, he was pushing her undergarments aside. The crown of his cock pressed against her entrance, teasing. Then he grabbed her by the hips with both hands, angling her toward him, her back pressed hard against the wall. She let her head fall back against the stone, her hips rolling.

With one firm, gasping thrust, he entered her. She couldn't believe how full she felt, how perfectly he seemed to fit. He kissed her, then let his forehead fall to her shoulder as he made slow, rolling thrusts with his hips.

'Elma,' he murmured into her neck, until her name became a string of nonsense syllables.

She couldn't contain the build of pleasure inside her, the tightness that grew and expanded to encompass the wholeness of her being. And when she finally came, Rune reached the peak along with her, biting down on the base of her neck as he spent himself in her.

He took her mouth in his, the taste of her blood on his tongue, and she felt so acutely that she had never wanted anything as much as she wanted him. As much as she *needed* him. But she couldn't have him. He was going to leave her when all she wanted to do was cling to him and beg him not to. Suddenly, horribly, she found she couldn't remember a time when she had felt so strikingly alone.

Seeing something in her gaze, perhaps, or in the tenseness of her body, Rune withdrew and set her gently on her feet, his fingertips still brushing her arms.

Elma bit her lip to bring her back to herself. She wasn't alone. Rune was still here. She had an entire kingdom laid out before her. Yet, not a soul could she claim as a true friend, an equal.

Rune fastened his breeches and smoothed them down, once more the picture of a hired killer. He watched his queen with a line between his brows, lips downturned. 'Your Majesty . . .'

She inhaled sharply through her teeth. A moment ago, she had been Elma.

'Are you all right? Have I done something?' His tone was lost somewhere between confusion and surprise.

'All right?' she echoed, unable to hide her scoff. 'I am more alone now than I've ever been. All that lies before me is isolation and death. My blood is a curse. And you . . .'

She saw no sarcasm in his expression, none of the laughter she was so accustomed to. 'And me?' he said. 'I'm not going anywhere.'

'But –'

'No,' he murmured, taking her head in his hand, his fingers curling in her hair. 'I'll be a thorn in your side, Queen Elma, until I have every reason to believe that Rothen will not invade my kingdom. Until the enemies in your midst are dealt with, until I decide I'm good and ready, I'm afraid you're stuck with me.'

The relief that flooded Elma was so vast and unexpected that her knees grew weak. While she had always assumed she and Rune would come to blows as soon as the crown was hers, that one of them would lie slain by the other's hand, Elma could no longer imagine it. She had so vividly fantasized about Rune's blood on her blade, the life draining from those ice-blue eyes, but now . . . when she tried to see it, to draw that imaginary steel across his throat, she couldn't.

Her hatred had curdled into something else. Something terrifying and dangerous, if Elma let it thrive. Something that might get her killed, or worse – heartbroken.

'This is a farce,' boomed Lord Bertram from across the table. He slammed a fist to emphasize his point, causing everyone's goblets to wobble dangerously.

'You think I'm in the habit of making jokes?' Elma said, her voice threateningly cool. She had called her advisors to meet at first light the next morning, eager to bring the traitors to justice. She had no desire to continue to fear for her life, lying awake in bed and wondering what ice-eyed monster might come prowling to her bed from the shadows.

'No, Majesty, but –'

'Come now,' Elma said, cutting off Bertram's protest. 'I am the Queen of Rothen. Arrows will always be notched and aimed at my neck. A protector is needed now, more than ever.'

'The deal, if I recall,' Ferdinand said, 'was that the assassin would be allowed to remain alive until Her Majesty's coronation. After such time, which has now quite obviously passed, his life becomes forfeit.'

Elma surveyed the room, her gaze catching on each of her advisors' – Godwin, Ferdinand, Bertram, and Maurice. 'Are you questioning your queen?' she said. No one spoke, though Bertram opened his mouth as if to say more. Elma held up a hand. 'Of course, you aren't. You wouldn't dare, would you, Lord Bertram? Even *you* are well aware that not only am I bound to pardon Rune now that his end of the deal has been upheld, but the agreement does not end there. I have agreed to seek peace with Slödava. Not only that . . .' She glanced toward the door, where Rune stood, half in shadow.

Now is the time, she thought. If she was ever going to do it, she had to expose her men now or risk losing credibility, destabilizing the throne. If she knew there were traitors in her midst and allowed them to continue . . .

The advisors watched her keenly, no doubt hoping that this hesitation was a sign of weakness, a slip-up. 'I have received evidence . . .' Elma said, the rest of the sentence catching in her throat.

Rune perked up as she spoke, understanding that she was about to have her advisors arrested for treason. Elma ran her fingers over the parchment in her skirts, Cora's evidence. The places her maid had seen Bertram and Ferdinand, the conversations she'd overheard, the documentation of money being sent to Slödava – an assassin's payment.

All she had to do was say it. She had them in her trap.

Her assassin watched her with bright eyes.

But then the trap would close, and Rune would depart. She would never see that wicked smile again, cross swords with him, or laugh. It would be exactly what she had wanted. But she didn't want it anymore.

'Evidence to indicate,' Elma continued, at last firm in her conviction, 'that Slödava is open to a treaty of peace with Rothen.'

Rune's eyes narrowed, the only hint of his surprise. She had not discussed this with him, though she knew he would play along. After all, she needed him if this plan was going to work, and he would see that. All she had to do was convince her men.

Grumbling broke out among the advisors.

'Peace? With Slödava?' said Godwin, incredulous. 'Impossible. Even if they deign to sign a treaty, they'll turn around and slit your throat by cover of night. Whatever evidence you may have received is clearly a lie, some weak attempt at misdirection. At first, I stood with you in this, but to avoid action now? War is *inevitable*. We must begin to gather forces. Three times, Majesty. Three times, they have tried to kill you. And now that you sit on the throne, it is within your rights to declare a legal war with Slödava, to seek aid from other kingdoms. None can question such a war. King Alaric may even send his sorcerer if . . .'

'His sorcerer?' Ferdinand interrupted. 'That unkempt, brooding creature?'

'We are the frozen fist of Rothen,' Bertram cut in. 'We need no magic.'

Elma stood abruptly, her chair skidding across the floor. She could not lose them now. This was her moment. Bracing her fingertips on the table, she leaned forward, catching each of them in the fierceness of her glare.

'There will *be* no war with Slödava,' Elma said. Icicles could have formed on her words. 'I am the Queen of Rothen. I will not send my subjects to their deaths. We do not have the resources for a full-scale war. We do not have the strength of arms. And even if we did, I will *not* begin my reign with the blood of thousands on my hands. If you continue to push for war, I'm in the mood to have your tongues removed.'

A smile unfurled across Rune's face.

'But Your Majesty,' said Godwin, the clench of his fists belying a barely-contained anger, 'we can't just sit here and do nothing in the wake of three assassination attempts. Rothen will be seen as weak.'

Elma spun on her uncle. 'I'm beginning to suspect you haven't heard a single word I've said, Uncle. Perhaps one ought to consider listening to one's queen before speaking, lest one sound *witless*. Was I not clear enough? Slödava is open to peace with Rothen, should we pursue it. My bodyguard has attested to the truth of this matter.'

'You would trust a Slödavan?' Godwin said. 'One of the very monsters who scale our walls, who raid our villages and scatter the guts of our people in the snow? It's a ruse, a trap –'

'Whatever it is, Uncle, it is up to me to decide whether the risk is worth taking. I am the Queen of Rothen, am I not?'

The advisors shared a look.

At last, Maurice, who had been utterly silent until then, folded his hands before him on the table. 'Your Majesty,' he said, 'how do you propose we negotiate with Slödava? Their men attack on sight. Pigeons cannot fly that way. No ambassador would ever agree to such a journey, as it is certain death.'

'You're right,' Elma said, silently grateful for Maurice's rationality. 'No ambassador would survive the journey. But a queen would.'

Again, the advisors began talking all at once, their gestures wild and their brows drawn low.

'Elma,' Godwin muttered, taking her hand. 'You cannot –'

She wrenched her hand from his grip. 'Silence,' she hissed. And as she spoke the word, steel rang as Rune drew his sword.

The advisors ceased in their protests, glowering.

'You will address me as *Your Majesty*,' she said to Godwin, cold as a glacier. Then, turning to Lord Ferdinand, whose face had gone white, she said, 'You will write to the courts of Navenie and Mekya to inform them of Rothen's bid for peace with Slödava. Notify them also that Rothen's new monarch, Elma I, will be brokering the terms. In person. Rune of Slödava will serve as her bodyguard and liaison. Make it clear in the letters that if any harm should befall the Queen of Rothen while she is away, Rothen will invade Slödava.' She eyed the men at the table. 'If such a thing occurs, the monarchs of Navenie and Mekya are aware that they must assist us, or we will bar them from trade. I will be safe.'

Lord Ferdinand nodded, scratching notes onto a parchment with pursed lips and a deep frown.

'Slödavans do not care for *treaties* and *trade* negotiations,' Bertram spat. 'They are animals. Brainless and violent. There is no language they understand but the drums of war.'

Rune shifted in the shadows. Elma caught his eye and held it – *don't say a word, or you belittle me in front of them*. The assassin glowered but kept his mouth obediently shut.

'The men of Slödava are no more brutal, no more violent,' Elma said, 'than the men of Rothen. Our own people are starving, Bertram. Who knows what the people of Slödava have had to endure for generations? Would you ask me to condemn both kingdoms to a slow and miserable end? That is what war will bring. But with peace, the heavens willing, we might bring an end to the cycle of death.'

She straightened, knowing how tall she looked from that angle, how imposing she appeared at the head of the table. Her advisors watched with wary gazes, and she was satisfied.

'I will hear no more arguments on the matter,' Elma continued. 'I will travel to Slödava as Rothen's queen and her ambassador for peace. In the event that I die on the

Frozen Sea,' she gave each of her advisors a long look, a dare to defy her, 'then it is your war to lose. I want a traveling party outfitted and prepped immediately. I will depart tomorrow.'

Elma swept from the room, color high in her cheeks. Her stomach was in knots, her heart thudding hard in her chest. As she made her way back to her chambers, her bodyguard and several guards trailing in her wake, the realization seeped in. She had made a decision that could end in her death, in the birth of a war that would bring widespread slaughter and would stain the Frozen Sea red with needless blood. A decision her father, Rafe Volta, would never have made.

Because if she was truly her father's daughter, she would be licking Rune's blood from her fingers. And with his head on a pike, she would lead the attack on Slödava. But that was another Elma, in another lifetime.

In this life, Elma now wanted something she had never wanted before – to be a good queen.

24

'You must be aware that they'll try to have you killed on your journey to Slödava,' Rune said. He closed the door to Elma's chamber neatly behind him, leaning back against it with arms crossed over his chest. His expression was unreadable in the firelight. 'You practically handed them your own assassination on a platter.'

She turned. 'That's why you're coming with me.'

'I only wish you'd told me sooner,' he said. 'About your plan.'

'It doesn't matter what you wish,' Elma said, her energy beginning to fade in the wake of her declaration of power. Would the crown ever feel right on her head? 'You're the thorn in my side, remember? Not going anywhere. And I promised you peace with Rothen. You'll get it.'

'That's all?'

A thousand replies came to her. Of course, that wasn't all. She couldn't kill him, nor could she let him go. She was stringing him along, making use of him when he ought to have been removed from the equation. Because she couldn't bear to be without him.

'Yes,' she said.

Rune pushed away from the door and moved toward her, catlike. 'I don't think that's it,' he said, circling her as he spoke. 'I know you. You thirst for blood, just like every other Volta. My blood, in particular. So why aren't you taking the first opportunity to have me arrested and executed? First me, then your advisors. It would be so easy. You have us in the palm of your hand.'

'I . . .' said Elma.

'You haven't lost your nerve,' he said, his voice thoughtful, as if speaking aloud his innermost thoughts. 'I saw you in there, with your men. You were . . . *inexorable*.' At that, he came to a stop in front of Elma, studying her face with a keen gaze.

She shivered at his closeness, her body reacting without her permission, as always, when faced with Rune. 'I only did what needed to be done.'

'What needed to be done,' he repeated, his voice quiet. The fire popped as a log settled. 'According to who? Your father would have called for war. He would have ripped out my heart with his bare hands if he could get through the ribs. And he would have enjoyed doing it, just as you might have not long ago.' He paused, running a hand through thick white hair. 'I knew your father. There was always a choice. And he often made the wrong one.'

Elma froze. 'You knew *of* him, surely.'

'No,' said Rune. 'I met King Rafe.'

As far as Elma knew, her father had never once left Rothen, let alone joined any of the attacks on Slödava. 'When? How?'

'I was just a child,' said Rune. His gaze was far away, remembering. 'Your father was a weathered old bastard, even then. Cruel and cunning. He rode with a small group of men, across the Frozen Sea, all the way to our city in the north. To treat for peace.'

Elma's brows drew together in incredulity. 'But my father . . .'

'Hated Slödava? Dreamt of invading us and taking Rime Ice for his own? Yes, I know.' Rune smiled ruefully. 'But his terms seemed reasonable. And you might recognize his reasons for wanting peace at long last. Not enough resources, too many deaths. And Queen Hildegard of Slödava, perhaps naively, took him at his word. King Rafe and his men were welcomed into the stronghold as guests, offered food. That was when his men attacked. Dozens were slaughtered in his failed attempt to murder our queen. Guards, courtiers, innocents.'

Elma had never heard this story. She had known her father, known him to be cruel and merciless. But he had always been honorable, in his way. Lived by a code.

But you were in Mekya for fourteen years, she thought. *And he, alive for decades before that.*

'That can't be,' she breathed, still unable to accept the truth. What queen would be so ignorant of her own lineage?

'It can,' said Rune, his jaw tense. 'Your father managed to escape with his life, but only just. And among the men he killed, slaughtered in his escape . . . was my father.'

Elma's knees threatened to give way. She reached for a nearby chair, steadying herself, unable to meet Rune's gaze. She had seen her father commit unthinkable violence, but always in the name of justice. Always within the bounds of the laws of war. If what Rune said was true, her own father had entered the home of another monarch in the name of peace, only to turn around and cut them down. It was an unforgivable act.

'You're lying,' she said at last. Why should she believe him? *Because you see truth in his eyes.* Her blood seemed to be made of ice.

'Tell me,' Rune said, 'what is your father's prized possession? Let me guess — a silver ring set with a blue-black stone.'

Elma froze. Her father had always worn the ring; it could have been a lucky guess. But to know that it was his prized possession . . .

'That was my father's ring,' said Rune, casually. 'King Rafe cut it from his finger. I watched him do it through all the blood. When the fighting broke out, I got in his way. He gave me this scar.' He tapped the jagged white line that marred his face.

Elma's world seemed to fall around her, blurring and morphing into something familiar, yet altogether foreign. What did she truly know of her own kingdom, her own family, this crown she'd been born to wear? *They were right*, she thought with wild misery, *I'm not ready to be queen.* Nausea roiled in her gut.

Rune's mouth, so close to hers, was set in a grim line. Was this it, then? He had been waiting to reveal this horror to her, to weaken her with the truth of her father's crimes, before he cut her down?

'Don't look at me like that,' Rune said, softening. 'I'm not going to hurt you. Not unless you ask me to.' But his lustful smirk was half-hearted. He reached out to her, his warm hand cupping her head, thumb against her jaw. 'I thought you already knew. But something in your eyes today . . .' he shook his head, closing his eyes for a moment. 'I was wrong about you,' he murmured. 'I've known it for a long time. I will protect you, Queen Elma, with my life, if it means true peace between our kingdoms. You are not your father's daughter.'

Grief, anger, and relief warred in Elma. She was ashamed, too, for not having known about her father's true cruelty. For not fighting it in herself. For allowing that bloodlust to live in her, to take hold, even in the smallest moments. And above all, she now understood why Rune had come to kill her. Not just for revenge, but because she was a Volta. He had feared the thing she might become.

'I *am* my father's daughter,' she said at last, her voice small and wet with unshed tears. 'It's my duty to be better than he was. A better ruler. A better person. I'm trying –'

'You *are*,' Rune said.

Then he kissed her, pulling her into a tight embrace, and his mouth felt like longing, his hands like forgiveness. 'I have wanted you,' he murmured, lifting her up and carrying her into the bedroom, 'since the moment I first heard your voice. I have dreamt every night of tasting you, of hearing my name on your lips.'

The words were like fire in Elma's belly, where a deep ache was already forming.

'Even in the dungeon?' she asked, unable to stop herself.

Rune tossed her onto the bed and crawled over her, lowering himself slowly to cover her body with his. 'Even in the dungeon,' he murmured, biting the soft lobe of her ear. 'Even in the Death Games. I saw you in the stands, and your eyes were so cold. I wanted you even then.'

Elma groaned, pulling him against her. He was already hard, and she was hot and wet with want.

'Now, now,' he crooned, nuzzling her neck, allowing the fingers of one hand to trail down her dress and circle her breast. 'Not tonight.' He brushed her nipple with a soft thumb, eliciting a soft whimper from Elma. 'If I touch you . . . I won't be able to stop. And we need rest before our journey. I need to be at my best to protect you.'

'Please,' she gasped, already delirious with Rune's smell, the heat of his body, his deep voice rumbling through her. She arched her back and lifted her hips to press herself harder against his erection. She needed this distraction.

'You're relentless, Your Majesty,' Rune said, but even as he spoke, he slid his hand underneath her, lifting her hips as he ground down into her. 'But imagine,' he said, his breath tickling her ear, 'if you came . . . just like this. Layers of clothes between us. Simply because you couldn't help yourself.'

The rising need inside Elma was insatiable. It was too much. She craved release, the euphoric comfort of it. She craved *Rune*. She wanted him inside her, tasting her, his hands and his mouth all over her. But if she couldn't have that, if he wouldn't let her . . .

He rocked against her, kissing her neck where he'd bit her before. It was sore, but the pain only fed the rising tide of Elma's pleasure. The pressure between her legs was building to a crescendo. Rune lifted her hips with one hand, holding her to him, rolling her slowly against the erection that strained under his breeches. His seeking mouth found her earlobe, and he bit down softly on her tender skin.

All too easily, Elma fell over the edge.

Rune held her against him as she rode the wave of white-hot pleasure, her sobbing breaths muffled in his neck. And then he kissed her, raised himself up on his elbows, and said, 'Are you always like this, or is it just me?'

Elma closed her eyes, still breathing hard, the spasms of release still fading. 'Don't flatter yourself,' she said, because more tender words wouldn't come. Then a sudden fear took hold of her, that he would leave her. That she would fall asleep alone, and wake in the morning to find him gone. A figment, a dream.

'Stay,' she said before she lost her nerve.

'Your men will be just outside,' said Rune, misreading the look in her eyes.

'No,' she said, 'I . . .' *I don't want to be alone.*

'Oh,' said Rune. 'You want me to *stay*?'

'How many times must I say it?' Elma asked. 'Don't make me hate you more than I already do.'

He grinned, gently moving a lock of hair out of her face and tucking it behind her ear. 'Of course, I'll stay.'

Elma fell asleep that night with Rune's arm draped over her, his breaths steady against her back. And while she could think of a thousand reasons why this was a bad idea, why this would only end in misery and pain, her only feeling in that too-brief moment was a soft and gentle peace.

25

Two dozen men were to accompany Elma and Rune to Slödava: Luca, Hugh, and a regiment of guards hand-picked by Elma. They were Luca's best men, guards who had been at her side and protected her for years. Godwin had been adamant that Elma ought to bring some of his personal men, men who excelled at navigation and survival, but Elma was stubborn – the guards would be her own. And if they turned on her, she would have no one to blame but herself.

Elma did her best not to think about the dangers of attack, from enemies, the natural cataclysms that might occur over the course of their three-day journey north, or even from within her own ranks. The path would lead them across the Frozen Sea, avoiding the well-traveled paths in the hopes of avoiding rumored camps of highwaymen.

The maps had all made the journey look like a death trap to Elma. First, the narrow road down from the Frost Citadel, and then a storm-stricken pass through the mountains, before the journey took them across the most hazardous of all, the Frozen Sea – the plane of glasslike ice, never melting, miles and miles of open land without any landmarks, and no protection from attack. This was the place where travelers got lost and froze to death on the ice. Where creatures, spirits, and demons came out of the fog; Slödavans wielding Rime Ice.

Elma imagined an army of men like Edvin, eyes gleaming blue, blades of ice bursting out from their fists like magic. Would it feel cold against her skin, biting like frost? Would it freeze the blood on contact? Or did it behave like any other weapon?

And then, if they survived the Frozen Sea, a great city would rise up from the ice – at least, it appeared imposing on the maps. Like a cluster of blade-like icicles bursting upward, out of the snow: Slödava. A mystery that remained unseen to most.

A tickle of something like curiosity fluttered in Elma's stomach. What would it look like, that fabled city? She had always imagined it as sinister, overrun with brutal men, a monument to hatred and war. But now, knowing Rune . . .

'Majesty, it is time.' Godwin's voice pulled her from her thoughts, his solid presence anchoring her to the present moment. He had personally overseen that the traveling party be outfitted with provisions, ensuring everything was up to his standards. Unrest pooled in the depths of his eyes. 'A storm is coming from the southeast. If you leave now, you will avoid the worst of it on the mountain pass.'

Elma gripped Godwin's arm with steady fingers. His face was worn and dangerous, as it had always been, but there was a kindness there. 'I will make Rothen proud,' she said, and she was just a girl then, assuring her uncle.

'You have always made me proud,' Godwin said, and his voice caught on the last word as if some strong emotion threatened to break his stolid demeanor.

A knot formed in Elma's throat. There was nothing more to say. She moved to the carriage, allowing her men to help her inside. There were pillows and hot stones waiting to keep her comfortable, and skins of spiced wine. Rolled-up maps in leather casings were arranged in one corner, as she had requested. Otherwise, the carriage was empty. Cora would not be joining her – the journey was too dangerous, and Elma had asked enough of her attendant already.

As soon as she had settled herself in the carriage, with a creak of wood and leather and the jangling of horses' harnesses, they began the journey. Horns rang out from the citadel, and flags hung from the battlements. Even her own carriage was decked out in the Volta colors, flags streaming from every surface. If Slödavans attacked on the road, this was meant to deter them – attack this carriage, and you attack the kingdom of Rothen. But Elma felt distinctly like a hare caught in the sights of a hawk.

The long, treacherous ride down from the Frost Citadel went without incident. Elma went through an entire skin of wine in the descent, but she deemed it a necessary loss. She had been glad Rune rode horseback with the other guards so he couldn't see her terror as the carriage rocked and swayed along the sheer cliff.

But now, as they made their way along the frozen road that would lead them through the Hell Gate between the mountains, Elma wished he was with her.

If the traveling party kept up their pace, they would reach the pass just before sundown. They would cross it at first light the next morning, and if all went well, just a few hours after that, they would descend to the Frozen Sea.

Elma couldn't help but think of all the things that might befall them on the way. Wolves swarming out from the scrubby alpine forests, highwaymen who built homes out of ice and waited for travelers to murder and rob, the unthinkable things that came only at the edges of reality.

I can't do this, Elma thought, her fingers twisting in the tassel of a pillow. She had to see the sky, the road before them. Sitting in that dim carriage, warm and queenly as it was, felt like tumbling blindly into a world of horrors.

Lifting the window latch, Elma leaned her head out and said, 'Stop the carriage a moment.'

'Stop the carriage!' came the cries from her men. 'The Queen orders a halt!'

Rune and Luca appeared then, concern written on their faces. Luca dismounted and bowed, approaching the carriage window. 'What is it, Your Majesty?'

'I wish to ride outside. On horseback.'

Luca blinked. 'But it's much safer –'

'It wasn't a request,' Elma said.

Behind the guard, still mounted, Rune smirked.

Luca's expression tightened into unease. 'I would much prefer it, Majesty, if you were well ensconced. The dangers . . .'

'I would prefer to see the dangers coming, Luca, rather than wait for them inside a wooden box. You know I can defend myself.'

Her guard's expression closed, an empty mask. 'You are the Queen of Rothen.'

Elma couldn't stop herself from rolling her eyes. 'Move aside, Luca. I'm coming out.' She pushed open the carriage door and jumped down daintily, landing on hard-packed snow. She had dressed appropriately for travel – leather boots and leggings, a woolen tunic, thickly padded surcoat, and her warmest fur cloak. Riding would not be a problem.

'Your queen wishes to ride,' Luca said, his voice carrying to the rest of the traveling party. 'Bring one of the spare horses.'

The spare horses were already saddled; there could be no delays in their journey. And so, Elma swung into the saddle, settling herself with a deep, grateful inhale.

Luca frowned deeply. Rune grinned at her.

'Thank you, Luca,' said Elma, gripping the reins in one gloved hand, raising the other above her head. 'Onward.'

With the word from their queen, the procession started up again. But this time, rather than trapped and vaguely afraid, Elma's lungs filled with vital air, her cheeks pinkened in the cold. This was unlike anything she had ever felt in Rothen, unlike the cold of the arena, the courtyards in the citadel. She felt alive and awake, cradled in the arms of her frozen kingdom.

Shades of white, gray, and blue spread out before them like a painting. The breath caught in Elma's throat as they rode, her eyes stinging. Mountains loomed ahead, grand and eternal. Elma had seen those mountains from the citadel and thought them foreboding; now, she found them beautiful. Snow blanketed their valleys, and great peaks of gray-black rock rose up from the white.

Even the growing storm, which roiled upward and began to daub part of the sky in rich blacks and wild grays, filled Elma with a sense of wonder. This was not a forgiving landscape, nor would it ever be. Nothing about it was soothing or calm. Yet Elma felt, for the first time, not joy . . . but something right and easy in her chest.

She had never seen it like this before, her kingdom.

'Haven't you traveled beyond the borders of your

city?' Rune asked, as if Elma's feelings were written across her face.

'Not since the day you tried to kill me,' she said, shooting the assassin a wry look.

Rune nodded, his expression thoughtful. 'It's a lovely country if you look at it with the right eyes. You're fortunate.'

'To rule a frozen wasteland?' Elma said, only half joking.

'To have experienced it at all,' Rune said, turning. 'How many Navenians do you suppose come up to Rothen for a holiday? How many Mekyans?'

Elma stifled a laugh. 'They wouldn't make it an hour. You should have seen me when I first came to Frost. I'd been floating around in Mekya with short hair, gauzy gowns, and bare feet. I nearly died of shock.'

Rune's face brightened in surprise. 'Gauzy gowns, you say? I'd love a more detailed description when your guards aren't looming in every direction.'

Elma snorted, glancing at Luca, who rode two horse lengths in front of her. 'I was fourteen.'

'But you aren't fourteen now,' he said, eyeing her appreciatively. 'Though you still have the short hair.'

She reached up self-consciously, pulling at the black curls where they brushed against her jaw. 'My neck is always cold. But . . .'

'It's a reminder. Of the girl you used to be.' Rune tilted his head, studying her. 'It suits you. Makes you look powerful.'

Elma bit her lip to keep from smiling. 'I'm beginning to suspect you killed Rune and replaced him with a doppelganger,' she said. 'I almost prefer you when you're cruel.'

'Oh,' Rune said, leaning sideways so only she could hear

his low voice, 'I can still be cruel. Next time I have you alone . . .'

'We approach the Hell Gate,' Luca's voice rang out. He twisted in the saddle, catching Elma's gaze with his own disapproving one. 'We make camp in an hour.'

By the time the pale sun was setting over the vast frozen plain to the west, camp had been made. It consisted of many squat tents, low enough to avoid being blown away, and a shallow hole that served as a firepit. Wood had been brought from the citadel for fires. The men worked so efficiently that a fire was already crackling and cured meats were being passed around within minutes of stopping to camp.

Elma's tent was larger than the rest and marked by a pair of wildly fluttering pendants in red and black. She wondered whether this was the best choice in the event of an attack – someone might creep in under cover of night, slit her throat, and sneak away, all without being caught. But Luca insisted that she have the best tent, that guards would be on rotation throughout the night.

And so, wrapped in furs, her feet tucked against a hot stone from the fire, Elma ate her dinner with the traveling party. As the sun's light diminished, orange firelight danced on faces old and young, all of them familiar to her. She prayed silently that no harm would come to them on this journey.

When she was finished eating, Elma noted that the men were solemn, their voices hushed as they spoke with one another. Even the skins of wine were being passed around quietly and only a few sips were taken by each guard. They wouldn't be able to relax while their queen sat among them. So, Elma took her leave, pressing a hand to Luca's arm as she did. Rune got up with her, trailing her to the tent.

'Your Majesty,' said Luca, coming up behind them.

Elma turned, blinking against the firelight that still danced in her vision. 'I'm going to bed,' she said. 'You and your men deserve time to . . . be merry.'

'I'll post guards around the tent,' Luca said, glancing at Rune even as he spoke.

'No need,' said Rune, his white hair and blue eyes shining ethereal in the firelight. 'I'm as good as ten of yours.'

'Majesty,' Luca said, ignoring the assassin and plying Elma with an adamant gaze. 'We are no longer within the walls of the citadel. Let me do my job.'

'Of course,' Elma said. 'You may ignore my bodyguard. He is full of himself.'

Rune's sharp glare in response made her skin tingle.

Luca inclined his head, returning to the fire. Within moments, half a dozen guards were arranged at strategic points around Elma's tent, and she was finally allowed to go in. She had to duck to enter it, but it was surprisingly warm and piled high with blankets, furs, and pillows. A pile of hot stones waited for her in one corner. Her men had been efficient, and she was grateful.

Rune had stayed at the tent entrance, where he claimed he would remain all night, barring a few hours' sleep. Elma didn't like the idea of her men freezing in the snow all night while she curled up in fur-lined blankets. But there was a fire, and hot stones for their boots, and spiced wine. It would have to do.

Elma undressed quickly, shedding only her cloak, surcoat, and boots. Tucking her ever-present knife underneath a pillow, she crawled beneath the blankets and tried to sleep.

She dreamed of blood and frozen crowns and a far-off city made of ice. And too soon she was pulled into wakefulness by the bustle of camp being packed up, of horses snuffling in the cold air.

It was time to cross the Hell Gate.

26

They broke camp just before daybreak. Elma was once again struck by the guards' efficiency. She had never seen anything like it before – the gathering and stowing of gear, the sure and strong movements of her men. Did she look anywhere near as confident in her own actions, she wondered? Or was she stilted and unsure, a queen in name alone? Such thoughts hung heavy in her mind as the sun's weak light crested the mountains, and she and her men began their ascent.

Despite the need for caution, the pass proved to be strangely quiet. The storm's approach thickened the air and darkened the sky, but no snow fell, and the howling winds were so distant that Elma found the sound almost calming. She was glad to be outside the carriage, which jostled and made horrible noises as it went. Out in chill air, with the cloud-heavy sky wide above them, her heart lightened; fear couldn't seem to find her.

She and her men spoke little through the pass. The way was treacherous, and Elma had no desire to clutter the air with pointless chatter when she was finding herself, shockingly, so taken with the landscape, the cold, and the wind. Without a cage of stone around her, Rothen was starkly breathtaking.

It took four hours to cross the pass. The road opened up to vast swathes of snowy hills and patches of scrubby trees, and beyond that, a seemingly endless bright expanse of blue-white.

'The Frozen Sea,' Elma breathed, relief filling her at the sight of it. A shiver teased her spine, and she knew it wasn't from the cold. They had made it this far, but the most dangerous part of the trip was yet to come.

'Isn't it lovely?' Rune asked, ever her shadow. He rode beside her, his hair catching in the wind and lifting about his ears, the fur of his cloak fluttering. Color marked his cheeks, and he looked so free and at ease in that moment.

'It's arresting,' Elma replied. 'Though I'm not sure I'd like to die there.'

'You're in no danger of dying,' he said, half-smiling. 'Not with me at your side. Not in such beautiful surroundings.'

Elma sniffed, her nose running from the cold. 'You have a very romantic view of things.'

'On the contrary,' he replied. 'But I happen to be in company that brings it out of me.'

Pulling up her hood to hide her blush, Elma urged her horse forward. She understood what this feeling meant, the soft warmth in her chest that spread out to her fingertips and hummed. She couldn't afford to feel it. Rune could not be anything more than a dalliance. A distraction, a pleasurable ride. He was Slödavan. Despite the fragile thing between them, until a peace treaty was signed, he was her enemy.

Under no circumstances could she let herself fall for him.

They crossed the Frozen Sea with precision. If they traveled too slowly, they would only be extending the time spent in considerable danger. But if they hurried, the sounds of their horses, the wheels of the carriage, would reverberate far along the ice.

The sea was loud enough as it was. Strange sounds rippled along the ice as they rode, almost as if the frozen water were singing. Every once in a while, there would be an echoing crack, the sound of the ice expanding in changing temperatures, Luca explained. Elma knew she should have been afraid out there on the Frozen Sea, so cold and lonely their procession was on that flat expanse. Instead, she found she liked it. It was so unlike the closeness of the citadel. The sky seemed to stretch on forever above the endless ice, and Elma felt as if she were expanding to fit.

As day faded into evening, Luca called for a stop to set up camp. To sleep on the ice was dangerous, but traveling through the night would only make everyone tired, paranoid, and clumsy. Elma was selfishly glad. Her thighs ached from riding, and her stomach twisted with hunger.

A fire was built on the ice, which was far too thick and too cold to melt through. And when they were finished with dinner, Elma stood to leave her men to themselves once more. As she passed Luca, she touched his shoulder – an indication that he should follow. Dismissing Rune with a word, Elma led Luca away from his men, just out of earshot.

'What is it, Majesty?' Luca said, a line forming between his brows.

'I'd like a report,' she said, voice low. 'On the journey so far.'

'There isn't much to report,' Luca said, clearly choosing his words carefully. 'Nothing Your Majesty needs to worry about.'

Elma raised a brow.

Luca exhaled through his nose, a puff of steam gusting out in the frigid air. 'The men are loyal to you and would never question their queen. But it is . . . unusual, this mission.'

'As it should be,' Elma said, chin high. 'When was the last time Rothen sought peace in earnest?'

'As you say, Majesty.'

'Anything else?' Elma asked, trying to hide the small crumple of disappointment in her chest. Luca's gaze was more distant than it had ever been, his stance more formal. But she was queen now, after all. And if they had ever been something close to friends, whatever connection they shared was all but gone in the face of duty.

'That's all,' said Luca.

He turned to go, but Elma held out a hand, stopping him short. 'Luca,' she said, the words hanging stubbornly on her tongue. *Say it*, she thought.

'Majesty?' He waited, curious.

'Thank you,' she said at last. 'You've been –'

But she never got a chance to finish the sentence. An arrowhead was suddenly protruding from Luca's neck, black-red in the firelight. He gurgled, his eyes wide with mild surprise. And then he crumpled to the ice. Unending darkness seemed to stretch out around Elma from where she stood.

'Luca,' she said, unmoving. 'Luca.'

Shouts rang out, and the twang of arrows loosed in the night.

'Elma!'

Rune's hand was on her arm, pulling her down to the

ground so roughly that she lost her breath. Guards trampled past, some issuing orders, others falling, arrows coming out of their bodies like pins from a cushion.

'Stop,' said Rune, when she tried to struggle free, to get up and help her men. 'You can't die. You, above all, cannot die.'

But she thrashed, wild and single-minded all at once, desperate to save them. Surely, she could save them. She was their queen.

'*Stop*,' Rune growled, practically dragging her as he crawled through the tents, away from the firelight. Chaos surrounded them as they went, as Elma's men were shot down again and again. Bodies slammed into the ice, eyes staring sightless into the night.

And then bodies she didn't recognize, men with strange armor and weapons, appeared in the camp. Their attackers. Elma looked for white hair or blue eyes, but saw none. These were simple highwaymen.

Highwaymen. That was all.

'Luca,' Elma said quietly. She no longer tried to struggle free from Rune's grip. Like a woman caught in a dream, she crawled obediently across the ice with Rune, not caring that it scraped her knees, that its cold was so harsh it threatened to burn her hands, even through her gloves.

They came to a breathless stop behind a tent. Elma roughly wiped her eyes, ashamed of the burn she felt at their corners. She was Queen of Rothen. She had known the risks. Peace was more important than . . . *than Luca?* came the unwanted thought. *More important than the life of a friend?*

'There was nothing you could have done,' Rune said, seeing her shaking hands, her terrified gaze. He took her face in his hands. 'There is nothing you can do now but survive. Do you understand, Queen Elma?'

She nodded. A world of anguish sat heavy on her chest, suffocating her.

'Then I'll get you out of this alive.'

A highwayman burst out from behind the tent. He was behind Rune, and fast – his masked face a pale blur in the darkness. Elma had no time to cry out, to warn her bodyguard. She watched as if in slow motion as the attacker's blade arced down, down toward Rune's neck.

I can't lose him too, Elma thought, but her body wasn't fast enough. She had only just begun to cry out, Rune's name rough and strangled in her throat, when the assassin moved.

The speed was something out of a dream, or nightmare. Rune fell back and spun, his back slamming to the ice as he dodged the highwayman's attack. And as Rune fell, his arm shot out and – one second, he was holding his sword, and then his sword was discarded, clattering to the ice. A crackling sound like shattering ice filled Elma's ears, and Rune's arm glowed white-blue, suddenly engulfed in a glittering, swirling mass of frost. In a breathless instant, the frost expanded and resolved, solidifying with horrifying quickness, into an ice-sharp blade that seemed to sing as it cut the air, frigid and deadly.

Rime Ice.

The highwayman, so terrifying and inevitable only a moment before, crashed to the ground in a heap, severed in half at a sickly angle, painting the black ice with sticky dark blood. He stood no chance against the magic blade. Because that was all it could be – *magic*.

244

Rime Ice was not some strange ice mined from the gla-ciers of Slödava, forged into weapons. It was magic.

There was no time to think, to consider what this meant. One after another, Rune cut down three more attackers with ruthless ease. He had leapt to his feet and was killing as if born to do it, his weapon a streak of icy glow in the night. He was preternatural in his movements, the ease with which he put men down. Elma had seen him fight in the Death Games, but this was visceral and close, his weapon a beacon of otherworldly power.

She watched in a trance-like state, watched her assas-sin's surety in combat, how efficiently he killed, how his attackers' blood stood out so starkly against his hair. The moment, horrific as it was, felt somehow intimate. Rune cut their lives short for her. He killed for *her*. The death cries of men caressed her ears, the smell of blood and gore assailing her nostrils.

It was as if time, for a while, stood still. Or perhaps it ceased to exist altogether. Elma could not tell how long she and Rune made their way through the camp, exterminat-ing highwaymen, Rime Ice crackling in her assassin's grip. She pointedly did not look at the bodies of her men, the blood-stained ice, the unseeing eyes in the night.

Instead, she fought. Rune did nothing to stop her from drawing her knife, from pressing her back to his and join-ing in the fray. Whenever a shadowed figure came at them from the darkness, they were a pair of blades, their move-ments in sync. And though Elma's blade was far inferior to his, somehow, she felt bolstered by him, stronger, faster, as if the frost were collecting at her arm too, as if a blade of ice extended from her hand as well.

When Elma's blow was knocked sideways by an enemy, when the man took her by the neck and would have snapped it, Rune easily dismembered him with two swipes of his blade.

Elma watched the man fall, then turned to Rune, who stood panting. His face was spattered with blood, his hair plastered to his sweaty brow, and in his gaze was the fierce flame of something that could have been love.

She had never understood life, Elma thought, until that moment. Blood and death swirled around them in a maelstrom. Terror warped her thoughts, made her lungs burn hot. But she was free, and the wind was on her face, and grief, sharp, painful grief embedded in the recesses of her soul. *Only a Volta*, she thought, heart slamming in her ribs, *finds life at the edge of death.*

She pulled Rune to her, fingers buried in his hair, and found his mouth with trembling, blood-flecked lips. She bit down and tasted iron, and the tang of it brought her back to earth. Back to herself. All was suddenly in sharp, vibrant focus.

And here was Rune, vivid, immovable. Strands of white hair clung to the muck of his face, curling against his ears. His lip bled where she'd bit it. He looked terrible.

Don't fall in love with him.

'That's the last of them,' Rune said, breathless. His Rime Ice blade was gone now, dissipated. Somehow, Rune looked more human then, his eyes dimmer, his hair less bright. But he was still very much alive, and it took everything in Elma not to let him consume her.

Shouts rose up from the remaining men about camp. Shouts of affirmation, of safety – *they're gone, we got them.*

But Elma looked around her and saw only death. The heavy reality of their situation fell like a mountain around her, and she staggered, Rune taking her arm to hold her steady. Was this fated to be her legacy, then? Not peace, but death?

'Take stock of the situation,' she said dully, her throat tight, as she tried to be a queen again. She shoved her bloody knife into its scabbard, and stood as tall as she could, though her hands shook, and her breaths were labored. 'I want a full report.'

Elma found Luca's body easily, retracing her steps. The fire still crackled merrily, free of the torment that lay cloak-like on her shoulders. Firelight illuminated Luca's face, handsome even in death.

'We have a report, Your Majesty.'

Elma looked up, and saw Hugh standing with Rune, at full attention. She searched Hugh's face for grief or terror but saw only the practiced calm of a man trained for war. How many deaths like this had he seen? How many of his men had fallen to the warriors of the north or highwaymen like these?

Elma was once again reminded of how truly sheltered she had been. How little she knew and understood of war, of her own kingdom, of the ways in which it interacted with the world.

'Hugh,' she said, his name an exhalation of relief. She gathered herself together, exuding as queenly an aura as she could manage. 'Report, please.'

'It was highwaymen, Your Majesty. Probably heard us from miles away and waited for the cover of night to attack.

We lost sixteen men. Two more are injured and must take the carriage.' He paused, glancing sidelong at Rune, who remained silent. 'There is a full day's journey ahead of us on the ice. Even if we travel at speed, we will not reach Slödava until after sundown. And with the carriage . . .' he trailed off, nostrils flaring, his jaw tight.

'Speak your thoughts, Hugh,' Elma said, her heart sinking even as she spoke. *Sixteen men.* With two injured, that meant only seven able men remained, including Rune.

'Her Majesty is asking for my opinion?'

'Yes.'

The guard shook his head. 'We can't continue like this. Not with only seven of us to protect you. There could be more highwaymen. Or Slödavans. Anything could . . .' he paused, his throat bobbing as he swallowed. A shadow crossed his face, the only hint that he was as affected by the slaughter as Elma was. 'I recommend returning to the Frost Citadel.'

By now, more of Elma's men had drifted over, their gazes sharp with grief and anger. She knew they must all be thinking the same. That this was folly, a suicidal mission across the ice. But if Elma turned back now, nothing would change. The aggression with Slödava would continue on and on, perhaps forever. Elma would begin to find comfort in the citadel, in the throne, and settle there until her body and the stone of the citadel became indistinguishable. She would watch the Death Games and call for blood. She would send her men on raids to Slödava, calling for death. More men, countless more bodies, would fall on the Frozen Sea.

Above all, if Elma turned back now . . . Rune had no

place in that life. No reason to stay, no reason to remain loyal to a queen who had given up on peace, on his people. Who had given up on him.

She caught Rune's eye, a safe haven among the rock-hard stares of her men. She knew he would follow her to Slödava, even if all others abandoned her. She read it in the tilt of his head, in the gleam of his eyes.

'I am not prepared to abandon the hope of peace for Rothen,' Elma said, her voice carrying across their small camp so that all could hear. 'I'm not prepared to let your children, and their children, inherit a legacy of war. If you wish to, you may depart, and return to Frost. I will not mark you as a deserter, nor will anyone blame your choice. Ahead lies likely death. But as your queen, I cannot give up hope. I will continue to Slödava.'

Her words hung on strained silence. The corner of Rune's mouth curved upward.

Hugh hung his head and sighed, a long and weary breath. The men shifted, sharing dark glances. They weren't happy about it, but Elma knew they wouldn't desert her. Their pride was too strong. At last, Hugh lifted his eyes to meet Elma's gaze. A small inclination of the chin was all he gave, his shoulders tight and his lips twisted in disapproval. But for Elma's purposes, it would do.

They would continue to Slödava.

27

Flames licked the gray sky of morning. A column of black smoke rose up from the bodies, expanding and spreading as it rose until it merged with the low cloud cover. A light snow fell, flakes landing cold on Elma's face.

All was quiet as the remaining travelers spoke prayers to the winter star, to the Frozen Sea itself. *Keep their spirits safe. Guide them well to the after.*

There was nothing to comfort Elma, no soft words or sweet drink. She did not want comfort in that moment. She welcomed the agony, the visceral stench of the bodies of her own men, burning on a makeshift pyre, two days from home. In one hand, she clutched the hilt of a sword. Luca's sword. She had taken the sword belt too, for safekeeping. When they returned safely to Frost – *they would return safely*, she assured herself – she would give it to his family.

How had her father lived like this, knowing so many men had died for him? Had he built a wall of stone around his own heart? Or had it always been there, and the killing had come easy from the start.

Rune's presence at her shoulder should have been a comfort, but it felt like a curse. She could not turn to him for words of warmth, and the memory of his Rime Ice hung bright in her memory. She hadn't asked him about it, and he had said nothing. The time wasn't right. Yet the knowledge of it burned in her, the revelation that this weapon her father had fought and killed for, a weapon that count-less men had died for . . . was magic.

But she could not think of it then, couldn't carry the weight of it along with everything else. Not yet.

Hugh broke away from the few remaining guards where they stood watching the funeral pyre. Heavy circles hung under his eyes, and his jaw was tense, his shoulders restless. 'Your Majesty,' he said, his gaze catching on Luca's sword at her hip. 'We must go now.'

She nodded wordlessly. There was never enough time for grieving.

The small company rode out just after daybreak. As the column of black smoke faded behind them, a terrible, itch-ing thing began to burrow its way into Elma's thoughts, more persistent and disturbing than the Rime Ice.

'Rune,' she said, when the thought couldn't be ignored anymore.

'Yes, Majesty?' He had ridden in silence beside her all morning, his usual sarcastic demeanor gone in place of a shadowy thoughtfulness.

'I've been thinking about the attack.'

He raised an eyebrow. 'And?'

She lowered her voice, hoping that only he could hear. 'We're not on the main road. We're not anywhere near it. Yet the highwaymen knew exactly where to find us.'

'I thought the same,' Rune said, and seemed to relax somewhat. Elma knew he had expected her to ask about the Rime Ice. 'But the ice song can travel miles.'

'All the way to the main road?' Elma asked, unconvinced. 'And even if it did, it would have taken the highwaymen a day to reach us. Maybe more. The ice is *vast*. I know that much.'

Rune's lips turned down in thought. 'You're saying they knew we were coming.'

'I'm saying that no other explanation makes quite as much sense. Could they have been hired by Slödava?' she asked.

He shook his head. 'The Queen of Slödava wouldn't have seen us coming until we reached the Frozen Sea. Not enough time to organize something like that attack. And anyway, it's not her style.'

Elma sighed. Frustration and suspicion knotted in her stomach. 'I don't believe it was a coincidence,' she said at last. 'It was a targeted attack. I'm almost certain of it.'

Rune leaned toward her, his voice low. 'You suspect Bertram and Ferdinand?'

'Who else?' she replied. 'They hate the idea of peace. War keeps their dicks hard. And you saw my guards – their loyalty to me isn't all-consuming. There was mutiny in their eyes. It wouldn't take much to turn them.'

A vicious wind rolled over the traveling company, and Rune's hair buffeted his face. Elma closed her eyes against the stinging cold.

'Surely,' she said, when the wind had died down, 'that was the only hand they meant to play.'

Her assassin pushed a mess of hair out of his eyes. 'Didn't I say you were handing yourself to them on a platter?'

Elma shot him a glare that stopped that line of discussion in its tracks.

Rune swallowed. 'It doesn't matter what I think. If your men set up two traps along the way, we're no better than dead.'

Elma's thoughts rolled away on the wind, a myriad of scenarios springing up unbidden. More highwaymen, Slödavan assassins, the advisors themselves, emerging from the mist to demand that Elma feed their lust for war.

But despite her fears, and the looming specter of what she'd seen the night before – the deaths, the Rime Ice, – they crossed the Frozen Sea with no further incident. At one point, just after midday, an enormous bird flew over their company. Its wings were snow-white, its talons blue-ish in the shadow of its body.

'One of the Slödavan Queen's snow hawks,' Rune said. 'She knows we're coming.'

'Will she attack us?' Elma asked, as if there was something she could do about it if such were the case.

But Rune only shook his head. 'The city is well fortified. There would be no point. If she doesn't open the gates, Queen Hildegard knows we'll either turn around and leave, or starve on the ice.'

'Comforting,' Elma murmured. She still had said nothing about the Rime Ice. But it nagged at her, an open question that was an itch in her brain. Why hadn't he told her? Why had he never used it until then? And was it truly magic? She had begun to wonder if it was all some trick of the light, her terrified brain, the chaos of the fray.

But something in Rune's eyes – a knowing glint – told her that what she'd seen was real.

Dusk crept up on them slowly. By the time night was falling, just at the edges of darkness, the city of Slödava loomed into view, solidifying out of a cold wet gray.

Elma had never seen anything so strange or impos-ing in her life. The city of ice, as it was sometimes called, appeared from a distance to be nothing but an enormous stronghold. It rose up vertically from a high wall at its perimeter, with spires and crenellations that defied Elma's understanding of architecture. As they rode closer, she saw that the city was built on a hill, its buildings tall and narrow, clustered closely together, and reaching upward toward the close sky like the spires of one massive citadel. Everything glimmered as if truly made from ice.

'Frost,' Rune said, apparently seeing Elma's awed stare. 'It's frost, clinging to the stone. From a distance, it looks like ice.'

Embarrassed by her obvious wonder, Elma bit her lip. 'It doesn't look real.'

He huffed appreciatively. 'I'm glad you think so. It's what they intended, centuries ago when they decided to build the ridiculous thing.'

Despite the city's beauty, Elma's wonder melted and gave way to anxiety as they approached its gates. She caught sight of the glint of weapons on its battlements, of armored guards. Deep blue flags waved from the gates, marked with the white symbol of Slödava – a white circle made up of complex symbols that looked like stars.

Hugh called a halt to their approach when they were within shouting distance of the gates. Riding back to Elma, he gave her a nod. 'Your Majesty, may I have a word with your bodyguard?'

She inclined her head.

'Rune,' Hugh said, turning to the assassin, who regarded him with one raised brow, 'this is your domain. How do we make ourselves known without . . .'

But his question trailed off as an echoing horn blast

rose up from the Slödavan walls. It was melodic and other-worldly, like the cry of a distant gale. Goosebumps tingled Elma's skin, a shiver running down her back. And then the gates of the city, fifty feet high and shining with the illusion of ice, swung slowly inward.

'I hate to be the one to break it to you, Hugh,' Rune said, 'but I *suspect* we're already known.' With a grin, he urged his horse forward.

No one protested as Rune rode to the front of their company, taking over from Hugh. Elma rode just behind him, the carriage clattering on in the group's wake. And it was like this, breathless and wide-eyed, that they entered the city of Slödava, shrouded in mist.

All Elma wanted to do was *look*. She wanted to take in the strangely intricate buildings, the white cobbled roads. What were the homes like? What sort of lives did they lead? But she would never be allowed to wander the city and learn its intricacies as an anonymous visitor – she was a queen on a diplomatic mission. And as they rode through the gates, there was only a moment of quiet before a regiment of Slödavans in shining armor intercepted them.

'Oh good,' said Rune, 'they've sent the full welcoming party.'

'Halt!' rang out a clear, melodic voice. 'State your business.'

Elma couldn't see who had spoken – there were dozens of guards arranged in a crowded half-circle in front of them, and beyond that, curious Slödavans poked faces out of windows and doorways.

'I am Queen Elma of Rothen,' she said, hating how small her voice sounded. 'I have come on a mission of peace.'

Scattered laughter and snorts of derision burst forth from the Slödavans.

'Peace?'

'With *Rothen*?'

Then one of the Slödavan guards held up a hand, a tall man at the front of their company, and the mutterings faded to silence. Elma noticed that the plume in his helmet was white, while the rest were a pale shade of blue.

'The manner of your arrival suggests a bid for war,' said the white-plumed man. His hand rested on the pommel of a sword, and his stance was tense, ready to spring. 'You speak of peace, yet you hold our Crown Prince hostage. If it weren't for our queen's mercy, you would be dead where you stand.'

Elma frowned. 'Your intelligence is false,' she said. 'We hold no hostages in Rothen.'

'Be still, Björn.' Rune's voice carried over the Slödavan force, interrupting whatever the white-plumed man had been about to say. 'You're making an ass of yourself.'

Elma wished she could reach over and clamp her hand over Rune's mouth. These may be his people, but this was a precarious situation, one that demanded tact. Precision.

But instead of lashing out, or worse, attacking them, the man whose name was Björn crumpled to the ground. And like a wave of shimmering armor, the men all around him did the same, and Elma realized they were *kneeling*. They pressed their fists to their chests, eyes downcast.

'Your Highness,' Björn said, his voice muffled by his position, 'forgive me. I did not recognize you.'

Elma glanced around and saw that her men appeared to be as shocked and confused as she felt. But when her gaze fell on Rune, he did not return it. Instead, he sat up straighter in the saddle and surveyed the kneeling men with sharp eyes.

'You may stand,' Rune said, waving a hand dismissively.

All at once, Elma saw him with new eyes. He was holding himself differently, his movements lazy and delicate. Haughty. He looked like a *prince*. But it couldn't be. There was only one Crown Prince of Slödava, and he . . . Rune could not be him.

But even as she thought this, Rune spoke with resonance, giving orders as if this were his regiment. His city. *His* Slödava. 'Björn,' he said, 'there are two injured men in the carriage. See to it that they're tended to. Bring in the rest for questioning. Oh, and tell my mother I'm home.'

A sense of unreality caught Elma in its grasp. It was as if she couldn't fully react to what was happening, lest her heart stop and her blood cease flowing. The only evidence of her pain was a slight shake in her fingers as she allowed the Slödavans to help her down from her horse, to bend her arms behind her, binding her hands. She watched in numb dread as they did the same to her men. And when Hugh shot a dark, meaningful look at her through the melee of Slödavan guards, she could not hold his gaze.

You are a queen, she thought. *Do something*.

But dozens of Slödavan guards surrounded them. They had ridden right into the heart of the enemy, broken and battered. There was nothing to be done. Nothing.

Her assassin's voice rose above the general din, making orders. He, too, had dismounted. But she did not want to see him. Even his voice was wrong, too formal, too like a prince. He wasn't her assassin anymore.

A slow creep of frost grew over Elma's heart as she was jostled and led roughly with her men through the throng of Slödavans. Hostile blue-bright eyes glanced off her as she went. Her knees weakened, but she remained upright, her chin held high.

She had trusted him. She had believed him to be a friend. She had thought foolishly that he might love her. That she might . . . But he was not her Rune, her assassin. He was Rune, the Crown Prince of Slödava. His mother was Queen Hildegard.

And he had led Elma straight into a trap.

28

Björn himself led Elma to what she imagined must be the Slödavan palace. She had been separated from her men and tried not to think of what the Slödavans would do to them, without her protection. The walk to the palace wasn't far from the city gates, but the climb up to its doors consisted of several stone stairways and steep narrow roads. By the time she was led roughly inside, Elma's lungs burned with exertion. Her legs, still sore from riding for three days, shook.

But she said nothing, tried not to pant. There could be no sign of weakness or fear. At last, when she had gathered her breath enough to stop gasping, she spoke. 'Where are you taking me?' she asked, glancing around them. Björn and a small contingent of guards were leading her through eerie corridors, lit only with quivering candles. Unlike the heavy low-ceilinged corridors of the dark-stone Frost Citadel, this palace towered like a spire. The ceilings were impossibly tall and arched, and something high above them in the rafters seemed to glow blue-white.

'Down,' said Björn. That was all.

So, Elma followed him down, down to the belly of the palace. They had spent so much time climbing up, and now they descended into a dismal cold. The clatter of guards' armor echoed in time with their footsteps. Elma was glad to be wearing her traveling clothes; if she had been in one of her gowns, she would have been shivering in the chill. This was colder even than the dungeons of the Frost Citadel.

At last, a narrow stair leveled off into a corridor, along which were barred cells. Elma peered in as they passed but saw no one.

'Where are my men?' she demanded. 'If you harm them or me, it will be war with Rothen.'

'Isn't it always war with Rothen?' Björn replied, sardonic. 'Your men are being taken to another location. We can't have you strategizing.'

Elma wanted to say something sarcastic, cutting. *Thank you for assuming we can strategize our way out of a fortified dungeon in a fortified palace in a fortified city.* But she was no longer a haughty princess; she must be a stately queen, even as a prisoner. She would remind herself of that until the belief held.

At the end of the corridor, Björn halted. They stood before a dark cell, furnished only with a blanket draped over a pile of straw and a bucket.

Elma balked. 'You cannot be serious,' she said, despite herself.

'Can't I?' Björn said. Without pausing, he unbuckled Elma's sword belt and handed Luca's sword to another guard. Then he patted her down, locating two other daggers and handing them off.

Elma seethed. Her teeth were clenched so hard her head began to ache. But she said nothing. Petulance would get her nowhere. Instead, she tried to imagine what her father would do. He had been welcomed into the court of Slödava once and treated like royalty, until he slaughtered them without cause. But if she could leverage the Slödavan sense of honor, perhaps . . .

'Björn,' she said, turning to face the guard.

He raised his eyebrows, gesturing for her to enter the cell. 'Can I get you something, Majesty? A hot bath, perhaps? Someone to braid your hair?'

'Only this,' Elma said, standing her ground. 'I believe it would behoove you, my lord, to treat the Queen of Rothen with the proper respect. If Navenie and Mekya hear that I've been tossed in a cell like some street rat –'

'Navenie?' scoffed Björn, turning to his men to laugh. 'Mekya? They are leagues away. Another world. Nice try, though.'

'Not as far as you think,' Elma said, speaking louder. Allowing her chest to fill, to project her voice just as her father had. 'King Alaric and Queen Antigone are aware that the Queen of Rothen is on a mission of peace to Slödava. If they hear that you have taken me captive, they will join Rothen in declaring outright war on Slödava.'

Björn snorted, but the mirth in his expression faded. 'You're bluffing. And even if you weren't, Mekya and Navenie would never go to war if they knew what you'd done to our Crown Prince. They'd let you take the beating you deserve.'

Elma raised her eyebrows. 'Is that a risk you're willing to take on behalf of your realm?'

He regarded her with reluctant thoughtfulness. 'You're in no place to make demands.'

'A room with a bed and a fire in the hearth,' she said. 'That is all I ask. Is this a request that the honorable kingdom of Slödava would deny its neighboring monarch?'

Björn sighed, rolling his eyes. Then he waved a gauntleted hand, gesturing at his men to turn around and go back the way they'd come. 'The Queen of Rothen has made her request,' he said, 'and the hospitality of Slödava will not deny her.'

Elma was silent as she allowed Björn to lead her back out of the dungeon and upward toward the warmth and light. And with every step, she felt a faint warmth bloom in her chest. Something like pride. Something like power.

The room contained a bed, and the hearth was wide, a crackling fire within. It was more than Elma had hoped for. Björn had shown her in without fanfare and left her there alone. When Elma put her ear to the door a moment later, she heard the low voices and creaking of leather and metal that indicated Björn's men had stayed to guard her.

She hadn't expected any less.

Elma was standing in the middle of the room, wondering what to do next, when a knock sounded at the door. Before she could answer, it swung open. The boy at the door, flanked by guards, appeared to be a pageboy. He was decorated in blue and white livery, a floppy velvet hat on his head. He carried a bucket and a sponge.

'For Her Majesty's bath,' he said when Elma stared questioningly. 'In case she desires to smell less . . . potent.'

Elma bristled. 'Thank you,' she said stiffly, knowing that a pageboy was not the source of her pain or her ire.

'With pleasure,' he said pleasantly, setting the bucket and sponge near the fireplace. He turned back to her and gave her a pertinent once-over. He had the sharp blue eyes and delicate features of the Slödavans that Elma had come to know, but his hair was pale gray. 'Surprised they don't have you locked up in the dungeon,' he said. 'The Volta name doesn't inspire much kindness here.'

There was no way to respond to this comment without sounding sullen or ungrateful, so Elma simply returned the boy's stare with her own.

He shrugged. 'The Queen will see you in an hour. See that you're presentable by then. Ring the bell if you need something.' He pointed to a length of rope that hung from the ceiling near the bed. 'No one will bring you anything, of course, but the bell sounds nice.' Then he bowed at the waist and took his leave.

The door slammed behind him, and Elma was alone again. She wished she had thought to question the pageboy, to ask after her men or Rune. Then again, she knew exactly where Rune was – lounging somewhere, reveling in being a prince, no doubt. Probably laughing at her, her naivete, the way she'd been so easily taken in. He had undoubtedly colluded with her advisors, planned her death, perhaps planned all of this, from the start.

Elma squeezed her hands into tight fists until they ached, her nails digging into her palms. After a few long breaths, she willed her fingers to relax.

I will get through this alive. My men will get through this alive.

The mantra did nothing to soothe her, but it distracted her from more dire thoughts. Since there was nothing else to do, she went to the bucket and was surprised to find that the water was, indeed, hot.

Unwilling to undress in the enemy citadel, Elma made do with washing her face and hands. The hot water was a welcome relief from the grime of the road, the chill of travel. But her spirits remained cold, her heart rimed with subtle agony. She could not keep the image of Rune, head held high as he gave the order to arrest her, out of her thoughts. It gnawed at her, pulling her down and down.

Despair is what he wants, she thought desperately. *Give in and he has you exactly where he wants you.*

When she was finished washing, Elma inspected the room more thoroughly. It was small, but fine – in the Frost Citadel, such a room would have been given to traveling merchants who held favor with Rothen, or members of court without a title. But this far north, in the isolated city . . . Elma could only imagine who might need a room for the night. Like the rest of the Slödavan palace, this room's ceilings towered upward. All was made of white stone.

The only item of note, other than the bed and hearth, was a decorative sword hung over the hearth. Elma spent several minutes trying to pry the sword from the wall but only succeeded in loosening its fastening. It wasn't a proper weapon, anyway – it would not protect her from Slödavan steel, let alone Rime Ice.

She was on her hands and knees behind the bed, feeling around for any weapons or sharp objects that could have been abandoned and forgotten there, when another knock sounded at the door.

Certain that an hour had not yet passed, Elma stood abruptly. Blood rushed to her head. A man in the most beautifully ostentatious clothes she had ever seen strode into the room.

He wore dark leather hose of navy blue, a pair of gray leather boots reaching almost to the knee. His doublet

266

matched the hose and was embroidered at the shoulders with intricate silvery threads that looked like a light snowfall. The full sleeves, narrowing at the wrist, were slashed to reveal pale gray damask silk beneath. The collar of his doublet hung open just enough to reveal a tan chest draped with silver chains of opal. A sword hung at his waist. Fingers heavy with silver rings, he tapped the pommel of his sword and regarded Elma with a thoughtful expression.

'Your Highness,' Elma said, the chill on her heart solidifying to ice, expanding through her until she was frozen with unspent rage.

Rune smiled and closed the door behind him.

29

The air lay taut between them, a held breath, both Rune and Elma waiting for the other to make the first move. Rune's scar seemed out of place here in his finery, in this palace. There was still a ferality to him that wasn't to be contained. Elma hated that she saw it in his eyes – the man she thought she knew.

'What do you want?' she finally said, breaking the silence as she made her way casually toward the fireplace. It would do her no real good, but if she could wrench the display sword from the wall, she might at least give Rune another scar.

'You, obviously.' Rune moved toward her, almost brash in his swaggering confidence.

He truly doesn't care at all, Elma thought. *He never did.*

'I've only just managed to speak with the Queen –'

As Rune spoke, Elma made her move. She darted to the hearth, and using all her strength, at last pried the display sword free from the wall. It was far too light, its edges too dull to pierce properly let alone kill.

But she could take an eye.

'Oh for –' Rune said, and Elma lunged.

She had meant to go for his face, to further mar those perfect features, the full lips and slightly arched nose. But Rune was far too fast.

In one moment, he stood wide-eyed, hand still resting

on his sword pommel. Then, with a flash, his blade caught Elma's, and there was a ring of steel on metal, their faces only inches from each other. With one deft twist of the wrist, Rune disarmed her. The display sword went flying, bent at a ridiculous angle.

But Elma's rage was boiling over. She had been so stupid, so naive. She had *trusted* a Slödavan. Taken him under her wing, into her bed. Her advisors were right – she wasn't fit to be queen.

In a burst of passion, Elma struck out with her bare hands. As she reached for his sword arm, hoping to hold him off just long enough to cause him pain, she kicked upward with her knee, aiming for his groin.

But again, he was too fast. With infuriating ease, he avoided her attacks and caught her under the knee with his free hand. There was a loud, ringing clatter as he tossed his sword aside and swept Elma's legs out from under her.

Her back slammed to the floor, the breath fleeing her lungs in one violent burst. Rune moved like a serpent striking. In a breath, he had both of Elma's wrists clenched in one hand, holding them above her head so that she was stretched out beneath him. His other hand pressed to her throat.

She writhed, kicking, but Rune had settled himself on top of her, straddling her hips, his body weight holding her down.

'Stop,' he said, his face only inches from hers.

She couldn't read the emotion in his expression; he was flushed, eyes bright, but she saw no hatred there. No cruelty. What new trick was he about to play? Instead of replying, she spat in his face.

Rune closed his eyes for a moment, letting out a sigh. 'You're being ridiculous. If you'd only give me a moment to speak –'

'How dare you try to speak to *me*,' Elma growled, unable to hold back. 'I should have let you die in the Death Games.'

'Oh please, you don't really feel that way.'

Elma bucked, trying to dislodge him, and he made a low, satisfied sound in his throat in response. Her body was beginning to betray her, the raging fire of anger and betrayal tightening, drifting lower until it began to thrum deep in her belly.

'I haven't betrayed you,' Rune said, leaning down until his lips brushed her ear. 'Will you *stop* writhing? You're going to make this impossible for both of us. I'm having a hard enough time as it is, keeping my hands off you.'

'Haven't betrayed me?' Elma said, her voice cracking with disbelief. 'What do you call this, then?'

'Self-defense,' he crooned. Then, as if he couldn't help himself, he bit down on her earlobe.

Jagged desire, undeniable, cut through Elma from Rune's teeth on her ear to the ache between her thighs. 'Fuck you. Get off of me.'

'But if I let you go, you'll try to kill me. And while dying at your hand would be my greatest privilege, I'd at least like a chance to explain myself before that happens.' He paused and took a long, shaking breath. '*Please* stop moving around like that, I am distracted enough as it is.'

Elma laid still, breathing hard. Emotions, fiery and confusing, warred within her. She wanted to hurt him, to make him suffer. But when they locked eyes, she saw only her Rune there and the hazy fog of lust. The haughty Crown

Prince of Slödava from the gates of Slödava was gone, but he could return at any moment, turning on Elma. There was no knowing who the real Rune was. But now, in this moment, he was hers, and she could not pretend she didn't want him.

'Speak,' she said at last. If he was so desperate to try to absolve himself, then so be it. And when he was finished, Elma would find some way to kill him anyway. But just the weight of him, his obvious arousal, his fingers tight against her neck, was almost enough to render her incoherent.

'Thank you,' Rune said, his fingers on her neck loosening. His other hand, holding her wrists, remained firm. 'I have an image to maintain. There are rules. You must understand that. Until the Queen of Slödava commands it, you *must* be a prisoner here. I don't have the power to defy the law. And if our people suspected that I've been . . . well, *fraternizing* with Rothen, then I've compromised myself, and you can take a peace treaty off the table. Forever.'

Elma listened with stubborn incredulity. Trust lost was not easily regained. 'Why didn't you warn me?' she demanded. 'Why didn't you tell me who you are? Is your name even Rune?'

'Of course, it's my name,' he said. 'And I didn't tell you that I'm the Crown Prince of Slödava because it would have been incredibly stupid, that's why. You'd have held me hostage, had me tortured or executed or some such nonsense.'

The rationality of it gnawed at her. She would have. She knew it, and so did he. But his words were not enough. 'Let me go,' she said, teeth clenched. And then, because the truth rankled, she added, 'I would *not* have tortured you.'

He grinned. 'Don't lie.'

Elma made a sound of frustration, bucking upward in a vain attempt to dislodge him.

'Good gods, what did I say about writhing?' Rune said, breathless. 'If I let you go, will you promise not to stab me?'

She considered. There was no reason to cling to honesty here. But some part of her, the weakest part, was sick with the desire to believe Rune. To trust him again.

'Fine,' she said at last. 'I promise not to stab you.'

'Or otherwise harm me fatally,' he added.

'*Fine.*'

'Good,' Rune said. He freed her hands and throat, and then leapt up to his feet, backing away, giving Elma room to breathe, to stand.

She did so slowly, warily. And with every movement she made, Rune watched her. She felt naked before him, despite her layers of traveling clothes. She no longer knew for certain which man looked at her – Rune, or the Crown Prince of Slödava. It was unfair that despite his treachery, he still knew *her*. Still saw through to the soft core. She wished she could steal herself back from him and build armor with it to keep him out.

'You *can* trust me,' he said, bending to retrieve his sword, returning it to its sheath. 'I spoke to the Queen, my mother. I hope you find some satisfaction in the knowledge that she lectured me quite severely.'

Elma narrowed her eyes. 'I had assumed that perhaps she colluded with my advisors. That you were sent on her orders.'

Rune snorted. '*Her* orders? Absolutely not. I left of my

own accord, hellbent on disposing of your father after what he did to mine. It was, regrettably, a mission of revenge. The fact that you overheard your advisors talking about me was coincidental, I'm afraid.' He lowered his eyes. 'I was a bit of a fool. And when I saw you for the first time, asleep in that carriage, well . . .' He shrugged. 'I knew what a cocksure dunderhead I'd been. As if I could have killed you.'

Blood roared in Elma's ears. She didn't want to hear this. Didn't want to *feel* about him.

'Anyway,' said Rune, at last meeting her gaze. 'My mother isn't particularly happy with me, which puts you in a far better position than if I'd been a good little boy. Compared to me, you look practically honorable, despite being a Volta. I've explained everything to her. How you spared me in the Death Games, the deal we made, your desire for peace above all. You do still desire peace . . . ?'

For a moment, Elma considered lying. Rune's expression seemed to teeter on the edge, ready to fall should she change her mind. And it would have felt good, for a short while. The satisfaction might have cured her pain for a moment. But she couldn't bring herself to do it. Cocksure dunderhead or not, Rune deserved peace. Rothen and Slödava deserved peace.

'I do,' Elma said.

Rune brightened visibly. 'In that case, I've been given the authority to free you from this drab little room and declare you an honored guest of the court of Slödava. An ambassador for peace, by order of Queen Hildegard.' He held out his arm, bent at the elbow. 'Would you do me the honor of accompanying me to dinner?'

She ignored his proffered arm, crossing her own across her chest. 'I want Luca's sword back.'

Rune blinked. 'Was it taken from you?'

Elma gave him a long, withering look.

'Of course, it was. I'll have a word with Björn. No doubt they've put it somewhere for safekeeping. And before you ask, your men are perfectly safe. They, too, are to be treated as guests. I've already sent word to have them rescued from whichever dreadful dungeon they're in and given rooms of their own. Are you going to take my arm or not? It's getting tired.'

'Then put it down because I'm not touching you.' Relief filled Elma at the mention of her men, but she refused to show it.

He lowered his arm, his mouth twisting. 'Will you at least come to dinner?'

'Is this an invitation from you or the queen?' asked Elma. If the latter, she had no choice but to attend. But if it was an invitation from Rune, if she spent too much time with him, allowed him to crawl back under her skin a second time, she might be lost forever.

If I'm not lost already.

'Me,' Rune said.

Elma pressed her lips together in a thin line.

'Please,' he said. The single syllable was heavy with resignation, but for a glimmer of a tempered hope.

Elma took him in, the man who had been her would-be killer, her bodyguard, her assassin. He was the same man, yet utterly new. And he stood open to her in that moment, ready to let her in. His explanations had made sense, despite her misgivings. Letting out a breath, releasing herself from the cage of stubbornness and mistrust, at least for a short while, Elma held out a hand.

'Fine,' she said. 'But only because I'm starving.'

The Crown Prince's eyes, somehow bluer than ever against his finery, lit up like a constellation in the night. He took her hand with warm and gentle fingers, holding it for a breathless moment. While the bond of trust had been broken, the air between them hung taut like a bowstring. And Elma knew that if she loosened her fingers even slightly, the arrow would fly true, piercing the muscle of her heart.

30

Elma had expected Rune to take her to a dining room, or perhaps even to meet the Queen of Slödava herself. Instead, he led her on a winding path through the palace. When the guards at the door had tried to join them, Rune ordered them to stay. *Don't worry,* his eyes had seemed to say, glancing sideways at Elma as they walked together through the corridor. *I'm still your assassin.*

And so, even deep in the belly of enemy territory, Elma began to shed her all-consuming distrust, her fear. The Crown Prince would protect her, loath as she was to accept it.

When at last they came to a pair of great doors, a chill wind dancing underneath and across her ankles, Elma realized they were about to leave the palace. She wasn't dressed appropriately; she would freeze. But before she could protest, Rune snapped a finger. In a moment, a page-boy appeared, carrying a pair of heavy fur-lined cloaks.

'Thank you,' said Rune, taking them and handing one to Elma. He slung the other across his own shoulders. He was almost too beautiful then, like a painting rather than a man, a princely figure wreathed in night-dark raiments, his blue eyes shining as he stood half-turned to face her, expectation and affection lingering in his impossible gaze.

Elma had to look away while she donned her own cloak. *I am a queen,* she reminded herself. *I can survive this, along with everything else.*

Stepping out into the night, Elma couldn't help but be overwhelmed by the unfamiliarity of it. She had walked the same stone, stood under the same sky, for the past several years of her life. But Slödava was nothing like Frost. Where Frost felt as if it clung stubbornly to the mountains, angrily holding off winter storms with its solid walls and dark stone, Slödava seemed to rise out of the landscape. It was part of the fabric of the north. There was no sense of stolid strength, no push and pull between the landscape and the people who resided there. It felt peaceful. As if this city, with its rising spires and delicate arches, had simply formed at the beginning of the world. As if it belonged there.

They walked along narrow and steep roads, free of snow and ice. They were largely empty, though Elma could hear laughter and smell the aroma of cooking as they passed well-lit windows. When they did come across the odd Slödavan, no one seemed to notice Rune, or care that the Crown Prince was out walking among them, unprotected and unannounced.

Their path took them vaguely downward, away from the palace, toward slightly busier streets. And with every step, Elma became increasingly awed by the beauty of the city. It was unlike anything she'd ever seen. Not even sun-drenched Lothyn, with its lush gardens and colorful mosaics, was so arresting in its intricate architecture, the balance and design of buildings and shop fronts.

'My father never told me how beautiful it was,' Elma said, unthinking. They passed beneath a series of buttresses, vaulting outward from a cathedral that seemed to glow from within, blue and glacier-like.

'Well, he wouldn't,' Rune said, glancing up to follow Elma's gaze. 'I'm well aware of the way they paint us in Rothen. Brutes from the north, practically inhuman, probably living in caves and practicing cannibalism. Inaccurate, of course, but I suppose it fosters a sort of superiority among your people. Justification for your crimes, etcetera.'

Elma bristled. 'You speak as if the Slödavans have done nothing wrong, but I've seen the slaughter. I've heard your men – the things they've said to me while in chains.' Her lip curled at the memory of a particularly vile Slödavan, one of her father's many hostages, a man who had leered at her with the empty gaze of a hungry lizard.

'Tell me who it was, and if he's not dead already, I'll have him killed for you.' Rune's words were lazy. He didn't even meet Elma's eye as he spoke.

'This isn't a joke,' Elma said, stopping dead in the street.

Rune paused, blinking. 'I never said it was. And if you're determined to have this discussion here, *now*, I suppose you've conveniently forgotten about the fact that the Rothen nobility have no qualms about capturing and enslaving my people.'

Bile rose in Elma's throat. The bed slaves offered as a birthday present, executed in the wake of her father's death. The white-haired men she'd seen slaughtered in the arena or dragged through the dark citadel corridors, down toward the dungeons. She said nothing.

Rune studied her closely. 'You'll notice a distinct lack of Rothenian slaves in Slödava.'

Elma remained quiet as she followed the Crown Prince in ashamed silence, hating herself for her ignorance, the lack of self-awareness. But how could she have known better? Until now, she had imagined Slödava to be, while not exactly as brutal as Rune said, a land shrouded in mystery and darkness. A place where Rothenians would be slaughtered on sight. A warlike enclave.

But while Elma was subjected to the occasional inquisitive glance from the people they passed, no one regarded her obviously Rothenian features with anything more than passing curiosity.

'I thought we were going to dinner,' Elma said when they had been winding through the city for quite some time.

'We are,' Rune replied. 'It's not far. The Snowbitten Stoat.'

'The what?'

He grinned. 'You'll see.'

Rune spoke true – they turned down another narrow street lined with shop fronts that spilled honey-thick light out onto the cobbles. He stopped short in front of one of the shops, which Elma now saw was an inn of some kind. An ornate, white-painted sign hung out front, decorated with a dancing weasel-like creature.

'We're having dinner *here*?' she said, incredulous. Elma had never taken a meal in the city of Frost, not outside the arena. Not even in Lothyn had she been inside an establishment like this.

'It's a tavern, Your Majesty. The purpose is to eat and drink and, if you're not the Queen of Rothen, perhaps even be merry.'

'I know what a tavern is.'

Rune smiled. 'Then why don't you indulge me,' he said, pushing open the door.

Sound and light and music swept over them. Elma was momentarily set off balance. She was used to cacophony, the sound of drunkenness and lechery. But there was joy in these sounds, true laughter. The carefree intimacy in the atmosphere was so unlike anything in the Frost Citadel that it weakened Elma's knees.

'In you go,' said Rune, guiding her inside with a hand at the small of her back. 'Before you let the cold in.'

They found themselves at a wooden bar that was sticky with spilled wine and things Elma couldn't begin to identify. She perched uncomfortably on the stool that Rune had shown her to, arms crossed over her chest. There were bodies everywhere – laughing, raucous, and drunk. The couple closest to her at the bar was playing some kind of game, both of them placing bits of bone in small designs and bursting out in peals of glee whenever some unknown achievement had been reached in the game.

People kept bumping into her, practically shoving. And when Elma spun accusingly, she saw that the offenders were pink in the cheeks, eyes shining, and so drunk that they likely wouldn't have understood her even if she tried to demand respect. Not that any of these tavern patrons owed it to her. They were Slödavan, down to the last person. And from the looks of it, none of them had any idea who Elma or Rune were.

'Doesn't anyone recognize you?' Elma muttered in Rune's ear. He had finished ordering for them, a task which Elma had outright refused to attempt.

Rune turned, eyes bright. He shoved a tankard of something sweet-smelling and hot toward her. It struck Elma that he seemed different here, more at ease. No more was he the haughty prince, nor was he the bloodthirsty assassin he had seemed to be in Frost.

'Of course they do,' he said, taking a long swig of his drink. 'I come here all the time.'

'I mean, do they know you're . . .' Elma lowered her voice, 'the *prince*?'

He chuckled, leaning toward her conspiratorially. 'It might shock you to learn that they do. I try not to let the expectations of royalty cast a pall over the joys of life. Nor did my father. He's the one who brought me here when I was young. It used to be his favorite tavern. He wanted me to know our kingdom and our people, to understand them. Not just as my future subjects, but as individuals.'

Elma was suddenly embarrassed. She had been so eager to pick apart this new Rune, to find cracks in the facade of Slödava. But so far, all she'd done was highlight the humanity in Rune and his people. 'Your father was wise.'

'He was.' Rune studied her face, his brows drawn. 'I wish I could say the same of yours.' It wasn't spoken as a joke or an insult, but simply fact.

Elma's throat tightened. 'So do I,' she said, looking away. 'My father had many defining traits, but . . . none were wisdom.'

'He can't have been all bad,' Rune said.

'You don't need to placate me,' said Elma. 'I'm well aware of my father's sins.'

'I only mean that he raised a wise daughter.'

Heat burned Elma's cheeks at the unexpected compliment. She reached for her drink, letting the steam curl around her face. 'I don't know if I'd say the same.'

'You came here on a mission of peace,' Rune said,

matter-of-fact. 'Against the direct wishes of your advisors, with a Slödavan assassin at your side. You chose to risk your life and your reputation, on several fronts, just for something you believed in.'

Elma sipped her drink. It was hot and sweet, honeyed, with a hint of ginger. 'I had no other option,' she said at last.

'The option was war,' Rune said. 'You would have had an entire kingdom behind you, and all of your advisors. You'd have been cheered and applauded up and down the streets of Frost.'

'Maybe I was just being selfish.' Elma spoke quietly, thinking that maybe if he didn't hear, if she said the words anyway, she might be absolved.

Rune cocked his head. 'Oh?'

She sipped her drink again, not meeting his eyes. 'I wanted to arrest Bertram and Ferdinand. More than anything. My heart, my gut, *everything* told me that I had to put them down. But the reality of it, two lives would have been taken . . . their blood would be on my hands. And most painful of all, it would have meant that our deal would be done. And that you would leave.' Gripping her tankard with white knuckles, she stared hard at the wine-stained wood of the bar. 'So, I found another use for you.'

Anxiety twisted in her gut, a horrible knot that wouldn't relent. Rune would hate her, she knew. He'd realize that everything she'd done was for herself, her own interests. And while she did want peace, there was no telling if she would have made the decision to travel to Slödava on her own unless Rune was there with her.

Rune's tankard slammed on the bar, hot droplets flying everywhere. But instead of going cold and turning away or denouncing her as a villain, he was grinning. His face was flushed with mirth, eyes shining.

'Why are you smiling?' she asked, accusing.

'Because,' he said, leaning toward her as if they shared some terrible secret. 'There's something I haven't told you. Something about our deal. When I said the involvement of your advisors was incidental in my mission to kill you, what I meant was . . . they weren't involved at all.'

Elma stared. 'How strong is this drink you've given me?'

'I know,' he said, shaking his head, 'and I'm sorry. I never outright *lied* about it, exactly. When you came to me in the arena and told me you suspected your men of betraying you, I simply allowed you to continue believing it.'

'But . . .' Elma couldn't make sense of this. Her mind was lurching along, trying to remember every conversation she'd had with Rune, every suspicious glance from her advisors. 'But I *overheard* them. They were talking about me, how I wasn't fit to be queen. And they mentioned you. And . . . Cora's evidence.' Elma blinked, staring at Rune with incredulity.

Rune's expression twisted at the mention of Cora. 'I'm certain that you did overhear your men speaking ill of you. And perhaps they did, or still do, want you dead. But they never came to me about it. And I, well . . . I stopped wanting you dead the second I laid eyes on you. But rationality has never been my strong suit. My mother always said I'm relentlessly romantic.'

'Cora's *evidence*,' Elma said again, refusing to allow the puzzle pieces to fall into place.

'That, I can't explain.' But Rune's expression was clear enough.

'You think Cora betrayed me,' Elma murmured. 'That she manufactured the evidence.'

'It wouldn't be out of the realm of things Rothenians have done,' Rune said, his tone apologetic. 'I tried interrogating that assassin about it in the high tower. Someone paid him to look like a Slödavan; he admitted that much. But he was well-trained, and his tongue didn't budge after that.'

'Why didn't you tell me?' Elma asked, too lost to be angry.

Rune reached out as if to lay a comforting hand on her, then thought better of it and withdrew. 'It's only a hunch,' he said. 'No more than a guess. I just . . . saw the way you two argued. She was the one who claimed to have seen a Slödavan assassin. Your advisors are far too bumbling to have orchestrated two assassination attempts, let alone three. And who, other than your maid, had full access to your chambers? Edvin didn't sneak in there on his own merit, I can tell you that much.'

Just then their dinner arrived, steaming bowls of stew and hunks of warm bread. Elma's stomach turned, the blood draining from her face. The mention of Edvin made her gut roil even worse. Rune had killed his own man for her. For *her*.

'Elma,' Rune said, 'eat. Nothing has changed. I thought you would be glad to know. You and I don't have to be enemies. And I'm not even sure that –'

'I don't believe you.' The words were no more than a whisper. She pushed her food away, wishing she were somewhere else. The room was too hot, too loud. The laughter that had been so joyful earlier now felt like a wave that would drown her.

'Of course, you don't,' Rune said, in the tone of someone desperately backpedaling. 'I hardly believe myself half the time. I'm a fool and a romantic with a brain of mush.'

She shot him a scathing look. 'Don't patronize me.'

'I'm not, I'm –'

'You've just told me that my only friend in the world is trying to have me killed.'

Rune's earlier mirth was utterly gone now, replaced by a cold understanding. He held Elma's gaze, and she was unable, despite herself, to look away. 'You are a queen,' he said. 'Monarchs don't have friends. We can't afford to.'

'Edvin was your friend,' Elma managed.

'He was anything but. An unwanted acquaintance, at most.'

'Cora was all I had.'

'And you still might have her. But to trust in those who are far below us, whether it makes sense or not, is folly. The mistake goes both ways. Cora trusted you to reinstate her family's title, and you failed her.'

Elma's eyes flashed. 'I couldn't. Godwin wouldn't.'

'See? Even queens are subject to the wisdom of their advisors. Cora sees you as all-powerful, thinking that if you had wanted to, you would. And you see her as an equal, when in fact you are worlds above her. She *dresses* you, Elma. Tends your fire. Brings you food. Keeps you alive, some might say. And when she asked something of you, something real, something difficult, you couldn't give it to her.'

'You don't know what you're talking about,' Elma said, even though she knew he was right. She felt it in the tangle of regret in her stomach. She had been so naive.

'Perhaps,' said Rune. 'But there are worse things than being alone. Betrayal is one of them.'

'I don't want to live like that,' Elma said. She imagined a world without friendship, human connection, without love. 'I couldn't.'

'That's why I come here,' Rune said, indicating the rowdy tavern with a jerk of his chin. 'It's human, real, and raw. For a short time, I can pretend that these are my friends. That I'm welcomed, loved, part of a community. When in fact,' he said, hopping down from his stool and extending a hand to Elma, 'I'm afraid I'm seldom more than tolerated.'

Instead of going back to the palace, as Elma had expected, Rune led them down a series of narrow alleyways, some steep enough to warrant steps in the white stone. She allowed him to guide her down the steepest of them, one hand at her waist, the other holding her hand, in the manner of a gentleman.

Some part of Elma wanted to rail against Rune. To strike him, to fight him, to let loose the emotions that twisted inside her. But it would have meant admitting to herself that she believed him. That Cora was not, as she had believed, a trusted friend and confidante. And even if Rune's suspicions were untrue, if Cora had not betrayed her, the heavy weight of lead in her stomach told Elma that she had never truly been Cora's friend. She had never been Luca's friend. And as a child in Mekya, the place she missed so sorely that it still woke her in the middle of the night . . . she had been alone there, too, but for her mothers.

So Elma remained silent, allowing Rune to lead her through the city, as the reminder of her isolation seeped inward and joined with her sinews to become a part of her.

'Here we are,' said Rune, turning into a walled sort of courtyard off the street. It reminded Elma of the smaller parks in Lothyn, hidden gems in the middle of a bustling city, somehow quiet in the noise of civilization. But the night was quiet, and even though there were no thick hedges or flowering trees to muffle the sound of the streets, there was no need.

A few stone benches were scattered about the courtyard, and in the center stood a statue. At first, Elma thought it was carved from ice, but as they drew closer, she saw that it was marble. Ice had formed a layer on top of it, slightly warping the figure's shape. But even so, she recognized the work.

'A De Rixiis,' Elma breathed, walking around it to confirm. The statue was of a woman, similar to the one in the Frost Citadel courtyard. This statue wore a more substantial gown, and in her right hand, she held a sword, delicately cradled against her chest. On her other hand perched a dove, wings unfurled; upon her head was a delicate crown.

'One of my ancestors was a great fan of his work,' Rune said, coming to stand next to Elma where she admired the statue. 'In fact, I read in one of his journals that he journeyed all the way to Mekya to commission a series of statues for the courtyards of Slödava. He was joined by an ally of his. A friend, in fact. One he wrote about often. The King of Rothen.'

Elma turned sharply to stare at Rune, whose gaze was still fixed on the statue. 'My great-great-great-grandfather.'

'No one bothered to tell you there used to be peace between Rothen and Slödava, I suppose,' Rune said. 'And not just peace, but friendship. Part of the reason why it rankles so much to see it all tossed away, abandoned in the name of a pointless war.'

'That can't be true,' Elma said, reeling and reluctant to reveal yet another point of ignorance. 'I've read my ancestors' accounts, their histories. There was *nothing* about friendship with Slödava.'

'And it's impossible, of course, for pages to be ripped from books and burned or for passages to be rewritten.'

'Why should I believe you?' Elma said, frustrated, angry, and most of all, hating how small she felt in the wake of so many revelations that she ought to have already known. 'For all I know, this is a tactic. An attempt to make me docile, unsuspecting, before you stab me in the back.'

'Remember your father's mission of peace,' Rune said softly. 'If your father's own actions were shielded from you with ease, just think what generations of Volta monarchs might achieve. One misunderstanding and two kingdoms can so easily turn on one another. A grudge sits comfortably in one man's heart, but to convince his children and his children's children to cling to such poison . . . that is no easy feat. The Volta have always been determined and well-versed in the art of bitterness and resentment.'

Elma gazed up at the statue's face, her stone eyes turned ever southward. 'You have to understand how difficult this is for me to hear,' she said, 'let alone believe.'

Rune turned to her. 'I brought you to this courtyard because I used to come here as a boy. I'd stare up at this statue, this eternal queen, and wonder who she was. As if she was real and not just some hunk of rock. I wondered what she believed in. I had this ridiculous idea in my head of a queen so brave, so defiant in the face of the inevitable, that she would do anything to uphold what she believed was right. My imaginary queen was idealistic, probably to a fault. But I wanted so badly to be her or to love her. I don't know which. Both, perhaps. But I can tell you that my idea of this perfect queen, the projection of a woman who didn't exist . . . she reminds me painfully of you.'

Elma recoiled at this pronouncement. 'Of me?' she said. 'I'm no idealist. You heard what I said back there at the tavern. This mission of peace was —'

'Selfish, yes, and so forth. You say that, but I don't think you believe it.'

The words hung between them. Elma knew what she believed and what was important to her. She knew what she'd lay down her life to achieve. Above all, she knew that she wanted to be a good queen. Perhaps she always had, in some way. Until recently, her father and the Volta name had kept her trapped in an unseen cage of inevitable cruelty, that being a Queen of Rothen meant gripping her subjects in an iron fist, calling for blood with wild abandon. But now … seeing Slödava, its unearthly beauty, the people so unlike the thoughtless creatures her father had described, she knew what kind of queen she would be.

'I don't want to rule the way my father did,' Elma said at last.

Rune smiled. 'That much is obvious.'

They stood in companionable silence for a moment, studying the statue. Elma glanced sidelong at Rune, his moonlit profile, his snow-white hair. She wanted to let him in altogether, to trust him in the way he seemed to trust her. But so much of him, his life, was still a mystery.

'When were you going to tell me about Rime Ice?' Elma asked.

He didn't turn to her, kept his gaze on the statue, but raised his brows slightly. 'I'm shocked it took you this long to ask.'

Elma pursed her lips. 'I've been somewhat *distracted*.'

Laughing, he spun to face her. 'I suppose you noticed it's actually magic.'

'I saw enough men fall to your glowing ice blade to draw that conclusion, yes,' she said, crossing her arms. 'But . . . why keep that a secret from Rothen? We've been at your doorstep for decades, trying to steal it for ourselves. My father was obsessed with Rime Ice. If he'd known it was magic . . .'

'You think he would have called a happy truce and become my mother's best friend?' Rune said, sardonic. 'I'm not sure your father didn't know the truth of it. He'd seen it wielded, how the blades work. It's possible he wanted us to teach him how to use the magic, or . . . maybe he was simply jealous. Either way, your family's vendetta against Slödava didn't start with King Rafe. It's been that way for generations. Old dynasties get stuck in their ways.'

Elma frowned, mulling it over. 'And generations-old grudges don't just disappear,' she said, thinking aloud. 'My father's stubbornness would have kept him hammering at your doors, Rime Ice or no.'

'Didn't I say you were wise?' Rune said, grinning.

'Show me how it works,' Elma said, ignoring him. 'Magic. I've never . . .' she trailed off, not knowing what to say. She had always believed in other realms, the heavens watching over her, the power in her seven candles. But this was visceral, physical magic. Power that split the sinews of living muscle. It was new and frightening, and she was aching to understand it.

'Never seen it before? You're in for a treat,' Rune said. 'I'm not sure I can teach you, but I'll show you. I've never done this for anyone before. Not like this, outside of combat.' He looked almost shy as he spoke, as if Elma were someone to impress.

And as she watched, something in the man's bearing changed. His sheepish expression faded, and in its place, he began to radiate what could only be described as *kingliness*.

Like hoarfrost gathering on stone, shards of glassy ice burst from his outstretched arm, piling on top of one another to form a thick layer. It crackled and hissed as it grew, until his entire forearm was encased in it. Within moments, the frost on Rune's arm extended outward, crawling over his skin and into his fingers, until it became a hissing blade of ice gripped in his hand. The blade shimmered and moved like a river flowing beneath a layer of glassy ice.

'It's beautiful,' Elma breathed. More beautiful than she had remembered.

'A bit overdramatic, when you think about it,' Rune said, running a finger along the flat of his blade, 'but effective.'

'How does it work?'

Rune shrugged, and as he did, the Rime Ice blade contracted, shortening with the loud crackling of melting ice until it was gone. 'We actually don't know. Isn't that convenient? The legend says that the first Slödavan king was given Rime Ice as a gift from the people of the snow, the fair folk. According to the stories, Rime Ice comes from the blood of the land, passed between those with royal lineage. If you're feeling particularly philosophical, some believe that the land chooses who is blessed with Rime Ice. If a heart is ruined with greed or selfishness, supposedly, one cannot manifest Rime Ice properly. It will turn on you.'

'I see,' Elma said, frowning. 'Could I learn how to wield it?'

'Thought you'd never ask,' said Rune, his mouth quirking in a half-smile. 'But unfortunately, I have no idea. As far as I'm aware, no one but Slödavans have ever accessed its power.'

'I want to try,' said Elma. 'I'm a queen, aren't I?'

Rune's gaze heated. 'I love it when you're haughty. But let's not get ahead of ourselves. We have a peace treaty to write, and you look . . . well, for lack of a better word, exhausted.'

Elma had to accept the truth of his statement – she *was* exhausted. The long journey north was weighing on her eyelids, weakening her limbs. That morning, she had lit a funeral pyre and watched its smoke fade into the distance on the Frozen Sea. Though it had only been hours, it felt like lifetimes ago.

'It's quite late,' Rune said. 'Allow me to escort you back to the palace.'

Elma did not speak for the entirety of their walk back up those steep, narrow alleys, the winding thoroughfares, until they were standing at her new chamber door. Thoughts and questions hung like ripe fruit in her mind, but she did not pluck them. She needed to sleep, to clear her mind.

'Thank you for dinner,' she said.

Rune's eyes shone with unsaid words as he took her hand in his, kissing it once. 'Sleep well, Your Majesty.'

Her skin burned where his lips had touched it. Even then, she longed for him. 'Good night,' she said, closing the door behind her and returning to the familiar cocoon of solitude.

32

A frenzied thudding tore Elma from the clutches of sleep.

It was just after sunrise; she could tell from the angle of the pale sunlight glancing through the tall windows of her room. She had been given better accommodations as Rune had promised, with a soft four-poster bed and a far larger hearth, the floor piled with fur rugs. And despite the constant swirl of her thoughts, Elma had slept peacefully.

The thudding came again, and blinking blearily, Elma realized it was someone at her door. Scrambling out of bed, she went to the wardrobe and was gratified to find a robe there. Draping it about herself hurriedly, she went to the door.

The pageboy from before stood pink-faced in the corridor. 'Your Majesty,' he said, 'You are needed in the strategy room. If you'd come with me?'

Elma blinked. 'The strategy room,' she repeated.

'Yes, Your Majesty. Come with me, if you please.'

'I'm not dressed.'

'I can see that, Majesty, but there isn't time. I was sent to fetch you with the utmost urgency.'

Sighing, Elma shoved her feet into a pair of slippers, glad of the robe's warmth. 'Very well,' she said. 'Show me the way.'

The page obliged. He led her on a circuitous path

through the palace, often ducking into narrow servants' corridors, no doubt to speed their progress. Elma was relieved that no guards had been placed outside her door, nor did any trail behind her and the page. Rune had spoken truthfully – she was not a prisoner here.

At last, the page came to a halt outside an unassuming door, his chest heaving. 'Here we are, Majesty,' he said. He knocked once, then threw open the door and announced, 'Her Majesty Queen Elma I.'

'Thank you,' said Elma, and she passed into the room.

Elma had seen her father and his men holding strategy meetings. They were often in the same low-ceilinged room, stuffy and hot, with several men arranged around a table and pushing wooden pieces about on a map.

The room she entered now could not have been more different. Like the rest of the palace, the ceiling was high and arched. At the center of the room stood a white stone table that seemed to grow out of the floor, its shape perfectly resembling that of the Continent. Clusters of glass figures in varying colors were scattered about the board.

But the room itself only held Elma's attention for a breathless moment. It was the woman standing over it, her face twisted in a frown, from whom Elma could not look away. The woman was slight in stature. She was draped in night blue robes, cinched at her waist with a belt of silver discs. Her hair, snowy white, hung loose down her back. She wore no crown, but there was no doubt in Elma's mind – this was Queen Hildegard of Slödava.

'Ah, there you are,' said Rune. Elma hadn't even noticed he was there she'd been so enchanted by his mother. 'Mother, this is –'

'I can see who it is, darling.' Queen Hildegard's words were soft and drawling. She spoke like a woman who had all the time in the world, a woman who feared nothing. 'Your Majesty,' she said. 'Welcome to Slödava. It's been such a long time since we welcomed a Queen of Rothen.'

'I'm grateful for your hospitality,' said Elma. She resisted the urge to curtsey – she, too, was a queen. 'Might I ask how my men are faring?'

Hildegard's gaze sharpened. 'Your men are safe, fed, and housed. In fact, they've been of particular use to me this morning. Are you aware that an army marches north from Frost?'

Elma glanced between Rune and his mother. 'I'm afraid you've found me at a disadvantage,' she said, choosing her words carefully.

'An army,' Rune said, his voice edged with warning. '*Your* army, to be precise.'

Cold dread crawled up Elma's spine. 'What do you mean, my army?'

Rune opened his mouth to speak, but Queen Hildegard held up a hand to stop him. 'Last night,' she said, her gaze searching Elma unrelentingly as she spoke, 'I sent my hawks to seek out the men who attacked you on the Frozen Sea. I make a point of knowing who is on the ice: who poses a threat and who is an ally. I'd received no reports of highwaymen so far off the main road, so I grew curious. In the small hours of the morning, my birds returned. They had discovered two things.'

'I trust you'll tell me what those are,' Elma said, keeping her voice level. Dread curdled in her stomach. She had a feeling she knew what the other queen was about to say.

'Some of the men who attacked you managed to escape unharmed,' said Hildegard. 'My hawks followed their tracks for some time across the ice. The tracks led south, back to Rothen. It was not long before my scouts saw the army, camped on the southern side of the Hell Gate pass. They wave the Volta banner.'

'Is this an interrogation, then?' Elma asked, not bothering to ask how the queen had obtained so much information from mere hawks. If Slödava had magic weapons, who knew what other mysteries lay behind these icy walls. 'You believe I mustered the forces of Rothen in secret and ordered them to follow me?'

'No,' said Rune, 'but . . . there's more. Another banner was raised alongside yours. Your men confirmed it this morning, based on description. The banner belongs to Lord Godwin.'

'This is a trick,' Elma said. Ice gripped her heart. 'Your hawks must be incorrect.'

'My hawks,' said Queen Hildegard, her face a mask of calm, 'are never incorrect. They pride themselves on sharp hearing and even sharper vision.'

'This is very much not a trick,' Rune added quickly, 'though I'm sure we both wish it was. Your uncle rides on Slödava against your orders. His own men waylaid you on the ice, killing their own in an attempt to get to you. Whatever it is he intends to do now, it won't be in the name of honor.'

Elma's knees threatened to buckle. She had no choice but to reach out for the table, steadying herself. She exhaled shakily. 'One by one, you've declared my allies traitors. My advisors, then Cora, now my *uncle*. How am I supposed to believe you? That this isn't . . . some means of getting me alone and taking my throne from me.'

'Elma,' Hildegard said, her voice kind. 'We would not deceive you in such a way. But we couldn't, in good conscience, hide this from you. In a few days' time, the army of Rothen will be camped on the Frozen Sea with your banner on display. Your men are sending a message, clear and undeniable.'

She hated to acknowledge it, but Elma felt in her gut that the other queen was not lying. Elma had not called for war; her banner's use alone was tantamount to treason. But for Godwin to fly his own colors, green and gold, alongside hers, when she had clearly stood against this war her advisors so desired . . . her fingers, splayed on the table, curled into a fist. Godwin had been on her side.

'When my uncle arrives,' she said, 'I would like to speak with him alone.'

'He's very clearly intent on war,' Rune said. 'Do you really think a few words from you will change that?'

Elma spun on him. 'I am Lord Godwin's queen. Those are *my* soldiers riding on Slödava, betraying me. The last thing I'll do is hide from them behind some pretty wall. If they're determined to commit the highest form of treason, they will do it to my face.'

An expression almost like admiration hovered on Queen Hildegard's face.

'I'll go with you,' Rune said. 'If nothing else, let me be your blade.'

Elma was tempted to refuse; she didn't want to need him. But she was alive now thanks to Rune. And there was no telling what Godwin might do if given the chance.

'Fine,' she said, 'if your queen allows it. But I need you to be my bodyguard, my shadow. If my uncle doesn't know your true identity, I'd rather keep it that way.'

'A good queen always has at least one ace up her sleeve,' Hildegard said, thoughtful. 'Let my son be yours and prove himself useful for once.'

'I beg you,' Rune said to his mother, 'at least refrain from harming my ego until *after* we've eaten.'

'My son is more than tolerable,' said Hildegard, moving around the table to offer her arm to Elma, as a close friend or confidante would, 'but only when he's fed.'

'Ha,' Rune said, trailing behind the two queens as they took their leave. 'Always making jokes, my mother.'

Breakfast was an intimate affair, located in what seemed to be one of Queen Hildegard's personal parlors. Rune perched on a rather uncomfortable-looking chair, while Elma and Hildegard sat together on a grand settee. Trays were brought in, laden with steaming bowls of honey and cinnamon porridge, sausages, coffee, hot wine, and even fruit.

When Elma asked about the fruit, wondering how they kept it fresh, Hildegard explained that it was packed in ice and cold stones, and sent directly from Mekya. Apparently, a vibrant trade had blossomed between Slödava and other countries of the continent. Slödava offered artisans and blacksmiths, musicians and painters, in return for food, resources, and things that could not be obtained in the isolated north.

With Rothen's inability to offer more than weaponry, and King Rafe's obstinate personality that had bordered on antagonism, Elma realized that her kingdom sat isolated, unwilling and unable to give Navenie and Mekya what they needed. And so, it, like Elma, huddled untouched in the frozen north, alone and feeble.

Even as the conversation turned toward lighter things – music, art, and culture – Elma's thoughts clung to Rothen. Her birthright, a dying thing. Her father had hungered so much for war that he had left her a shriveled throne, carried on the backs of its slowly starving people.

After breakfast, Hildegard pulled Elma aside. 'I have great hope for your kingdom,' the other queen said. 'But until your men are firmly under your thumb, there can be no peace between our nations. Many lives hang in the balance. My son believes in you.' She held Elma's gaze with ice-blue eyes. 'Don't fail him.'

Elma's heart was in her throat. This was more than she deserved, yet the words stung. She hardly believed in her ability to speak sense into her uncle, let alone call off the dogs of Rothen.

Even so, she said, 'I won't.'

'Good. Then please, for gods' sake, go and entertain him for a while. He's spoken of nothing but you since you arrived.' Her smile was tinged with sadness. 'He has been lonely for such a long time.'

'So have I,' Elma said, unthinking.

'Then perhaps your meeting wasn't by chance,' said Hildegard. Her smile brightened, and she took Elma's hand in hers. 'In a few days, we don our armor, if we must. But today, we rest. And find joy where we can.'

Rune was waiting for Elma in the corridor, leaning against the wall. Before he turned to greet her, she saw him in profile, his features so elegant in the palace, his frost-white hair, the dark tan skin, the curve of his neck above the frothy doublet collar.

As he turned to her, he smiled, his face lighting up. There was a soft disarmament in him that had not been present in the Frost Citadel. 'Well, well,' he said, pushing off from the wall. 'If it isn't my mother's new favored confidante. What did she tell you? Embarrassing tales of my wayward youth?'

'No,' Elma said, 'though now I'm tempted to go back and ask for some.'

Rune made a face. 'Please, at least wait until I'm dead or something. The things I got up to . . .'

'I'm sure they're not nearly as bad as you think,' Elma said.

They stood for a moment in awkward silence, as if without something to argue about, without blood dripping down their fingers, they were strangers. Elma wanted to be near him. She wanted to devour him, to be devoured. Yet here they stood, worlds apart.

'Do you –'

'I was –'

They spoke at the same time, their words colliding and tangling in the air between them. Elma's cheeks burned. 'Sorry,' she said.

'It's all right,' said Rune, studying her intently. 'I'll show you to your room. You must not have slept well last night.'

'Yes,' Elma said. 'I mean, no.'

When she took Rune's arm, she felt his heat as if he were on fire. Her nerves seemed to buzz with his proximity. As they walked, she shot sideways glances at him, noticing the lift of his chin, the sway of his sword at his hip.

'What?' he asked, obviously noting the way she couldn't stop looking at him.

'It's just . . .' Elma said, swallowing. It would sound ridiculous, the truth. Saccharine and nonsensical. But in two days, she would go to her uncle, and there was no telling whether she might come back from that alive. 'I feel as if I'm seeing you for the first time,' she said at last. 'As if your armor's come off.'

'Well,' he said, 'you're a weapon. I had to keep my guard up in case you tried to pierce me through the heart. The only difference now is that I no longer fear such an attack. You could puncture me full of holes, Your Majesty, and I'd only beg for more.'

33

In the dreamlike city of Slödava, Rothen seemed as far away as a childhood memory. Elma understood that she teetered on the brink of war, and yet all she felt in her first day as a guest of Slödava, was an inexplicable peace. Her advisors no longer lingered in shadows or cast her dark glances across the dinner table. The heavy stone of the Frost Citadel no longer pressed in upon her from all sides. And her duties as queen, while they lay heavy on her shoulders, seemed to have temporarily lightened.

She was an honored guest here and was treated as such. The first day passed with relative ease. After breakfast, Rune took her on a brief tour of the palace, rambling on about his family's history as they went. Elma found it fascinating, her gaze locking on paintings hung from the walls, on intricate tapestries. This was a wholly new Slödava, a city so unlike the one she'd been brought up to understand.

It galled her, knowing that her own father had seen these halls. He had seen Slödava as it truly was. But he'd kept it from her, as he'd kept everything else.

'Don't you have any siblings?' Elma asked as she and Rune made their way out into a frosted courtyard. He had shown her paintings of his parents, his cousins, and aunts and uncles.

'No,' said Rune, kicking at a tuft of snow. 'I'm technically my mother's heir, but without a daughter to sit on the throne, the Belgard line would die with me.'

'Belgard,' Elma repeated, her breath steaming in the frigid air. 'Your family name?'

'Quite.'

'I had no idea,' Elma said, her new refrain.

Rune regarded her softly. 'There's no reason to be ashamed. We like to keep our secrets, us Slödavans. Your father never actually knew the royal name, or if he did, he was saving that knowledge for some later purpose. He was granted my mother's name before he tried to kill her, when we believed that peace was on the table. That was all.'

Elma looked away. She was so full of the desire to undo her father's wrongs, to create a new legacy for the Volta name. But the image of her own army, flying hers and Godwin's banners, burned in her mind.

'My men,' she said, eager to turn the subject away from her inadequacies, 'have you seen them today?'

'They've been given the freedom to come and go as they please, on the condition of pledging loyalty to you, of course. I've no idea where they are. Could be drunk in some tavern, for all I know.'

'Loyalty?' Elma repeated. 'I'm surprised. I led them into a death trap.'

'You did,' Rune said, a hint of sarcasm glimmering in his eyes, 'but what queen hasn't led her men to certain danger?'

'You say it as if it's inevitable.'

'Perhaps it is. For kings and queens, morality isn't black and white.'

It wasn't until later that evening that Elma, at last, came upon Hugh, striding through a palace corridor with two of her men in his wake. His expression was stormy, his shoulders tense. When he saw Elma there alone, he stopped, eyes momentarily wide with surprise. She was on her way back to her room to change for dinner, for once enjoying a moment of solitude.

'Your Majesty,' said Hugh, bowing his head once he collected himself. 'I'm gratified to see you're well.'

Elma's tongue felt dry and heavy in her mouth. As she rallied herself, seeking the words a queen should speak, her gaze fell on Hugh's sword. It was as familiar to her as the storms at her citadel windows. Luca's sword. Hugh balanced a light hand on the pommel.

'If there's anything I can do to . . .' Elma said, faltering. What else was there to say? 'Godwin's army is only days away,' she went on, standing taller. 'When he arrives, I'll see that he is brought to justice.'

'You are most gracious, Majesty,' said Hugh, bowing again. 'We are at your disposal.'

When the guards went on their way, as Elma approached her rooms, a shadow seemed to pass over her. *I will be a better queen*, she thought. *If I must, I will die for them.*

And so, over dinner that night, Elma asked Rune – quite formally, and with every intention of holding him to it – to teach her how to use Rime Ice.

In the two days that followed, Elma distracted herself with Rune and, to a lesser extent, Rime Ice.

He was more than willing to oblige her desire to be near him, and he appeared to have no other duties or tasks to otherwise occupy him. And though Elma was never unaware of the crackling tension between them, his warm skin and deft hands and strong arms, she made no move toward intimacy. The layer of ice on her heart had been renewed since arriving in Slödava, and even though she was drawn to Rune like a moth to a flame, he would not so easily melt her.

'You have to *feel* it,' he said, gripping Elma's arms with intensity. 'Here. And here.' He touched her heart with a gentle hand.

Her cheeks heated despite the cold. They stood high on one of the palace battlements, a dramatic locale that Rune declared would suit best for teaching Elma how to wield her Rime Ice. Somewhere cold, where she could embrace the ice and her power. That is, if she even had the power to begin with.

The pair had been at it, on and off, for two days, returning to the frigid battlement while Elma's hope waned. 'I don't think I can,' she said, not for the first time, gritting her teeth against the chill. 'Your instructions are esoteric at best. *Just access the land with your heart. Try to embody what it means to be a queen?*'

'Well, it makes sense to me,' Rune said, airy. 'Maybe it's because you're so old.'

Elma made a derisive sound.

'Compared to me, when I learned,' Rune laughed. 'I was only a child. Things come more naturally when you're that young. We'll keep trying.'

But she had tried it all. She had reached into herself, closed her eyes, and imagined whatever grand visions Rune recommended. None of it had worked. Not even a hint of frost tickled at her skin. Maybe she *was* too old, or too Rothenian. According to Rune, no one in Slödava had ever heard of a

Rothenian monarch wielding Rime Ice. Then again, no one truly understood exactly what it was, or how it worked. All he knew, he'd said, was that only those in royal families could wield it. And then, usually only monarchs. His was stronger than most princes', but 'Compared to my mother's blade,' he'd said, 'I may as well be carrying a frozen fork.'

Rune moved toward her, into her personal space. No one else was on the battlement, and Elma's belly twisted pleasingly as he raised a hand and ran it down her arm, an affectionate touch. 'We'll try again tomorrow.'

Another sensation in Elma's belly: heavy foreboding. 'My uncle's army will arrive tomorrow.'

Rune dropped his hand, his expression lighting as if something had just occurred to him. 'Come with me,' he said, taking Elma's cold hand in his rough, warm one. 'Let's see if we can catch a glimpse.'

'A glimpse of what?' Elma asked, but Rune said nothing, only flashed her a knowing look.

They didn't go far. Rune led them to a nearby tower and up its coiling stairs until they were at the top, far above the ice-bright city. Narrow windows looked out on the buildings below, which looked like sugary confections from so far above. And beyond them, the wall, and the expanse of the Frozen Sea. Elma thought she saw a blurry shadow on the ice, perhaps the distant approach of Godwin's army. Or perhaps a low-hanging cloud; it was impossible to know.

'Look,' said Rune, going to a contraption by one of the windows and patting it lovingly. It was a strange thing. It was cylindrical in shape and balanced horizontally on a wooden tripod. One of its ends was pointed toward the window.

'At what, exactly?' Elma asked, unimpressed.

'A *telescope*,' Rune said, his voice tinged with awe. 'We had it shipped in from Lothyn; one of the few in existence. Want to try it?'

'Fascinating,' said Elma, crossing her arms. 'And it does . . . what?'

He huffed. 'It sees things that are very far away. Here.' He took her by the arm and led her bodily over to the telescope, before bending over and pressing one eye to the glass end. He muttered and twisted a few pieces on the cylinder, pushing his hair away as it fell repeatedly into his face.

Elma watched, trying not to laugh. *Sees things that are very far away?*

'Ready,' said Rune, standing straight at last. He gestured for Elma to put her eye to the thing. 'Look.'

Incredulous but in the mood to humor him, Elma put her eye to the glass. At first, she saw nothing but blurry shapes, smudges of white. And then she lined her eye up properly and gasped. There before her, clear as day, was an approaching army. She could make out pennants in her own colors and some in Godwin's. She caught the flash of weaponry, the movement of bodies.

Lost for words, she stood up, gazing out the window. All she saw was ice and a distant smudge of brown. She turned to Rune, who was beaming.

'Incredible, isn't it? The technology they're developing these days,' Rune said. 'Almost like magic.'

'Rothen has nothing like this,' Elma said, amazed. 'We make war machines, great ridiculous devices that fling boulders or fire massive arrows. Even when I lived in Mekya, I saw no telescopes.'

'Certainly, it hadn't been invented yet,' Rune said, eyes

softening. 'And you're the queen now. Imagine all the books you can have brought in, the scholarship, science, and agriculture.'

'Rothen would be unrecognizable,' she said, unable to stop the smile that tugged her mouth.

'The Golden Age of Rothen,' Rune said, his voice low. He was so close to her, just as he had been for nearly two full days. Every movement, every breath he took, was so painfully bright to Elma. He was a star, and she was the night, yearning for his light.

They stood in silence for a moment, a palpable ache in the air between them. Rune's gaze flickered to her lips, and Elma's belly dipped pleasingly, a twist of excitement deep inside.

'Rune,' she said, unable to look away from him, his mouth, the obvious lust in his eyes.

'That's my name,' he murmured.

She swallowed thickly. What could happen between them now? Even if she trusted him completely, even if her heart saw fit to melt, he was the heir of an enemy kingdom. She was Rothen's queen. Where did love fit in?

'The sun is setting,' she said, pulling away from Rune. 'Your mother will expect us for dinner soon.'

She couldn't be sure, but she thought a shadow of disappointment crossed Rune's face. 'As you say,' he said, offering her his arm. 'Shall we?'

They descended from the tower arm in arm. Elma savored the feel of his strength through the woolen fabric of his doublet, his sidelong smiles, the sway of his sword at his hip. He would not be here like this, with her, a friend and ally, for long.

Godwin's army would arrive the next day, and everything would change. Elma would stop this war, or she would fail, and Godwin would do what he deemed just. There was no guarantee that Elma would survive a meeting with her uncle, or that Rune would want to see her in the wake of it.

But for tonight, at least, she held his arm in hers.

Throughout dinner, Elma couldn't take her eyes off Rune, couldn't stem the tightness in her chest or the ache in her belly when he so much as glanced at her. She found herself unable to focus on her food, on Hildegard's questions, on anything but the man who had been her assassin. *You should be grateful to be rid of him*, she thought, watching him laugh at his own joke, eyes crinkled and bright with mirth, his countenance so relaxed and assured. As if he wasn't worried at all about tomorrow.

His gaze snapped to Elma's as she stared across the table, and his expression sharpened. As if he could sense her hunger. She thought about how his mouth felt on hers, his skin under her teeth, the way he undid her slowly and masterfully with tongue and hands.

She needed him to chase her, to pin her down, to free her from her worries and surrender again. She needed him to give her that, but she had no idea how to ask for it.

When dinner ended, the three exchanged pleasantries. Elma could tell that Hildegard was preoccupied, the woman's brows were drawn, and her mouth pulled tight. Elma was relieved to be set loose from the duty of conversing with the other queen; she was nearly drowning in thoughts of Rune.

I need you, she thought, nearly incoherent as Rune led her out of the dining room, hand in hand.

'I'll show you to your room,' Rune said, almost as if he were asking a question, his gaze searching Elma's.

Elma said nothing, despite the roaring of blood in her veins. Her tongue lay heavy in her mouth, her heart bright and raw within her breast. She ached for him; she burned at his slightest touch. And when they came at last to her room, Rune bowed – a polite and distant gesture. He meant to take his leave, and Elma would be alone again, wishing she had done something.

She stood still, her breaths coming shallow and heavy.

Rune was the Crown Prince of Slödava. She had no idea where they stood beyond their allyship – if he still wanted her the way she wanted him. Whether he had only enjoyed tasting her when it was so sinful, a servant and his lady. Whether he cared more about propriety, now, in his own kingdom and his own palace. But Elma couldn't contain herself; something fraught and hungry blazed inside her. Politics were politics.

But this? She wanted this too badly to care.

'Come inside,' she said, opening the door to her room, turning to Rune.

Rune's gaze met hers – questioning but lit with subtle eagerness. He wanted her. 'Is Her Majesty sure –'

'I'm sure,' she said in a rush and pulled him inside, slamming the door behind them.

34

Rune's mouth was on hers the second they were alone. He shoved Elma back against the door, lifting one knee to brace himself between her legs. She groaned into him, rocking against his thigh, her teeth fastened on his bottom lip. She kissed him as if she were dying, and his immediate hardness, his shaking breath, told her that her desperate desire was reflected in him.

This was what she wanted. This would feed her, keep her warm at night.

'Elma,' he murmured against her throat. 'I –'

'I know,' she gasped, burying her fingers in his hair as her head fell back against the door. He was working her into a senseless frenzy of want, knowing what would sharpen the ache between her thighs, what would make her moan his name.

As he held her in his arms, his body against hers, his touch opening her like petals in the spring, she felt herself at last begin to melt. This was not the violent, hateful desire she'd felt in her room after the assassin's attack, fueled by bloodlust and fear. And as Rune so gently rocked against her, as if pressing his erection against her belly was the holiest thing he had ever done, she felt utterly safe.

This pleasure was gentle. It was soft. And she trusted him.

But Elma knew what she liked.

'Rune,' she said, breathless against his throat, 'I want to see you bleed.'

He huffed, pulling back to regard her with hazy eyes. 'Still hate me that much?'

'No,' she gasped, as his hands roved inside her bodice, his mouth lowering to her breast. 'I want you to surrender to me.'

Rune kissed her nipple sweetly. 'You say that like I haven't already.'

'I'm your enemy,' Elma said, half groaning as she spoke, as Rune rucked up her dress and slid a hand underneath, feathering light touches on her bare thigh. 'I'm the queen of Rothen.'

'My apologies, Majesty,' he said, a devilish smile curling across his features. 'I forgot to pay my respects . . . properly.'

Without warning, Rune swept Elma into his arms and carried her to the bed. He kissed her and then tossed her onto the soft mattress, crawling up after her. He looked every bit the predator, his eyes lit with desire. She arched her back with the anticipation of pleasure and closed her eyes.

'Your Majesty,' Rune said, rucking up her skirts and pulling her underclothes aside. 'I am your servant. I'm nothing. Allow me to grovel.'

He lowered his mouth to her pussy, the heat and pressure of his devoted mouth driving her so quickly toward the apex, too quickly.

'Not,' she gasped, 'not yet.'

Rune sat up, smiling lasciviously. Somehow, his doublet had come undone, his shirt loose at the throat, and Elma wanted to bite through his perfect skin. As she watched, still overwhelmed with pleasure, he drew a small dagger from within his doublet. 'Where do you want it, Your Majesty?'

A sharp thrill ran up her spine at the sight of him, flushed and compliant, ready to bleed for her. *I am your servant. I'm nothing.* 'Your chest,' she said, lying back to watch him, hungry, her own hand snaking thoughtlessly down to between her legs.

Rune unsheathed the dagger, tossing its scabbard aside. With agile fingers, he unlaced his doublet all the way and pulled it open, revealing his undershirt. By the time he was finished with its ties, the entirety of his bare chest finally on display, Elma was writhing with need. A tight ache pulsed between her legs as she touched herself, her body reacting to the sight of Rune's pink-brown nipples, the few hairs on his chest. He was fit but not overly muscled, and a few faint white scars marked his skin.

'Keep touching yourself,' Rune ordered, and despite her smoldering need to lay her hands on him, she obeyed, burying two fingers deep into her wetness.

Rune groaned as he watched, his expression almost pained. 'Elma,' he said, 'you're going to kill me.'

The uncontained need in his voice made her lightheaded. She felt as if she would go mad with pure unadulterated desire, but she wasn't the only one. Rune's lips were swollen, his eyes bright, and she saw something warm and gentle in his gaze. Something that threatened to thaw her heart completely.

But she wanted more. So much more. She would never have enough of him.

'Your blood,' she said, gasping slightly as she spoke. She hardly knew what her fingers were doing anymore, pressing and circling, following her pleasure. All she could think of was Rune. There was nothing in her world but him, his blue eyes, the blade in his hand, the weight of his knees pressing divots into the bed.

Never taking his eyes off hers, with a precisely delicate movement, Rune dragged the blade down his left pectoral, just inches from his nipple. He hissed in pain, and Elma let out a corresponding moan of pleasure. It was only a small, shallow cut. But blood welled from the wound and began to drip down Rune's abdomen.

'You're so beautiful when you bleed,' she managed to say, her vision blurred with tears. Unable to keep her fingers from him any longer, she pulled herself to a sitting position.

Rune watched through a haze of lust as she reached out, drawing her fingers across the line of blood. She had never understood why it made her breath catch, why violence had always been tangled with lust in her mind. All her life, she had seen it as a problem, a strange mistake of nature.

But Rune didn't seem to mind. On the contrary, when she glanced down, she saw a wet stain on his breeches, where his hardness strained against the leather. His breath hitched when she bent to kiss the wound; he moaned softly at the back of his throat.

The knowledge that he would hurt himself for her, to feed her strange yearning for his surrender, his lifeblood sticky on her fingers and wetting her teeth, was almost enough to make her come.

He was going to *ruin* her. Her head spun with arousal.

Hot blood coated her fingers. She pressed the heel of her other hand to Rune's erection, sighing with satisfaction at the desperate little sound he made. It was infinitely intoxicating, Rune's willingness to do this with her, to bleed for her. Once, they had been at each other's throats. Once, they had been enemies.

They were enemies no longer, though the spilling of blood remained.

And now, Elma realized, with a spark of clarity, that the bloodletting was a promise. Mutually assured tenderness. Elma knew then, the tang of Rune's blood filling her senses, that she could have opened her chest and shown her beating heart to him, and he would not harm it. Instead, he would light her from within, melting away the years of cold and ice until she was herself again.

'If you don't remove my breeches in the next two seconds,' Rune said, voice shaking slightly, 'I'm going to die.'

'If you die,' Elma said breathlessly, reaching for the fastening, 'I'll follow you into the after and drag you back here.'

'Elma,' he murmured, and kissed her with teeth and tongue, making the removal of his breeches even more difficult.

When, at last, he was free of his clothes, Rune set about dealing with Elma's dress. It was a more complex affair, but Rune's fingers were surely made, Elma thought, to remove her garments and toss them on the floor. As he unlaced her bodice, he kissed her neck, murmuring in her ears. He ran his hands up her thighs, brushing her stomach with his fingers, and as the last of the dress came off, he kissed each of her breasts with a hungry mouth.

She gasped at the sensation, wanting him desperately. His body heat scorched her skin as they lay back on the bed, and he braced himself on his elbows, skin against skin. His blood, already drying, clung sticky to her breasts and stomach. His erection pressed to her lower belly, and this time, it was her turn to feel like dying.

'Please,' she said, opening her mouth to him, allowing him to engulf her, arching her back against the bed to grind her hips against him.

Groaning, he slid a hand underneath her body, lifting her to meet him. He adjusted himself to hover at her entrance, pressing, teasing. She wasn't about to let him do this to her, not again. Elma wrapped her legs around his waist and, with a well-practiced leverage of weight and movement, rolled him onto his back.

He let out a breathless laugh, eyes bright with amusement and lust. He was so clearly happy to be controlled by her, to let her command him. Before he could react further, Elma lowered herself onto his hard cock, almost painfully slowly, until he was deep inside her. He filled her so perfectly, and Elma had to bite her lip to muffle her choked moans of pleasure.

Rune's eyes fluttered shut as he tilted his head back into the mattress as if in agony. His fingers fisted in the blankets as he said, voice taut, 'God, Elma, if you don't start moving, I'll –'

'You'll what?' she said and rolled her hips ever so slightly.

In response, he bit his lip so hard that a pinprick of blood appeared there. 'Never mind,' he managed, his breaths coming shallow and fast.

Elma loved the way he looked spread out beneath her, his flushed tan skin, the needy lust in his expression. She loved the way he felt inside her as she rocked against him slowly, riding, savoring the tightly building pleasure.

'I'm going to come if you're not careful,' Rune said after a few moments, his voice hoarse and utterly wrung out.

Elma's own pleasure was threatening to reach its peak, the tightness between her legs growing sharper, more urgent. She sped the motion of her hips, angling herself to allow him even deeper, grinding harder. As she did, she leaned down and delicately licked Rune's open wound.

As she had hoped, this was his breaking point. And as he lost himself, growling Elma's name as he came, she, too, fell over the edge, almost destroyed by the sheer magnitude of their shared pleasure.

When, at last, they came down to Earth again, they stared at one another, breathing hard.

'That was . . .' Rune said, breathing hard, his chest heaving and sweat-slick.

Elma only smiled and kissed him.

They fell asleep curled up together on the bed. When Elma woke in the middle of the night to pull the blankets over them, she paused, studying Rune's face, gentle in repose. A coil of undeniable warmth grew in her chest. This was what it felt like, then, to bloom unharmed in a frozen wasteland. This was softness and trust.

The next morning, Elma woke to news of the Rothen army camped on Slödava's doorstep. *Her* army. Though she wondered if the use of her banner was only some half-hearted attempt by Godwin to sow confusion and resentment between her and the Slödavans. This was his force of arms, not Elma's, no matter who wore the crown.

Queen Hildegard called Elma and Rune to one of the palace's great towers, which afforded a view of the city spread out below them, the pale Frozen Sea beyond. Clustered at the edges of the sea, dotted with rising columns of smoke and tiny tents with flags of green and gold, was the Rothen army. From here, it looked like a plague of vermin, scratching at the doors.

But Elma knew better. Those were trained warriors, many of them since boyhood. To fight and to die for one's kingdom . . . there could be no better fate.

'He can't be planning to lay siege to the city,' Elma said. 'Your scouts were right – no ballistae. Perhaps he isn't quite the brash fool I thought he was. He came here to intimidate. He still thinks he can win me over.'

'Or the siege weapons are still a day's ride out,' Rune mused.

'It doesn't matter,' Elma said.

Queen Hildegard wordlessly handed Elma a steaming cup of coffee from the breakfast tray. Food and drink had been brought up by the servants, but Elma found herself unable to eat. Her gut would not stop roiling. Delicately, she sipped her coffee, peering out over the rim of her cup to regard the army below.

'He'll be waiting for you,' Rune said. 'Do you still plan to go and speak to him? You know I'd happily creep into his tent and slit his throat if that's what you want.'

'*Rune*,' Hildegard said sharply, directing a look at her son.

He held up his hands in mock surrender. 'I never said it would be *honorable*. But war is war.'

'He hasn't declared war yet,' Elma said, imagining that if she stared hard enough, she might be able to make out Godwin's individual tent in the scattered mass on the ice.

'That's not entirely his call to make,' said Hildegard. 'I hate to be reactionary, but the Rothen army sitting at my doorstep feels distinctly like an aggression.'

Elma sighed deeply, setting down her coffee. She turned to Rune and Hildegard. 'It's time.'

Rune nodded, a terse, businesslike dip of the chin. He was already in his assassin's gear, sword at his waist. 'I'll meet you below,' he said, and took his leave.

Only the queens remained.

'Elma,' Hildegard said, her delicate brows furrowed, 'Lord Godwin is as likely to gut you as he is to hug you. There's no need to put yourself at risk. My men are more than capable of dispatching him, should that be your wish. Just . . . not Rune. He's seen enough violence.'

It was painfully tempting. Elma bit her lip, knowing she couldn't accept. Godwin might still have some explanation. Perhaps this was all a misunderstanding. And while Elma knew in her heart of hearts that it wasn't, that her uncle had betrayed her, she couldn't make the call to have him eliminated. Despite herself, she still loved him.

'Thank you, Hildegard,' Elma said, bowing her head in deference. 'But it's unnecessary. I'll have Rune by my side.'

The other queen's lips formed a tight line. 'He has few weaknesses, my son. But you are one of them. I'd rather you both came back from this in one piece.'

Elma softened. 'I will do all I can to ensure his safety.'

'I wish it were within your power alone,' said Hildegard. 'Treachery opens up a world of dishonor to those who embrace it. Do not underestimate your uncle's capacity for ruthlessness.'

While Elma knew that Hildegard spoke truthfully, the words caught bitterly at her, thorn-like. She understood, now, why treachery was such an abhorrent crime, punishable by death. It was a violation of the heart, and those subjected to it would bear the injury for a lifetime.

35

Rune took Elma aside at the stables, where they waited for their horses to be saddled. Pulling her into a shadowy corner, he wound his arms around her waist and held her against him as if he could save her from death.

'Elma,' he said, breath steaming in the cold air, 'you don't have to do this. The danger is unimaginable. You'd stand alone against an army. If they decide to end you . . .'

'I am the queen of Rothen,' she said, taking his face in her hands. For the first time since coming to Slödava, she felt as if Rune needed her reassurance more than she needed his. 'I have made my choice.'

She pressed a slow, sweet kiss to his mouth, tasting the wound his teeth had made the night before. He leaned into her, like water forming against the shape of a shore. Pulling back, she studied his beloved face – his slightly drawn brows, downturned mouth, the gorgeous white scar that lanced jagged across his eye.

'And I won't be alone,' she said.

Rune smiled wanly. 'And you never will if I've anything to say about it.'

She wished he wouldn't say such things, not if he didn't mean them. Not if he couldn't stand by them. But Elma pushed the thoughts away, focusing on the image of her uncle, hard-eyed and waiting, somewhere in that army on the ice.

The ride through Slödava, with Rune at her side, was interminable. The streets were packed with frightened city dwellers, gossipers, and soldiers. The energy seemed to vibrate with anxiety. The Rothen army had, at least according to Elma's education, never come to Slödava in such force.

But perhaps that, too, had been a lie.

'What are you going to say to Godwin?' Rune asked as they approached the massive city gates. He glanced at her, hair blowing over his eyes.

'I don't know,' she said.

I don't know.

Rune smiled with encouragement, and she was glad that he was with her.

As they passed through the gates, Elma saw that the army had set up camp a significant distance from the walls. This meant that she and Rune had to ride alone across a wide stretch of ice, clear targets for any arrow that sought to find them. But no projectiles came streaking out of the sky, and when they were close enough to see the faces of individual men sitting around campfires, a lone rider came out to greet them.

At first, Elma didn't recognize him.

Only about a week had passed since her departure from the Frost Citadel, yet it seemed as if everything had changed. The man approaching on horseback, resplendent in shining armor and bright heraldry, a warrior out of legend, was Godwin.

He came to a halt not far from them, though a distance remained. A clear indication of where they stood, who they now were to one another.

'Hello, Uncle,' Elma said, her voice clear in the morning air. 'I see you brought an army to join me in my bid for peace. How unique.'

Godwin's grin was bright, white teeth shining against his gray-flecked beard. 'I see you brought your Slödavan prince plaything to meet with me. How quaint.'

A spiky anger lodged itself in Elma, along with something worse: How did he know that Rune was the prince? 'Let's not play games, Uncle. I came to speak with you.'

'So, speak. Unless you have something to say that the men of Rothen cannot hear?'

Elma pursed her lips. Godwin knew exactly how to put her on edge. 'I appreciate your desire for candor, but I must reject it. As your queen, you'll do as I say. Unless . . . you believe you've accomplished something with all of this?' She waved her hand to indicate the army.

'They're loyal to me,' said Godwin.

Rune let out a muffled snort.

'Either we speak in private,' Elma said, growing impatient, the anger in her growing large and thorny, 'or I withdraw and allow the Slödavan army to crush you, as is their right under the circumstances.'

Godwin knew it as well as Elma – his encroachment on the Slödavan land was a declaration of war. Only Elma stood between him and an all-out slaughter on the Frozen Sea, and if Rune was right, his siege weapons were not here.

Godwin shrugged, a careless gesture. 'Very well,' he said. With a wave of one hand, he turned and rode back to the encampment.

Rune and Elma followed. Elma wanted to share a glance

with Rune, to seek his reassurance just as much as she yearned to reassure him. But to do so would show weakness, and she knew her men – no, Godwin's men – were watching.

When they came to Godwin's tent, an attendant took the horses while Godwin led them inside. A fire burned in a brazier at the center, and the small enclosure was lined with rugs and furs. A few chairs were arranged around the fire, and near the back of the tent stood a table, piled high with books and parchments.

'Sit,' said Godwin, indicating the chairs. He settled himself in one, kicking one leg out in front of him.

Elma sat primly, her back straight, hands folded in her lap. Rune practically stalked to his chair and hunched there, eyes blazing, an attack dog ready to lunge. Elma was glad of his presence.

'So,' Godwin said, leaning back in his chair and propping his elbow on the armrest, chin resting on fist. 'Where do we begin?'

'I suppose,' said Elma, 'we ought to start with you explaining why you've chosen to betray the Crown. It's unlike you, Uncle.'

'Is it?' he said, deep lines forming between his brows. 'I have always been loyal to Rothen. That hasn't changed. The Crown is a symbol, nothing more. I am beholden to the people, the land, the legacy. And you, dear niece, have polluted our legacy.'

'Polluted?' Elma exclaimed, unable to contain her anger. 'I've done nothing but what my father asked of me. I am a Volta. The legacy is *mine* to carry on, not yours.'

'And yet you allow the enemy prince to share your bed,' Godwin said carelessly, not so much as glancing at Rune.

'That is irrelevant,' Elma bit out. She knew it wasn't. How had her uncle discovered Rune's true identity? The truth of their relationship?

Godwin's jaw clenched. 'It is an aberration.'

'And this is why you've declared war on Slödava?' Elma said, incredulous. 'A war you can't possibly win?'

A cruel light glinted in Godwin's eyes. 'Will you not ask how I've discovered the truth of your conspiracy?'

Anger no longer nestled in Elma's chest; it consumed her, a roaring fire. 'I made him my bodyguard because I feared for my life in Rothen. And clearly, I was right to do so. I had no idea Rune was the Crown Prince of Slödava until we arrived here. The only conspiracy to discuss is yours.'

'Hmm,' said Godwin, rubbing his bearded chin against curled fingers. His hands were large and square, like King Rafe's, and like so many of the men of Rothen, as unyielding as the mountains. 'That's not what Hugh told me.'

Elma's anger, so bright and loud, turned suddenly to ice. *Hugh.* But he was in the palace, he was –

'Don't look so shocked,' said Godwin, seeing Elma's obvious surprise. 'Did you truly think he would so easily betray his kingdom for you and this princeling? That he would not make every effort to come to me, the moment he was given a chance?'

It was as if Elma had swallowed a boulder. Her men had been given permission to move freely throughout Slödava. It would have been no trouble at all for Hugh to slip past guards, to make his way out to the Frozen Sea.

You should have seen this coming, Elma thought. But there was no use berating herself now.

'My presence here is simply a warning,' said Godwin, continuing as if he hadn't just sunk a blade hilt-deep into Elma's metaphorical spine. Then he leaned forward, elbows on his knees, hands clasped. He regarded Elma with a sharp but careful gaze. 'You are within your power to stop a war. There's still time, Elma. You haven't lost Rothen. Not yet, not entirely.'

'Rothen is mine by blood and by the law of the land,' Elma said between gritted teeth. 'You have no right to take it from me.'

'And yet.'

Rune remained silent throughout the exchange, perfectly still. Elma wondered what he thought of her, of Godwin. Had Slödava ever been so messy? So rife with intra-family politics?

'And yet what,' said Elma, raising a brow, 'you commit treason?'

'None who are loyal to the kingdom of Rothen would stand against me. It is you who have strayed, *Your Majesty*.' He spat the words as if they were an insult. 'It's nothing personal, Niece. It's not my place to tell you whose prick to open up for, but as queen –'

There was a sudden movement to the left of Elma, and Rune held a knife in one hand. He spun it casually, his head tilted slightly. 'Speak like that again,' he said softly, 'and you'll lose an eye.'

Godwin huffed a sarcastic laugh. 'Leash your dog more tightly, Niece. He's embarrassing you. I know you're a rational woman. You learned from the best. But there's a streak of softness in you, no doubt absorbed in Mekya and yet to leave your system. Such things, fortunately for you, can be fixed. But that would take time, and time is one thing your people don't have. Do you see these men all around you? They rode here for their families, for the future of Rothen.'

'That is why I came,' Elma ground out, barely able to refrain from grabbing Rune's knife and plunging it into her uncle's face herself. 'Slödava engages in active trade with Navenie and Mekya while Rothen rots between them, too violent and unpredictable for anyone to trade with. How is a war going to –'

'You know nothing about it,' Godwin spat, cutting her off. 'You're practically a child. Your father and I have given our lives to Rothen, bled and labored for the future of its people. You do not need to yoke yourself to the weak-lings of the north. With Rime Ice firmly in the hands of the Queen of Rothen, we could bend anyone to our will.'

Elma took a slow breath. 'I do not wish to bend anyone to my will,' she said quietly. 'If we make peace with Slödava, there's a chance that they, and other kingdoms, will open trade with us. We don't need Rime Ice if we're not at war.'

'That is idealism,' said her uncle, leaning back again in his chair, eyes narrowed. 'Something I thought your father would have warned you against.'

'I've met with the Queen of Slödava,' Elma continued, determined to salvage this rift that was ever widening between her and Godwin. 'She and Prince Rune welcomed me as a guest. They could have held me as a hostage, but they didn't. Is that idealism? Or are you too stubborn to see that your way of doing this, my father's way, is old and decrepit?'

It was the wrong thing to say. Godwin's countenance

grew stony, and Elma knew then that she had widened the gap between them, perhaps permanently. 'I have not slept soundly,' he said quietly, eyes fixed on Elma, 'since ordering your death. The poisoning, the disguised Slödavan . . . even that barely competent creature your toy made easy work of. I lay awake in the small hours, wondering if I'd done the right thing. If you might be a great queen after all, if only you could divert your path and return to the one laid out for you by your father. A conqueror's path, one fit for a queen of Rothen.' He sighed and shook his head.

Elma sat frozen as the words sunk in. Her fingers curled slowly into fists, grasping at the wool of her skirts.

'Volta means power,' Godwin continued. 'Steadfastness. But you insisted on capitulation. I had no choice.'

'I should have you gutted slowly,' Elma murmured, her voice hoarse. 'I should have your body hung from the battlements in pieces.'

Her uncle shrugged. 'Perhaps. But the time for that has passed. Your people stand with me, not you. There's one choice for you now, one chance to reclaim your birthright, Elma Volta.' He held out his hand, palm upward, and lay it on his knee. An offering. 'Join me under the Godwin banner. Give up this silly dream of peace.'

Elma didn't have to look at Rune to know that he was seething. He radiated ire, practically vibrating with all the strength it took not to silence Godwin, once and for all. Elma understood. She felt the same. But more than rage, she was overcome with grief. Godwin had been like a father to her when hers was too busy with his duties as king. He had trained her in combat, offered advice, shown her what it meant to be the Volta heir.

But Godwin had never seen her as a loved one, a child, a girl who needed love and support. He had seen her as a figurehead, a bloodline, the wearer of a crown. Perhaps she had always felt it, in the practiced distance between them. The way his eyes glazed over when she spoke about her favorite pastimes, how easily he dismissed her when she simply needed someone to talk to.

Even with Godwin's pale sort of love, Elma thought, studying her uncle's craggy face, *I was alone. Always alone.*

And she could go back to that if she wanted to. He was giving her a choice. She would sit upon the throne of Rothen, an island, her heart frostbitten and black. But at her right hand would be Godwin, her once beloved uncle. And she would have a chance, finally, to rule her people with as much compassion, love, and fairness as she could manage under Godwin's warlike shadow.

But in making such a choice, Elma would be condoning a war and making an enemy of Slödava. An enemy of Queen Hildegard, who had shown her kindness. And Rune, who was her assassin. Her prince. Her beloved.

Could she ever truly shed the Volta destiny? What if she chose Rune? She thought. What if she chose the intangible thing that shone between them, the fragile care that might grow into something even more – and what if she broke it? With her clumsy hands, her bloody fingers. She was just as liable to break love as to embrace it.

At last, she turned to Rune. He was watching her, his eyes shining in the firelight. She realized that she had never asked him how he had learned to cope, as a child, learning that he might one day be destined to sit on a throne. 'No matter what you choose,' Rune said, 'I cannot fault you.'

Elma's chest ached. Her hands were clammy, the fire too hot.

'Godwin,' she said, controlling the waver in her voice as best she could, 'you have admitted to committing treason against the Crown. Were I more like the late King Rafe, I'd have you executed here and now. But I'm not my father.' She stood then, and Rune, ever her shadow, did the same.

Her uncle remained seated, one finger tapping at his knee.

'I'll spare your life,' Elma said, 'on one condition. You'll agree to open negotiations with Slödava on the subject of peace between our nations. If you refuse, your life becomes forfeit. You have until sundown today. I await your decision.'

She spun on her heel, not waiting to see how her uncle would react, no matter how her heart seemed to break and bleed within her, no matter how every cell in her body said to stay, to make things right again. She was finished arguing with him. And she could not give up on her kingdom, not now. Not like this. All she could do was act as a queen would and see how the bones scattered.

A sound of warning came from Rune and was cut off.

Before Elma could turn to see what had startled him, he slumped to the floor, a bloody gash at his temple. She froze in horror, unable to look away. She had misjudged her uncle's sense of honor.

Godwin wasted no time. He stepped easily over Rune, taking full advantage of Elma's shock. She was unarmed, swathed in furs and a heavy gown. She attempted to block him as he came for her, but it was no use. She had been utterly outplayed and was outmatched in strength and speed.

In a flash, Godwin had both of her arms twisted behind her. 'I gave you a chance,' he said, and he sounded almost sad. 'I would have followed you, had you only been more like your father.'

Then he barked a command, and the tent flap opened, and in a moment, the place was swarming with soldiers. Rothen soldiers. Elma's men.

She grit her teeth, too enraged to cry, though her heart was breaking. She had failed.

'Secure the Slödavan prince. Put him in one of the wagons,' said Godwin, handing her off to one of the soldiers. 'Tie the traitor queen's hands, but leave her with me. She and I depart for Frost within the hour.'

36

Elma was allowed to ride alongside Lord Godwin, and her hands were freed accordingly. Rune had been loaded into a supply wagon that now served as a traveling jail, but Elma was not permitted to go near him. And within the first few hours of riding, they lost sight of the wagon behind them, its small retinue of guards fading into the snow-lashed landscape.

The last Elma had seen of Rune, he had still been unconscious, his hair matted and red where it stuck to the wound on his head.

'If he dies,' she had said, her voice thick with blood and spit, 'I'll rip the flesh from your body with my bare hands and shove it down your throat.'

Godwin had only chuckled and left her in the hands of his men while he'd prepared their horses to ride out. Elma hadn't bothered trying to reason with the soldiers. None of them were known to her by name, a failing which fell all the harder on her heart when she realized that, had she gone out of her way to get to know them, to earn their loyalty, perhaps she wouldn't be their prisoner now.

But it was too late to try to turn any of them now. The army remained camped on the ice at Slödava, waiting for the arrival of Godwin's siege weapons. And when those were within range of the city, all-out war would break out.

And once Elma and Rune were back in Frost, made examples of before the people of the kingdom, Elma was certain that the desire for war within Rothen would boil to a frenzy. They would see Elma as a traitor queen, a Slödafucker who cared nothing for her kingdom.

Nausea, a persistent headache, and a writhing fear for Rune's safety were Elma's companions as she and her uncle rode, mostly silently, across the Frozen Sea.

At least she was allowed to ride, she weakly consoled herself. She would have been miserable inside a wagon or carriage, not knowing where she was, unable to breathe the air. She had briefly contemplated escape, but where would she go? Back to Slödava, where an army waited to arrest her? Or forward to Rothen, where she'd be welcomed in kind? There was no hope of running off into the frozen landscape – such a move would only end in death.

Her thoughts often went to Queen Hildegard. She wondered what the woman was thinking, back in her tower. Did she assume Elma had betrayed her? There was no reason to think otherwise. Elma was a Volta, after all. For all Hildegard knew, it took more than a few romps in the bed to turn a Queen of Rothen against her own uncle.

The thought of it made Elma's blood curdle, her stomach writhe and knot.

'Stop twisting the reins,' said her uncle, glancing sideways at her across the ice. 'You'll confuse the horse.'

Elma said nothing.

They had been riding all day, and dusk was beginning to fall. They would camp on the ice that night.

When the sun was nearly below the horizon, Rune's carriage and guard contingent caught up to them. Tents were quickly erected, and Godwin himself escorted her to her tent – private but hemmed in on all sides by guards. She turned to her uncle. 'Let me see him,' she said, the words falling out despite herself. 'I need to know he's alive.'

'You have my word that he is,' Godwin said icily.

'And I have no reason to trust you,' Elma shot back.

For a moment, she thought he might relent. That the human part of him, perhaps some remnant of softness in his heart, would allow him to buckle just once. Just for one small thing. But his expression hardened. His jaw worked as if he might say something more, but at last, her uncle shook his head and turned away.

Elma stood there for a moment, wondering again if she ought to make a run for it. If she could just get to Rune, if he was safe . . . if the wound hadn't been as bad as it looked . . .

But soldiers stood all around her, most regarding her with outright hostility, and the rest ignoring her as if she were nothing. As if she were vermin, skittering through camp.

'Into the tent, Slödafucker,' said the nearest soldier.

As if struck, Elma's breath caught. She ducked inside her tent, hot with shame and anger. These were her men, her army, and her own uncle had reduced her to nothing but a disgrace.

Or have you reduced yourself? came her traitorous thoughts. *Rune is just one man, a man who came to kill you. How do you know he and his mother weren't manipulating you?*

Her mind was at odds with itself, accusing and jagged with self-loathing. Elma curled up on her furs, fully dressed, and allowed herself to cry. Just one tear, a hot, pathetic thing, but even that felt like poison sucked from a wound.

Sleep came slowly, and when it did, it was fitful. Her dreams were nightmarish, painted red with death and gore, full of broken hearts and disembodied heads. When she awoke the next morning, just before light, Elma washed her face with snow. She straightened her skirts and arranged her hair; she pulled herself together and strode tall to join her uncle at the head of the traveling party.

Slödafucker or not, she was Elma Volta, queen to her last breath.

Godwin was oddly talkative that morning. They had ridden the first few hours in silence, Elma sullenly chewing dried meats, when Godwin began to point things out in the landscape.

'That peak in the distance, the one by itself, do you see? A temple sits atop the thing. Madness, I always thought, but the ancient religions are nothing if not ridiculous. I went there once. It was cold, though inside the temple, a raging fire burns and never goes out.'

'Which deity presides there?' Elma asked, interested despite herself.

'Mm, I can't remember. A strange one. Fasta, or Fleet, or something.'

Elma didn't reply, but a few minutes later, Godwin pointed out another mountain, this time some sort of remnant of a centuries-old volcanic eruption. She listened reluctantly, hating how much it hurt to ride alongside him, to hear him speak as if things were the same as they'd ever been. As if she was simply his niece, and he was beloved Uncle Godwin.

A lump rose in her throat, and she tried to swallow it

down with brute stubbornness. There was no going back from this. He had betrayed her; hurt her in ways that no one had ever managed to hurt her before. He had cut her from sternum to naval, reached inside, and pulled out her organs. She was an empty shell.

And she wanted the same for him. She wanted to twist every knife available to her.

'Uncle,' Elma said abruptly, when he was in the middle of waxing poetic about the glacier that used to occupy the very sea they rode on, 'you know your quest for Rime Ice is doomed, right?'

'Is it?' he said, uncaring. Elma knew he would see this as a desperate last-ditch effort to set him off-balance.

'Do you even know what it really is?' she asked, glancing at him as she spoke to make sure the words hit home.

Godwin's look was sidelong. 'Let me guess. You claim to know and hope to manipulate me in some way with this knowledge. It won't work.'

Elma shrugged. 'I just thought you ought to know, before you send innocents to death in service of your pointless war, there is no Rime Ice to steal. They don't forge the blades from some ancient glacier or whatever the legends say. The weapons are magic.'

'The same thing.'

'No,' said Elma, 'it's not. Only monarchs, or those with royal blood, can call it forth. But it's not an object, you can't simply *take* it and use it for your own purposes. This war will be your ruin, Uncle. If you take Slödava, you'll have nothing but a mountain of corpses to call your own.'

She didn't know what exactly she meant to accomplish with this truth. Perhaps if her uncle realized that what he pursued didn't exist after all, he'd give up on the aggression with Slödava. If he believed her at all.

Godwin was silent for a moment, his brow creased. Then he turned to her at last, and said, 'You believe I have but one goal in mind, one aim. I was wrong. You're very like your father, but in the worst way. You miss the bigger picture. War is money, it is power. It is glory. You're short-sighted in the extreme if you believe that the nature of Rime Ice will keep me from the battlefield or stop me from using it.'

Elma nodded, a silent acknowledgment. *Fine, then. Let him be cut down on the Frozen Sea.* She was done reasoning with a warmonger.

The Frost Citadel had never looked less welcoming. A heavy, dark sky hung behind it, blackening the stone with deep shadows. Thick snow began to fall as they rode up the winding ascent to what had once been Elma's home. It felt like a prison to her now, more than it ever had. An isolation sentence that would carry on through life and, if she was unlucky, beyond.

Her rooms were exactly as she'd left them over a week ago. A stray, fur-lined glove lay draped on one of the chairs by the fire, which roared brightly in the hearth. A small pile of books sat on the table by her bed. Snow fell in soft, heavy flakes outside the window.

Standing alone there, still in her traveling clothes, Elma couldn't stop the tears from burning in her eyes. It was as if nothing had changed. Yet outside her door stood a ret-inue of guards, ordered not to keep her safe, but to keep her on a short leash. She was no longer free. She was no longer a queen. In a day's time, or in a week, however long it took for the paperwork to be drawn up, Elma would be ousted from the throne and executed publicly.

Disgraced queens did not die peacefully.

No one would give her any news of Rune. He was taboo, as if speaking his name might strike down the speaker. Her guards were utterly useless. She wondered, vaguely, had Luca been there, whether he would have answered her, spoken kindly to her. But Luca was dead. She couldn't bear to think what might become of her few remaining men if they had stayed behind in the Slödavan palace. They were hostages or prisoners now, undoubtedly.

When she had changed into her warmest robes, her furriest slippers – at least her clothes were all still intact – Elma retrieved her seven candles from their drawer. She arranged them by the fire, one by one, and lit them. When at last her mind was clear, she asked them: *Are my men safe?*

Breathing in the pungent smoke, her eyes closed, she listened to the snap of dark wicks, inhaling the candles' wisdom. When she opened her eyes, the smoke trailed upward like narrow ghosts. But no messages lay within, and no comfort came.

'They'll be all right,' she said aloud, wrapping the candles in twine, tucking them away. She would have done anything to see her mothers, to speak to them just then. But she wouldn't be allowed to write them or send for them. Not even for her execution.

37

Two days passed in utter isolation. Elma had lost the will to be angry; the rage deep within her could no longer be stoked, weighed down by her despair. She couldn't look her guards in the eye. Their whispers were sharp, their gazes hateful. And when she asked after Godwin, or the rest of the advisors, she was given blank stares.

Not knowing was the worst of it.

So when the knock came on the third day, late in the morning, Elma assumed it would be her summons to the execution. Death, now, came as a welcome relief.

But it was only Cora in the doorway, pale and wide-eyed. Her fingers twisted together, and she swallowed as if words caught unsaid in her throat.

Elma stared. 'You,' she said. Her rage flickered weakly, a distant light in the dark.

Cora paled further. 'Please, Your Majesty. I see in your eyes that you know what I've done. But . . . I need to speak with you.'

A great exhaustion fell over Elma. What could Cora possibly have to say that hadn't been said already by Godwin, by the guards at Elma's door? But . . . Elma hesitated. The maid had addressed her as Your Majesty. Perhaps a habit not easily shed, or perhaps she was still, incomprehensibly, loyal despite everything.

'I would speak with my maid alone,' Elma said, addressing the guard just outside her door.

He frowned, his expression stony.

'If I'm going to die,' Elma added, 'you may as well let me bid farewell to the one person who still deigns to speak with me.'

The guard sighed. 'Five minutes.'

He searched Cora for weapons before she was allowed inside, which struck Elma as vaguely funny. She doubted Cora had ever carried a knife on her in her life, let alone spirited one to her queen. And if she did have a weapon, it would be destined for Elma's heart, not her hand.

When Cora was at last declared clean and allowed to enter Elma's rooms, she closed the door behind her carefully, still fidgeting as if she didn't know where to put her hands, where to look.

Elma settled herself in a chair by the fire, not caring what Cora did or said. If she had something to convey, she could do it in the next five minutes, or not. More likely than not, her attendant had come under the weight of her own conscience and desired to shed what remaining guilt she carried after betraying her queen. If it would ease the girl's life, then so be it. Elma would listen.

After a moment of strained silence, though, Cora came around to stand before Elma. And before Elma could stop her, the attendant knelt before her once-queen, bowed her head, and pressed her forehead to Elma's knees.

'Forgive me,' she said, her voice low and muffled.

Was she crying? Elma couldn't understand.

'Forgive me,' Cora said again, and again. Her words came as a chant, a prayer of absolution. 'I didn't mean to.'

Elma gently laid a hand on Cora's head. 'It's no use begging for forgiveness from me now,' she said. 'I'm already dead, just as you wanted.'

Cora sat up, her eyes wet with tears, her face stricken. 'Lord Godwin promised to reinstate my father's title if I . . . helped him. I was afraid. There's hardly any food, even with my brother's work. Trade has dried up. We needed –'

'I understand,' Elma interrupted. 'A queen in exchange for your family's survival.'

A tear ran down Cora's cheek.

'It's my own fault,' Elma said, looking away. 'I saw you as a friend. An equal. I was naive, and you were desperate.'

'You've always been so generous . . .'

Elma scoffed. 'Generous? I gave you a few trinkets here and there, thinking a necklace would keep you fed. Keep you thriving in this rotten kingdom. I was more concerned for my own safety than the needs of my people. I would have tried to kill me, too.'

Cora wiped her face with her hands, sniffling. 'You couldn't have known.'

'Get up,' Elma said, 'stop kneeling. It's awkward for both of us.'

Wordlessly, Cora got to her feet and went to the other chair, settling herself on the very edge of it as if she couldn't risk the comfort.

'I did know,' Elma said, gazing into the fire. 'I knew your family struggled. I knew, factually, distantly, that many families in Rothen were struggling. I was aware of the state of our trade with Navenie and Mekya. But it was all numbers to me, you see. Words from the mouths of my advisors. I didn't truly understand the situation until the parade before my coronation, and by then, anything in my power was too little too late.' She sighed, speaking as much to herself as to Cora. 'I never made the effort in those seven years, never set myself up to be a good queen. I cared only for myself, how lonely I was, how much I yearned for a life that had never truly been mine.'

'You mean Mekya.'

Elma nodded. 'It was easier for me to ignore the weight of my responsibilities if I believed they were wrong for me. That somehow, I might avoid them if I tried hard enough.'

'And you feel differently now?'

'Yes,' said Elma, the admission raw on her tongue. 'Now that it's far, far too late.'

Cora caught Elma's gaze. 'I am truly sorry for what I did.'

'I know,' Elma said. 'I understand why you did it.'

A sad smile caught at Cora's lips. 'There's another reason I came to you. Rune.'

Fear, and a pale hope, sliced through Elma's gut. She tensed, expecting the worst. 'What of him?'

Cora leaned toward her as if worried the guards outside might overhear. 'He's alive. They're keeping him in the dungeon, which shouldn't be a surprise to you. And I overheard the men talking. Lord Godwin and the rest. They mean to have him executed in the arena.'

'Again?' Elma said, clutching the arms of her chair so tightly her fingers ached.

'Since it didn't take last time . . .' Cora shrugged, her eyes sad. 'I thought you'd want to know.'

'Thank you,' Elma said, the words coming from a mouth so far away she hardly heard herself. 'When?'

'If I heard right, tomorrow.'

'I see.' Elma swallowed, forcing down what felt like a lump of glassy ice until the feeling sat heavy in her stomach.

Cora said goodbye then and drifted out of the room with a bowed head and watery eyes. Elma hardly noticed. Rune was still alive. By sundown tomorrow, he'd be dead. She had known they shared this fate, knew it was only a matter of time, but to have heard it from the lips of someone else somehow made the horror cut sharper. A ghost weapon made solid.

Elma went to the door again, catching the eye of the nearest guard. 'I need to go to the dungeon,' she said, as firmly as she could manage.

The guard raised an eyebrow. 'Planning to collude with your lover?'

'I wish only to say goodbye.' The words felt like jagged glass tumbling across her tongue, hurting and hurting.

'I think not,' said the guard.

An older guard, only a few feet away, turned to his colleague. 'They're bound for the chopping block,' he said. 'May as well have a little pity.'

'Pity,' said the first guard, incredulous, 'for a traitor queen?'

The other shrugged. 'Doesn't hurt us any. Could use a change of scenery, if I'm honest.'

'Fine,' grumbled the guard. 'For you, not for her.'

'Cheers,' said the other guard, peeling away from the wall. 'Come along then, Majesty.' He colored. 'I mean . . .'

She waited, not caring what they called her, as long as they brought her to Rune.

'Slödafucker,' said the first guard, smirking cruelly. 'That's her name.'

'Elma,' said the second guard, avoiding her gaze. 'Come along.'

Five guards in total escorted Elma to the dungeon. It was overkill in the extreme – she was no Slödavan assassin – but she knew Godwin would not take any risks. He had taught her the art of combat himself, after all, and knew her abilities well.

She was allowed to go into the dungeon alone, with only one of the dungeon guards accompanying her. Her retinue stayed at the top of the narrow stairs, knowing there was nowhere else to go from the dungeon but up.

Her way lit dimly by the guard's torch, Elma made her way to Rune's cell. Nothing had changed since the last time she'd been there, when Rune was nothing but an enemy. Even then, what felt like lifetimes ago, Elma had been drawn to him. His wild eyes, the cruel curve of his lips.

Had she ever truly hated him? Or was hatred so close to some other emotion, some clench of the heart, that it had been all too easy to fall?

At last, they came to the final cell in the row, and Elma bit back a small gasp that might have been a sob. Rune was hunched in the corner of his cell, hair falling over his face, his head hanging in defeat. The tang of blood, sweat, and misery assaulted Elma's nose. She couldn't see in the light, but Rune was undoubtedly covered in bruises and abrasions. Godwin would have seen to that.

'May I speak with him alone?' Elma asked. The guard narrowed his eyes, but handed her the torch and moved a slight distance away. She was certain he would still hear, but at least she could pretend to be alone with Rune.

At the sound of her voice, Rune stirred. He lifted his head, squinting in the torchlight. At the sight of Elma, his bruised face split into a wavering grin. 'There you are,' he rasped.

'Rune,' Elma said, her voice breaking. 'What has he done to you?'

'Nothing I haven't endured before.'

Elma's heart fell and shattered, scattering like ash on the Frozen Sea. 'You're going to the arena tomorrow,' she said, biting out the words. Her knees felt weak, and she put out a hand to brace herself on the cell bars. She wanted to say something deep and true, something that put her heart into words. But it all clung like a sob to the base of her throat.

'I figured as much,' said Rune. 'They've been roughing me up all day. I'm sure Godwin will stick me in the kidney right before the first fight, just to make sure.'

'Don't say that,' Elma said, words tumbling out like desperation. 'You can still –'

'What,' Rune cut her off. 'Win?' He snorted dismissively. 'There is no winning. I could use Rime Ice to defeat every last one of your arena's heroes, and your uncle would simply put an arrow between my eyes.'

Elma knew he was right. 'He'll force me to watch,' she said. 'He will make me watch you die, and then he'll have me executed in front of the city.'

'You sound resigned,' Rune said. He got slowly to his feet, flinching as he did, and came to lean on the bars. They were only inches apart, but it felt like leagues and leagues.

'Of course I am,' murmured Elma.

'One thing I've never seen in you is resignation.' Rune

curled his fingers over hers, and they were dry, cracked, and caked in blood and dirt. Elma had never felt anything so comforting. 'You're still a queen,' he said, holding her gaze, his eyes bright and rimmed in red.

Elma swallowed hard, the tears at the corners of her eyes, all the words of love, held just below the surface. 'They will strip it from me before the end. Every humiliation will be mine to endure.'

With a soft clang, Rune let his head fall against the bars. 'You would have been a good queen,' he said. 'The best kind of queen. You love your people. My mother saw it in you, just as I do. We could have had peace.'

Tears began to stream down Elma's face. She hadn't wanted to cry. What message would it send? But there was no one left to see it or to care. A soft sob escaped her. 'I'm sorry,' she choked out. 'My trust in the wrong people has doomed us both.'

'You saved me,' Rune breathed, kissing her knuckles. 'I should have died in the arena, all those weeks ago.'

'It was selfishness,' she protested, the words muffled by her tears.

'I don't believe it was,' he said. His gaze caught hers, his eyes clear even in the face of death. 'You're afraid of your compassion. It never fit within the bounds of what your father expected, what you learned. I think your mothers would have saved me, too.' He smiled. 'And I am honored to die as your weapon.'

Elma sobbed, a wracking sound, so small in the echoing black dungeon. 'I don't hate you,' she managed. 'I never did.'

Rune huffed a sad little laugh. 'You never fooled me for a second.'

Then he kissed her through the bars, soft and quiet. And while only their fingers and their lips touched, Elma ached and burned for him like a sun. Her fingers were stars in the night, his mouth a beacon of homecoming.

'None of that!' came the guard's sudden bark. He wrenched Elma away from the cell, away from Rune. 'Time to go, *Your Majesty.*'

Elma wanted to tell him. Her heart ached to say it. *I love you, I love you, I love you.*

'I'll see you,' she said instead, drinking in that last sight of him, his wan smile, the curl of sweaty hair at his ears, the cocky tilt of his head, even now. 'I'll see you in the after.'

He raised one hand in farewell. 'In the after.'

38

That night, Elma was stripped of her crown with little ceremony. She was taken to the throne room, perhaps for the sake of tradition, since she wasn't allowed to sit on the throne, nor was anyone present but her advisors. Godwin had drawn up a document that outlined her offenses, which he read out one by one in a ringing voice.

Treachery against the crown, fraternization with the enemy, collusion against Rothen. The list went on and on.

Listening from where she stood in the center of the great room, Elma allowed her mind to wander. She thought about Lothyn and Orchard House. Was the sun shining there? Perhaps a warm breeze danced through thick green leaves. With any luck, the winds were blowing harshly to the southeast, and her mothers wouldn't hear about her disgrace, or her death, for quite some time.

'Do you contest it?' Godwin's voice was sharp, and Elma realized he had repeated the question.

'No,' she said.

'Very well,' said Godwin. He laid the document on a small table and signed it with a flourish of ink.

'Elma Volta,' said Lord Bertram, clearly relishing every moment of this, 'you are hereby stripped of the crown, which was afforded to you by right of birth. As a result of your treachery, you forfeit the crown of Rothen and your life.'

Elma tensed, thinking she would be expected to speak again and not knowing if she could trust herself to do so over the lump in her throat.

But the ceremony seemed to be over. Godwin rolled up the document, tucking it into a sleeve. He gave Elma a searching, thoughtful look. And then she was taken roughly by her arms and ushered from the room, her retinue of guards in tow. She was no longer the Queen of Rothen. No longer even the traitor queen.

She was simply Elma Volta. And the world felt colder than it ever had.

When dawn crept in the next morning in gray curtains of snow, Elma was already awake. She hadn't slept. Today, she would watch Rune die, and then she, too, would be put down. There was no preparation she could make, no way to quiet the rising tide of panic in her mind. She wished she could at least relax, at least rest, before the grip of eternity took her.

She couldn't stop wondering if it would hurt, the blade through her skin, her muscles and sinews, her spine. Would she feel her head separating from her shoulders? Would she see blood spreading out below her, the last seconds of consciousness blessing her with one final glimpse of violence?

Elma was already dressed when the summons came that she would join Godwin at the Death Games before her execution. She had worn her best, as only seemed right. She would die draped in silks and furs, fit for a woman who had been queen. That, at least, was in her control.

Her guards escorted her out of the Frost Citadel and into a quiet, snowy morning. She wondered if this would be her last glimpse of it. Knowing Godwin, he would have her executed in the arena after the Death Games. What better way to make a spectacle of her and to secure his future as king of Rothen?

Elma wasn't ignorant; she understood that Godwin stood next in line for the throne. But he would not be crowned until after her death, as was the custom. And by that time, Elma's worries would be over.

To her surprise, Elma climbed into her carriage and found that it was already occupied. Godwin sat straight-backed in his lord's regalia, his eyes colder than the sky. Elma wanted to turn around and leave, to request her own carriage, but of course, there was no point. Godwin wanted to ride with her through the city; to gloat 'til the very end. She had seen him behave with pettiness before, but it hadn't occurred to her that it was in his nature to be cruel and boastful.

'What a lovely surprise,' Elma said scathingly as she settled herself across from her uncle. 'Taking my crown in disgrace wasn't enough? Had to get a few additional blades between my ribs as well?'

Godwin made a mirthless exhalation through his nose and tapped his fist on the ceiling. As the carriage lurched forward, he tilted his chin, regarding his niece with narrowed eyes. 'You think I act out of some personal vendetta rather than the good of the nation.'

'The uncle I thought I knew would have trusted me,' she said, her throat tight. 'Of the two of us, I would have thought I'd be the bloodthirsty one. The heartless one.'

'Instead, you were weak,' he said as if this were a regrettable fact of nature. 'I advised your father against sending you away to those women in Mekya. I knew their tender-hearted notions would pollute you. I should have seen it sooner. You can be mean, Elma. And you've always been cold, perhaps even bloodthirsty – to a point. But you lack the requisite cruelty. You cannot rule Rothen with love. The only reason Rothen still stands is because it has always been led by one who is willing to kill, and kill, and kill again.'

'Rothen clings to life by an unraveling thread,' Elma said between clenched teeth. 'You know this. The men in your army eat nothing but dried meat. The people of Frost are starving, little by little.'

Godwin listened with a cold gaze, almost distantly amused.

Elma sat back. 'But you know that. That's what you want. You want a weak kingdom, easily crushed beneath your bootheel. What's next after you conquer Slödava, then? Navenie? Mekya? You realize it's impossible to –'

'You speak of things you don't understand,' said Godwin, his voice dangerously soft. 'You're a confused little girl, nothing more. And you've given me everything I need to conquer whomever I choose.'

'A crown will only get you so far,' Elma said, crossing her arms tightly and gazing out the window. They had already descended from the citadel and were approaching the city of Frost. They sat in antagonistic silence as the gates of Frost swung open, and the carriage, along with its retinue of guards in Godwin's colors, entered the great city.

Elma stared out the window as they went and, knowing it would be her last glimpse, she saw the city as if through new eyes. The streets were wide enough for a carriage to travel with ease, much wider than those of Slödava.

Buildings of dark stone were painted pale gray by snowfall, already the steep eaves of their rooftops collecting layers of powder. Elma had always thought of Frost as a dour city, colorless and cold, just like the citadel. But as they passed shopfronts and inns, and rattled through squares marked with frozen fountains, she saw that it was beautiful in its way.

Tavern signs were painted with bright colors, and the doors of many homes were painted with flowers or suns, as if in defiance of the frostbitten landscape. Passing one home, Elma heard the sound of a harp and singing voices drifting out from within. A few people gathered along the streets to wave at the passage of Godwin's procession, mostly children with wide eyes, their parents gripping their shoulders with white fingers.

Are they afraid? wondered Elma, studying their faces. Most were pale and drawn. And there were far fewer people in the streets than there had been at the parade. Perhaps they weren't eager to show deference to a dethroned queen.

But as they drew closer to the arena, the streets began to fill, though most still wore frowns, their brows drawn.

Elma wanted to make some cutting remark, to draw Godwin's attention to the fact that nobody seemed particularly excited to witness her execution or the downfall of the Slödavan Crown Prince. But the words stuck in her throat. She didn't have the heart or the energy to trade more insults with him.

At last, the carriage stopped just outside the area. Elma scrambled out with as much dignity as she could muster and stood waiting in the snow as Godwin followed. She supposed they would now go to his seats, where she would be forced to witness Rune's death in aching detail. Godwin would not let her look away – it was the perfect opportunity to fully crush her spirits.

While Godwin was busy issuing orders to the guards, a figure broke free from the press of people entering the arena, darting around a guard. She skidded to a halt in front of Elma, her eyes wide, her cheeks pink. It was a child, a young girl. She held out her hand, offering something to Elma.

Elma stared, taken aback. It was the girl from the parade, the same girl who had made a pennant of Elma's colors with her initials sewn lovingly in the center.

'Winifred,' breathed Elma.

The girl beamed and held out her hand, palm up. 'For you, Queen Elma,' she said. A smooth green stone lay in her palm, no larger than a knuckle.

'Thank you,' said Elma, and unable to think of anything else to do, she plucked the stone from the girl's hand. It was warm, no doubt having been clutched in the child's hand for quite some time.

Before she could ask the girl what it meant, or why she'd given it to her, a lanky man came hurrying out of the crowd, his expression apologetic. Elma recognized the girl's father from the parade. 'Winny,' he gasped, breathless. 'Come.' Then he glanced at Elma, and she recognized a glint of fear in his eyes.

'It's all right,' she said. 'Your daughter gave me this.' She held out the stone, assuming the girl's father would take it back. For all Elma knew, it was an important item and shouldn't be given to a woman about to die.

But the man shook his head, his expression softening.

'She meant for you to have it. She's been talking about it all morning, though I *told* her she was forbidden from trying to give it to you.'

'What's all this?' said one of Elma's guards, striding over to investigate.

'Nothing,' said the man, growing pale. 'I'm sorry. We're going.'

'You're not permitted to speak to the prisoner,' said the guard, shooing them away. He turned to Elma. 'And you're not permitted to speak to the populace.'

But she ignored him, watching the girl and her father go. Winifred clung to her father's hand, but before they were swallowed by the crowd, she turned and waved to Elma. It was a silly thing, a tiny gesture, but Elma's chest ached as she fingered the stone, clutching it firmly in her hand. She had failed this child, just as she'd failed the rest of them. Whatever hope that had lit in these people's hearts when Elma was crowned, it was just as surely snuffed out in the wake of her disgrace. Godwin had no intention of feeding them, of paving the way for trade, of holding the people of Rothen in a gentle embrace. Instead, he meant to bleed them dry, use them as kindling in the blaze of war.

Elma hated him. She wanted to rip his throat out with her fingers.

'This way,' the guard said gruffly, steering Elma away from the crowds and toward the arena entrance reserved for royalty and members of the court. Her usual five guards flanked her. She knew there would be no chance of escape once she entered the arena, but even if she tried, she couldn't imagine where she'd run if she made a break for it. She would freeze to death as soon as she escaped.

There was nowhere left to go but the fate that had been laid out for her.

Godwin had disappeared while Elma was distracted, no doubt in search of hot wine and hot stones. Elma would be subjected to him soon enough and didn't bother to ask. But as they approached the arena, Elma's guards shuffled her past her usual entrance, aiming instead for a nondescript side door.

I'm not even fit for a noblewoman's door, she thought bitterly. This was the criminals' entrance, where those destined to die in the Death Games were funneled down into the belly of the arena and outfitted for their final battles.

The realization hit Elma when they turned to descend a narrow stair, rather than taking the corridor that would lead them up to the arena seats. She froze for a moment, until the guards prodded and swore at her to hurry up. She could have asked for confirmation, turned, and asked where they were going.

But she knew. She was going to be stripped of her clothes and outfitted in armor. She would be handed a sword, or a pike, or perhaps even a bow and arrows. She was going to fight in the Death Games.

There would be no clean kill, no blade through the spine. Even in death, she'd be stripped of all honor. The Death Games were brutal, bloody, and horrific. She would likely die scrabbling desperately, sliced up, and sobbing like a hare in the jaws of a hound.

She clutched the green stone in her palm and prayed to the stars or whoever might be listening. *Let me die quickly. Let me go home soon.*

39

Elma was given her own armor to wear when she died. She had expected one of the usual affairs, a dented chest piece and perhaps a pair of chainmail gloves if she was lucky. Instead, after being handed off to the gruff men who ran the Death Games, Elma was presented with a set of queenly armor.

She had never worn it except for a painting her father had commissioned on her eighteenth birthday, the year she came of age. It was ceremonial but functional, made up of interlocking plates of steel that shone in the torchlight. Her shield, which had once been bright with the Volta colors, was painted over with flat black. A black plume fluttered from the helmet in place of a red one. But the intricate gold filigree carved into the edges of her armor remained, and Elma felt a bitter sort of pride swell within her as the men laced her into her armor.

'What weapon will I be given?' she asked when she was fully outfitted. The usual roar of the arena seemed subdued, but she could still feel it vibrating above them like a great creature breathing. She tried not to think about Rune. Whether he was there in the arena with her, whether they'd be forced to face one another in battle, or if she would simply be led out into the arena to see his body there, crumpled on the packed snow.

'Sword, if you like,' said one of the men genially, smiling

365

through his beard. These were not the hateful soldiers or citadel guards. They were trained men of the arena, used to outfitting criminals and traitors, motivating them to fight well in battle. A disgraced queen must be a treat for them.

'I would like very much,' Elma said.

'Want to know who you're fighting first?' asked another man, though he was barely more than a boy, his beard thin and patchy.

A third handed Elma a sword, which he'd retrieved from a rack of weapons. It was old and the blade was chipped in places, but it was sharp and sturdy. Elma twirled it once, twice, testing its balance. She would have to adjust for its weight – it was heavier than her own sword, but it would do.

'I'd rather not,' she said, answering the question.

'But you *will* fight,' said the younger man, somewhat pouty. 'I bet my lads three coppers you'd win the first three, easy.'

Elma gave him a long, withering look. 'I'd prefer not to drag out my inevitable death if it's all right with you.'

'You're just going to sit down and die, then?' the bearded one asked, sounding disappointed. 'You may be many things, Queen Elma, but you're not a coward, surely.'

She sheathed her sword with a clang. 'I'm not a queen anymore.'

The men exchanged a look that Elma couldn't parse. 'As you say,' said the bearded one.

They left her alone then, bustling about nearby, cleaning weapons, and chattering amiably. Elma was glad they hadn't put her in a cell, another show of respect that she had not foreseen. Food was brought to her after a time, and while it was only dried fruit and cured meat, she was grateful for it. She hadn't been able to stomach breakfast, but she was hungry, and it would be so pointlessly sad, she thought, to die on an empty stomach.

As she chewed, she couldn't stop her thoughts from wandering to the other champions who might be waiting for battle. The arena belly was massive. Whoever her first opponent was, he would likely be entering from the other side. They would not interact before the battle, nor would she see who it was. Better that, she thought, than playing out the fight in her head beforehand. Anticipation would only make her sicker than she was already.

When the horn sounded to signal the start of the Games, Elma's gut twisted. She suddenly regretted all the dried meat she'd eaten.

'Here we go,' said the bearded man, holding out his arm to guide her way.

Elma strode toward the stairs that would lead her up, and up, and into the arena. Her limbs felt infinitely heavy, her heart a vibrating rhythm in her chest.

'Wait,' cried the man with the patchy beard, running up to her. He held out his hand. 'You forgot your rock.'

She smiled. 'Keep it safe for me, will you?'

But he shook his head. 'Take it. It's a protection stone.'

'That's superstition,' the bearded man called from where he stood on the stairs.

The younger man rolled his eyes and said in a conspiratorial whisper, 'You and I both know it's not. Most of the soldiers carry them. Didn't know queens subscribed to the beliefs of the masses, but, well . . .' he shrugged, glancing away. 'We had hoped you'd be different.'

Elma closed her eyes tightly, took a shaking breath, and opened them again. 'I have nowhere to put it.'

The man grinned. 'Give me two seconds. There should be a pocket in your armor lining.'

In a moment, he had untied her chest armor just enough to allow her to slide a hand in. She patted her velvet doublet, and sure enough, there was a pocket sewn into the side. Wordlessly, she took the stone and tucked it inside, standing tall while the young man tightened her armor once more.

'Good luck out there,' he said, giving her a jovial pat on the arm as if this weren't the prelude to her execution. 'Remember . . .'

'Three coppers,' Elma said. 'I know.'

Elma stepped into the arena in the wake of another deep, vibrating horn blast. The crowd roared. It was impossible to tell if they were cheering or jeering, but Elma supposed it didn't matter. A faint glimmer of warmth held fast in her, the kindness shown by the arena men and Winifred.

She may be disgraced, a traitor queen. But there were some who still believed in her. Godwin would win the game, but not wholly. Hope for a happy Rothen still lingered if someone rose up against him.

It was too late for Elma, but she would do what she could to die with something resembling honor.

From the other end of the arena, Elma's opponent emerged from a tall dark archway. It was not, as she had quietly dreaded, Rune. Instead, it was a brute of a man, not one of the arena's champions, but some criminal whose life they'd decided to toss away that day.

He moved with slow precision, sizing up his opponent

no doubt, just as Elma was sizing up hers. The man was tall and muscled, but he would likely strike and block slowly. If she could get past the reach of his arms, a lethal blow would be easy enough.

As she and her opponent sidled toward one another across the arena, she glanced up to where she knew her uncle was sitting. She imagined the smug look on his face as he watched his sick game play out exactly how he'd wanted it to. If only she could devise some way for him to come down to the arena.

Her opponent's attack came unexpectedly. Instead of moving slowly forward until they met at the center of the arena, when Elma was close enough to see the whites of his eyes, he let out a horrific bellow and charged. He moved like a loose boulder beginning its descent down a mountainside.

Elma could see exactly how he was going to swing his great-ax. The way he held his body as he charged gave him away neatly. And so, when he was close enough to bludgeon her skull in two, Elma nimbly dropped to her knees, skidding sideways while the much larger man stumbled past, his weapon hitting nothing but air.

It was only a matter of leaping to her feet, darting up behind him, and burying her sword in his spine.

He fell with a loud thud, his ax clattering to the snow beside him, half-hidden in fresh powder. The horn sounded to mark the end of the battle. The crowd nearly drowned it out. Were they cheering?

But Elma had no time to wonder. The horn signaled both the end of the first battle and the beginning of the second. Her next opponent was already on the field, rushing toward her like a phantom. Heart hammering, Elma wrenched her sword free, blood gushing onto the snow in its wake. She backed up, knees bent, and studied the figure that drew toward her.

They were slight and, unlike the last opponent, frighteningly quick on their feet. A pair of daggers was clenched in their hands, a black mask half-hiding their face. The rest of their body was encased in black leather. A moment later, Elma saw that this was a woman, one of the arena's resident champions. She hadn't seen this champion fight in years and had forgotten her name.

But names didn't matter in the Death Games.

Snow flew up in tufts as the two women crashed together. Elma blocked her attacker's first flurry of blows, but she moved almost as liquid-like as Rune. And a sword could only do so much against the close proximity of daggers.

Steel glanced off steel as Elma took a blow from the side, causing her to stagger, but the blade didn't pierce the armor. Elma swung in response, barely missing the leather-clad woman.

They circled each other, breathing hard.

'I don't want to kill you,' said the woman in black, grinning. 'But I'm going to. You may as well surrender. What's the point of drawing this out?'

Too out of breath to speak, and weighed down by her armor, Elma didn't respond. *Three coppers*, she thought.

Her opponent smirked and went in for the kill. Elma hadn't expected an attack so direct, not yet. She'd assumed Godwin, or the arena men, would have instructed Elma's opponents to drag out the spectacle. But the woman in black didn't seem to care or saw an opening she couldn't pass up.

Her knives were too fast, her leap almost wild, and she twisted in mid-air, falling upon Elma like a bird of prey. Elma's armor slowed her response, and she fell, tangled up with the woman on top of her. She dropped her sword, instead choosing to grapple with her opponent. At these close quarters, a sword was useless anyway.

Blades bit into her arms, her chest, the force of them reverberating through her armor. But the woman's thrusts weren't strong enough to pierce it. So Elma, using that to her advantage, leveraged herself up with one arm, rolling on top of the other woman.

Elma's opponent struggled and would have freed herself, but Elma did the only thing she could – she slammed her head, helmet and all, into the woman's face. A horrible crunch emanated through the metal, and blood spurted from the woman's nose. She let out a horrible scream of pain and frustration.

Elma could have ended it there, slamming her helmeted head into the woman again and again until her face turned to bloody pulp. But the thought of it turned her stomach. Even knowing that it might mean her death, that her man wouldn't get his three coppers, Elma scrambled to her knees, still straddling her opponent, whose face was bright with blood.

Forcing herself not to think, not to wonder who this woman was, why she had initially been brought to fight in the arena, whether she had any family or people she loved . . . Elma picked up her sword.

'Your man's next,' said the woman in black, coughing. A splash of blood colored her lips. 'Thought I'd try to kill you first. So you'd –'

Elma slammed the sword tip down through the woman's neck, severing her spine, killing her instantly. She didn't want to hear whatever the woman had been about to say. Didn't want to hear of mercy, of kindness. This woman was nobody, a dealer of death, that was all she could be. Elma couldn't afford this regret, this pain, not now. Not in the arena, with death on the way to welcome her home.

She wrenched her blade from the woman's body, unable to stop herself from shaking. Her knees wavered under the weight of her armor.

Your man's next.

40

The horn sounded, though Elma barely heard it. For the second time, she stared up at the stands, where she knew Godwin was sitting. Frustratingly, she couldn't make out which shape in the crowd might be his. She hoped he was enjoying the show. It would be over soon.

From across the arena, movement caught her eye. She turned, pushing up the visor of her helmet to see him better. He moved with the usual confident swagger, but his gait was uneven. He was injured more than Elma had thought when she saw him in the dungeon, or Godwin really had stuck him with a blade before sending him out.

She grit her teeth, anger boiling up in her. She would kill Godwin for that. She would wait for him in the underworld if she had to and gut him with a blade in the after. Pulling off her helmet, she tossed it to the side, snow pluming up around it where it landed.

Rune's smile lit her heart. It didn't matter that one of them was inevitably going to kill the other. All she knew was his face, the wind in his hair as he jogged to meet her, the way her armor no longer felt heavy, the relief in just seeing him again.

They fell into one another, embracing in the snow, hearts hammering together as one. Elma thought she could feel his, even through her armor and his leather getup.

'Elma,' he said, wrapping a hand around the back of

her neck. 'Your uncle's a fool if he thinks we'll cut each other down.'

'He knows me,' she said, breathless, searching Rune's face for injury. His jaw was bruised, and the remnants of a black eye was fading from one of his eyes. Cuts marred his lips and eyebrows, as if he'd been struck repeatedly by a bare fist. 'He knows I'll take my own life before taking yours.'

'Then he doesn't know me at all,' Rune growled, 'because I'll dismantle this arena stone by stone before I watch you die.'

Elma sobbed hopelessly.

The horn sounded then in a sorrowful peel. And Elma realized that the arena had gone quiet. It was still packed with onlookers, but not a soul was cheering; no chants emanated from the stands. The air was as still as the eye of a storm.

'This doesn't seem promising,' Rune said.

And out from the same archway Rune had come from, slavering and grinning like demons, stalked the Fang and his wolves.

'Shit,' Elma swore, quickly retrieving her helmet from the snow. Perhaps this was her uncle's attempt at irony. 'I'll take the Fang; you go for the wolves.'

Rune stood fast beside her, his chest heaving. 'I'd better tell you now, before it's too late and it becomes awkward . . . your uncle may have given me a bit of a slow-bleeding wound before the fight.'

Elma's heart stopped. 'But you can fight?'

'It depends.'

The Fang, unaware and uncaring for their hurried

conversation, pelted across the arena, his wolves flanking him, the kill count ribbons bright in their fur.

'The wolves,' Elma repeated, and then the Fang was upon them. Snow burst up as he skidded into battle, the roar and snap of wolves' maws filling the air.

Elma was good with a sword. She had never doubted that fact. But she was not as good in full armor and worse than Rune, even in his current state. Had they both been in full health, Elma with her own sword and a full breakfast and a body that did not threaten to collapse under the weight of dread, then they might have made easy work of the Fang. The fight should have lasted longer. Elma should have been able to protect herself and Rune.

As it was, the battle was breathless, painful, frenetic, and slowly going in the Fang's favor. No matter how many times Elma swung at him, sure she would at least catch an artery with her blade, he managed to dodge her. He seemed to be playing with her, seeing how far she might stagger about, swinging uselessly at him until he could easily push her over the edge into death.

Rune kept his back to hers as much as possible, but they were far from immovable. The wolves kept attacking from different directions, driving them apart, until Rune was forced to take the wolves on alone while Elma held off the lanky Fang.

It seemed as if the battle was only just beginning when Rune fell. Elma had just blocked a blow from the Fang, her arm throbbing in pain with the force of it, when she saw Rune from the corner of her vision.

He staggered, a hand pressed to his side, then stumbled to his knees. He lifted a hand, and something glimmered there, as if he were about to summon Rime Ice, to give away his secret. But the frost at his fingertips disappeared, and, in that brief moment, the wolves took their opportunity.

Elma had no time to think. No time to breathe. Knowing its extra weight would only slow her down, she dropped her sword and *ran*.

She reached him just as the wolves did. She acted on pure instinct, not a coherent thought in her head. As the wolves fell upon Rune, she dove between them, putting herself in the way of their jagged teeth.

Elma's sudden appearance made the wolves pause – just for an instant. For a breathless moment, Elma put up her arms, hoping against hope that if they killed her first, Godwin would call off the Games. In her heart, she knew it was futile, but she had no choice.

She loved Rune. She would gladly die just to give him one more second of that world. One more second of cold air on his cheeks, one more second of snow, one more second of glorious breath in his lungs.

The wolves fell upon her. She hadn't expected their teeth to pierce her armor, but they knew how to kill. They had done it countless times before. They went straight for the neck.

She heard Rune's voice from far away, but it didn't matter. She felt a hot gush of blood at her throat, felt it seeping into the seams of her armor.

No, she thought. *This isn't how it ends. I'm the Queen of Rothen. And I don't die like this. Rune does not die like this.*

An inexplicable sensation took hold of her, then. It began in her heart and spread outward, an icy chill. As if the mountains and the frozen rivers and the snow were all inside her, flowing through her veins, filling her up from head to foot. The sensation heightened, almost blinding her, vibrating through her skin. A prickling cold, coalescing at one single point – her hands.

Crackling and glinting against the snowfall, its blade extending with the speed of a flash freeze, a sword grew out from her hands. Bright and deadly and firm in her grip, the blade of Rime Ice swung as if bidden by her thoughts.

It cut through the first wolf, severing its head with unbelievable ease. With a sweep of ice, the second wolf was dead, and blood spread out before the Queen of Rothen.

Elma sat up, then staggered to her feet. The wound in her neck was throbbing, but somehow, she knew the bleeding had stopped. It was as if she had been waiting for this all her life. The snow, the ice, the land – reverberating in her veins, anointing her with the power and wisdom of a thousand queens before her.

It was all too easy to put down the Fang. Without his wolves, he was nothing but a man. And with Rime Ice in her grip, it seemed as if he moved in slow motion. Her blade was like a living thing, its surface changing like the frozen sea, and it sang in the voice of a glacial wind as she drove it through the Fang's heart.

His body fell with a thundering sound, snow flurrying outward from his body. Elma stood for a breathless moment, the snow swirling around her, a blade of magic in her hands. She stared up at the stands where Godwin sat.

'Come and face me,' she said, though of course he couldn't hear, not from that distance and over the crowd's low, agitated hum.

Movement in the snow caught her eye. Rune. As if

waking from a dream, her thoughts clarified as the Rime Ice withdrew. He was crumpled on the ground, still alive, and she fell to her knees at his side.

'Rune,' she said, cradling his head in her lap. He smiled, though he was deathly pale. 'Use your Rime Ice,' Elma said quickly, her words falling together like tumbling stones. 'Your secret's out now, use it, hurry. It healed me.'

'You're a queen,' Rune murmured, lifting a blood-encrusted hand to tangle in her hair. 'The land needs you. I'm just a prince. Not as powerful for me, I'm afraid.'

'Well, you can't just . . . *die*,' Elma sobbed, not caring that she sounded like a petulant child. 'I love you.'

Rune grinned, slow and self-satisfied, his blue eyes bright with emotion, even as the snow grew redder all around him. 'Come here.'

Elma leaned down, pressing her cheek to his, her hot tears dripping down her nose and onto his neck.

'And I love you,' he murmured, so quiet, as if it were a secret they held between them, a gentle spring flower untouched by the frost. 'I didn't expect to love a queen of Rothen. I couldn't help it. I'm sorry. You are inescapable.'

She kissed him where his jawline met his neck. 'Don't be sorry. I'm fine. You'll be all right. If we can get you to a healer –'

'Stop,' he said, and with every word, his breaths grew slightly more labored. 'I'm not sure you're aware, but these are called the Death Games for a reason.'

'Do not give up on me,' Elma demanded, sitting up to hold her assassin's gaze.

'I'm not,' he said, grimacing with pain. 'It's just . . . I seem to be losing an awful lot of blood.'

The arena horn cut through the air.

Elma started, suddenly aware of the silence in the arena, an extended hush. Whoever they sent out next, Elma would cut them down. She would do it again and again until no one was left to fight her. She would carry Rune out of the arena herself if she had to. She would cut her way through Godwin's soldiers. She would carry him over the mountain pass, across the Frozen Sea, back home where he belonged.

They could not have him. She would not let them have him.

The crunch of snow drew Elma's attention – someone was approaching.

'Stay alive,' Elma murmured, lowering Rune's head to the snow. 'Just do that for me.'

She stood then, steady on her feet, placing herself firmly between Rune and the new opponent. Snow was falling so heavily now that she couldn't quite make out the champion, but she could see that it was someone tall. A man armed with a sword.

'I hate to interrupt what appears to be a touching farewell,' he said with an achingly familiar voice.

41

Snowflakes clung to Godwin's hair and beard, at last near enough for Elma to recognize, to see with clear and seething hatred.

'If you touch him again,' she growled, 'I'll kill you and feed your entrails to the citadel swine.'

Godwin tutted, stopping in his slow approach. 'I should have twisted the blade,' he said, glancing over Elma's shoulder to aim a scornful glance at Rune. 'He should be dead by now.'

'What do you want?' Elma demanded. 'Was that not enough of a spectacle for you? Thought you'd come and end things on your own terms?'

He smiled ruefully. 'You know me too well, niece. I could have been patient, waited for the Slödavan to bleed out. And then, in your anguish, called for your beheading. It would have been poetic, I'll admit, and more than a little tragic. But I'd rather not risk the people seeing you as some kind of martyr, or, gods forbid, a hero. Better you go down swinging, with bloodlust in your eyes.'

'Fine,' said Elma, and already she could feel the cold burning in her, the glacial power. Now that she had found it, calling it forth was almost nothing. She had spent a lifetime seeking some connection to Rothen, a meaning, and now that she'd found it, the land would never let her go. She was its rightful ruler, and the man who stood before her was a usurper. Somehow, the land understood that.

I am the Queen of Rothen.

The air snapped with cold as the Rime Ice blade extended from her hand, long and angry. She yearned to drive it through Godwin's blackened heart.

'Whenever you're ready,' she said, waiting for him to draw his weapon. Or perhaps he would fall to his knees, crumbling in the face of her magic, to the true queen.

But he did neither. He only smiled, a cruel curl of the lips. And then, to Elma's distinct horror, her uncle's arm seemed to grow a layer of frost. Ice leapt out in jagged angles over his flesh, like a sped-up snap freeze, until – from one breath to the next – Godwin brandished his own blade of Rime Ice.

A distant gasp rang out from the crowd.

Elma's blood ran cold, her heart seeming to sputter to a stop. All her queenly confidence began to teeter, her stomach lurching as if she'd been walking down a flight of stairs and missed a step. 'How?'

Her uncle hefted his blade and ran one finger along its flat, the ice crackling as he did. His smile broadened. 'Last night, dear niece, I was crowned King of Rothen. A small and intimate ceremony, of course, but it did the job. You were kind enough to tell me how Rime Ice worked, that it could only be wielded by monarchs. And there was no point in delaying, so . . .' He twirled his blade, and it sang in the snow.

Elma thought, distantly, that something about the ring of Godwin's Rime Ice resonance sounded wrong. Like a note played just out of tune. As if his cruel nature had tarnished the magic itself.

She grit her teeth, allowing the pain of every hurt

her uncle had caused her to flood her veins like wildfire, tangling with the ice until her heart was aflame. There was no need to speak. With a guttural roar, she lunged for her uncle.

He parried her first attack, and their blades seemed to sizzle where they met. With the power of two glaciers crashing into one another, Elma and Godwin fought toe to toe. They were evenly matched – Godwin was taller and stronger, but Elma was faster, and she wore full plate armor.

Shards of ice burst outward each time their Rime Ice blades clashed, and Elma settled into combat, the flow of give and take, parry and lunge. But she knew better than to get comfortable. The second she let her guard down, her uncle would take the opening.

As they fought, the crowd reacted, though Elma couldn't tell who they were cheering for.

'Haven't you wondered,' Elma said, parrying a heavy overhead blow from her uncle, ice scattering from where the blades met, 'why I'm able to use Rime Ice even though you took my crown?' She had no answer for this but hoped the question might throw Godwin off balance, cause him to doubt.

On the contrary, her uncle only laughed, easily parrying Elma's next attack. 'How should I know what capricious rules this magic abides by? As long as you're dead, it hardly matters to me.'

Elma took shallow, heaving breaths as she skidded in the snow, her body drenched in sweat despite the strength and speed of the Rime Ice. She was reaching the end of whatever burst of energy she had been given, and Godwin was matching her hit for hit. Even her attempt at hurting his morale had failed, and she was beginning to see an end to the battle that wasn't in her favor.

Just then, Elma's boots skidded in a patch of unseen ice. She flailed, regaining her balance. Godwin took his opportunity to strike, elbowing her in the face. She fell hard on her back, the armor dragging her down like a cumbersome sack of metal.

Godwin knelt over her, the cold from his blade washing over her face as he pressed it to her neck.

'Before you die,' he said, 'I think you ought to know. Your maid Cora . . . that poor, foolish girl. We found her outside the arena voicing traitorous rhetoric in your favor, spouting nonsense about your devotion to the people. We arrested her of course, along with dozens of dissidents who claim to believe that you're their rightful queen. That you,' he scoffed, 'seem to *care* about them. A Slödafucker Volta? Care about the citizens of Rothen? How tragic when they find out what you've really done. That you've all but sentenced them to death, just by claiming their loyalty to you. All for a frozen prick.'

Elma struggled against him, her vision black but for Godwin's face. She was out of her mind with rage. But her throat smarted in pain as her uncle's Rime Ice blade cut her, and she knew that he wouldn't stop at a surface wound. Rime Ice could not heal decapitation.

'It's a shame, really, about your maid,' Godwin went on, clearly savoring the desperation in Elma's eyes. 'She had been so helpful to me until now. At my order, she claimed to see the false Slödavan assassin, lied that she had seen him wielding Rime Ice. Pity I hadn't known its sensitivity to royal blood at the time . . . a foolish mistake. It should have been rectified by my next gambit, assisting a true Slödavan in entering the citadel. Cora herself led him to your room. The silly girl thought all of it was to *scare* you, to start a war with Slödava. Like you, she hadn't the taste for blood. I should have guessed she would turn on me when she realized the truth. That I needed you dead. I'd let you live to see her execution,' he said, smiling in a sickly, self-satisfied way, 'if I didn't think you'd find some way to kill me first.'

No, Elma screamed silently, as if with one thought she could crush her uncle's skull to nothing. *No, no, no. Not Cora. She doesn't deserve this.* But who would fight for one maid, one woman in a vast frozen kingdom? Cora and a few citizens of Frost were nothing in the face of Godwin's army. And if Elma were to win this fight, then what? She would be swarmed by guards, arrested again, and dragged to the chopping block.

'There, there,' said Godwin. 'You see, it's no use fighting. You are finished, Elma Volta. Done. You'll be remembered only as a traitor until you are forgotten altogether, your memory faded into the snows like every disgraced monarch before you.'

He was right. No matter how Elma railed against him, no matter how strong she was, no matter how much she loved Rune . . . there was no winning. She had already lost. Perhaps there had never been a path for her that didn't end this way.

And then an image came to her: Winifred. Winifred, watching her at the parade, calling her name. Winifred, sewing a pennant with Elma's initials because she believed so strongly in her queen. Winifred, handing Elma a tiny green stone.

Her protection stone.

Winifred believed in Elma. Cora believed in her and was willing to die for her. Perhaps there were others. More who wanted peace instead of war. Those who would support Elma if she stood against her uncle. Godwin was no true king — he was a usurper, who would be a tyrant.

I won't let him. Rothen deserves more than this from its queen.

The fury inside Elma, the ice-hot rage that had so quickly subsided, now exploded forth in a sudden, uncontrollable burst. Letting out a guttural yell that seemed to tear her throat, she heaved her uncle off of her, striking out with her blade at the same time.

He staggered back, and as he did, she scrambled, breathless, to her feet.

A deep gash ran across the front of Godwin's chest, and he stared, momentarily caught off guard. But even as Elma watched, the gash began to heal. He was King of Rothen, after all, usurper or not.

Godwin advanced on her, unperturbed by his momentary wound. Elma held him off, but she was growing increasingly tired. Her armor began to weigh too heavy on her, and even with the advantages of Rime Ice, she could not fight forever. She had lost a considerable amount of blood. And her uncle was relentless — with every attack she dealt, he made two more.

She was beginning to stumble as she backed away in rhythmic circles, parry, parry, lunge. Block. And while her energy faded like water from a sieve, his seemed only to grow. As if her Rime Ice was passing to him, from the old monarch to the new.

A horrible light grew in his eyes. Death lust. She had seen it in her father's eyes and felt it in her own.

And then it came at last, the attack Elma did not see until it was too late. She had thought it was a feint and had moved to block a blow from the other side. So when her uncle's blade pierced her armor, the Rime Ice having no trouble slicing through the steel plate, Elma fell to her knees in shock.

Like a candle blown out in the darkness, her Rime Ice receded. *Come back*, she urged it, desperately, but the snow and ice in her veins were gone. She had already given up. There was no winning here; not even the protection stone could help her. The fire in her heart had burnt out.

She prayed that Rune's death would be quick. She prayed for Queen Hildegard's peace. Bitterly, she remembered the souls who had given themselves for her – Luca and his men. And now Cora, who would soon be gone.

Fractures of pain, unending and indescribable, wracked Elma's chest.

Perhaps, she thought, *it's right that I die now. Before more give their lives to the woman I should have been.*

And then something happened that Elma did not expect. Godwin had been advancing on her, his eyes blazing with eagerness, his Rime Ice blade held out before him for a death blow. But as he raised the blade high, Elma's death laid out before him, he stopped.

For a wild moment, Elma thought he had been struck with a change of conscience. He seemed to have frozen as if he were encased in ice. And then, in a sudden and horrific burst, his Rime Ice blade exploded backward into a thousand glassy shards. In one moment, the blade was raised before him, ready to kill. In the next, his hands were empty, and he was punctured full of ice.

Elma stared in disbelief.

Godwin fell slowly, a few of the shards having thrust all the way through his body, protruding bloody from the other side. Snow burst up around him as his body thumped to the ground.

It will turn on you, Rune had told her, back in Slödava. *If a heart is ruined with greed or selfishness . . . one cannot manifest Rime Ice properly.*

Whether it was Godwin's cruelty, his hatred for his own niece, his desire for war, or perhaps his rotten heart itself – whatever it was, the Rime Ice had deemed him unworthy.

And though this was what she had wanted, what she had fought for, Elma stood over her uncle's frozen body and felt nothing but sorrow.

No horn sounded in the arena. For a moment, all was silent but for Elma's heavy breathing. And then a yell went up from the crowd, a deafening roar that washed over Elma like a wave.

But she only had eyes for Rune. Falling to her knees, she gathered him in her arms. Miraculously, he was still breathing, and still awake. His eyes fluttered open, and the corner of his mouth twitched. A hesitant joy pressed at Elma's heart, wanting to be let in.

'You'd better not die,' she said, hot tears streaming down her face, 'or I'll follow you into the after and drag you back here to me.'

'I have no doubt,' Rune said, squinting up at her, still half smiling. 'But how embarrassing for me, to need saving by a Volta.'

Elma laughed through her tears, kissing his brow, brushing the hair out of his face. 'The moment you're well again,' she murmured, 'I'm going to hurt you for that.'

A slow grin spread across Rune's face. 'I look forward to it.'

The crunch of footsteps sounded in the snow, hundreds of footsteps coming down from the stands to join them in the arena. Whether they were coming to kill her or celebrate her, Elma couldn't tell. In that breathless moment, she didn't care.

Epilogue

A festival day was held to celebrate the arrival of the ambassadors from Mekya and a new dawn of trade between nations. It was the height of summer, but even then, a weak frost clung to the carriage as it rolled to a stop at the foot of the Frost Citadel. The ambassadors wasted no time in clambering from the carriage, swarming around it to greet the queen of Rothen.

Elma Volta rushed forward to meet them; all thoughts of propriety and queenliness fled in the face of her mothers. Dae, Tammire, and Sharra crashed into her like a hot summer wind, and they stood in the courtyard for a long time, embracing and weeping.

At dinner that evening, Tammire leaned close to Elma, her words and wide smile barely hidden behind a hand. 'Your man is something to look at,' she said. 'Did you give him that scar?'

'She may as well have,' Rune said, cutting himself a dainty bite. 'Bloodthirsty, this one.'

'Only where it counts,' Sharra laughed, raising a glass.

'She means in bed,' Dae added, giving Sharra a playful shove.

The three women erupted in laughter, tears streaming from their eyes, wine sloshing from their cups as they rocked together with mirth.

Elma shot Rune a long-suffering look. *I'm sorry*, she mouthed.

But Rune was laughing too, refilling the ambassadors' goblets. He had been taken with them immediately, leading them around the citadel, sharing histories that Elma had only just learned, truths about the Volta legacy that had been lost for generations. Stories of friendship between Rothen and Slödava, of harmonious relations with Navenie and Mekya. Rothen had thrived, once.

And Elma would help it to bloom again. She would plant a garden where there had only been stones.

After dinner, Rune and Elma took a carriage with the ambassadors to the festival grounds, so brightly lit and joyous in the night. Colorful bunting fluttered in the chill breeze, and lanterns hung from barren trees and sat in clusters on pale, frosted grass. A bright moon hung overhead. There was music, and dancing, and ridiculous games that only ever ended in embarrassment. But Rune and Elma played them, making spectacles of themselves along with the people of Frost, donning crowns of flowers – brought in from Mekya – and spinning in the moonlight.

When the festival had begun to quiet, Rune found Elma standing at the edge of the festival grounds, twirling a flower between her fingers. It had fallen from her crown, and she hadn't had the heart to leave it on the ground to be trampled.

'Everyone loves your mothers,' Rune said, coming to stand next to her, and she loved that he wanted to be in her personal space, to share her warmth.

'Almost as much as I love them,' Elma said, turning. She

hesitated, knowing what she was about to ask, and still not certain of the answer. 'But . . . what about you?'

'Do I love them?' Rune raised an eyebrow. 'I suppose, although –'

'No, no,' said Elma, 'I mean, would you . . . like them to be your mothers, too?'

He blinked. 'I'd rather not be your brother if that's what you're asking.'

She laughed, pulling him to her and wrapping her arms around his neck. 'I mean, you idiot, that I would like to marry you.'

'Oh,' said Rune, his eyes bright, as if not quite under-standing. Then his gaze sharpened, and he grinned. '*Oh.*'

Elma kissed him, weaving her fingers in his hair, enjoy-ing the feel of him, the knowledge that they were together, alive, and that she loved him. She was the queen of Rothen, and she loved him.

He had stayed in Rothen to heal after the Death Games. At first, she had thought she might lose him. It had been the worst day of her life. And now that he was whole and hale again, she couldn't stand the thought of him return-ing to Slödava, living so far away, ruling another kingdom. The idea of their fates forever branching apart, growing more and more distant . . . it wasn't a future she had the strength to bear.

She wanted him. She wanted him all the time, to touch him, to be with him, laugh with him, spar with him. He was her star, and she was his.

'Marry me,' she said, kissing his ear. 'Join our kingdoms. Be my king. Spend every day at my side and every night in my bed, for the rest of your life. You'll be far from home, but –'

'*Elma*,' he said, interrupting. She could feel the heat in his voice, his excitement in the languorous way he nuzzled her neck. 'Home? What do I care about home? I could never see Slödava again and die happy, just for the chance to spend a week of nights in your bed. Even for one night, really. I mean, all you'd have to do was ask. Want me to declare war on my mother? I'll do it.'

Elma couldn't help laughing, couldn't help kissing him until they were both breathless. 'That won't be necessary,' she said, removing her flower crown and placing it on top of his. 'Just marry me.'

'Then I'm yours,' said Rune, meeting her gaze with his bright blue one. 'I always have been.'

Dark, snow-laden peaks rose up beyond them, the moon slowly curving across a black sky. Far beyond, the Frozen Sea spread out like shining glass, and the city of Slödava glittered at its edge. Great civilizations raged afar, their heights and declines unknown to Elma, a faraway dream. Rune's hands were vivid and warm, his mouth spoke love, and she was a blooming flower in his embrace.